Dave Spence is a Manchester-based creative director whose advertising headlines are as short and punchy as they need to be. Ironically, he discovered a passion for writing much more when his fiancée, Angie, encouraged him to enter a national writing competition for which he was awarded first prize and a dream holiday for two to the Caribbean. This amateur literary success prompted Dave to start writing his heart-warming, tear-jerking, laugh-out-loud, homage to the eighties: *Gate-Crashers*.

For Angie.

Dave Spence

GATE-CRASHERS

AUSTIN MACAULEY PUBLISHERS™

LONDON · CAMBRIDGE · NEW YORK · SHARJAH

A CIP catalogue record for this title is available from the British Library.

ISBN 9781398400320 (Paperback)
ISBN 9781398400337 (ePub e-book)

www.austinmacauley.com

First Published 2022
Austin Macauley Publishers Ltd®
1 Canada Square
Canary Wharf
London
E14 5AA

Chapter One
Twilight's Last Gleaming

With foreboding circumstances, the beginning starts with an end.

A captivated child gazed wide-eyed in wonder, button nose pressed to frosty lead-lined panes as a jaw dropping luminescence appeared to turn night into day. The windowsill-knelt silhouette plucked from icy glaze to cuff clear, then with breathing reduced to a controlled pursed lip minimum and through ember-shielding cupped hands, the fascinating sepia night watch resumed.

Within minutes, an expansive white blanket flourished, magically transforming the dark, twiggy, lifeless garden into an animated winter wonderland, enticingly beckoning as bedtime frustratingly loomed.

The young boy pleaded for permission to venture out, desperate to experience 'Jack Frost Land' as he'd seen erstwhile children do in idyllic Christmas scenes, perchance build his own adorable snowman. His tired father wearily succumbed knowing it was his parental duty to acquiesce, wrapping his little darling in oversize winter clothing and wellingtons he'd been expected to grow into.

Outside, the rosy-cheeked child watched gleefully as his father patted a circular ball of snow and dexterously rolled it like a crown green bowl over the fresh white carpet where the front lawn had been. As if by magic, the six-inch ball trebled in size with snow gently grafting onto the rolling orb. The mass creaked as it adhered to the rotating sphere, millions of microscopic crystals tightly compact into one solid block. He heaved the huge heavy boulder with great might until he could move it no further. It had gathered enough snow to become a three-feet round base. He crafted another slightly smaller and less dense sphere pushing it close to the first and with great strength lifted the torso boulder onto the first with a gentle thud. A third smaller one, the size of a football was placed on top as a head. It was spellbinding to see the creation of their six-feet-tall sculpted snowman manifest in no time at all.

The sky blocking feathery white confetti cloud continued its infinite descent, gracefully and gently settling, fusing a super abundant terra-softa touchdown, shimmering mass of heavenly diamonds. Industrious scattered footprints and quarried trail lines were soon covered with a new layer of fresh, neat, delicately settled, weightless celestial fluff; erasing any hint of creation as if the snowman had suddenly and miraculously appeared out of nowhere... Hey pressed-snow!

"By jingo, he's cool! A most admirable snowman and I'm... A snow angel!" His father exclaimed, falling backwards and panting a great chuff of steam into the night's sky, waving his arms and legs to create the impression of angelic wings and gown.

The little boy leapt on his valiant daddy who laughed another great exhalation and took a clean, neatly ironed handkerchief from his coat pocket to gently wipe his son's nose, tucking him into his warm fluffy sheepskin jacket. Leaning on his father's chest, with gloved left hand, the boy carved an elliptical halo above his daddy's head.

Nestled together within the angel imprint, they admired their bold statuesque creation as the snowman was decorated with objects from the house. The boy's mother dressed him front and back so he had two faces, one looking towards their home and one facing the golden street-lamp and cold dark road ahead. She said he was like 'Janus' the Roman god of time who looked to the future as well as the past. As snowflakes landed on their faces, his father snapped to catch fluffy ice crystals in his mouth. The little boy laughed, cuddled into his father's warm shearling coat and asked, "What's 'jingo', Daddy?"

"Magic, Son. Magic." A flake caught on the boy's eyelash and melted into warm saline creating a cool tear of happiness. This rare half hour of pure glittering joy fleeted far too quickly, in a flash.

They returned to the safe bosom of home; pyjamas, dressing gown, slippers and sugary hot chocolate. Standing on the windowsill, the infant cuddled his daddy's warm soft neck as they admired their tall frosty figure from the comfort of the front room. The heirloom pipe in the mouth of the snowman's face pointing towards the house hidden from 'magpie eyes'. As the snow continued to fall, his father's angel was soon buried along with all the deep, hollow footprints.

One treasured memento captured the winter snow scene thanks to the last bulb on the Instamatic camera. A precious 'happy families' childhood moment framed for all eternity. His smiling father lying deep in the snow, strong safe arms cuddling his beloved son tucked within his furry trench coat, the most handsome snowman at their side. A simple 'aide-memoire' to re-ignite happy thoughts of joyous paternal love.

* * *

This photo was one of the oldest, most precious pictures in Nick's cube picture frame. It looked faded now, washed-out and short of life. White as a sheet, Nick placed the ornamental six-sided photo cube back on the windowsill and continued his eerily sinister night watch.

Tonight, Nick Hopper's outlook was bleak, the antithesis of his childhood memory. Every light in the four bedroom detached house has remained illuminated for days; the front room was a beacon with curtains permanently open as Nick kept a solemn vigil at the now double-glazed bay window. A scolding radiator cathartically chastised his burning thighs through his thick grey cords as he cursed the arctic tundra that had once again engulfed the region. The severe weather filled Nick with dread, not like a miserable commuter scraping windscreen on a cold dark morning before navigating cautious traffic to work; nor as a frail pensioner who fears slipping and breaking fragile bones on an icy path. Nick's angst had developed from a real life-threatening situation and unfortunately his worries were all too real and well-founded. To Nick, now a seventeen- year- old on the cusp of adulthood, the thought of an incarnate snowman was abominable and he prayed for guardian angels to manifest.

Helpless to the crisis as it unfolded, Nick anxiously watched any movement on the bleak, white road from the front window as dusk brought ominously dark nimbostratus clouds. The angry maelstrom battered tortuously cruel biting gusts, relentlessly whipping up blizzards of lethal icy snow as it piled in dune-like drifts anywhere hidden from the driving wind.

With no foliage on the deciduous trees in the smart wooded South Manchester suburb of Sale, it was possible to glimpse far up the quiet powdery road. It was twilight's last gleaming and a hazy dot appeared through the blizzard veil on the horizon. Nick's eyes followed the dipped headlights

9

anxiously as it appeared to slow but then accelerated past. At that moment, Nick realised another vehicle had drawn to a halt from the south, banking the pavement outside. He recognised the white Rover with luminous red and orange stripe markings. No lights were flashing or siren but that was the norm for panda cars plodding about their business. Many different police officers from Manchester and Trafford Constabulary had arrived at Nick's house recently, but this one was different. Its livery was emblazoned 'CHESHIRE CONSTABULARY POLICE'; news from further afield.

A hair-raising shiver ran down his spine. The car parked motionless for longer than a moment. Nick's heart sank. He called up the staircase to his mother who had been instructed to try and rest. Two officers waded through the deep snow to the front door; custodian helmets off, respectfully held over their hearts, half-mast. White caps of snowflakes mockingly settling on their solemn heads under the porch light.

It was late November 1984 when this devastating tragedy struck home. The senior officer weightily announced that he was the bearer of bad news: Nick's father had been found, twenty miles away in Northwich; alone, by the side of a quiet rural road and unfortunately he had passed away.

Nick's dad had passed away.

Nick contemplated: His dad hadn't simply 'passed away', that's what old people do peacefully in their bed surrounded by generations of loved ones after a long and happy life. The reality was quite the opposite.

Chapter Two

Spare Us the Cutter

Seven days earlier, late at night. Nick awoke to an 'aurora borealis' celestial apparition dancing across his bedroom ceiling. The same rhythmic movement, colours and patterns over and over. Gradually coming to his senses, he rationalised the spectrum was in fact flashing lights, refracting through the tall, multicoloured, stained-glass windows on the stairway at the front of the house flickering through the gap in his bedroom door… emergency vehicles outside.

Nick leapt from his bed, wrapped his dressing gown then pulled the door wide. The flickering lights now targeted him, strobe-beaming, painfully awakening groggy dilated pupils, blinding and grafting shadowed patterns onto the back of his retina. He quickly shielded his vision, blinking wildly as he walked along the corridor across the landing and leant over the balcony to observe the commotion below.

The hall was usually a welcoming room. A formal space for first impressions. Tonight, it was a very different, unwelcoming and odd sight: Full of tall strangers dressed in black. Two people were kneeling down with boxes and cylinders. Someone lay on a stretcher. The centre of all attention. The master of the house.

Nick then realised that his dad had tried it again.

Over Nick's seventeen years, his father had attempted to commit suicide several times… Sorry to be frank, it was usually by lacerating his throat with a bare razor blade in front of the bathroom mirror. Sorry to be Frank Hopper. Not a clean deep confident cut ear-to-ear as you see in horror movies, but, many short stabbed, terrified hacks in one concentrated spot on the right of his neck. As if his arm and eyes couldn't believe what his brain was instructing.

Two tall, helmeted policemen stood to attention facing the host whilst writing notes and relaying phonetic messages into loud clicking walkie-talkies as

11

steaming ambulance men with wet yellow fluorescent jackets busied themselves attending to Nick's dad bound motionless into a stretcher. The front door was wide open as was the porch door beyond. The cold winter's night whistled gusts of light snowflakes in to observe, hovering as warm air held them aloft.

Inevitably, as light crystals turned to heavy tears, gravity brought them down to melt slowly into the cream Axminster carpet. The stretcher was jolted up and the host was swiftly escorted out to the ambulance. As he crossed the dark ambient-lit room under the light-shade, the unmasked beam floodlit and Nick could see his dad covered in blood, head to toe. Bloodied gauze wrapped around his neck and his smart silk smoking-jacket was splattered blackcurrant-red. Nick couldn't see if his dad was dead or alive, in fact, he was just thankful that he'd not opened his eyes to see him spying.

Nick's mum was hurriedly putting her thick faux-fur coat on with a cigarette in one hand, the last to leave. She was about to pull the door shut when she noticed Nick.

"Go back to bed, darling. We'll be okay." Then with a puff of smoke which was blown at him as a kiss, fresh blood-red lipstick on the inside of her fingers, she flicked the light off and pulled the front door shut.

Silence once again. Darkness.

Chapter Three
A Million Random Digits

Nick opened his eyes to morning. His idle gaze drifted lazily around the bedroom. Familiar faces looked down at him, 'Rise and shine, Nick!' A mish-mash of childhood idols: Evel Knievel, James Bond, a time-capsule of his youth. Once safe and reassuring but now immature and childish.

It was time to grow up, after all he was nearly eighteen. As an art student, he couldn't invite a potential muse back to this nursery. 'Would you like to come up and see my Etch A Sketch-ings?' Who was he kidding, he didn't even know any girls.

Other posters included Frankenstein with his electrified bride. Nick's mum had asked how he could wake up looking at that monster every morning. Why did things seem clearer in black and white? On the door was a poster from a Queen LP featuring hundreds of naked women on bicycles. He had hoped his mother wouldn't spot it by blu-tacking it behind his door but she had and, surprisingly, rather than preach feminism she'd declared it art not pornography and Nick was an artist. A 'red-blooded' artist she'd proudly added.

The most recent addition was Salvador Dali's 'Metamorphosis of Narcissus'. A fascinating window into a magical world of Greek mythology. This spellbinding image depicted the tale of 'Echo and Narcissus'. A frail young man with head propped on his knee leaning into a pool, gazing at a beautiful reflection for the last time at the moment of death. The same shape echoed to the right as a huge rock-solid hand statue held a fragile egg hatching into a daffodil.

As Nick lay on his bed, the dying Narcissus figure brought to mind the childhood memory of his father and their admirable snow creation. Nick recalled days after building the snowman when the forgotten, thawing figure no longer commanded attention and his mother dressed him down: retrieved the cherished grandfather's pipe, trilby and scarf and recycled the chunks of coal into the sooty, coal shed. She even wiped the carrots and returned them to the vegetable rack. The withered, once handsome but now wasting away, featureless, abandoned and unwanted icy figure hunched over, gradually melting away.

Nick remembered the night before and wondered if his dad was alive. When his mum had said, "We'll be okay," Nick had a feeling she wasn't including her husband.

No one had turned the central heating on. He looked at his digital clock. The big luminous neon-red LED numbers indicated it was 9:14am. Nick had been diagnosed with glandular fever 'the kissing disease' his mum liked to tell everyone. He had a sick note for two months of isolation but felt better now and was bored out of his mind. He would go back to college soon but lazing around suited him at the moment. He decided to get up.

He looked into the bathroom. The rug was stained red with his father's letting. He walked down the stairs across the hallway dampening his socked feet into the morning room. His mum always communicated with him via notes in the same spot by the telephone. The pre-printed hippy-masthead recycled-paper notepad had words of wisdom printed on the top of each page.

'Be the best you can be.' His mum had written, 'Back at 5.30. Courgettes au gratin for dinner.' There were two courgettes out on the work surface with a book turned to the recipe page. Next to the note was an egg-cup containing several vitamins as well as the gobstopper-sized horse-tranquilliser he'd been prescribed. He stated out loud, "I know the rules of the game," chugging them all down in one with fresh orange juice.

There was another note which read 'Seize the Day'. And in biro below in capital letters, 'BATHROOM, BIN BATHROOM RUG, KITCHEN, MOP, VAC.' The black biro was placed neatly to the right. Nothing about his father. Nick imagined the trauma of having to mop blood from the scene of an attempted suicide. Surely it wasn't a domestic cleaning task and professionals ought to be called. The phrase 'in the blood' literally had a whole new meaning. Flicking the switch, the gas central heating ignited with a gentle roar.

Upstairs, he grabbed a towel from the airing cupboard, hung it on the warming rail by the shower cubicle, leaning-in to turn the faucet. Dropping his dressing gown by the blood-stained rug, he stepped into the hot steam. Closing his eyes, he lathered his hair then heard the front door shut.

"I'M IN THE SHOWER!" He shouted, pausing to hear if there was a reply, suds in his eyes.

This wasn't an invitation; it was a warning. Mrs Burns their cleaner, was an elderly lady and totally deaf. Because she came to the house to work alone she never wore her hearing aid so Nick would shout out loud upon her arrival so the fragile old-dear wouldn't jump out of her skin when she saw him. He continued to sing loudly into the sponge, 'Welcome to the house of fun', knowing there was no lock on the bathroom door and there was a distinct possibility Mrs Burns may not have heard him.

He was well-lathered with foam in his eyes, when all of a sudden the shower door opened. A hand appeared at waist height reaching in. Nick jumped to the side avoiding the wrinkly old claw which was going straight for his nads, with a shriek, Mrs Burns jumped back. Nick could see her dart off through the steamy glass door. She had probably been reaching for cleaning products stored in the shower base.

Nick shouted, "IT'S OKAY MRS BURNS, DO YOU WANT SOME JIF?" He opened the glass door slightly to toss the plastic bottle, lobbing it towards the bathroom door. He wiped the steamy glass to see if she was still there but there was no sign. The rug had gone as well.

When he was dry and dressed, he returned downstairs wearing moccasin slippers this time and walked through the morning room into the kitchen where the cleaning lady was busy at the kitchen sink.

Mrs Burns always wore a hood when she was working, a square cloth folded in half diagonally. Like a bonnet. With a matching apron. This was her 'cleaner costume'. Not something his mum had requested but Mrs Burns looked the part. She was very proud to have this job, earning cash to top up her pension.

"SORRY TO MAKE YOU JUMP, MRS BURNS," Nick shouted, waving to draw attention. Today's near cheb-brush was something he didn't want to repeat.

Mrs Burns tearfully shouted in a Scottish accent, "I'm so sorry to hear about your father, you poor dear." Nick wondered what she knew. Maybe his mum had phoned her earlier at home, when she'd be wearing her hearing-aid. His mum hadn't phoned him. He didn't know anything other than his dad had been taken away covered in blood, obviously after attempting suicide.

He started to shout back, "IT'S OKAY, BUT THANK YOU."

He knew she couldn't hear him. Every day started with pleasantry upon arrival then they'd ignore each other for the next few hours. As Mrs Burns went about her business, they mutually closed the conversation and Nick took a mug of tea and bowl of cereal into the sitting room. As he turned the TV on and sat down, the doorbell rang.

With a huff, he looked over his shoulder to his dad's heat-saving door-hinge hoping he'd hear Mrs Burns answer. But of course, he knew she wouldn't have heard a sound. Spooning a huge mouthful of Alpen in, he got up and walked through the hall, opened the door and swallowed quickly.

There was nobody there. He could see fresh footprints had trudged up the drive to the door, then turned and disappearing on the other side of his car, a 1970 Volkswagen Beetle which was hidden under a mound of snow and permanently parked in the bay between the lawn and the front of the house. His 'green bug' currently resembled an igloo.

Eighteen months earlier, he'd asked his parents if he could have a motorbike for his sixteenth birthday. His mother had cried and his dad had gone ballistic, saying he'd never assist the purchase of a death-trap, wrecking Nick's Evel Knievel dream. On the positive note and a deal to keep him off two-wheels, they promised to help him with a car at seventeen. They paid for lessons, test, insurance, road tax and half towards his five-hundred pound car. Supposedly, he was the 'driver of his own destiny' but the reality of being a student meant he couldn't afford petrol so he still walked everywhere and the old shed just sat rusting. Occasionally, his mum would give him a five-pound note so he could take a few trips out locally over a weekend with his friends to stop the car completely seizing up. The fiver would usually go on a couple of pints, three pounds' worth of petrol and some pocket money for college dib-dob machines.

But who had rung the doorbell? Was someone playing 'knock-and-run' then hedge-hopping through the gardens? Nick heard crunches in the snow behind his car. The strange little 'Pools Man' lurked out. Every week, the Littlewoods Agent called around to collect his dad's football prediction form with the prospect of winning a big cash prize. His dad had a book of randomly generated numbers he meticulously went through each week, crossing off spent numbers and selecting the next in the sequence. Nick accepted it was a good a system as any but he'd never won.

The pools agent was also deaf and Nick always tried to communicate with him as seldom as possible. He was a very skinny man and stood with a stoop, hunched over in the dirty beige shopkeeper's coat and a striped red and white bobble-hat. He was unshaven and had deep-set mad eyes, missed most of his teeth; he had the appearance of a vagrant and carried a scruffy Tesco carrier bag full of heavy copper coins and entry forms. Most people would have considered him the 'village idiot' but Nick didn't. He knew the fact he was deaf made his loud droning monotone-voice sound humorous to some. Nick had always been taught to not mock the afflicted but his mates would have played merry-mischief with this poor unfortunate. The little man was clearly dedicated to his players, out in all weather. At this time of year, even paper boys get cold feet and throw in the scarf.

Nick's dad usually left the form and thirty-six pence in an ornamental vase on the windowsill by the door so the entry would always be submitted. Nick checked. No form or money. He then looked out at the frail man hopping from foot to foot like a weightless marionette puppet attempting to keep warm. Nick braced himself, entered the porch and opened the front door. Prioritising, he leaned out, balancing on one leg to keep his slippers dry, stretching for the semi-buried daily pinta.

"NO!" he shouted angrily, raising the glass bottle to inspect the punctured silver foil lid.

"Little robbing bastards," Nick muttered to himself. Blue tits had helped themselves to the top of the milk. He leaned back and dropped the germ-ridden bottle back into its snowy grave for the milkman to liquidate. From his balanced poise, he looked up at the little man and with an empathic opener shouted, "BLOODY TIT!" with a tut.

On the other side of the road an elderly neighbour paused from wind-screen wiping.

"POOLS PLEASE!" The Littlewoods man shouted in his loud deaf tone, not looking up from his stoop, a drip dangling from the end of his big nose.

"HI, SORRY. MY DAD'S NOT HERE. HE HASN'T LEFT ANY MONEY," Nick said as clearly as he could, pointing to his mouth and saying the words as phonetically accurate, slowly and clearly as possible. No response.

"HE'S... NOT... LEFT... ANY... MONEY!" screamed Nick at the top of his voice. On the other side of the road, the neighbour shook his head and scowled. Nick could only imagine what he was thinking: 'Police constantly at their house and he's moaning about having no money. Bring back the birch.'

"WHAT?" shouted Mrs Burns from inside the house.

Nick turned, shouting, "IT'S OKAY, MRS BURNS, I WASN'T TALKING TO YOU."

The pools man quipped back belligerent in his monotone, "If you weren't talking to me then who were you talking to?"

Nick turned sharply to look at the pool's man, giving his sternest glance, studying his expression to see if he was taking the piss. He wasn't as deaf as he made out.

"Look… just wait here." Nick said in his normal voice. Leaving the door wide open, he ran back into the hinged-door sitting room, where a library of books propped up one of the walls. He quickly found the hardback book his dad referred to weekly and observed the cover, 'A Million Random Digits with 100,000 Normal Deviates' by the RAND Corporation, published 1955. No words just page after page of randomly generated numbers. All numbers at the start of the book had been carefully, neatly and meticulously crossed, obviously over many years of pools playing. But the thing that caught Nick's eye was the bookmark holding the page of the next sequence.

It was an old sepia photograph. All the black parts of the picture had turned ruddy-brown and the white paper had become cream with age. He studied the photograph. He had never seen this picture before. It was obviously an old glossy print, from the 1960s that had been kept flat, probably hidden from light within the leaves of this book for decades.

It was a photograph of a young couple, one being his dad but much younger. Maybe a few years older than Nick. He was smiling and had his arm around a beautiful blonde girl. She wasn't his mum. Nick's mum was a brunette. She was nestled into him and they fitted perfectly. He was very handsome wearing a smart dinner suit and bow tie with a cigarette smouldering in his right hand like James Bond and she was wearing a beautiful ball gown flashing her cleavage. But who was she?

Obviously, an old girlfriend before Nick's mum. But the fact that his dad had kept this picture hidden for himself in this very boring book, a book that his mum would NEVER have picked up, possibly a secret bookmark he may have kept for only himself to view on a weekly basis for two decades. It was very strange to Nick. He looked over at a framed photo of his parents on their wedding day displayed for all to see. His mum looked so happy and his dad looked regal with chin up. Not beaming like he was in the long-time kept secret picture with the blonde bombshell 'Marilyn Monroe' doppelganger!

Nick walked out of the room studying the photograph. The girl was stunning, like a film-star or a centrefold model. No wonder his dad was beaming with pride. Nick had never seen this expression on his dad's face before. "What a fox! Ding-dong, you dark horse." Nick whispered to himself as he walked into the kitchen, picked up the biro and walked back into the porch still transfixed by the photo.

"Sorry, I don't know your name," Nick said pleasantly to the pools man. He'd changed his tune.

"WHAT?" Barked the little man.

"I'm Nick," Nick said pointing at himself. "AND YOU ARE?"

"MALCOLM," he said innocently.

"Great. Listen Malcolm, I'm only seventeen but will it be okay if I fill out the form for my dad?" he asked as clearly as he could, getting close to Malcolm rather than shouting.

Malcolm handed Nick a blank form looking up and down the street as if he'd just sold Nick drugs. Nick bent over leaning the open book on his raised thigh and copied the next sequence of numbers onto the form. Filled out FRANK HOPPER, a passable squiggle signature perfected for school notes and address in capitals handing the form back.

Nick fished in his pocket and found fifty pence and passed the warm pentagon to Malcolm saying, "Keep the change," then muffled a cough. "Have you seen this photograph before?" He held the photo near Malcolm's face.

Malcolm said he had seen it many times over the years. When Nick quizzed him further, it appeared that Nick's dad had never discussed the photograph and Malcolm had just assumed it was a picture of Nick's parents. Anyway, it became apparent that this had always been the bookmark, hidden in this particular book for many, many years.

Nick thanked Malcolm and closed the door taking the biro back to the cleaner's note and the book back to the bookcase. With one last look he closed the page, the lovers Frank and 'Marilyn' ensconced in digits for seven days until their secret love affair would ignite again. He returned the book to its innocuous hiding place and went back to his Alpen which had gone solid.

* * *

At five-thirty, Nick had prepared the evening meal as his mother returned home. He'd lit a candle in the middle of the table which his mum blankly considered then with a questioning glance asked, "What's that for, you Nelly?"

He shrugged. This wasn't an Oedipus moment but for an old woman in her early forties, she was doing well and looked radiant in the candlelight. Still slim and pretty. She deserved better.

He'd set the table with a wine glass and chilled bottle for his mum, which she found more to her liking than the romantic candle. No wine for Nick, he was on prescription medicine. They sat, his mum at the end near the kitchen and Nick ninety-degrees to her right, alone together for the first time since last night. Unimaginable secrets between them. In the darkness at the other end of the table was his dad's vacant chair. The elephant in the room had gone: The real Nelly. It was time to talk honestly. Nick unfolded his serviette and placed it on his lap. His mum lit another cigarette which she puffed at a couple of times and then leaned, smouldering into an onyx ashtray, red and gold 'by royal appointment' crested Dunhill's and a thin packet of matches stacked neatly next to Nick. Unused smoke habitually wafting into his face.

"This looks delicious, Darling, thank you." She took a big glug of Chardonnay to wet her palate and pensively whet her tongue. Then after a moment, began to explain calmly and slowly in carefully prepared words, what had happened the night before.

Chapter Four

Love Lies Bleeding

"Your father is stable and being treated in the Secure Wing at Withington Hospital for his self-inflicted, non-life-threatening wounds. Fortunately, he didn't sever any arteries." His mother reached for her cigarette packet then bravely finished, "And he has been detained for his own good."

The codes 'Secure Wing' and 'Detained' meant his father had been 'sectioned' under the Mental Health Act, again. Nick encouraged his mother to continue, silently striking a match.

"Thank you, Darling. It's such a relief knowing I can talk to you. 'A problem shared is a problem halved'," she said in an attempt to sound cheery.

Nick reached for the bottle of truth-serum and topped her glass. Now was the time to listen, not talk. Time to direct his mum to full disclosure.

"Why don't you start at the beginning," Nick offered maturely as his mother took a long, pensive draw through the mist of time.

"Back in the early sixties, long before you were born, your father and I met at University. We weren't courting, just friends. I heard that he'd had a serious motorcycle accident so I rushed to the hospital. He was in a coma but I'd visit his bedside, day and night until he came around. My bleeding heart fell for his in this injured state, they call it Florence Nightingale Syndrome."

She tried to laugh but her tired eyes welled-up, dark memories hidden behind a veil of smoke. Nick knew not to ask questions. To just listen and nod sympathetically. He passed a box of tissues. The accident was a revelation to Nick, it certainly explained his parents' anxiety towards two-wheeled motors.

"Your father doesn't choose to be unhappy, miserable and sad. He has a mental illness, which was triggered by the accident." Nick's entire life, he calculated but allowed his mother to continue.

"He suffers from Paranoid Schizophrenia Depression. Sometimes hearing cruel voices in his head mocking him. But he is no danger, his medicine pacifies his troubled mind. Recently, he's taken a turn for the worse. It's possible he may have stopped taking his drugs. Have you seen him scowling and frowning for no reason?"

Nick thought his dad's sneers towards him were just normal everyday behaviour, but gave his mum a considered expression. She continued, "He's been battling cruel messages from angry demons. He sometimes scribbles vulgar messages from the internal voices on anything to hand: newspapers, matchboxes even library books. Promise me you will never read his notes." She leaned forwards and put her hand on the top of Nick's looking earnestly into his eyes.

"I won't, mum," Nick said reassuringly. "Could I go and visit him?"

His mother was quick to reply. "No Darling. You're ill, you have to stay in. Anyway, the doctors say he isn't well enough for visitors. He's in a very fragile, confused state of mind. They're planning to increase his medication and experiment with new ground-breaking antipsychotics."

"Sounds dangerous," Nick said quietly, not wanting to alarm his mother.

Nick was actually relieved that he wasn't permitted to see his dad. When he had visited Withington with his mum as a child, he had become aware that many of the patients in that ward weren't there for physical injuries but for their mental health. They scared him. The shouting. The mad crazy-eyes of other 'inmates'. It was disturbing to see his father in such company. He was obviously very ill and therefore in the best place. The physical scars on his neck were only scratching the surface of the torment within. What glimmer of hope could Nick possibly have offered?

A tear rolled down his mother's cheek as she calmly announced in a brave voice, "I have suffered your father's demons for two decades and I am emotionally and physically exhausted." With a sniff and pursed lips, wavering semi-smile she added. "And you're an adult now," patting the back of his hand proudly.

She withdrew her hand and folded the serviette. "The mental abuse has been too much. I visited your father in hospital today and told him I want a divorce." She then broke down in tears.

Nick rose from his seat and hugged his sobbing mum's head in his chest. She couldn't take it anymore. Neither could Nick's dad. It was just normal daily life for Nick.

"If ever a woman suffered," She wailed.

As his mother wept, Nick considered the hidden photo no longer a burden. It was best not to mention. Perhaps when his father was better and after the divorce he'd find the blonde beauty, remarry and she might become Nick's stepmother. But who was he kidding? His dad was a shadow of his former self, had absolutely no self-esteem and the blonde beauty would have been snapped up by a rich, successful suitor years ago. Furthermore, his dad currently resided in the loony-bin; everything was going to change.

Nick suggested his mum rest in front of the telly, wine and cigs in tow. As Nick cleared the table and filled the dishwasher, he started to wonder whether it was possible to genetically 'catch' his father's mental illness as an inherent bloodline time bomb. A terrifying thought. He'd never considered that his dad had an illness; he knew him no other way. Nick had always tried to be like his mother, viewing everything with optimism and positivity, enjoying life to the full and leaping obstacles with uninhibited enthusiasm. She was like the strong stone sculpted hand holding the precious egg in Dali's painting, Nick being the egg. His dad was like the lost boy withering away.

* * *

Nick sat silently alone together with his mother in the dark smoky lounge to watch World in Action '28 Up'. As Nick stared at the screen contemplating his own upbringing, it dawned on him that dependency had never been an option. From childhood his mother had hatched a long-term plan to toughen him up and give him the independent mindset and cognitive skills required to survive without parents.

They'd always been busy, career driven business professionals; his mother a journalist, father in management. Nick's requirements were outsourced from the start. His earliest memories were of young foreign au-pair girls living with them, as Nick's nanny. Walking him to school, taking him to the park, helping with homework, cooking and putting him to bed. Inevitably each July the surrogate umbilical cord was severed as the young guardian returned to their continental home. Within days, Nick would be packed off to summer camp until September. From the age of seven, he'd travel alone by train, bus and ferry to remote corners of the British Isles to be met by hippy camp officials. Camp toughened him up and taught him independence, giving him a broad education in ways school and home could not. He may have left as Christopher Robin but returned as Rambo.

By the age of seventeen, starved of affection he was an independent teenager who didn't require reassurances or parental guidance; he could fend for himself.

The TV presenter announced earnestly, "Give me a child until he is seven and I will give you the man." Nick's mother was sobbing again; he left her to it. He had learnt from an early age the futility of emotion and dependency, which on balance must have upset his mother but equally reassured her knowing he would be able to cope with the inevitable.

Chapter Five

Lilac Time

On the Tuesday after his dad's incarceration, Nick and his mother were sitting to dinner when the telephone rang. His mum sprang to the phone, removing Filofax from handbag and flicked to the ruler-bookmarked notes page. With receiver in one hand and biro in the other she sat at the phone desk, ready. Looking over at Nick she gave a 'tutted' eyebrow gesture.

"Press office," She answered officially.

Nick's mum was often 'on call' with work and the office phone would be diverted to their home number in the evening so there was a twenty-four-hour contact to give emergency press releases. It was quite normal to receive phone calls at all hours.

Her face dropped and she lowered the pen. She then said, in a crackly, less confident voice, "Okay, thank you," and put the phone down.

She looked dazed and the colour drained from her face. Lighting a cigarette but not using it she said, "That was the police. Your father has absconded; he's gone missing from the hospital. He's escaped. They're going to send a police officer here, just in case he tries to come home."

"Are we in any danger Mum?"

"He's run away with no coat or money," his mother sobbed.

"Mum, are we in any danger, what happens if he comes here?"

"The snow is inches deep and he's out there in his pyjamas and slippers," she blubbered.

"Do you want him to come here?" She didn't answer. Nick immediately remembered the firewood chopping axe in the unlocked potting shed five yards from the back door. Were they safe?

Food abandoned, everything stopped at that moment, frozen in time. They went to the front room with the lights off to look out of the window. A police car sped up the road no lights flashing leaving rail lines on the white powdery road and traversed the pavement outside their house. An individual officer emerged from the car and darted out, putting his hat on as he ran up the drive. Before he had a chance to ring the doorbell, Nick had opened both front and porch doors.

The officer was led into the rear lounge and they all sat. Nick's father was missing and there was no way of finding him. The policeman asked if he had phoned or been to the house. They were asked to compile a list of phone numbers or addresses of Mr Hopper's friends, family and colleagues, anyone he might go to for help. This was a very serious matter, it was for his own safety, not to re-incarcerate him but to protect him from the weather outside; the officer gravely advised pointing at the window.

After a couple of hours, Nick's mum insisted it wasn't necessary to have a police guard. Her husband didn't even have a key, so if he did show up she would phone them before letting him in.

"If it's all the same to you Mrs Hopper, I'll wait outside in the car."

"But you'll scare him off!" She sobbed. As the police officer left, Nick said. "I thought you'd told him you wanted a divorce?"

"Yes, but I don't want him dead." She looked out as the snow poured down.

* * *

Over the next three days Nick's mother's friends formed search parties; mainly women she'd befriended from the 'Housewives Register'. Nick was aware his dad didn't have any friends of his own. Nick remained at home hoping his dad would phone or knock at the door. Bobbies would arrive throughout the day for coffee and biscuits and to see if there had been any news.

Nick spent his days watching the snow engulfed road, beyond the hibernating-beetle outside their house, cursing the weather. He'd also ventured to the garage, shed and greenhouse to check those potential hiding places. As a precaution, he'd moved the log-splitting chopper from the unlocked potting shed and put it safely away in the garage. From the front room bay window he would study every movement in the distance until it passed, knowing he was helpless in the search. His mum had insisted someone had to remain at home in case his dad showed up and with Nick's glandular fever he wasn't fit to go out.

It was Friday afternoon. Nick had guided his mum to bed insisting she catch a moment's rest. He folded the duvet over her and kissed her furrowed brow, then maintained his vigil in the front room.

His mum had left The Guardian on the windowsill, neatly folded into quarters with the cryptic crossword face up. A lipstick-smeared, white porcelain Verona coffee cup and saucer acted as paperweight. She had solved the entire crossword, as usual. Nick's eyes were drawn to the 'X' in one of the answers she had given, written in neat black biro cap letters 'XMAS'. Looking out at the snow, Nick contemplated it would soon be Christmas. Everything was going to change. He then pushed the obstructing saucer aside, looked through the questions wondering what four-across could be. He read out loud, "The Time of Nick."

* * *

It was the third day of his dad's absconsion, late afternoon when the Cheshire Constabulary police officers arrived at the family home to break the news Frank Hopper had been found. Frozen to death twenty miles away in Northwich.

His dad had died. Confused, sad and alone. On the run. Outside in the winter. A fugitive: worse off than a down-on-the-dumps, homeless tramp. Furthermore, the police officers gravely added that he may have committed suicide. He'd been found in pools of blood; he'd tried to cut his neck and slit his wrists with shards of broken glass.

There was no way of knowing what Nick's dad had done over the past three days. The facts were that he had walked out of Withington Hospital, wearing nothing more than pyjamas and slippers and his light silk dressing gown, with no cord belt. He would have had a packet of cigarettes with him: His wristwatch. He had probably walked past the reception area, waving a cigarette and a smile. Perhaps even asking the guard for a light as he slipped past. Out into the snow in his nightwear then sneaked past the gate and walked and walked. He didn't head for home.

Nick's father was originally from Delamere, a semi-rural village in deepest Cheshire. Perhaps he had been heading there. Trudging through snow in his ice cold slippers. If he walked west along Chester Road, he could keep going straight like the Romans. Perhaps he was heading to his former home. But he had no family left in Delamere. There would be no welcoming door. No friends there. No friends anywhere. No one to help. What about the blonde in the photo? Perhaps he was going in search of her.

He had walked for up to seventy-two hours in the freezing cold and got as far as Northwich. Exhausted, terrified and literally freezing to death. With no one around to stop him, he curled up by a lonely gate on the sharp bend of a deserted rural road and smashed a bottle. Taking the biggest shard, he attempted to cut his throat and wrists but his heart-rate dropped, too cold to bleed. His only escape from his tormented mind was unconsciousness as the lilac time sky blew away.

* * *

When the older police officer hesitantly asked if Nick had any questions, Nick wondered about his dad's watch, the only item of value he carried. A silver quartz diver's watch with black bezel and luminous hands. Dumbfounded the policeman didn't know what to say. Nick could see the man carefully consider his reply.

The gruesome things in his mind.

He tactfully said, "You don't want the watch, Son. It was covered in blood and… Other matter… Near the slit wrist, you see… It's at the coroner's office… Evidence… It may be returned in time."

Did Nick observe a twinkle in the policeman's eye at his play-on-words 'in time'? Nick made a mental note of badge 'PC Murray'. The Police Constable stopped talking and looked down, aware of his tongue slip.

An autopsy would determine the cause of death: hypothermia or suicide? Nick knew the truth but hopefully the post-mortem would be kind. He looked at his mother. Rocking backwards and forwards, hunched, elbows tucked in with her forearms running parallel to her thighs. Her hands clasped together on her knees, cigarette between her locked fingers. Was she praying? It was too late for that. Her husband was dead now and he'd gone in the most gruesome way possible.

A female support officer came to the door.

Chapter Six
Dead Man's Boots

What had happened to Nick's dad was horrific, his life had tragically ended with a shocking conclusion. He was only in his forties but had finally achieved the solace he had sought for so long. At that moment, Nick felt ashamed. Why hadn't he done something to stop him? Insisted he visit him in hospital. Shown him he was loved and supported even though he had tried so hard to repel everyone. Why hadn't his mum stopped him? Why did she have to talk about divorce when he was so vulnerable? Nick felt responsible. He knew his mum would be feeling even worse. The support officer had stressed that there was nothing they could have done to help and tried to reassure them it wasn't their fault.

* * *

Nick was in the kitchen dutifully making percolator coffee, the expensive ground coffee his mother insisted on. He poured it into coffee cups with saucers, adding a matching Verona jug of cream and a bowl of brown sugar. He placed the tray in the serving hatch then walked to the sitting room where the two policemen and support officer were comforting his mum. Nick overheard the woman compliment the chandelier. What was the comfort in that?

As he walked over to the hatch, the phone rang. Nick expected it would be his mum's work or perhaps a relative or family friend asking for updates so he didn't want to answer. He hadn't composed himself for what to say. It rang out for about three seconds and the female officer asked Nick to answer as she went in the direction of the tray. He decided he would just lie and say there was no news, be as brief as possible.

"Double-one double-four?" Nick answered.

A heavy breathing voice whispered quickly, "First of all I'm going to break into your house, sneak up to your bedroom, then I'm going to gag you and tie you up, and then I'm going to… CHOPPER, YOU FLID, IT'S ME, HEFF! CALL THIS NUMBER NOW!"

It was Nick's best mate from school, Heff, who gave him a number and hung up. What a relief! Nick looked around, shrugged as if it was a wrong number, walked out of the spring-loaded room and went upstairs to the phone in his parents' bedroom.

He threw himself backwards onto the double bed and stared up at the woodchip ceiling; sighed, leant forwards and picked up the phone. The cord was over-twisted, so he spent a few seconds, dangling the receiver to unwind, spinning to release its stranglehold.

* * *

Heff, or Richard Hefferan, was a big, jovial, confident lad who could appear menacing; adults and teachers weighing him up with caution. He liked to be called 'Heff' because it was the nickname of the Playboy magazine magnate Hugh Hefner, a real ladies man. When Nick wanted to tease Heff he'd call him 'Heffer'. At Summer Camp he'd learnt a Heifer is the name for a young cow that has never had a calf, literally a big girly virgin. Only vengeful teachers dared call him 'Dick'.

Nick's friends called him 'Chopper'. It rhymed with his surname but when he was younger he liked to think he was named after the Raleigh Chopper, the bike his parents had given him when he started secondary school. It was supposed to be a present for passing his eleven-plus, but he hadn't. He'd perfected a one handed wheelie adding an Evel Knievel V for victory with his right hand as he unicycled into the bike-sheds. It had taken him ages and a lot of scrapes to perfect.

Nick and Heff had been friends since the first year. They had both worked at Derek Smith's newsagents.

Nick was a Sunday paper boy but Heff, who looked older, had been promoted to shop assistant giving him access to the top-shelf 'adult' magazines which he'd steal and sell to kids in the playground, reinforcing his Hugh Hefner porno-mag magnate persona. He was generous with Nick and they would spend Heff's ill-gotten gains on ice cream or cakes from Mrs McCarthy's Bakery.

Heff was particularly keen on rum truffles, which contained alcohol and he'd gurgle if they had enough they could blackmail Mrs McCarthy for being a paedo and getting children drunk like a pervy, old witch. They'd scoff cakes whilst flicking through left over dirty mags, thumbing chocolate prints over all the dirty bits.

* * *

Nick looked at the number, lay back and with another sigh prepared his thoughts. None of his friends knew about his home life. They didn't even know his dad had been unwell. How was he going to explain that his dad was dead? At least it was going to be easier to talk to a friend, with no adults in the room. He tried to remember the last time he'd had a serious conversation with Heff but couldn't think of one.

He dialled around the digits which appeared to be a premium rate number, meaning the caller was charged a lot more than normal local calls. Nick wasn't bothered, his mum's company paid their phone bill.

"WELCOME TO THE PARTY LINE! THE PLACE TO MEET NEW FRIENDS. Your-call-is-being-monitored-so-please-do-not-swear-or-insult-other-guests. Your-call-will-be-charged-at-twenty-pence-per-minute... NOW JOIN THE PARTY!" The crackly, pre-recorded message was an over-played tape of a really excited American gameshow host voice with a cheap electronic fanfare. Nick tutted but waited for the message to finish. God knows who used these things. One of his friends had a CB radio in his car, that was the future of communication.

On the line a couple were having a conversation about school. Then faintly in the distance Nick could hear, "Chopper, it's Heff. Where are you Chopper? I love you!" It was very faint but made Nick chuckle.

Nick started to reply in a monotone voice, trying not to be heard downstairs. "I'm here Heff, it's Chopper." They did this back and forth for about forty-pence worth until the operator paired them up and linked all lines at the same volume.

Heff was reclining on his bed. His bedroom has recently been redecorated red and white. The focal point of the big room was a massive mural Nick had painted on the wall: An exact replica of a 'Kentucky Fried Chicken' salt packet. Seven-foot tall by twelve-foot wide. Colonel Harland David Sanders proudly looking back at Heff wherever he was in the room like a priceless oil-painting. It had taken Nick two days to complete, with help from Heff to 'fill in' areas. They affectionately called Kentucky Fried Chicken 'Rat-Meat' after Heff

31

claimed he could eat anything battered in the Colonel's delicious blend of top-secret herbs and spices: even an urban-myth endorsed scabby rat.

Heff lived in a huge modern detached glass house on a cul-de-sac in leafy and spacious suburbia. His dad had built the house to his own futuristic specifications a couple of years earlier and there had been no expense spared redecorating. The room smelt brand new: linseed oil paint, wallpaper paste, woollen carpet and Habitat furniture. Heff even had an unused bargain bucket as a Kentucky-Shrine, the centrepiece of his bookshelf. On the windowsill was a stack of beermats, souvenirs from pubs he'd been taken to. There was a telephone socket on the landing so he could stretch the phone cable to have the luxury of a phone in his own bedroom.

Heff was holding a new white push-button slimline phone in one hand and the other teased his fat bulldog, Winston, with a beer mat; trying to excite the dog by stroking its old-feller with the edge of the card. Winston was lying on his back in a state of bliss with his tongue panting upside down as Heff was fascinated by the dogs growing reaction. He sat up when he heard Chopper on the line.

"Alright love, do you come here often?" Heff asked the couple who's line they'd hijacked. The girl audibly yawned.

"Hey, can you do that again? Open your mouth really wide this time." Heff quickly thrust the phone down his pants for a few seconds.

"Thanks luv, do you spit or swallow and how's your bum for spots?" Heff then continued, "Easy tiger, not you, I was talking to Rennie. Oy mate, what do you do if a bird shits on your bonnet? Finish with her!" The couple retorted but left saying they were reporting him and hung up; Nick and Heff had the chatroom to themselves. "I was in there! You scared them off, Chopper." Nick hadn't said a word. The operator warned Heff about his behaviour.

Winston had decided to finish himself off and was now dragging his nether regions across Heff's cream shag-pile carpet, pulling himself along with his front legs, back legs akimbo sitting upright, his tongue merrily dangling. Heff sat up and flicked the beermat through the air at poor Winston who ran out.

"Soz boz, but she led me on, she was flirting with me. Gagging for it. Didn't you hear her heavy breathing? And I'm sure she was licking the phone. Did you hear her rimming me?" (Silence). "Anyway, Chopper, are you better? Has that VD gone yet? Everyone's going to The Vine at seven tonight. I've got a surprise for you, something to do with the Rat-Meat wall."

Heff had obviously cattle-raided a small group of their old school mates to go to the pub nearest his house. Nick hadn't planned on going out, considering he'd only just been told his father had died plus he was sick. But not wanting to share his news with the eavesdropping operator, Nick decided he ought to tell all his mates together, but stay off the booze, being on prescription medicine.

* * *

Nick went to the cloakroom under the stairs and put on his denim jacket. He was already wearing a white t-shirt and over it a thick red tartan shirt. He then considered he may need more layers, possibly to compensate for his dad's death due to lack of clothing. He reached for a burgundy scarf. Then his dad's new long Abercrombie coat. He tried it on and looked in the mirror inside the cloakroom door. He had so many layers on but it seemed right considering the deadly weather outside. The black coat swamped him, but this mishmash multi-layered ensemble made him actually look quite cool. He also put on his black 'Steptoe' fingerless gloves. He pulled his tucked-in shirt out and turned up the collars of his jacket and his dad's Abercrombie. He brushed his hair back and posed in front of the mirror to see how cool that might look but his hair just flopped back into a non-descript, unstyle.

He then looked down and saw his dad's steel-toe capped biker boots; old but extremely well looked after. These days his dad only ever wore them axe-chopping firewood by the potting shed. They were in very good condition. Old scuffs had been treated and professionally repaired. His dad always said, 'Look after your boots and they'll look after you'. They were probably the boots he'd been wearing when he'd had his motorcycle accident.

Nick reached for the heavy boots. Many art students wore sixteen-hole cherry-red Doctor Martens, but these were black and had reinforced caps. Heavy like army boots. Nick delicately placed his slippers on the shoe-rack, sat on the second step up and looking at the closed lounge door carefully squeezed his feet in. They fitted perfectly as he laced the thick boot straps. His tight grey stretch corduroy trousers crumpled above and couldn't fit over the clod-hoppers. He stood up, another inch taller and looked in the mirror again, 'Rock Star!'

He then rummaged through the pockets. There was a smart Parker pen, with his dad's company logo engraved along the side. In one pocket was a

Bryant and May matchbox. He slid the box open and noticed amongst the matches a piece of paper. It was very small, probably about 5mm square. It must have been carefully cut from a sheet of paper and then folded over and over. Incredibly neatly and accurately. Nick unravelled the microscopic piece of paper and after four folds the strip was unravelled. He remembered his mum warning him never to read any of his dad's messages. There was a very neat 'V' marked in the centre of the last fold. Or perhaps it was a greater than '>' sign or lower than '<' or an arrow pointing up.

What did it mean and which way up had it been in the box? It didn't matter now. He placed the box back in his pocket. There was also a neatly folded, new and clean handkerchief with initial 'F' embroidered into a corner. Like Q's gadgets in 'James Bond', these items may become useful. They were his now: Nicked.

He popped his head around the sitting room door. "Is it okay if I go out mum, will you be alright?"

She waved him off with a hankie and one of the police officers gave him a thumbs up. Nick opened the front door and his mum's friend Judy, was tottering up the drive with a bottle of sherry. She smelt like it was her second and gave Nick a kiss on the cheek as she went in.

"She's not eaten much." His mum would be okay. Judy would flirt with the police officers, scare them off, then they could relax with food and hit the drinks cabinet. Nick could get some Rat-Meat later.

The police car outside was fortunately covered in snow so neighbours wouldn't wonder what the police were doing there again. Nick pulled his dads jacket close and trudged up the road in the dead man's boots which fit extremely well. He didn't live near any of his school friends so walked up the road alone, considering how deadly this weather had been for his father or was it suicide?

Neighbourhood gardens looked so neat with the new fallen snow, sparkling crystals twinkled prettily in the lustre as snowflakes danced through the orange lamplight. His dad's boot prints were the first on the pavement and gave a determined impression. There were no cars or pedestrians. No one in their right mind would have ventured out in this weather. He thought of his dad freezing to death in his nightwear.

As he trudged onwards, a gritter lorry passed, ploughing snow and spraying slurry onto the pavement. No consideration given to pedestrians, the dark grey slush was hurled at Nick, soaking his legs, closely followed by a round of rock-salt chunks which pebble-dashed his now wet and cold legs, lobbing grit from a spinning device behind the lorry. The huge chunks hit him, stinging his wet backside as he twisted around and jumped into a hedge to try and avoid the rocks hitting his naughty-bits as the lorry charged on.

The once-neat privet hedge he'd flung himself into was slightly higher than waist high, covered in a layer of fresh snow about four inches deep. Nick plucked himself out and looked around to check no one had witnessed his slapstick routine. He could feel the pain of the rocks on his cold wet legs and reached down to rub his thigh. Both his front and back had been completely hammered by the elements within minutes of leaving the house. With a deep inhalation he once again buried his face into the snowy bank and held to feel the icy burn. A moment went by as the freezing pain hit him and he raised his head with a gasp. His ancestral print was eerily visible. The outraged red-faced house-owner stared out and bawled, "Clear off yobbo or I'll call the police!" Throwing the curtains shut.

* * *

Plodding up the main road, Nick eventually arrived at The Old Vine Inn, a Victorian coaching house. The streets on either side were smoky two-up-two-down Lowry-esque terraced houses originally built to house factory workers. Nick disliked this pub. It was frequented by short, bitter faced, bitter drinking, miserable old men in flat caps chain-smoking cheap cigarettes with nicotine-stained fingers and lips, propping the bar to drown their sorrows. The sombre atmosphere was upheld with a lack of entertainment; no space invaders, no jukebox, no pool table, not even a dartboard. The sort of pub where patrons cheer when last orders is called. No girls ever went in there. Nearest to Heff's house it was the first pub they'd all managed to get served in, so they'd continued to meet there out of convenience.

It was a small desolate pub and probably hadn't changed its decor since the war. His friends were grouped around their usual booth in the gloomy tobacco tinged lounge where the ancient wooden seats were afforded dusty, beer-stained, shallow, squashed cushions to match the tired old brown curtains.

Heff had managed to rustle together Salty, Lanks and Eggy: 'The Bang Gang'. A rogue's gallery of the most profoundly sanctimonious and sarcastic people

Nick had grown to call friends. Telling these sarky sods his dad had just died was going to be a challenge.

Chapter Seven
Friends of Mine

Best of a bad bunch Heff, Salty, Lanks and Nick had been 'Prefects' in the fifth form. Keeping warm and dry whilst the rest of the school soaked, the monitors claimed the cloakroom as their own common room and during one wet break, flicking through Heff's 'Readers Wives', Salty had nudged Nick bragging he'd 'banged one out' at school. Playing along, Nick also confessed to having a secret break-time tug and so the auspiciously titled 'Bang Gang' was formed and challenge set. Heff had immediately snatched the dirty mag away to the bogs, loath to be excluded… Playing right into his hands.

'Salty' was so called, not for 'banging out the salty stuff' but because the old sea-dog was a champion yachtsman and keen to sail the seven seas with the Royal Navy. He'd been head boy; a hostile-humoured authoritarian, cocksure of his levity and despised by many a lowly dreck. Being short and belligerent he suffered a real 'Napoleon Complex'. Associating with giants, Heff and Lanks didn't help.

'Lanks' had been the tallest in school from the first year and was at least six foot seven but thin and gangly, weighing maybe only twelve stone. He too had a chip on his shoulder about his height. In first year English he'd been christened 'Lanky' because of his resemblance to the long-limbed outcast in John Wyndham's 'The Chrysalids'. He was now the only one with a job and money, but the mutant never shared, he was as tight as a duck's arse. He claimed to have banged one out on the school hall stage but no one believed him, although the tall red velvet curtains did have some suspicious out-of-reach white splattering.

Heff and Salty were now studying A' Levels at Altrincham Grammar where they'd met 'Eggy', their new crony. Eggy lived locally but had no friends, having studied at boarding school. Because of his posh education The Bang Gang christened the egg-head, 'Eggy'. He'd protested it was a name for someone who farted a lot, so the decision was unanimous and the name stuck. He also became the butt of any fart jokes. Literally being the new member Eggy was coerced into 'choking the chicken' at school to earn his wings. The phrase 'Are you chicken?' re-ignited the age old question: 'What came first, the chicken or the egg?'

* * *

Lanks was sniffing a bag of 'Scampy Fries' and whispering in a dream-like state, "Smells like pussy!" inhaling the pungent, fishy savoury bar-snack treat. Sweet, tangy, intoxicatingly fishy. Catnip to a tom. Common knowledge after eating Scampy Fries, fingers were a phantosmia, invoking the aphrodisiac scent of a ripe woman via the holy-grail act of digital stimulation: The third quarter of the mythical sexual act measurement cycle, strangely associated with the American bat and ball field game baseball.

Eggy was begging for a whiff but Lanks held the bag out of range. He brought it close to his chest, saying, "Mine" in a trance-like voice, smacking his mouth open and shut, then stuck two fingers into the bag, covered them in dust and pulled them out, wafting them near Eggy and raising them, pointed the V's directly in Eggy's face viciously sneering, "Get your own, Scav."

Lanks brought the V's closer to his own mouth, inverted them and stuck his tongue between them, licking disgustingly, covering his fingers in crumby slather, mimicking orgasmic groans. He then parted his scissor fingers a few times, encouraging a gooey-window of goz. This really was too much and Heff's thump in the ribs stopped him. Eggy barked, "You can only dream of getting fishy fingers!" Annoyed and winded, Lanks pulled Eggy's head down to fart in his face.

Coughing Eggy shrieked, "Lorks oh lordy, que profungus?"

Lanks replied, "The one who smelt it, dealt it, Eggy-farts, old bean." Wafting the foul odour towards Eggy's nostrils, then grabbed noxious gas from behind himself to throw across the table at Salty and Heff.

Salty quickly picked up a matchbox from the overflowing ashtray, lit a match and launched it towards Lanks who ducked out of the way of the burning arrow.

"You tight get! Give me one!" Eggy demanded.

Heff's innuendo-radar was always on red-alert and he quickly heckled, "One up the bum, no harm done!"

Lanks placed the packet on the table in front of Eggy with the open bag facing him; obviously a trap. Before Eggy had a chance to reach in, Lanks quickly bashed it with his shovel-like hand, smashing all the remaining crisps into smithereens. "Help yourself!" he said.

Salty snatched the pack of dust and poured it all into his own pint pot and downed the beery 'taste of a woman' aphrodisiac cup-a-soup in one. Not the reaction Lanks had hoped for.

"Tastes like victory. Your round Chopper." Salty held the empty upturned pint over his head with a belch as he looked at Nick in the doorway.

"Who've you come as, your dad?" Salty added looking at Nick's coat.

The Bang Gang: These were the people Nick had hung around with since school had finished. He was growing tired of their venom towards one-another. It really was time to grow up. He needed some love in his life: The company of people who were kind, caring and compassionate.

Nick's friends chose to drink pints of 'mixed', which was half a bitter and half a mild together in a pint pot. It was cheap and they discerningly called it 'gut-rot'. Nick had heard that rugby and darts players drank bitter and football-players and rock-stars drank lager. He wanted to drink lager but was forced to drink this slop so the price of a round was even.

At the bar, Nick was thinking about the sophisticated, colourful people he'd met at art college, the month before getting glandular fever. He'd like to get to know them but never bumped into them socially. No wonder, frequenting The Vine. Nick wondered what his school mates would make of his college friends and vice versa. The loving artists would think his school friends were hateful geeks. Art versus science, imagination versus logic. Two worlds collide. Mind-fucking pandemonium!

When Nick returned from the bar with five pints of gut-rot on a sticky tray Salty was talking homebrew.

"Look out lads, I'm brewing!" warned Eggy. He grimaced and went cross-eyed letting out an audible cheek-squeak guff and with his feet and back firmly wedged against the cubicle-seat he raised his torso, without moving his arms or head, like an explosion below had shot him up four inches. Like Stan Laurel's bowler hat trick, where he blows into his thumb and his hat raises: Except from the other end.

Salty's dad had bought the equipment to make beer at home and if they chipped in thirty-five pence each he could make fifty pints, ten pints each, that's three and a half pence a pint! It would be ready to drink for an all-day major drinking sesh at Christmas. They could all go around and get rat-arsed. He was looking for commitment, putting his upturned hand out to his sponsors. Over a gallon each. Better than this gut-rot? Nick doubted it. He wanted to meet new people not sit in Salty's Artex house getting plastered on home-brew with these four nerdy bitter fools.

All this technical chemistry was a different language and Nick drifted off again. Imagining what 'positive' was to come. When something bad happens, there's always something good around the corner. But you have to look for it. It would have to be monumentally brilliant to balance his dad's death. He really wanted a change of direction, to start a new exciting adventure. He'd always believed in positive thinking, that there was a great life out there, all you have to do is look for it; choose your direction, create a path and go for it. It certainly wasn't going to happen here in The Vine. He just had to get up and go and find it.

He decided he wouldn't tell this lot his sad news. They'd burst, trying to hold back laughs. This glum venue was sapping the life out of him, he could feel his mood getting low and the half empty pint of tepid gut-rot was a symbol of everything wrong with his life. He wanted a half full pint of cool European lager and a fun environment surrounded by pretty girls and happy people their own age.

He pushed the grog tankard to the centre of the sticky mahogany table, clinking the overflowing ashtray, stood up and said, "Who wants to come to The Little B? I'm meeting friends from college there… Girls." Starting to wrap the scarf around his neck and putting his dad's coat back on, he slowly threaded buttons.

He hadn't arranged to meet anyone but wondered if Heff's cattle-raiding 'everyone's coming' ploy would work for himself. The Little B was popular with young people who'd dress for a night out, with music and girls.

Heff exclaimed, "Odgeamowey!"

Salty said, "Nah, it's full of twatty posing bastards, transvestites and 'Fluff Boys'."

"What's a 'Fluff Boy?" Heff asked.

"You know…" Salty crossed his legs and waved his hand down theatrically. "Bit of 'fluff', They fluff up their hair, like girls." His eyes opened wide and he looked around with a shocked pout.

Eggy said in a Yorkshire accent, "I'm 'appy 'ere wi' me pipe, flat cap and whippet!" Returning to his game of balancing beer mats.

Lanks also declined, "Nah, it's Salty's round next. Anyway you'll freeze your tits off! I'm not walking in this tonight, a couple more pints here then taxi home," flicking the house of cards.

Heff was Nick's only hope.

At that moment, a distracting knocking-bulk navigated the entrance. The 'Prawn Man' in his white fishmonger's coat and hat barged into the pub with his large wicker basket heavily stocked with small white polystyrene cartons and cling-film covered trays full of fishy treats from the distant sea. 'There's nothing like fresh fish' and that was nothing like fresh fish. He greeted the patrons with a deep and cheery, town-crier bellow, "COCKLES, MUSCLES, PRAWNS AND WHELKS."

For a moment, the pub was united in lively groans, taunts and jeers as noses were held and red-top newspapers wafted, cracking smiles on even the most miserable faces.

A heavily sellotaped, homemade card crudely advertised the basket's wares in black felt pen 'SUPER COCKLES'. The Bang Gang had christened the 'hardcore prawn-star' vendor 'Les'. 'Super Cock' Les.

With a deep inhalation Salty pointed up at Nick, standing white-faced alone ready to go and asked, "What's that whiff? Oh, I think your mum's come to pick you up, must be your bedtime."

Lanks announced eagerly, "Crabsticks for me." Smacking his chops, he leaned forward and raised his arm.

Heff moved his head into the gap behind Lanks's back projecting his voice. "Cooie, Les! Show us your cock!" Lanks tried to sit back and crush Heff's skull.

Nick's rally-cry moment had passed with no success. All attention had moved. He was standing alone with the 'ripe' vinegary smell-of-the-sea uncomfortably close. He dug deep into his pocket's shrapnel and pushed a stack of coins to Salty.

"Here you go, Shrimp, homebrew squids." He hoped he would never actually have to attend the horrendous homebrew sesh. No doubt Heff would be keen to start a game of trying to fill Salty's bath with vomit.

In fairness, his friends were comfortable having their mundane predictable Friday night together in familiar settings; warm and safe. They didn't know about Nick's dysfunctional family-life of late: That only just an hour earlier he'd learnt of his father's horrific death. Whether hyperthermia or shard artery hacking

41

suicide… And Nick felt responsible, a heavy weight on a young person's shoulders.

Surely, if his friends had known, they would have rallied around. Nick imagined their sympathetic reactions and the embarrassment he would feel. Eventually, they would all see the funny side and laugh. That was inevitable. Everything was a big joke to them. The last thing Nick wanted was sympathy or insincere words from these piss-takers. He didn't need comforting. No one is taught how to come to terms with a parent's death, especially as a child. He needed professional counselling, to coax out and expose deeply hidden emotions, grieve his father's death and not blame himself. Perhaps he ought to have stayed at home with the chandelier light-seeing support officer. He came to the conclusion going to The Little B wasn't such a good idea after all. He needed to be dismissed by all his friends and sent home to his mum.

Preparing to face the chilling reality, Nick leaned into the table and downed the remaining half pint he had previously discarded in a final attempt to wipe his mind then fumbled to buckle his last button, steadying himself. He felt dizzy, light-headed and shaky.

Heff was the only one yet to reply. Unbalanced and requiring support Nick leaned on the wooden chair; ready to go, chin up awaiting Heff's pungent put-down and sarky rejection.

"Heff?" Nick bravely prompted, in sight of the gallows.

Heff stopped laughing, sat upright and looked into Nick's sad dilated eyes, trying to read his mind. Nick had decided the conclusion would be to go home to address his father's death and drink sherry with his mum and Judy. He must have looked destitute because after a moment's pause Heff said, "Girls eh? Fuck it, why not?! I'll come with you, you randy little sod. You can stick your fishy-fingers up your tight-arse Lanks. We're going on-the-pull!" And stood up rubbing his hands together excitedly.

As he turned, Nick knocked the chair into the table and Eggy was quick to steady drinks. Nick stumbled out of The Vine with Heff to cries of, "Mutiny!"

As they left Heff turned and taunted, "You're not our friends, you're just people we hang around with!" His gloved hand stuck the V's up at the three remaining Bang Gang through the closing door, which then became a 'wanker' gesture as his hand disappeared.

Chapter Eight

What Difference Does It Make?

Nick stumbled out into the cold air feeling dizzy, head spinning and seeing double. He grabbed for a 'No Entry' post to support himself; fortunately contacting the correct one narrowly missing a fall into busy main road traffic. Angry car horns beeped past, inches from his head, spraying cold slush as lights flashed before his eyes. He steadied himself and pulled his hand back off the post, ripping bare fingers away, stinging his senses. Pain showed he had feelings. For a moment, he had escaped reality and forgotten. It felt good to not know. Good to be out of his mind. He had hardly touched a drop of alcohol but the fresh night's air had stirred his senses and he wanted to continue forgetting, desperate for the night to continue on a drug and drink fuelled rollercoaster binge of amnesia. He needed more, to excess.

As Heff pulled the Vine door shut, he turned to watch Nick sway from the post then throw himself to the right into the narrow road, his legs quickly following his torso. He quizzically laughed at Nick, who jabbered, "I'm feeling a little bit light-headed Heff. Didn't eat any scran earlier so I'm just getting some Rat-Meat. Not wise to drink a lot on an empty stomach full of drugs."

An umbrella-sheltered old lady walking past scowled at the self-confessing drug addict.

"Oh, I'm always up for drugs and the Colonel's finest Rat-Meat. What drugs anyway? Are you pissed Chopper?"

"I'm absolutely plastered!" Nick replied stopping to steady himself.

"You've only had a pint you lightweight."

"Yeah well, you're not supposed to mix alcohol with the antibiotics I'm on. It makes the alcohol stronger and the drugs weaker."

"You jammy sod! Have you got any spare? Does that mean you're taking it easy or going for it?"

Nick reached into his back pocket and pulled out his wallet which was stuffed with notes. He'd not spent pocket-money in ages. Being ill was a great way to save up. Showing his wallet Nick said, "Check out these spondulicks, I'm wadded! Fuck it, why not? Let's go for it!"

"YE-HAR!" Heff shouted, throwing his arm in the air. "Get pissed, destroy! The Colonel's scran will do you the world of good. That vegetarian slop your mum insists on isn't good for you. It might keep her slinky but she needs some meat inside her! What was it tonight, Henna Lentil Ragu? No thanks."

They crossed the narrow road to the hallowed 'Kentucky Fried Chicken' on the corner, conveniently only twenty yards from the pub. The Colonel's illuminated face beaming down at them, 'Welcome back lads'.

"Who've we got in tonight doing the Colonel's good work? Algernon, Stanley and Don. Fry that chicken with a smile!" Heff shouted like a missionary clapping his hands together, pointing his praying hands and smacking his chops excitedly as he recognised regular staff. He only knew them from reading their name badges on previous visits but acted like he was their regional manager.

Heff always talked to people serving him. He believed that if you interact with servers personally and keep them talking they actually give you more food. Mrs McCarthy, the baker over the road knew his life story.

"Two pieces of chicken please, no chips or drink and could you make one a breast and one a rib please?" Nick politely asked Algernon, the black albino behind the counter wearing a paper sailor's cap, short sleeved red logo shirt with white stripes and a thin black-lace gambler tie. No one ever seemed to ask for rib or even know it existed as a cut, but it was the best piece in Nick's opinion. It looked smaller than a breast but had no bone, just a strip of cartilage so you actually got more white meat than other cuts like leg, thigh or wing.

"Two for me as well, please, breasts," Heff said as if the albino's name was Breasts, for Nick's amusement. As Heff fished in his pocket for more money, he added, "And a corn on me knob."

"Say that again?" Algernon growled.

"Corn on the cob, please. Sod it, make mine a three-piece meal of breasts with fries and a Coke. Diet Coke," he said, patting his belly with a wink. "And a large tub of gravy… And a cheeky cinnamon apple pie."

The fast food was handed to them. Nick's wasn't in a box his two pieces were in paper-thin boat shaped envelopes that 'fries' were usually served in. He removed his fingerless gloves and put them in his pockets. They both grabbed handfuls of salt, serviettes and lemony hand-wipes from the end of the counter, stuffing their pockets as they exited.

The usually-familiar Rat-Meat bench at the bus top was hidden under inches of snow. They brushed each end and sat.

Heff started, "Come on Chopper, tell us about the Colonel's secret spices!" As Nick bit into the succulent golden crispy covered boneless chunk of rib, steam rose from the deep fried deliciousness.

"Okay, it's given there are eleven herbs and spices. Salt and pepper to start with obviously. Nine left." Deliberating as he chewed, steam rising in his face. Heff knew Nick was a keen cook and always made meals from recipe books rather than ready-made pies or tins. His kitchen had all the herbs and spices known to humanity. Heff was fascinated to have the secret revealed, it was like a bedtime story.

"Sure to be: Oregano, paprika, celery-salt," Nick had another bite to taste the coating for added effect. "Thyme, basil, dried mustard, ground ginger and garlic salt."

"But that's only ten!" Heff declared furiously, having carefully counted on his chicken-fat covered fingers. Nick chomped then continued with a smile. "The secret is… he used both black and white pepper!" Nick added proudly.

"Genius! So if we buy all the ingredients we can make Rat-Meat ourselves?"

"We'd need flour and I'm not sure if they dip the chicken in beaten egg before seasoning, did you see any eggs behind the counter? Oh, and we'll need a deep fat fryer. My parents don't have one of those."

Parents? Nick had taken a few chomps out of the second piece of 'breast is best' and tossed the bones onto the overflowing bin pile, licking his greasy fingers.

At that moment, a lone skinhead stopped suddenly and turned to Nick, "Did you just throw that at me?" snarling menacingly.

"No, I threw it into the bin," Nick replied calmly.

"It came fucking close. You were throwing it at me!" The angry skin came a step closer. Nick then recognised him as 'Mental-Rentil', a lunatic who'd been expelled from school. He'd always looked intimidating with borderline crew-cut but now he was practically bald and his eyebrows were shaved for full psychotic effect.

Nick reasoned, "Look if I had wanted to throw it at you I would have got you. I was aiming for the bin."

"Go on then! Throw one at me!" Rentil goaded.

Nick took a lemony wipe from his pocket, careful not to stain his dad's coat or handkerchief and wiped his hands. "I've none left." He showed his hands to the yob as he started to put his Steptoe gloves back on.

"What about that tub of gravy?" The fool was pointing at the carton between them.

Nick and Heff both looked down at it. Nick looked at Heff, who had his mouth full but calmly gave a shrugged expression as if to say, "It's okay I've had enough, take it," pushing the pot towards Nick, dipping a final handful of chips in the thickly congealed peppery chicken broth. Nick picked up the carton and weighed it up.

"If I throw this at you, you're just going to try and twat me," Nick reasoned.

"No, I won't," Rentil laughed, starting to roll up the sleeves of his bomber jacket. He was rocking, shaking his arms and dodging his head from side to side, warming up like a pre-match boxer. He snorted, clearing his nasal passages and hawking up a big greenie, gobbed on the snow at his feet. Clearly 'try' he would not.

Nick stood up fearless, estimating the weight of the carton and the distance about six foot. He raised it to the side of his head in the palm of his left hand then steadily held his fingers around the base to aim, closing his right eye and looked directly at the yobbo. He stopped and looked down at Heff for any sign of concern. Heff did a nonchalant shrug, biting into his final breast.

Returning to his aiming, Nick pulled his arm back and launched the steaming tub to the side, into the bus lane, over Rentil's shoulder, missing by about two foot, launching it steadily so the gravy wouldn't escape its container. Purposefully missing but not backing down from the challenge. At that second the ruffian came charging for Nick. Quick as a flash, Heff leapt into action and stood between them, protecting Nick, towering menacingly over the little thug growling his scariest voice, "Have you got a problem?"

Weighing up giant-haystack Heff, the skinhead went white as a sheet and backed away. Heff stamped his foot glaring at his opponent and the troublemaker legged it. Looking over his shoulder as he shot off, slipping and running up the terraced street Rentil shouted, "Fight your own battles."

Heff called back, less intimidating this time and a bit camp, "And don't spit!" Nick and Heff smirked at one another then sat back down on the bench resuming as if nothing had happened.

"Right, when Salty's homebrew is ready we'll make Rat-Meat," Heff declared. "The only breasts and thighs those blankety-blankers are going to see this year!" He took the scorching-hot deep-fried cinnamon apple pie from his pocket, wiping dust from the front of his coat and bit into the deep fried burning magma.

"Motherfucker!" He grimaced with scalded mouth wide open, trying to blow on the molten lava. He hastily sucked on diet coke to extinguish the fire within, grabbing a handful of snow and patting it onto his swollen tongue.

Heff's attention moved from the welding pie as he looked down at Nick's boots then up at his coat. "Nice threads, Chopper. You're looking more and more like a trendy art student every time I see you. Are they new?"

"No, they're my dad's," Nick said absentmindedly. Starting to feel the cocktail effect of near-scrap adrenaline.

"You're brave, he'll go off his fucking trolley when he finds out!"

Nick had visions of his dad's corpse rolling off the mortician's slab at that precise moment.

"Yeah," Nick said distantly. He was plastered but needed more booze. Try to forget again. He got up from the bench. It was fifteen minutes' walk to the promised land.

Excited by Nick's close-call with the little skin, Heff marvelled the new boots. "Blakey segs as well! You could've kicked his head-in in those! WE'RE THE BALMY SKINHEAD ARMY, NA-NA-NA-NA-NA!" He bellowed, now walking backwards with his arms locked on Nick's shoulders in an aggressive intimidating pumped-up mental skinhead wrestler's stance. He rubbed forehead into Nick's temple and snarled menacingly, grinding his teeth breathing cinnamon-appley-chickeny-beer fumes into Nick's face which would have been truly terrifying to anyone else.

"You're a good skin you are. Us skin's stick together," he added toughly, calming from faux-rage, wiping spit from around his mouth and rubbing Nick's hair scruffily. He put his arm around Nick's shoulder and turned to continue walking forward. He'd seen a documentary about skinheads and was trying out some of the phrases he'd heard. The fact he had a basin cut with choirboy birdwing parting made him very un-skinhead. Nick was glad of the support and put his arm around the back of Heff gripping coat.

Heff continued, "You'll be wearing a beret and blind-man's glasses next, walking a r o u n d pontificating poetry, you bloody poser!" He reached into his inside pocket and pulled out a silver hip-flask, took a swig a n d grimaced, "Bastard!" Then passed it to Nick and started reciting the first poem he could remember.

"*On the breast of a barmaid in Sale,*" Heff prodded Nick to summon the next line.

"*Is tattooed the price of brown ale,*" Nick continued and sniffed the flask: Southern Comfort, yuk. Took a tight swig and passed it back.

"*And on her behind,*" added Heff.

"*For the sake of the blind,*" carried on Nick.

"*Is the same information, in braille!*" Heff theatrically bowed to the bus shelter umbrella lady.

"Why as I live and breathe, if it ain't Mary Poppins!" Heff said in a cockney accent. He tap-danced around her then scooped up a pile of snow from the low wall outside The Vine and patted it into Nick's face running ahead, dancing like Dick Van Dyke. Nick attempted to run but it was more of a stumble, scooped up some snow which he threw into the air above Heff, not even packing it into a ball.

"The barmaids in 'The B' are supposed to be the fittest in Manchester," Heff said, taking a long swig. As he exhaled warm boozy breath, a huge mist cloud blasted like a fire breather.

Nick asked, "Why chat up barmaids when customers aren't working?"

"Ah, you see. If they're working you don't have to buy them drinks, they might even give you one for free and they finish at eleven to go home to bed. Working girls have their own bedsits," Heff said cheerily, glugging the last of his Comfort down. He nudged Nick with a wink, "Give you one, get it?"

It was funny hearing Heff trying to sound sage-like and worldly-wise. He was so confident and self-assured. Quite the opposite of how you would imagine a big fat virgin to be: It was endearing. Must be all the 'confidence-building' readers-letters he read in his porno-mags.

As they trudged through the snow, Heff occasionally stopped to throw snowballs at pedestrians on the other side of the road. He was a very good shot.

Nick considered it odd that just because it had snowed Heff thought it was acceptable to lob things at complete strangers.

A turquoise Invacar came into sight, trundling slowly northbound on the other side of the road, hidden from view by the four mist-spraying lanes of traffic. Nick hoped Heff hadn't spotted the fibreglass-framed electric wheelchair which, as it came closer, stood out like a sore thumb.

"A moving target. Injured for sure… Let's put you out of your mystery, old chap," Heff said distantly, cold-hearted deer-stalker eyes locked on the elderly debilitated stag. With intense concentration the hunter slowly crouched to scoop ammo, angle-poised with wolf-like prey-fixed vision. No hand-eye co-ordination required. Motor skills instinctively knew to pack tightly a deadly spherical shot without losing sight of the game like an emotionless assassin loading his weapon.

Disgusted, Nick objected, "Picking out the weakest members of society for target practice? Does your moral compass know no bounds?"

Heff then cried dementedly, "GET THE SPACK CHARIOT!" Throwing his arm into the air, dummying a throw then paused with his arm coiled back once again. He gave Nick a 'try and stop me' grin. Then relaxed his intimidating pose with arms by his sides and asked, "What would a skinhead do?"

"You're not one of them, Heff," Nick cautioned.

Heff mimicked camply, "Ooh, you're not one of them!" Then he growled, "YOU are!" After a pause, he said, "Seriously though, attack a spaz-mobile? How much of a twat do you think I am?"

Rhetorically and with a sudden burst of energy, Heff leapt into action, yelling, "ODGEAMOWEY!" His arm swerved in the air at the last minute to hurl the ice grenade at a different target, the orange sweet-shop window of their former newsagent employer. The icy mass exploded with a slushy thud as it hit the 'Paperboy Wanted' poster sellotaped to the centre of the huge sheet of thin glass. It visibly shuddered, briskly rattling backwards and forwards like a bowl of jelly within the putty-wood frame; logistically weighing-up whether to buckle and shatter. Amazingly it remained intact. The boiled-sweet protecting anti-fade amber covering had stopped the great fragile glass pane from smashing into smithereens.

"How did you know the window wouldn't break?" Nick asked.

"I didn't!" Was the gruff reply.

* * *

A steamed up orange and white 263 double-decker chugged past, slowly accelerating juddering diesel. Heff quickly packed snowballs and bombarded the side, saying they ought to aim for the little gaps of open window to cause as much distress to passengers as possible. The bus was a hard enough target for Nick, let alone specific part of it.

The bus had stopped at the traffic lights and a row of girls were on the back seat of the top deck, probably heading to the ice rink. Wiping the window of steamy condensation, they'd spotted Nick and Heff. The first one started blowing kisses and the one in the middle stood on the seat, pulled her jeans down and mooned at them through the wet glass, rubbing her white bum cheeks on the window. Her friends laughed hysterically and the kneeling girl on the right lifted her glittering mohair pink sweater and flashed her huge bra-less boobs as Heff lobbed two snowballs directly hitting the bum-titty targets. Nick had never seen a naked girl in real life and quickly knocked the next round of ammo out of Heff's hands complaining, "What did you do that for? We can't see anything now!" as the bus drove off.

Nick was having fun. A great distraction from the sadness of the day; from the misery of the last seven days. He wanted to pretend everything was okay and continue as normal. He wanted to get pissed out of his head tonight. The antibiotics were a good start. He was excited to be heading somewhere new. Heff was like family to him, the brother he'd never had. Heff was the closest person to Nick, even closer than his mother; but he decided to save telling his sad news until later. He didn't want to spoil the night. He'd not even told Heff that his dad had gone to hospital or that he'd been unwell. What difference did it make when he told him? Nick was feeling comfortably drunk.

The Little B was one of the biggest pubs in South Manchester, a mecca hang-out for fashionable underage revellers. The most glamourous, trendy teens from miles around paraded themselves there, it was like a prestigious, exclusive youth club for the most elegant.

The building had the appearance of a grand old Tudor manor house: symmetrical with black and white wattle-and-daub beam architecture and stained glass windows. In the snowy winter the beer garden front was a void barren tundra guarded by two bouncers. No one dare mess with or walk across the neat snow for fear of being turned away. At busy times an orderly, queue would form along the yellow-grit path down the central walkway.

Nick could only dream what it would be like inside. It was clear that the fittest, most desirable girls went there. He'd seen them queuing. Like a beauty pageant. It appeared to be packed out every night. That's why there were always bouncers on the door. The doormen could afford to be fussy. It made the place even more chic. Turning away riff-raff: anyone in jeans or trainers, anyone showing up already drunk or anyone who couldn't produce fake ID. This list basically described The Bang Gang, which is why Nick had never attempted to go there before.

About fifty yards from the entrance, out of sight of the interrogating bouncers they stopped and turned to check each other. Heff said, "Only a true friend would tell you this: You've got chronic dandruff. You need to see a dermatologist, I think it's scurvy." He brushed snow flecks from Nick's shoulders then patted his damp hair into a Sunday School parting. Nick swayed.

"I could do with some of those drugs to catch up with you, you jammy bastard. Just pretend you're sober for a few mins, I'll do your talking for you," Heff advised, turning down Nick's collar and tidying his scarf.

Facing each other, Nick weighed up Heff and said, "Okay: Monkey boots not trainers, check. Trousers not jeans, check… Are they your school pants, Heff, you scruff?"

"Says you, what are you wearing? They look like YOUR old school kecks!"

"These aren't SCHOOL kecks! They're grey stretch denim jumbo-cords. Like Millsy used to wear."

"At school!" Heff added. "Anyway, what do you want to dress like that dreck for?"

"It's style. You wouldn't know," Nick continued. "Big long coat with scarf covering up your terrible dress sense, check."

Heff pulled Nick's scarf to one side and added, "Check shirt, check. Is the lumberjack look making a comeback? Hanging out in bars?"

Nick said, "I'll be okay talking, it's you I'm worried about. You're a threat to them. Just try not to look too hard. Slouch a bit and bend your legs so you're not as tall as them and don't look them in the eye. Grovel. Be polite. Smile and if they ask you your date of birth, just add a year to your actual birthday. I mean take off a year, okay?"

A big grin appeared on Heff's face as he started unbuttoning his thick coat like a burlesque dancer, then pulled his scarf to the side and quickly gave Nick a glimpse of what was underneath, like a flasher.

"What was that? What are you wearing?" Heff flashed again, but held his coat wide open this time.

"Is that a Rat-Meat shirt?" Nick asked, gob-smacked.

"It is indeed, Sir," Heff replied proudly, slowly turning around with hands in his pockets, coat held out to show off like a courting peacock fluffing its feathers. It was a red shirt with collar, buttons down the front with three vertical stripes running down the side and an embroidered Colonel Sanders logo with the words Kentucky Fried Chicken over his heart. He was even wearing a lace gambler's tie.

"Where the hell did you get that from?" Nick asked.

"I sent a photo of the Rat-Meat wall to Kentucky Fried Chicken telling them what we'd done. They've sent us both real staff shirts. You've got one as well, it's at my house they arrived today. We've also got chicken vouchers and we're going to appear in their newsletter!"

"Wow, that's amazing. I'm surprised you actually wanted to wear it on a night out though."

"And why not?" Heff sulked.

"You look great, mate." Nick pulled Heff in for a hug and straightened his hair into a side parting.

Re-buttoning, they started the final walk in view of the doormen. "It's Snowtime!" Nick could hear the thumping baseline of Frankie Goes to Hollywood. With no turning back Heff was putting on a stupid leg-dragging limp which wasn't going to help them get in… Nick was trying not to show anger as they were within sight of the door. Was Heff trying to sabotage their evening? Relax Heff, don't do it. Turning to walk up the cleared, gritted path towards the guarded entrance the queue was short, no one in front when they arrived at the checkpoint. They tried to look mature, friendly and harmless. 'Eighteen' was a difficult look to perfect. They didn't want to appear 'hard', easy for Nick but difficult for Heff. Likewise, they didn't want to look 'young' easy for Heff but difficult for Nick. They walked up the path, awkwardly crushing rock-salt as they approached the bouncers.

The doormen were blocking the central gabled entrance. They too wore long coats, similar to Nick's dad's, black trousers and shiny policemen's boots. Their arms were crossed aggressively. Leather punching gloves. Nick could see they were also wearing black turtle neck jumpers underneath. Bouncers usually wore dinner suits and black tie but a Chuck-Norris Kung-Fu top was probably more flexible for the modern meat-head doorman thug to leap into action. Both bouncers were stocky and dressed the same with identical facial hair. Nick was expectantly and politely rubbing hands together with a smile anticipating a warm welcome, kicking snow off his boots, stamping his toes to knock ice behind himself, not wanting to wet the carpet. But could this be a sign of aggression? Drawing attention to his skinhead-steelies? Like a bull, kicking the ground before charging at a red flagged matador.

The doorman on the right casually weighed-up Heff and didn't bat an eyelid at Nick as he reached back and started to open his side of the door. It appeared that amazingly, on their first attempt, they'd managed to make the grade, with thanks to his dads boots and coat. Suddenly the bubble burst, just as Tweedle-dee had opened the right side of the door, the doorman on the left moved forwards, standing in the way of Nick.

Expecting a confrontation or at least a humiliating rejection. Nick looked up, trying to focus on the face of the goatee-bearded thug for the first time.

"Bloody Hell Rick, not seen you in ages you left-hooking sprog!" The bouncer said gruffly. Rick? There was only one person who called Nick 'Rick'.

The sturdy security was Steve Benson, an acquaintance from Nick's youth. Not someone he knew through family, school or the neighbourhood or someone he had kept in touch with; he knew him from church! Nick had been member of a Sunday School football team which had become over-run with an influx of street-urchin ne'er-do-well tough-kids. The hapless leaders tolerated and probably feared the hijackers, trying to make them 'see the light'. The team was a rogue's gallery, a dirty dozen of Sale's most wanted, 'colourful' villains. Opponents jaws would drop when they saw 'The Crusaders' expecting 'God Squad' choirboys. Nick never made it onto the subs bench but they were a notorious winning team by all accounts.

It was no surprise that Steve Benson had become a bouncer, he was a few years older than Nick, he wasn't the sharpest tool in the box and was a double-hard bastard. A good hooligan to know. Best to be on the right side of him. Nick had never had the nerve to correct Steve so the name Rick stuck. It would have been rude to correct him after so many years. Especially when bouncers policing 'the most important doors in the world' were concerned. Steve probably knew Nick wasn't eighteen. Nick was plastered, struggling to converse and reluctantly turned, thinking he was being ejected.

Steve reached out and put his huge goal-keeper hand on Nick's head with his big glove, stopped him walking off and turned his head around, aiming him towards the goal. Nick had expected to be sent off so the shock took a moment to settle in.

"Get inside, Rick, you prick. It's freezing out here." The friendly bouncers welcomed them. Saved. Crusader sanctuary, into the hallowed temple of the holy grail. Promised land goal.

Chapter Nine

In with the In-Crowd

A pleasant blast of warm air greeted them. The exotic coconut scent instantly evoked halcyon memories of serene, carefree days basking under the fiery sun. With all senses curiously stimulated, Nick's mood switched in the blink of an eye. A huge contrast to the icy cold, deadly world a thousand miles away on the other side of the Narnian door. Enthused by his first glimpse of the wondrous inner sanctum Nick raised his arm stopping Heff in his tracks as a dancing conga of twelve or more brushed past creating a temporary path through the horde into the endless crush. The trench vanished in seconds. 'The Little B' was literally buzzing! It was packed with a chattering colony of beautiful young people grouped in receptive circles like busy bees relaying important messages; a hive of activity. Girls and boys excitedly communicating. The birds and the bees. As far as the eye could see, beautiful young people, fashionable revellers, chatting, drinking and laughing trying to make themselves seen and heard above the sound of the crowd.

Heff waded to the right with Nick in his slipstream, attempting to follow the previously cleared route formed by the human chain seconds earlier. It would have been difficult for Nick to navigate through the packed area but the buzzing mass parted for bulldozer Heff. Nick apologised to anyone pushed in Heff's wake as they barged through the nest; breaking hexagons, avoiding the sting of cigarette tips and the agitation of precarious glasses of nectar. Narrower gaps were navigated sideways and Nick found himself rubbing past hot, sweet-smelling girls. His shoulders and chest physically contacting silk wrapped breasts as he continued through veils of brightly coloured, thickly sprayed candyfloss crimped hair; onwards, politely nose jousting perfect strangers; nether regions brushing past curvaceous bottoms and thighs. Nick was greeted with alluring honey-sweet smiles as displaced individuals nonchalantly returned to their tight-knit honeycomb groups. Routine to keep the arterial route and testosterone flowing.

Heff stopped in a raised area close to a cigarette machine surrounded by an abundance of green flora. Nick felt like he'd been transported to an exclusive five-star tropical island resort. A cornucopia of exotic enamel jardiniere's adorned terraced ledges opulently distributed throughout the predominantly black mood-lit 'hall-of-mirrors' labyrinth; overflowing with brightly coloured, ornate ferns and lush palm trees flourishing hydroponically with artificial photosynthesis.

Bright red and electric-blue neon lights flashed rhythmically and lasers fired at mirror balls diffracting onto the crowds below through the smoky atmosphere.

Half a dozen silhouetted beauties efficiently glided the L shaped bar attending to the raison d'etre spring of youth as the focal point white lightbox glowed in the dark mood-lit vastness behind. Barmaid's breasts were at eye level with the huge range of coolly alluring condensation-dripping frosty-chrome European draught lager pumps.

Spotlighting targeted dozens of replete bottles identified via inverted labels with brand logos suspended upside-down in a regimented line optically measuring their way through the perpetual cocktail hour. Above, stretching to the heavens was a heavily stocked and dust-free shelving system of mixer-bottles: every colour, size and shape eagerly awaiting their call. More enticing liqueurs and spirits than Nick had ever heard of. Elevated, out of the reach of mere mortals. The angels' share. Nectar for the gods. And with your spirit? Sunday school had paid off, Hallelujah! Heaven on earth.

Nick had noticed dancers in a sunken terrace area in the depth of the pub where a disc jockey was spinning records. The Hawaiian shirt and Wayfarer wearing DJ with tight-perm and moustache was watching the dancefloor and playing on his twin deck avoiding silent gaps with a cross-fade. Since they had arrived, the music had played non-stop, seamlessly mixing 'Woodbeez' by Scritti Politti into Sister Sledge's 'I'm Thinking of You' and then 'All Night Long' by Lionel Richie. All the newest chart music from this week's 'Top of the Pops'. The DJ's toppy assistant sprayed a knee-high gust of dry-ice swamping the pillar cornered sunken dancefloor. The crowd gave an audible gasp when the smoke appeared up to their waist and changed rhythm to the slower beat. Couples smooched together and small circles of boys honed in on larger circles of girls dancing around handbags.

Looking around at the crowd, Nick could see only happy sober sociable young people. They weren't here to get wasted, ridicule one another and antagonise strangers. No overflowing ashtrays. No crisp packets. No empties. No crabsticks. No miserable old folk. It seemed so alien. So friendly and inviting.

It must have taken people hours to get ready: Hairstyles a spectrum of proudly-overstated, heavily-styled thick and flowing bouffant locks, held in position with breath-taking amounts of hairspray. Girls and boys!

A parade of biological-ornaments. Uninhibited, bright and fashionably dressed debutant(e) peacocks and hens boldly strutting past their mates, striking confident choreographed poses in a fervent attempt to command attention. Seemingly the biggest show-offs were the most attractive and most successful. These courtship displays faltered only momentarily as the posers glanced aside into the mirror to preen their reflected pout. Androgynous Human League eyes attracted bright and bold admirers with bright pink smiles of appreciation.

Girls dressed like Madonna, The Bangles, Bucks Fizz or Bananarama with huge looped earrings, Perspex bangles and large crosses with layers of silver chains; neon spandex or brightly coloured jackets with upturned collars and sleeves rolled up to their elbows. Boys dressed like whoever was in the top ten, many wearing sunglasses. Mannequins in the latest fashions, or designer suits with huge box-shoulders straight out of Smash Hits.

Glancing down at his dad's boots and coat, his own denim jacket, lumberjack shirt and grey cord trousers Nick felt under-dressed. As he looked up, he noticed a group of girls watching him. Maybe they were mocking his clothes. Embarrassed and uncomfortable he pretended not to notice and looked away continuing his people-watch. Two stool-seated girls were repeating their metronome synchronised pout, smile, wink and straw suck. As each wave of posers passed, they'd head to head giggle, blowing bubble-gum bubbles, amused by whatever reaction they received.

Every inch of the pub was packed with trendies drinking colourful cocktails, looking like they were having the time of their lives. Straws, parasols, glacé cherries and plastic monkeys hung from martini glasses. This was more Nick's scene. He had sampled a taste of honey and he liked it. He never wanted to get caught up in The Vine again!

Nick wondered whether anyone from school or college may be there. He recognised one lad, known as 'Monkey' at school who was now a George

Michael from Wham! look-a-like with big bouffant hair, tan, designer stubble and Choose Life t-shirt. He would have been ridiculed for that look at school but now he was confidently chatting to a pretty blonde girl in pink boob-tube and yellow tutu. Go for it Monkey, Nick thought. He then noticed one of the drecks from school who now had the most eye-catching hair. He was trying to look like Limah from Kajagoogoo or perhaps the lead singer of A Flock of Seagulls. The vaguest connection being his dodgy bleached mop was defying gravity, standing vertically upwards like a fan, he wore white boxer boots and some kind of yellow parachute jumpsuit, that was a little too tight around his nuts. A very odd ensemble for one of the tough kids. Nick decided to guide Heff off the platform.

As they stepped down to ground level, Nick noticed a glamourous couple had just arrived striding in side-by-side arms-linked, commanding the crowd to part with ease as everyone turned to admire them, clearing a path in the direction they strode. The beautiful girl was a pretty big-lipped curvaceous blonde with flowing locks of golden hair. Her long coat was unbuckled revealing a slim hourglass figure, voluptuous cleavage and sexy long tanned legs. She reminded Nick of the girl in his dad's hidden photograph. The guy was tall, slim and handsome with neatly manicured hair, possibly bleached. He wore a long expensive-looking light-caramel knee-length coat. Nick and Heff stopped to stare at them with the rest of the crowd. As the cool girl smouldered past, she looked Nick in the eye and gave him a slow eyelash flutter wink.

Heff said she looked like Barbie and the boy was like 'Peter Perfect': Penelope Pitstop's beau in Wacky Races. Nick tried correcting him saying surely it was Barbie and Ken or Penelope and Peter. But Heff insisted they didn't look like a matching couple, although perfectly dashing.

The atmosphere was humid and stifling. Nick couldn't believe it was winter outside, tanned sunbed-worshippers were in here dressed for summer: miniskirts and t-shirts. Heff unbuttoned his coat, turned to Nick wiping his beaded forehead with the back of his coat-sleeve and said, "I'm sweating like a cow's fanny in a field full of bulls!"

Nick scoffed, "Randy Heifer!"

Heff shouted into Nick's ear. "Have you seen that yavin' over there?"

Un-hearing correctly, Nick looked to the bar where Heff was pointing and shouted, "What yavin'?"

To which Heff replied, "A pint of cider and black. Cheers easy!"

Nick had bought the previous round, but knew Heff was good for it, the night was young and he was loaded. He squeezed his way to the bar. Barmaids were dressed up to the nines like models, the bees' knees. The pot-lad was the only male dutifully collecting glasses, emptying ashtrays and wiping down tables with 'piss-boy' bucket.

The barmaids were incredibly cool, thin and sexy wearing cropped bra-tops with shorts or miniskirts, tanned skin and bright fluorescent team war-paint make-up dancing on the spot in synchronisation. Nick had never seen night-time make-up apart from on the white-coat wearing department-store beauticians in Lewis's: Beautiful to behold yet sadly spiritless with 'rescue me' glazed bottom lip pucker; distressed daytime damsels hoping for a knight. But in here the heavily made-up barmaid expression was a pushed out purse of concentration not boredom. It was a very sexy sultry pout broken only with an echoed repeat of order, returning to serene disposition after an acknowledging gum tongue-stretch or bubble pop, flexing cheek muscles with time-keeping, jaw clenching minty chews.

Nick caught the attention of a barmaid with short neat blonde bob hair, side parted with a long asymmetrical Phil Oakey flick-fringe below a tinsel-stared iridescent deely-bopper headband waving on springs above her pixie-esque head. She had day-glo pink stripes under her eyes, like an American football cheerleader, and an ultraviolet light made them glow fluorescent. Huge page-three breasts bowed forward into the black marble bar leaning closer as she brushed her straight golden locks behind her small studded left ear to take Nick's order. She looked him in the eye and repeating his order with a pouted nod; reached above the bar for glasses and her amazing tight pink cropped t-shirt-covered breasts lifted up and down, blatantly no bra.

At that moment, he got an eye-full of her athletically thin sun-bed tanned slender stomach. She wore a small black and white tartan mini skirt and above her shoes pink legwarmers. Nick leaned on the dry marble bar and quickly glanced at his reflection in the mirror behind. He awkwardly wiped his fringe into a parting, which surprisingly held its damp position. He then turned his attention back to the barmaid who placed the pints in two different shaped glasses on a black drip-tray. Nick put his thawing Steptoe-gloved fingers into his tight corduroy trouser pockets and passed her two pound coins.

Carefully balancing the heavily filled pint glass, Nick slowly and delicately lifted Heff's with two hands over the crowd of heads to an outstretched arm as it was clumsily grabbed, spilling a glob of cider and black into the hood of some unsuspecting poser's white jacket. Nick scowled at Heff who returned a shrugged 'couldn't give a toss' raised eyebrow and downturned pursed-lips expression as he purposefully poured out some more to show it hadn't been an accident. Ignoring Heff Nick picked up his long-stemmed vase but remained at the bar, waiting for change and turned towards the dance floor.

Beyond the dancers, along the far wall close to the smaller 'club bar' was an area seemingly reserved for and populated by the most attractive, desirable visually important people. The exclusive meeting place and hangout for rich-kid models and Adonises, the in-crowd. Nick recognised some faces from the art block at college; people whose names he didn't know, they weren't on his course, but they were the designer-suit wearing 'Duran Duran' look-alikes: The posers Salty had called 'Fluff Boys'. The people Nick's punk artist friends sneered at and openly mocked. It seemed they didn't just wear expensive designer suits for college, they had even better clobber for going out in! Each was immaculately groomed, slim and handsome, oozing charisma, surrounded by adoring debutante Durannies. Barbie and 'Peter' had just been welcomed into their fold, fitting in perfectly.

The 'Fluff Boys' had self-confidence. Not just the self-preservation, barrier-building defence the Bang Gang had taught Nick. Real self-esteem and an ability to comfortably talk to and befriend girls.

As Nick scanned the harem, his heart instantly skipped a beat and thumped back at a higher pace when he noticed one face. A truly beautiful girl from his psychology class he had developed a major crush on. He couldn't believe his fortune on this of all days to find the rarest, most beautiful and sweetly fragrant of all ornamental flowers: Jasmine.

Nick's heart began to thud, blood-pressure shooting up at an alarming rate. His chest started to pound uncontrollably, banging like a frenzied bongo drum. He could feel his whole body pulsating to the deep boom, boom, boom. The artery in his neck visibly pumped in time to the percussion making his windpipe tighten as an overcrowded race of pressurised blood coursed up his thickened jugular bulging through the narrow channels of his inner ear, racing around his brain energising freshly activated neurons, connecting synaptic gaps and stimulating his over-active adrenaline-boosting hypothalamus. The sudden rush of blood and lack of oxygen turned his cheeks crimson and small beads of sweat appeared on his forehead. Dizzy and light-headed he sensed a zinc metallic taste, a sensation he'd only ever had after falling off his bike. Relax and breathe, he thought to himself. With a cold, visibly-shaking hand he took a large gulp from his narrow pint glass to calm his nerves.

As everyone around him seemed to slow down and disappear into darkness, he observed the gorgeous beauty through the crowd. Perhaps it was the addition of strong lager to his internal antibiotic cocktail but he seemed to be able to see through dancers vanishing from sight. The music muffled to silence and the emptying room faded to darkness. Jasmine and Nick were the only two people in the whole room. The only people in the whole world. A bright spotlight from the heavens appeared to shine down on Jasmine.

In a flash, the crowd and music returned. Nick exhaled a deep sigh.

Jasmine was sipping delicately on a straw looking into her tonic or lemonade drink and smiling as a girl-friend spoke closely to the side of her face. She laughed demurely showing her pearly white teeth and turned to continue the secret conversation in her friend's ear, mouth smiling sweetly.

She had not noticed the infatuated Nick ogling her, but Heff had. "Look, there's 'Jizzum'!" Heff noted.

Chapter Ten
Cupid and Psyche

Along with art, Nick had chosen to study psychology at college. Odd for someone so creatively minded to select a 'science' considering he had failed any school exam requiring facts, reason or logic; but Nick had a personal interest in 'the workings of the mind' and genuinely hoped the subject might help him understand his father's 'disposition'. He was also keen to discover how to read body language and perhaps learn to project himself more confidently. It was also common knowledge that psychology was an easy, course-work-based A' Level to pass: Win, win, win.

On the first day, Nick was early to class and selected a position halfway a round the horseshoe, open rectangle of tall laboratory desks, a good spot to see the projector and also weigh-up his new lab-rat peers. It was the first class of the day and the room was clean and tidy but oddly there was a single banana placed precariously on the inner edge of the horseshoe about nine feet to Nick's left which he chose to steer clear of. All psychology students had been required to purchase an obligatory course book at enrolment which Nick placed in front of his notepad. He'd noticed a diagram of a brain on the far wall so on foolscap sheet began to doodle. The room filled to its dozen capacity, an even split of male and female subjects.

It was his first experience of a 'normal' higher-education classroom where students were keen to attend and actually learn. No 'anti-education' artists who believed 'creativity couldn't be taught'. Just fact-seeking academics. He was looking forward to unravelling subconscious, possibly with the psychoanalysing can-of-worms opener: 'Tell me about your childhood'. In his doodle, the brain was now relaxing on a 'Magnus Pike' shrink's couch. However, Nick's long awaited introduction to perception and human behaviour began before the tutor had even arrived.

The room was filling evenly on either side as classmates bustled in dropping their bags at vacant spaces, hanging their coats over stools and plonking down at available seats.

Then a vision of absolute perfection walked into the room and a cataclysmic, heart-striking Cupid bolt walloped through the centre of Nick's chest.

The demure beauty elegantly removed her long coat with a pirouette and hung it smartly on a lone coat-hanger she attached to a lab-coat hook on the right hand wall. No one else had even considered hanging up their coat; how chic. With a joyous swish she pivoted to her chosen seat, about three o'clock to Nick's right, only two people on a corner between them. She had a jaw-dropping sexy, slender and curvaceous physique: stacked breasts, slim waist, peach-like bottom and long athletic legs; accentuated with a lightweight figure hugging sweater and tight stretch denim jeans.

Her flowing long, dark curls bounced vivaciously as she turned and gently lowered to prop at the side of the stool, back straight with perfect posture. Gracefully poised she brushed aside an auburn tress, tucking it neatly behind her ear as she leaned down to reach into her bag. Her dainty left hand with natural, manicured shiny fingernails revealed no bracelet or ring. She wore no earring, although Nick could see from a microscopic, pore-size dot her ear had been pierced. She instantly turned to converse with the girl on her right so Nick could now only view and appreciate the features of her profile. She had a perfectly regal silhouette with a film star's nose. He was struck by her natural beauty and tilted his head to view her love-heart shaped lips. Her complexion was flawless with a tanned, healthy holiday glow. No need to dress up, flaunt jewellery, or plaster on make-up. This perfect flower was not for gilding. Natural and absolutely blooming lovely.

Until then, Nick had only been introduced to the scary 'everyone look at me' non-attention-seeking horror-show 'goth' girls in the art block. He hadn't fancied any of them. But THIS was the perfect girl.

Looking down at his pad, he could see the couch-reclining brain-doodle had become entwined with a peachy heart shape with long hose-like umbilical cord extending from the cerebral cortex wrapping around, probing and penetrating the curvy intersection, joining together as one. One step ahead of the perv, Sigmund Freud, Nick quickly screwed the sheet into a ball and lobbed it, 'eighty-six' over his shoulder at a small empty bin in the corner of the back wall.

Nick's muse-studying appreciation resumed, carefully sketching the pretty girl's profile in secret. No threat of detection, she would have had to turn and look towards him to detect his gaze. Her complexion was immaculate; English rose. A sweet and innocent princess or the 'girl next door' he had always dreamed of. They were in the same class. Did she know how beautiful she was? In Nick's eyes, she was a perfect ten.

His vision drifted to the left of the bridge of her elegant nose, catching sight of perfectly geometrical cheekbones and butterfly lashes in an attempt to reveal her ocular palette.

For a second, he found himself looking directly into a pair of dark brown eyes. Two eyes, but she hadn't moved her head. Nick then realised the beauty's friend had shifted aside and was staring back at him. They had both tilted to the side. Their eyes had locked, holding sight for over a second. With a flinch, reflex motor-skills kicked-in and Nick quickly flopped his head down to study his notepaper, cringing with embarrassment he held his view like a naughty schoolboy, trying to calm his beetroot cheeks.

Through his eyebrows, Nick noticed a scruffy long haired, pube-bearded, simian-like middle aged man in a baggy suit, spectacles and plimsolls, enter the room with a dramatic ape-like leap, bounding spritely onto a chair and then hop onto the horseshoe of tables with a gentle thud, hunched above the class at ten o'clock. The room fell silent.

The strange little crouching man swayed with his knuckles touching the desk for a few seconds. He lifted his arm and pointed at the first girl he was stood above with a 'grunt'. She looked back at him recoiling in her seat, confused, with a beaming, embarrassed smile. The hunched man jabbed his finger at her several times with further grunts, then, irritated and breaking from character, whispered through clenched teeth, "Your name PLEASE?"

Satisfied with the reply, he scuffled along the desk to the next person with another grunted point and onwards around the room still on all fours atop the horseshoe anti-clockwise; stealing the suspiciously 'planted' banana enroute he began to peel on two feet, growing in Darwinian stature from ape to troglodyte then to man pointing at each individual, as the banana became more interesting than their reply. No further prompt required as everyone called their name loudly for the whole class to hear.

With this visual distraction unfurling, Nick decided it was safe to look up as the monkey-man hopped off the desk half way around into the central arena now an 'evolved man' stretching his vitruvian arms and legs wide. Breaking from the star pose with a banana bite he pointed at Nick.

"Nick."

As he looked up, the class welcomed him. The two girls turned to each other, repeating 'Nick,' under their breath with giggles.

The monkey-man turned and pointed over his shoulder with a half-eaten banana without looking at the next boy.

"Philip, but everyone calls me Pip… Not because of my size though, I'm no pipsqueak!" He said in a broad Mancunian accent snapping into an aggressive pose, pointing his raised hand around the room trying to look tough, eyeballing with a humorous glare. He was short, about five foot three and proportionately slim. Everyone was smiling back at him, Nick guessed the girls would probably have described him as 'cute'. Although he must be Nick's age Pip looked about fifteen. His styled hair was thick, straight and black and his tall parting was raised up about three inches on the top of his head to deceive height. He wore white shirt, jeans, new white Adidas trainers, white socks and an expensive Fila tracksuit top. Similar sports casual fashion to Nick. He had a friendly, cheery persona and turned to Nick giving him a welcoming self-assured and cocky nod-wink.

The tutor bent forward and with mouth full pointed upside-down between his legs, with the banana skin. The class giggled.

"Roger… You can call me Todger BECAUSE of MY size!" The next boy said, continuing Pip's cheeky ad-lib, looking over the brim of his Wayfarer sunglasses scanning the girls in the room for the first time. The class chuckled. Todger appeared to be wearing what could only be described as an oversized dinner suit with bow tie and Converse All Stars. His sleeves and trouser legs were rolled up to make the ensemble fit. His large white shirt wasn't tucked in and he wore a white pocket handkerchief and had long curly, slicked back Brylcreem hair. The stylish misfit was sat in a very cocky manner with one foot on the edge of the desk leaning back balancing on two legs of his stool, coolly chewing on a cocktail stick like a 1950s gangster.

Then it was time for the most beautiful girl in the world to reveal her name. The tutor, now centre stage facing the audience did a thespian polite upturned hand gesture with his left hand combined with a slow single nod of appreciation. Evolution had taught it was rude to point.

"Jasmine." The goddess said greeting everyone in the room with a warm engaging smile and glossy plump pink lips, the shape of cupid's bow, framed pristine calcite-white teeth.

As Jasmine, the most beautiful, rare and precious flower looked directly into Nick's eyes for a split-second magnetic tractor beams drew their souls together at the centre of the universe. All around a gentle wave of turquoise ocean ripples reflected warm ultramarine summer skies with an abundance of sapphire and azure treasure, floating, sparkling iridescent, weightless in space. The blue planet outer circle iris merged indigo centrifugal radii, earth to space joining soul to soul in the centrally dilated heavenly gateway. The most precious cobalt shooting stars binding infinite sky with sea and the celestial constellation universe beyond, from here to eternity.

The now vaguely human tutor lobbed the banana skin into a bin at the front and turned to the last girl. "And finally you are?" he spoke.

"'And FINALLY you are?' I'm Jane," she echoed with a cocky laugh and gave a quick wave to the rest of the class, "But FINALLY it ought to be your introduction, surely."

Jane had cow eyes and was a bit too gobby and self-assured for Nick's liking.

The tutor started to pontificate arrogantly that 'final' was the introduction to the students, that it was HIS class and they already knew his name. It was in front of them, on the cover and spine of every book, the author of the obligatory reference material.

The projector was switched on with a gentle hum and the first acetate sheet indicated the start of the actual lesson. People started to bow their heads, scribbling personal notes. With lights dimmed and heads down Nick thought it would be safe to look up. The two girls were still trying to catch his eye. The one at the end gave Nick an eager smile, a secret wave and quickly wrote a note on the paper in front of herself; showed it to Jasmine with a chuckle, folded it twice and then pushed it to Jasmine who looked into Nick's eyes, gently holding her bottom lip between her teeth with a sweet smile.

Jasmine passed Jane's note to Todger who flicked it to Pip who then slid it to Nick. The quarter folded note said 'NICK' and once unfolded, read, 'DIBS: I LIKE YOU X'.

Dibs! Everyone knows unwritten childish playground law bequeathed that if someone declared or calls 'Dibs' first over someone then they have the right to claim them as their own before anyone else present; all must respect dibs and never get in the way. How immature and utterly devastating.

* * *

At the bar Nick's secret infatuation switched to anxiety as he recalled the following Saturday when he had introduced Heff to Jasmine.

* * *

Cutting through 'Sale Snips', a bric-a-brac shop in Sale town centre, Nick was navigating a busy narrow aisle when Heff suddenly appeared, thundering towards him knocking small bargain-hunters aside like a skittle-striking bowling ball.

"Incoming!" He shouted in an excusing tone, raising his arms overhead to narrow himself like a belly dancer as he barged at Nick.

Short of breath and with a mischievous look on his face, Heff held Nick's shoulders and turned him to face the entrance. "I love the smell of toothpaste in the morning. Smells like Victory!" Heff said, flicking his head and eyes to the side behind himself, indicating Nick observe the door as Heff squeezed his eyes shut and put his fingers in his ears.

Suddenly behind Heff, Nick saw a huge white squirt appear on the window, there was a brief unexpected scramble outside and cries of distress came from the open doorway. A tube of toothpaste had been planted on the camber of the crossing which had been squashed by a passing vehicle indiscriminately splurging the pavement and anyone at the entrance with a quick-fire, jet blast hose of minty white ectoplasm.

"Did YOU do that, you fucking dreck?" Nick asked in disgust.

"I'm not at liberty to divulge that information." Heff replied as he turned to face the central aisle, reaching up to grab a huge catering pack of Cadbury Flakes.

"Well, I hope you didn't splurge all those people for my benefit, Fat Sam."

"Oy, less of the 'fat'. I'll have you know I'm on a FAT FREE diet. I was just in Tesco sampling the FREE stuff on their cheese counter the FREE stuff on their sliced meat counter and the FREE stuff on their bakery," he unwrapped the box of Flakes and scoffed two as he joined the till queue. He shovelled another two in and mutely nudged the unpaid-for box towards Nick with a 'help-yourself' nod.

"No thanks. Are you feeding a tapeworm? Anyway why such a big box you greedy get? Have you got a job as an ice-cream man on the sly?"

"No, I've got to replace my old bid's supply before she comes home," he chomped. "She knows there's less than half a box left so if I replace it with too many in, she'll know I've eaten them all." There was method in his madness, Nick considered.

"There were thirty Flakes in that box so you're planning on eating fifteen now plus you've already eaten another fifteen at home earlier?" Nick calculated.

"Sounds about right," Heff smacked his chops. The young girl on the checkout looked up at Heff in disgust snatching the box off him to quickly check the price tag and till in the sale before there was nothing left.

They walked out towards the shopping precinct with aftershave next on Heff's freely foraged list. 'Sale Snips' sold aftershave but only cheap brands: Brut-33, Old Spice, Flint and Hai-Karate. Why have free cheap when you can have free expensive? Boots the Chemist was their next port of call.

Heff had shaved earlier in preparation for his usual Saturday night. The finishing touch was to smother himself in the most expensive aftershave tester, enough to keep the scent pungent well into the evening.

As they walked into Boots, Heff headed straight to the aftershave section and started his selection process checking the price-tag on each bottle to find the most expensive and then smothered himself in the 'free' tester. Starting with his face, chest and underarms even in his mouth and finally spraying down his pants for good measure until the bottle was empty. The scent didn't matter, he had no sense of smell.

Just then as luck would have it, out of the corner of his eye Nick spotted Jasmine, the beautiful girl from his psychology class. She was there in Boots working behind the medicine counter, preparing prescriptions for the pharmacist; a make-up-less nurse Florence Nightingale. Nick slowly moved to the side of Heff hiding himself from view relishing the opportunity to watch her from afar.

Heff realised that Nick's attention was elsewhere so he stopped showing off and looked to see what had caught Nick's eye. Nick coyly pointed Jasmine out, saying he knew her from college.

"Let's get a closer look at the 'stealer of hearts' shall we?" Heff growled, quickly mincing directly up the aisle towards her.

"No Heff, PLEASE!" Nick's plea went on deaf ears.

Fortunately, as Heff reached the condoms and cough-sweets Jasmine had moved to the store. Heff was leaning into the counter, trying to look behind the white screen. If there had been a bell, he would have rung it impatiently demanding an immediate return of service.

Jasmine reappeared looking startled but then a beautiful white smile formed when she saw Nick.

"Hi Nick, how are you?" Jasmine had remembered his name. She was wearing a white medical overall with name badge 'JASMINE BANKS'. She brushed her hair behind her ear and looked wide eyed, comfortable and relaxed as if she was happy to chat for a moment. Not in front of Heff. Nick wondered if, in her professional capacity, Jasmine may have determined that Nick was Heff's helper and that the poor unfortunate obviously required prescription drugs to pacify his madness.

Nick shyly said, "Hi Jasmine. Sorry." Quickly linking arms with Heff, practically dragging the bulk away wrestling him towards the side exit, praying for Heff to keep quiet.

Heff teased loudly, "Hi Jasmine I'm sorry. I'm so, so, sorry." In a pathetic weak voice continuing his attack, "Well, whatever you're into mate. Why don't you just go up to her, buy ten boxes of extra-large rubber- Johnnies and ask her out? What's her name… JIZZUM WANKS?!" Heff broke into hysterics howling with laughter as Nick pushed him towards the sliding doors. Nick hoped Jasmine hadn't heard.

What a mistake revealing his secret infatuation to Heff.

Chapter Eleven
The Beautiful Ones

Annoyed that Nick hadn't reacted to his perfectly witty 'Jizzum' goad, Heff walked to the bar and shoe-horned himself into the narrow space next to Nick, settling back and looking towards the dance floor, copying Nick's foot rail leaning, elbow propped stance but adding an over-exaggerated neck out, eye-popping, open mouth gawp he held for a few seconds. Still no reaction. Heff turned and cheerily shouted into Nick's right ear, "Actually when you think about it, her real name 'Banks' is better than 'Wanks'. It's a place to store a huge amount of jizz," bracing himself for a rib punch. It didn't happen.

He then delivered his best Queen Elizabeth II impression, "I name this vessel 'Jizzum Banks'. May God bless her and all who jizz in her." Wantonly toast-clinking Nick's motionless elbow-anchored vase and guzzling down-in-one his almost full pint of tinto 'gypsy-juice'. With a mouth sleeve-wipe he belched looking up into the air as if he was replying to divine intervention, "Yes, I know the rules of the game."

Heff turned to slam the empty pint on the bar near Nick's ear, demanding, "Do YOU know the rules of the game?" An invitation to down a drink in one.

But Nick remained motionless. He was captivated by Jasmine, an adorable fresh to the stage beauty pageant hopeful under the compelling bright lights of tinsel-town. He had never seen her dolled up and wearing make-up before. Impressed by her confidence to draw attention. He was mesmerised.

She wore a smart, light brown, Red-Indian style suede leather jacket with box shoulders and collar coolly turned up. From the jacket sleeves thick tassels dangled below and across the front pockets, swaying in front of her curvaceous breasts. Underneath a figure hugging electric-blue t-shirt the colour of her eyes; and around her neck a big, pearl necklace as white as her teeth. She wore a huge buckled belt and beige calotte shorts stopped above her knees with fishnet tights making her beautifully long, slim athletic legs look sun-tanned. Diamante high-heeled Chelsea boots made her just short of Nick's height, he guessed.

Her long, thick, light brown curly-permed hair flowed back, wind-tunnel-like over her shoulders as large, lip-pink, hooped Perspex bangle earrings dangled along her neckline. In contrast to the spellbinding dusky eye make-up her complexion was healthily tanned with rosy cheek-bones and her ripe, full lips were joyously fresh and tempting; sweet bubble-gum pink with a divine ambrosia gloss honey glaze, framing her perfect white teeth and the sweetest smile. She wore thick feline mascara which emphasised her alluring almond-shaped eyes in a smouldering Cleopatra style and a glittering flash of midnight blue eyeshadow complimented her natural celestial iris palette.

Suddenly, Nick froze to the spot. He swallowed without the aid of lager realising it was actually HIMSELF who was green behind the ears and naive. He had misjudged Jasmine. The sweet and innocent 'girl next door' was not an unworldly shrinking violet; she was the nucleus everyone desired at the heart of the beautiful ones. An intimidating, unapproachable siren. He daren't talk to her, how could he be so foolish to think she could even be interested in him. He looked like a tramp in his layers of clothing and fingerless gloves. Looking at Jasmine he accepted that she was completely out of his league and definitely too nice to talk to. With a shaking hand he took a large gulp from his comforting lager. He was a quivering wreck.

Heff was tired of Nick's Jasmine-induced trance. The expression on Nick's face was not a happy look of love but the self-pitying face of a sad, deflated person obviously struggling with weak and negative thoughts. The expression Heff had seen on Nick's face before they left The Vine. So Heff, being the good friend he was, patted Nick gently on the shoulder, heaved himself off the bar with a long sympathetic sigh and reluctantly said, "Right, there's only one thing for it…"

"I'M GOING TO ASK HER OUT FOR YOU!" With a demented grin and wide-eyes he was off, barging his way through the crowd towards the dance floor in Jasmine's direction.

He bloody-well would too, Nick thought shouting, "KEEP THE CHANGE, MWODGE!" to the pouting barmaid who had long since left Nick's coins neatly stacked on the bar. He rolled off his scruffy fingerless gloves, slid them into his pockets then charged after Heff taking a huge Dutch gulp from his exotic lager so it wouldn't spill as he threaded through the crowd shouting, "Excuse me, coming through, sorry." Then h e waded onto the dancefloor in search of Heff who was somewhere amongst the uninhibited posers.

Navigating through the merry-go-round of flamboyant cavorters, Nick found himself at the far side of the pub below the two-tier VIP area. No one seemed to mind that he had entered this exclusive zone. He couldn't see Heff through the crowd so he continued to squeeze past the footloose and fancy-free with his sights set on a higher-tier, ringside table. A vantage point occupied by 'The Fluff Boys' from college in front of whom, at dancefloor level Jasmine and Heff surely were.

'The Fluff Boys' had pride of place. A royal-box positioned sofa overlooking the dancefloor and evening's entertainment. The cool admirers were already surrounded by a harem of the most beautiful and attentive girls. As Nick observed the higher echelon at close range, he guessed some were wearing make-up, their healthy adolescent complexions were spotless with clear skin, well- defined, chiselled cheek bones and black-lined eyes. Each was immaculately groomed with stylish manicured hair obviously carefully sculptured regularly by fashionable salon hairdressing professionals. Three were casually seated, others were standing or propped on the back or arms of the leather sofa leaning on one another's shoulders poised as if they were posing for a Smash Hits centrefold. They were 'New Romantics' and wore stylish designer suits and fitted leather jackets like Duran Duran. They appeared more mature than Nick's friends; they didn't try to bellow over the music instead they held short, friendly and relaxed tete-a-tete conversations with gently considered movement, polite smiles and thoughtful pouts. No piss-taking or punches. Studying in the same year at college, they must be the same age as Nick, so he guessed they must have attended Sale Grammar School. The real A-List Elite. Nick felt inferior to them in every way.

As Nick bowed his head to the extended female entourage below, he squeezed into an open space and found himself in close quarters with Heff who was facing him and dancing like a nutter, strutting his funky stuff to Ray Parker Junior's 'Ghostbusters'. He had quite a space around himself as other dancers gave him a wide birth, compensating for his erratic movements. More importantly, directly to Nick's right Jasmine was sitting amongst a group of girls, elegantly perched, cross-legged on a stool. Heff had chosen a spot to make Nick stand right next to Jasmine so he couldn't simply admire her from afar.

He had to say something now, but what?

Jasmine may have successfully ignored Heff occupying her personal space but her face lit up when Nick appeared. She quickly slipped from her stool, tongue-flicking the lip-gloss adhered straw to the side of her glass and stood in front of Nick with a beautiful smile, holding his arm to gently stop him.

"Hi Nick, it's SO nice to see you," Jasmine beamed bouncing on the spot.

"Are you better now? I'm glad you've finally ventured into The B. Isn't it great?" She placed one hand gently on Nick's shoulder and one on his chest as she lifted her head up and leaned intimately close. For a moment, Nick thought she was actually going in for a kiss and started to pucker up but then realised she was aiming for his ear with secret words. He could feel himself going red but his pucker quickly became a thoughtful pout as he leaned forward turning his head to assist mouth to ear communication. He could feel Jasmine's nose or lips lightly touch his earlobe and with cool breath on his skin she whispered excitedly, "Are you going to THE PARTY?"

Grateful that Jasmine had commanded the conversation in such an unexpected direction, he stalled, pausing for thought, placing his pint on the shoulder-high table to his left so his vase clinked Jasmine's tall effervescent lemonade glass. Then he replied with a stutter, "W-What party, w-who's party?"

Heff had craned his ear in close, eaves-dropping and piped up, "Jeeeezus! If someone asks you, 'Are you going to the party', you say 'Yes I am going to the party, where is it?' Not 'what party', you div! Did Ghostbusters teach you nothing?"

Simulating some sort of gyrating hip, underarm-spray dance Heff shimmied to the side of them and turned to Jasmine over his shoulder saying coolly, "Where's the party, luv?"

Turning back to Nick, Jasmine asked if he had a pen. Not something he would usually carry in the evening but with a smile he reached into his inside pocket to pull out his father's smart Parker pen then clicked and presented Jasmine in his upturned open palm. Taking the pen, she gently turned his hand over and held it steady. As Jasmine's soft warm fingers held him securely, she carefully wrote letters on the back of his hand in neat capitals. The gentle caress, close attention and tickling sensation of being marked by Jasmine sent an ecstatic shimmer of orgasmic goosebumps tingle around his entire body.

Jasmine clicked the pen and clipped it securely back into Nick's inner coat pocket with a pat and a big smile. She then raised his hand to gently blow on the drying ink saying with a smile, "Hope to see you there." She hesitated as her face changed to a more serious expression and with a sigh she said, "I've got some bad news but I'll tell you later." She patted Nick's chest again then gave him a smile as she went with a spring of her toes.

Bad news? Nick had some REALLY bad news. What could Jasmine's be? He was sure it would be nothing in comparison to a freshly deceased parent. He'd not even had the bottle to tell Heff yet. It was probably that Jane had lawyers' documents written up to say 'Dibs' was legally enforceable. Well, he'd dispute it.

There was a sudden burst of movement as if a signal had been given. The dancefloor emptied with a single-line conga and seated people rose, wrapping themselves in scarves and coats. Jasmine turned and walked towards the steps, briefly waiting for her stool-seated a-la-mode friends to join her for a synchronised ascent. Nick then realised one of the girls on the other side of the circular table was the blonde Barbie girl who had winked at him and the other was Jasmine's friend Jane from psychology. She was beaming at Nick, waving excitedly. As she walked up the stairs, she kept turning and smiling over her shoulder and giggling. Nick gave her a friendly nod with a polite smile saying with ventriloquist's gritted teeth, "Please leave me alone." With a raised glass 'toast' held aloft.

Nick then looked at the drink he had raised in his hand realising it wasn't his vase of lager. It was actually Jasmine's cool droplet covered lemonade glass. He brought it to eye level, close-range inspecting the barber-shop-pole straw, specifically the enticing glossy pink lipstick marks which surely held traces of Jasmine's saliva. He gave the thin plastic tube a gentle sniff as effervescent bubbles tickled the inside of his nostrils then closed his eyes as he puckered up, preparing to touch the tip with his lips and tongue.

Heff was looking at Nick disgustedly. "There'd better be booze in that, you sick fucker."

Startled, Nick turned to Heff and coolly shrugged his shoulders saying, "Waste not want not! VODKA MINESWEEP!" Lifting the straw out he tipped Jasmine's glass back, gulping the refreshing citrus pop wide-mouthed, crashing the icy tumbler down as he feigned a bitter expression of hard-liquor rush. At the same time, he slipped the precious straw into his inner coat-pocket like a slight-of-hand magician.

"Spoils of war, eh? Good call Chopper... MINESWEEP FRENZY!" Heff yelled, rubbing his hands together as he eagerly launched himself into a nearby table heavily-stocked with exotic cocktails and half-finished pints, working his way indiscriminately chugging every glass as if it was a time-checked Generation Game.

The in-crowd was out. The exodus had cleared. Witnessing the evacuation, the horrified DJ quickly changed record mid-track and blasted out the 'Gitterbug' of Wham's dancefloor filler 'Wake Me Up Before You Go Go' as his assistant fumigated the 'left-over swilling' Heff with dry-ice as if he was an annoying wasp. The terrified pot lad was trying to clear remaining leftovers with the growling Heff shovelling glasses with both arms into his personal area, shouting, "On your bike, YTS!"

Within minutes, a new influx of joyous youth flowed through the pub as the dancefloor refilled and Nick and Heff found themselves surrounded by a new wave of gitterbuggers.

Nick turned to Heff and said, "It's not every day a beautiful girl invites you to a party." He held up the back of his hand as if he was showing Heff the time on a watch, pointing at the address as if it was time to go-go. The truth was they had never been invited to ANY parties, ever. Heff was happy to go wherever Nick wanted and partying with the beautiful ones sounded exciting. A quick leap up the social ladder from standing in the gutter, looking at the kerb to being elevated on a red flying carpet to the stars.

"There's one major problem though," Nick pointed out. "It's not Jasmine's party, she's a guest. We're going to have to GATE-CRASH."

Heff patted the air like an entertainer calming applause; gave a knowing nod inhaling deeply and slowly deliberated, "To gate-crash a party we're going to need a lot of booze, more booze than we can possibly drink ourselves, it's like an entry fee... and dodders. We're going to need a shit-load of rubber-Johnnies."

The bar crowd had dissipated as Nick and Heff returned through the pub towards the front exit. Nick sighed, "Another problem is that Jasmine's friend Jane fancies me, the one who was waving, she's in the same class and thinks she's got 'Dibs' over Jasmine."

"Oh, boo hoo, poor Chopper, everyone fancies him but the one he wants isn't interested!" Heff teased.

Nick was adamant Jasmine mirrored mutual attraction. Why else would she have invited him to the party? Unless it was to set him up with Jane. He started to feel confused and less confident. He HAD TO let Jasmine know that he liked HER. Forget 'dibs' or any 'sisterly-code' Jane didn't own him just because she'd expressed an interest first.

Heff continued, "Forget those two. Beauty is but skin deep. I'm attracted to intellectual, emotional and spiritual qualities." He patted Nick's back and rested his hand on his shoulder.

Nick considered Heff's words of wisdom. "Yeah right and big tits. But just one thing… WHAT ARE YOU TALKING ABOUT?!"

Heff was pragmatic. "Girls ALWAYS go out in two's. It's a known fact. So when you start chatting up some totty you fancy they'll have a friend at their side, yeah? Trying to stop your advances. Well, introduce the gooseberry to me and I'll graft on her while you cop off with your bit of trim. They'll be happy to go anywhere and do anything together, yeah? If I cop first, I'll do the same for you."

"If it's Jane you're after you're welcome to her," Nick declared. He started to think that Heff was asking him to only look for girls who had a friend interested in Heff. That would narrow his selection down enormously.

"I've moved on from them. You're missing my point. If you can't have your chosen one, go for a 'five'. Or even a minus five if it's someone you like to be with. Everyone starts off with a dog they'd be ashamed to take home to their parents. You don't look at the mantlepiece when you're stoking the fire."

What was Heff going on about? He'd never even been out with a dog, except Winston. Jane was hardly a dog. Annoyingly in the way and infatuated with Nick but certainly not a dog. Was Heff trying to steer Nick away from Jasmine, realising she was out of his league and perhaps didn't want to see his friend hurt?

As they walked out through the thick wooden double-doors into the golden street-lamp-lit neat white beer garden, the cool air was invigorating. Inhaling deeply Nick waved his arms, welcoming the freshness shaking off the deeply imprinted fumes of stale used cigarette smoke. They cheerfully thanked the doormen for their hospitality, offering friendly eye-contact to ensure a warm welcome on their next visit.

"What were those moves you were doing on the dancefloor, Heff? It looked like you were spacing out!" Nick asked putting his warm hands in his pockets for his gloves, carefully covering the freshly inked address as he gently exhaled a mist of steam.

Heff beamed, proudly turning to Nick looking for positive signs of encouragement. "Did you like it? I made it up myself."

"No shit."

"It's based on actions I do getting ready for a night out in my bedroom."

"What, like having a wank?" Heff ignored Nick's comment and started acting out his strange dance.

"I start by spraying under each armpit, left then right, left then right and making the deodorant spray sound 'Pssssst, Pssssst.' Then the disco bit, I pat on my knees four times and clap twice. I do this twice. Next I point twice down my left leg with both hands, then twice down my right leg, that's like pulling my trousers on. Then I pat aftershave on my face, pushing my palms up onto my cheeks, four times. Repeat until the song finishes. It works with nearly any song."

"Yeah, well, it certainly was special."

"You cheeky bastard. I'll teach you, if you like."

"No it's okay."

Heff grabbed Nick and put him in a headlock, messing his hair with his other hand.

"A non-believer! Kill the heretic. Mark my words you'll be doing it when you're pissed out of your head, the speed you drink, you alchy!" He bellowed then twisted Nick, who still had his hands in his coat pockets, into an unbalanced limbo position then released him so he fell onto the no-go snow carpeted lawn. Heff turned and waved to the bouncers, pointing at Nick, "Aaah, look, naughty Rick."

Nick sat in the deep snow as thawing slush melted through his cords. He leaned forward to respectfully brush ice away from the cap of his dad's cherished boots. Without the dead man's boots he'd never have made it into the pub and met Jasmine. He put his hand up for assistance as Heff gripped wet gloves and stepped on steely-caps to seesaw-haul him to his feet.

Chapter Twelve

Eat The Worm

Under golden lamplight, Nick held out his knuckle-clenched hand and with great anticipation carefully pulled the black knitted glove up and off to reveal the address on his skin beneath:

"No, no, NO!" Nick jabbered in disbelief. Horrified to see that his wet glove had smudged the address: '(??) ALCES (???) (???) D, SALE'

Keen to assist, Heff studied the remaining letters and read out loud, "Alchies of Sale," with a clear, assured nod. "Yup. She's got you sussed."

Determined not to be beaten, the sleuths studied the code and deciphered that the second word had to be ROAD and the name was likely to be ALCESTER in Brooklands, within walking distance. It was a double digit address but the number didn't really matter, there were probably only about sixty houses along the entire road, thirty on either side and surely there could only be one house-party happening tonight.

As pre-teen paperboys, Nick and Heff had learnt the location of every street name in Sale having covered all neighbourhood rounds. Holding his compass-like hand Nick moved his torso pivoting to determine the party's direction.

"First thing's first... Booze!" Heff declared in a serious tone, stopping Nick in his track and pointing at the shops. "We're going to need a GARGANTUAN amount of beer."

In the row of shops next to the pub was a convenience store known as The Dairy.

Heff continued, "What's the maximum amount you could possibly drink? Well, double it! How much can you carry... double or drop my dear cabbage. Let's see what offers Bren's got in The Dairy."

"Aw I don't want cheap offers, Heff. Not tonight. We don't want to look tight or give everyone gut-rot. Can't we just buy normal English lager?"

"Listen to Rockefeller! There's nothing tight about offering strangers free booze and anyway, what's English lager? The Dairy sells the cheapest, strongest and best imported pilsners known to humanity," Heff proudly boomed jousting the door open with his right arm.

The small bell attached to the doorframe rang as they entered.

Nick and Heff knew the humble shop keeper as alumni from school and although they were all the same age, Bren seemed old before his time. He greeted them theatrically, "Welcome discerning customers. Welcome. How may I assist your voyage of discovery this evening? Don't be guided by money, whether you're pinching pennies or raking it in, I've got just the tonic... I have the finest range of European lagers this side of Hull. Are we celebrating or commiserating this fine evening? Either way, you've come to the right place. Come in gentlemen, out of the cold."

Mild-mannered, easy going Bren worked the family business, contentedly guarding the cash-till alone in his 'Open All Hours' dust jacket, until the cows came home. Contrary to its name 'The Dairy' was not stocked with refrigerated cheese and yogurt or other milk-based consumables; it was packed with crates of fast-moving cheap imported lager, stacked shoulder high, crammed into every available space to tantalise the thirsty youth of Sale. Behind Bren's counter, expensive out of reach desirables were displayed: cigarettes, cigars, spirits, Champagne and condoms. It was these items Bren had indicated with the word 'Celebrating'.

Bren was affable, naive and undervalued: A perfect combination to nurture a relaxed attitude towards age and time restrictions on the sale of alcohol. A willing hostage, forced to keep shop every night whilst school-chums enjoyed the unbalancing and mind opening effects of his miracle cure, magic medicine. The cheery soul saw himself as a drinks doctor: a purveyor of mood enhancing social lubricants to the needy. He could never turn away a paying customer, no matter what age or the time of day. It seemed even 'notes from mum' were acceptable with the right cash. A local hero to the underage drinking youth.

There was little room to manoeuvre within the tightly packed shop as Nick and Heff stood in front of the counter looking in awe at the over-stacked crates. All around were illegible brightly coloured, hieroglyphic brand logos with 'letters' unrecognisable to any known European language. The collection of suspicious 'independently imported' beers were certainly not intended for UK market. Heff had pointed out on previous occasions that the only things that mattered were numbers: The price tag and the alcohol percentage. Anything under five percent was for wimps.

Close to the counter was a BARGAIN BIN full of stray individual cast offs, damaged or close to expiration cans, Heff's usual port of call for the cheapest grog but on this occasion he agreed to buy matching cans as Bren steered them in the direction of 'Scandia Green'.

Heff ripped a can from the plastic four-pack ring and studied it.

"Ah, good old faithful Scandia SMEG…" Heff tossed the can around in one hand, bottom to top, spinning it to study the Danish gobbledygook close to his face, carelessly agitating and awakening resting gasses.

"This is the reason the Danes are the happiest people in the world," He advised insightfully then started to flick the ring pull making an annoying high-pitched pinging sound turning his attention to Bren. With an eyebrow twitch side glance and over-exaggerated happy face, he added in a creepy whisper, "May I?"

Not waiting for Bren's 'But of course, anything for Sir' maître d'offy seal of approval, Heff cracked open the can which instantly fizzed a foamy eruption at himself, all over his face and down the front of his coat. He greedily slurped froth in a wide-mouthed attempt to guzzle. As the foam died down, Heff threw his head back gargling a mouthful, shaking his body side to side like a wet dog and then gulped down with a coughed exhalation. Teary-eyed with drips evacuating his nose he rudely flicked the ring pull over the counter shouting, "Eighty-six."

In an attempt to sound like a knowledgeable sommelier, he belched, "Biting and prickly on the taste buds; a generous blend of lead, hint of rust and cheeky zest of asbestos. The palate's aftertaste is certainly not subtle, like two black eyes! But it is a surprise to the lips…" Heff then pointed at Nick's mouth adding, "Like your oral herpes!"

Nick laughed, but advised Bren, "It's glandular fever."

Another deep gulp and this time Heff pretended to read from the can interpreting the Danish in a Scandinavian accent, "Strong Danish Pilsner Lager… Viking antidote for kraken bites… Ideal for the use in chemical warfare… Popular with the homeless… Drink chilled with rotten herring!"

"Just the ticket for us, Bren me old mucker! Cheers, I'll take twelve of the smeggers!" He said, glugging down the dregs. "Let's make it a baker's dozen, eh?" He winked, handing Bren the empty can with a crush.

"We also have the Gold and Special Editions for particularly rampant celebrations," Bren advised as he hoisted Heff's three sets of four green cans onto the counter, replacing the missing can with one from the 'bargain bin'.

"I'll just take eight of the green one's please Bren." Nick said politely, adding two pairs of four to the counter.

Heff barked, "EIGHT! Are you SHITTING me?"

The only other customer in the shop popped his head out from the back room, looking scornful over the brim of his glasses. Heff continued his tirade.

"Eight's not enough. When I said I'd give half of them away free, I didn't mean to YOU, you scav!"

"I'm on antibiotic medication. I'm not supposed to be drinking ANYTHING. The fact I'm planning to drink four is risky!"

"Too-oo WRisky?!" Heff said with a 'Jim Davidson' impression, "Yeah, right. Drugs? Who do you think you are… SID VICIOUS? Well, you're a lucky bastard. I'm doing it My Way… With good old fashioned binge-drinking!"

"I'm assuming sirs do not require gift wrapping on this occasion?" Bren said politely as he hesitated to place the cans in two Unigate 'Gotta Lotta Bottle' milk-branded plastic carrier bags, a fleeting remnant of the Dairy's heady lactose days. He then carefully doubled-up bags to reinforce handles.

Bren was about to ring the sale into the till but paused, placing both arms outstretched and locked on the counter glass, hunched over with his head bowed looking through his brow as if he was about to say something serious. Was there a problem? Surely he wasn't going to ask his seventeen- year- old school chums for proof of age.

Looking discreetly at the other customer who, still in eye-sight, had returned to study the label on a bottle of Thunderbird, Bren beckoned Heff and Nick closer then whispered, "Can I interest you two gentlemen in a couple of miniature bottles of Mescal? Just slipped through customs from South America." He leaned down hesitating to open a draw under the counter.

"Yeah, okay," Heff said quickly.

"What's Mescal?" Nick asked cautiously.

Heff replied, "Heroin substitute? I dunno, but if it's something that has to be whispered about and sold with a wink from under the counter, I want it."

"Fair enough," Nick said pulling a note out his wallet, "One each then. How much for mine?" Putting his tenner on the counter, Nick ought to get plenty of change back. He wasn't going to be caught out paying for Heff's party drinks as well.

Quickly snatching Nick's note before Bren could touch it, Heff objected, "Put your girly purse away, your money is no good here. It's my round. I insist." He added his own ten pound note and presented them both to Bren, probably hoping to receive all the change, "Oh, and a box of Johnnies."

Bren asked professionally, "Extra-large, Sir?"

With a sigh of faux modesty, Heff said, "If you've got any left Bren, mate. I've had a hectic Fresher's season. A pack of three should do it. Two for me to double-bag, you know what they're like around here! And one for Chopper to blow up on his head, bless him." He reached over and messily ruffled Nick's hair as if he and Bren were two adults talking about a scallywag youth.

Not wishing to be mistaken as Heff's stooge Nick retorting, "As if?! Fresher's season? You go to an all- boys school, you bummer!"

* * *

On the edge of darkness and the colder side of the bright shop door, they stopped within range of the incandescent nightlight. Resting their already heavily stretched-handle carrier bags in the deep snow, they studied their tantalising new discovery: The intriguing glass bottles of Mexican alcoholic spirit. Mescal: One hundred and ten percent proof. More than double the strength of tequila. Only sold in shot measures because any more would be a coma-inducing dose of deadly poison. Nick remembered maths teachers professing there was no percentage greater than one hundred; oh, how wrong they were.

But it was not the label's lure of impossible numbers that was mesmerising. The disturbing thing about the bottled translucent spirit was a dark brown, inch-long pickled grub, a 'worm' of some kind, floating motionless in the neck. Bren had told them that it was actually the larva of a moth that feeds on the plant the spirit is made from, 'live by the cactus, die by the cactus'. Poor little bugger, pickled to death in alcohol. Nick could think of worse ways to go.

"Okay Gringo, let me introduce you to my lil friend," Heff declared, reaching into his coat pocket to pull out two of The Colonel's Kentucky condiments saved from earlier. Ripping open a mini salt packet with his teeth he sprinkled a generous line of granules along the back of his left hand in a Tony Montana-esque mound and unwrapped the 'finger-lickin'-good' damp alcohol lemony-wipe which he pincer-held still neatly folded, between his outer fingers. Nick did likewise.

Heff then unscrewed the small tightly-sealed Mescal lid with a satisfying click and held the tiny bottle between forefinger and thumb, his little pinkie pointing delicately outwards and with an eyebrow-raised smile he held the bottle up and shouted the defiant battle-cry toast, "EAT THE WORM!"

Nick took a deep breath and with his best 'Speedy Gonzales' added, "Arriba, Arriba! Andalé, Andalé!"

They politely clinked bottles and with eye-to-eye synchronisation quickly lapped up the salty crystals, chugged the rocket-fuel down-in-one and bit into the lemony gauze: Lick. Gulp. Suck.

Heff lunged forward first: gasping, wheezing, breathless. He gripped Nick's coat forearm tightly. Veins popping from his neck he barked, rasping exhalation then began to Hoover deep hoops of air with tears streaming down his anxious face anticipating Nick's reaction sure to be worse.

Nick had tried to throw the shot centrally down his throat without touching the sides in an attempt to avoid his tongue and delicate 'alarm-bell ringing' taste buds, but his inner head chasm was now an inferno having been doused in what his central nervous system could only imagine was, flammable toxic pesticide.

He couldn't breathe. He was choking and could only summon weak convulsed hacks for unavailable air. For a moment, his lungs were paralysed but he instinctively forced the physical expansion of his diaphragm and exhaled through his core with all his might to resuscitate the cycle and breathe once more restoring the confused respiratory airways. A huge sigh of relief.

Gurning, Heff puckered his mouth then carefully felt his numb lips with his fingers to check they were still solid. Licking away citric acid and poison, gradually smacking his mouth open-and-shut he whispered hoarsely, "My... Tonsils... have... dissolved!" pointing at his neck and crossing his throat.

Jubilantly intoxicated and safely on the other side Nick stamped his feet with joy. With chin raised he inhaled the wonderful cool night's air; relishing the tingling sensation of micro crystals as they raced up his nostrils and gently melted on the back of his throat moistening his alcohol-abrased slippery-slip. Heff was now theatrically holding his head to one side, banging the top with his hand presumably to pour dissolved brains out onto the snow covered pavement. Glad to be alive they embraced and continued in the party's direction.

"Did you bite it?" Heff asked.

"Bite what?"

"The worm, divvie."

"No I just downed it in one. Why, should I have?" Nick asked.

"You might be farting butterflies tomorrow, mate!" He put his arm around Nick as they waded through the snow up the road chanting, "Eat the worm, eat the worm, eat the worm…" to the tune of Sousa's 'The Stars and Stripes Forever'.

They cut across the sunken rose-garden at Brooklands junction wading from entrance diagonally towards exit in the moonlight through the untouched snow blanket. With no clear footpath they took the brighter, ergonomic route straight across the lawn.

"I've got butterflies in my stomach," Nick told Heff.

"That's worm metamorphosis for you, Chopper," Heff replied sagely. "Is it burning? Might've been a glow worm. Bloody fast work osmosis. Must be the drugs. Are you going to chunder?"

"Nothing to do with the worm. It's just nerves, I wasn't expecting to see Jasmine. She'll be at the party and I look scruffy and I've never had a proper conversation with her. Even if I do actually gain confidence to talk to her I don't have a clue what to say and if I don't talk to her she'll think I'm not interested. I'll probably blow it."

"I can put a word in for you, 'my mate fancies you, will you go out with him?' Or just tell her that you'd like her to blow it."

"No thanks, mate. That won't be necessary," Nick replied with deep unease. He gave Heff a worried scowl, shaking his head.

"Why not? You'll just get pissed and hide in a corner watching her longingly from afar, whilst other less worthy suitors chat her up. She's probably already in a bedroom getting bonked by some spotty make-up wearing Grammar School posing twat right now."

"I don't think she's like that! But why am I so afraid to talk to her, why am I so shy? I don't know any girls. I don't know what to talk about."

"Gay."

"Cut it out, Heff, you know you can be a right dickhead sometimes. I need help."

"Mental help?"

"Maybe," Nick said distantly, remembering his dad's illness. He decided perhaps, this was the moment to tell Heff his news. He stopped walking and turned to Heff, "Look mate there's something I have to tell you, something serious…"

"That you're gay?"

"Look, forget it. I thought I could tell you something important but obviously not." Nick had had enough of Heff and started walking towards the garden exit.

In his defence, Heff had no idea what Nick was referring to. It wasn't the right time to tell him about his dad and Heff did seem to have a lot of good advice for some strange reason. Where did he get it from? He was so confident and Nick was timid and shy when it came to talking to girls. Looking at them anyone, would have thought it the other way around.

Heff ran up and leapt his bulk on Nick hugging him with a smile. "Look, it's okay. I was only taking the piss. The reason I'm not shy around girls is because my sister has her friends around so I'm used to talking to them. Practicing on them. You shouldn't be afraid of Jizzum just because you think she's pretty. Imagine if she was ugly, would you be able to talk to her then? Pretty girls want to be liked as well. Talk to her about the things that you like. Interests you have in common; Art, poetry, flowers, handbags, you know, that sort of thing," Heff winked.

"Seriously, find a common interest but not Psychology for fuck's sake. When she talks about something she likes, add to it, tell her about something similar that interests you. Get her interested in you. Once you've chatted her up then try and get her into the sack."

"I don't want to do that. I want to go out with her and get to know her. I really like her and I think she likes me. I'd like her to be my girlfriend."

Heff pretended to throw up.

"Sorry, I've got a little bit of vom at the back of my throat," He coughed. "GIRLFRIEND? Fuck me, you're serious. The worm that turned. You'll be talking marriage and babies next. God, roll on death. Why not play the field? Experiment? Cherchez la femme is the best game ever. First chat up the ugly girls then the plain one's. Until you get to a level where you are on equal playing fields, then try punching above your weight. I'm warning you, if you ask her out, you're going to have to go out with her every night instead of your mates. You're only seventeen for fuck's sake. And you'll go insane having to talk about Black Beauty, doll houses and dresses. Until she chucks you and you're left heartbroken. You'll come running back to me to pick up the pieces, mark my words."

"Why will she chuck me?"

"Because you're a boring bastard or your dicks too big for her tiny vaj! I'M ONLY KIDDING! Seriously, you're a handsome guy, you're talented, interesting and funny. Who wouldn't want to go out with you? It's people like me who have to do all the hard work. Ply the girls with drinks to make ourselves look more attractive to them and compete with all the handsome sods like you. Or get off with the drunk one's no one else is interested in at the end of the night. They just come flocking to you, you bloody handsome stud."

"You're embarrassing me now… but go on," Nick coaxed.

"Studley Moore, that's you."

"I race cars, play tennis and fondle women. But, I have weekends off." Nick delivered his best drunken Arthur/Dudley Moore impression with a bow to distract from the embarrassment of Heff's candour. He had never considered himself handsome and it was so unlike one of his friends to say anything complimentary. Thanks Heff. That was a real morale booster.

"You'll probably stay with Jizzum forever and she will hen-peck you until the day you die: 'Yes dear, no dear, three bags full dear'. God help you. Well, don't come crying to me, you little shit."

Nick silently noted Heff's John Gielgud quote.

They ascended the steps onto the salt gritted pavement, under the lamplight on Brooklands Road. Nick cracked open a can and asked, "How come you're suddenly so worldly wise, Heff?"

"Well, while you've been tucked up in bed, sipping Lucozade and gluing the pages together of worn-out porno-mags with man-porridge… I've been busy. Seize the day, not your battered old todger! You know my sister's at Uni in Brighton? Well, I went to see her and got off with one of her mates. I had drugs as well!"

"Wait a minute… you got off with a girl? Odgeamowey!"

"Don't sound so surprised you cheeky tosser. She was a skinhead with three earrings in one ear!"

"Nice. What was she like?"

"Look mate don't take the piss, I'm a realist. She was rough as fuck but up for it with a fat schoolboy. I'll take whatever I can get."

"How did you get to Brighton?"

"Well, Katie's in her second year so she's moved out of Halls into a big student house full of gash. Girls only. The fossils were taking some of her stuff down so I hitched along for a free ride."

"So your biddies took you?"

"They stayed in a B&B, it was only a lift. I stayed at Katie's. Anyway, she was having a house-warming party, invited all her mates, like ninety percent fanny. How could I not trap?"

Heff gave Nick a solemn look. "I did phone to see if you wanted to come, but your mum said, 'If you're not well enough for college, you're not well enough for weekends away'. Anyway, I was at Katie's helping set up, opening crisps, etcetera and a delicious baking smell was coming from the kitchen. I got there first and saved them from burning. A tray full of delicious chocolate brownies. I ate about six before my sister showed up. She freaked out saying I'd eaten her DOPE BROWNIES! I was off my tits on 'Space Cakes'!"

"Makes a change from dried banana skins. What was it like? Does she have any fit mates?"

"Well, my stomach became very warm and I started to feel dizzy. My heart was pounding. I was cloudy-headed but relaxed. Nothing I couldn't handle. Katie wanted me to honk it up but I was in it for the long ride. My whole body felt tingly, like I was pissed and everything went into slow motion. I didn't care what I was saying and met the skinhead on the stairs, we got talking and she dragged me into her bedroom."

"Are you sure it was a girl? You were 'high as a kite' on drugs after all."

"Blokes don't have fannies!" He waved his fingers triumphantly in Nick's face.

"In all fairness, it could have been his arse you were fingering," Nick laughed.

"Look she was a girl living in a girl only house, okay. No knob or goolies!"

"All right, all right. Keep your hair on Caligula."

"She said I looked like Simon-le-Bon out of Duran Duran…"

Nick sprayed a fine mist of Scandia Green breaking the drinking seal, unable to contain laughter, "Sounds like she was hallucinating on psychedelic drugs!"

Heff turned to Nick, holding up his hand, then parted his fingers, "I've fingered a girl before you've even got to first base. With drugs the portals of my mind were opened and I got exactly what I wanted."

"She sounds mental, what did you say to her to get her to drag you into her bedroom?"

"Well, these are my words of wisdom: us fat plain lads have to do more than smile at a girl to get their interest. I wooed her. Told her all about my interest in ska music, that I have a saxophone."

"Oooh, I bet that's what did it, the saxophone!" Nick scoffed.

"I talked about skinheads. Asked her about herself, where she was from. I teased out a few compliments and facts about London's East End, letting her know I was interested in her. If you ask the right questions, you don't have to do much talking. Get them to do all the hard work."

"Nothing to do with the fact she lives with Katie and knows that your family are wadded? She probably wanted to get preggers and claim child-support from your family. Talking of the hard work. Why didn't you give her one?"

"Well, to be honest with you, after their dinner out, my parents came back to pick me up to go to the B&B. Katie told my dad I'd stolen drugs and was trying to shag one of her housemates. He went mental and came bursting into the room and dragged me off her. The sudden force backwards made me heave. I chundered all over her and her bed. Not my finest moment. Don't think she wants to see me again."

"No shit, but seriously… Is that story really true Heff?"

"Yeah." Heff pledged sincerely.

"Swear?"

"Fuck yeah," He assured.

Heff had got to third base and he'd taken drugs. Nick wasn't being detrimental but if Heff could pull a girl surely he could. It was just a question of confidence and having an interest in the girl. Nick felt like life was flying by far too quickly and he needed to pick up the pace.

"You'd have loved it Chopper, creamed your pants. All they want to do is party and shag and take drugs. Student life is ace."

"My parents want me to go to Uni, not for those reasons though. Third base, eh? You jammy sod." Nick considered the word 'parents'. He ought to get used to saying parent, but it just sounded weird. Not yet.

Another long glug of cheap beer. Cooking-lager was a safer option at the moment than experimenting with mind-altering drugs.

"What did Katie put in the cakes?"

"She'd bought an 'Enry which is cockney rhyming slang for an eighth, 'Henry the Eighth'. A weight measurement of 'ganja'. That's why she was so mad with me. She'd spent five quid on her share of the marijuana. It looks like liquorice and they just crumble the 'five-pound wrap' into the cake mix, then cook them. Simple as that. No smoking doobies. Just easy drug taking. The only thing is, if you get too much there's no way of stopping the effects unless you puke. I could handle it though."

"Says Mr Drugs! Where did she get it from?"

"From a drug dealer!" Heff beamed encouraged, "I think she's going out with him. He's as black as the ace of spades. My dad would go fucking nuts if he knew. I can ask Katie to post us some ganja if you like. Two pounds fifty each, plus postage and packaging. Let's say three quid each. We can go to the post office and send her a postal order. We could make dope brownies for when Salty's home brew's ready."

"Like that's going to end well... Blind-drunk on moonshine we tuck into half-raw Frankenstein Rat-Meat, then finish ourselves off with an uncontrolled amount of illegal drugs! We'd definitely be able to fill the bath with puke. Nah, Drugs aren't for me mate... I get my creativity naturally I don't want to fuck with my mind. Have you gone cold turkey yet?"

Heff started clucking, waving his arms and strutting. "Cold? More like Frozen... Brrr!" He shook himself.

"It's a rocky road, mate. And turkey's gobble not cluck. You'll be on opium or chasing the dinosaur next. A pimp's bitch giving out free blowjobs in a crack den to feed your smack habit."

Heff gesticulated performing a blowjob in his open mouth, pounding his inner cheek with his tongue, "Gobble, gobble!" he slurped.

Nick continued, "At Uni I want to develop my skills and knowledge of art and design. I'd be happy to just meet a nice girl and get to know her, I don't want to charge to fourth base. First base or a kiss will do."

"Do you have any idea how gay you sound? You need to take drugs, live a little. All the greatest artists took drugs: Leonardo Da Nimoy, Pic-arse-hole and Tony Hart. All at it. Do things outside your comfort zone. Then you'll see the light and the true reasons for living without your parents."

It seemed Heff truly was full of wisdom, even if his knowledge of art was slightly limited. Nick then began to wonder whether University was still going to be on the cards for him. The future was very uncertain.

They ploughed onwards back-hand guided by intermittent golden lamplight, heavy boots breaking fresh snow with each satisfying crunch. As they trudged under tall lampposts, Spirograph shadows slowly grew in length stretching along the perfect gold blanketed pavement ahead like distorted hands rotating a diamond encrusted golden clock-face.

After three hundred yards, they turned left. This dormant thoroughfare was no priority to the busy gritter truck and a blanket had materialised more than twelve inches deep.

Hectares of sumptuous mansion houses set back within the peaceful, wooded copse indicated they were at the heart of the money: Millionaires row. With no traffic on the road Nick and Heff walked side by side in the middle along two tyre lanes forged through the pressed snow. The recently excavated icy tracks veered to the right and up the next road, Alcester. They stopped under golden lamplight in the middle of the wide junction to survey their destination.

The tracks led to what was clearly the party venue about two hundred yards away. The conspicuous house was gently rocking with a neighbourhood-respecting thud, thud, thud. Recently driven cars, clear of snow, were parked bumper to bumper along the driveway and in a neat pavement banking cluster. Nick also noticed a majestic black and chrome Triumph Bonneville motorcycle parked ninety degrees to the kerb.

As they stood at the end of the drive, Nick could now clearly make out 'Let's Go Crazy' by Prince along with the buzz of a crowded house. All internal lights were illuminated and curtains drawn. Heff pursed his lips and raised his eyebrows, trying to silently open the gate with no creak. They followed footprints up the glistening silver drive guided by ornate white garden lamps. To their right the untouched lawn looked like an iced cake. A 'welcoming' coach lantern wall-light overhead illuminated the Georgian doorway as they stepped up to the ominous hoop-mauling lion head 'party animal' door-knocker.

Chapter Thirteen

Gate-Crashers

Under lantern spotlight, they faced the solid front door, psyching themselves up to dare knock.

"You've 'gotta lotta bottle' gate-crashing a complete stranger's party!" Heff whispered looking down at Nick's milk-branded carrier bag. Nick laughed nervously, lifting the bag and supporting it with a loving hug from underneath at chest height. He whispered joyously to the closed door, nodding up to the bright lamp with a squint, "We were guided by a star. We bring gifts... Gold, Frankenstein, Beer." He nodded towards Heff as the second present and respectfully raised the package for first and third.

Heff delivered an angelic and ethereal, high-pitched "Laaaaaa!"

Neither of them had ever gate-crashed before. Nick hadn't even been invited to a 'real' party with girls and booze. He was genuinely gutted to have missed Heff's sister's monumental house-warming.

'Let's Go Crazy' was peaking, Prince sang 'Better live now before the grim reaper comes knocking on your door.' Definitely not the best time to knock. They wouldn't have been heard anyway so they waited patiently for the volume to die down.

Nick held the package with his forearms and air-guitared along to the heavy metal outro screwing his face in concentration. As Nick battled through the electric guitar crescendo, Heff, who probably didn't know the song, joined in head banging, holding his bag at chest height with P-Funk All Star/heavy metal devil-horn hands performing his best Gene Simmons, Kiss nose-touching tongue-stretch.

As Prince screamed his final tonsil-rasping 'CRAZY!', Heff looked at Nick and gave a scared expression daring to push his forefinger towards the lion's brass ring. Nick noted the hellish irony of a 'bestial rectal probe' but kept shtum.

"Wait!" Nick said, stopping Heff's arm, "What are you going to say?"

"I'll say 'We're friends of, er, John?' There are lots of John's, right? There's sure to be a John here somewhere. 'We've got an important message from his sister, no his mum, can we come in please? And we've brought loads of booze and dodders; which we'd like to share with you, all'."

"Okay, sounds plausible," Nick said, releasing Heff's arm. "Go for it."

Heff reached out to the door-knocker once more but the lion mask was suddenly yanked away from him as the door burst inwards and a tall, leather-clad defender in a motorcycle helmet barged out forcing them apart with a large shield-like 'buffer' raised to his chest. Nick instantly assumed their break-in attempt had been rumbled and The Force's 'Special Patrol Group' riot squad had been summoned to disperse the unwelcome intruders. But with a muffled "GERONIMO!" the motorcycle jacket wearing bobsleigh-wielder hurled himself head-first, ribs crashing onto the metal sled as it hit the snow-covered lawn and sped like greased-lightning down the incline, picking up pace torpedo-like as it crashed over the finish line; confetti-raining thorny rose-bushes and sledge-hammered helmet to brick at the front wall of the garden.

The glistening 'pearly gate' party door was now wide open and a posh crowd had emerged to spectate the stunt. Nick and Heff were actually standing amongst the very important invited populous and could easily have slipped into the house at that moment. But Nick, concerned the slider may have hurt himself, dropped his bag into the snow and waded across the lawn to assist the young man who had now risen to his feet, disorientated, struggling with his helmet. Nick brushed snow from the low terracotta wall and guided the slider to sit.

The tobogganist plucked his helmet off with a gasp to reveal a surprisingly gentle face. He was slim and had a healthy, tanned complexion. He was good-looking with chiselled cheekbones, friendly dark warm eyes and Marlon Brando-esque full lips. Forward leaning, his head nodded down to quickly scoop back his bouffant hair as he flicked his head up to observe the carnage he had created. With a wry smile he gave a victorious self-clasping handshake gesture above his head to rally the crowd, adding an underwhelmed "Yaaay," audible only to Nick. Evidently drunk, the slider began to brush snow from his clothing. Nick then realised it wasn't a motorcyclist's jacket, it was actually an expensively crafted, designer fashion item snugly-fitted, with no reinforced padding, to look like a 1950s biker jacket. He also wore designer jeans and a white t-shirt which probably wasn't plain. Very cool. Inappropriate clothing for motorcycling or playing in the snow. Nick deduced that neither helmet, sledge nor motorcycle were the slider's, thankfully. He was out of his head.

Nick asked, "Are you okay mate?"

The faux-biker turned slowly towards Nick, again brushing his highlighted mop back into place. It seemed checking his hair was his 'thing'.

"Hey, I know you. You're the guy who doesn't like me from the art block." He prodded Nick accusingly and his wet hair flopped down again over his dark eyes. Nick then realised he was actually sitting next to, talking to, one of the Duran Duran wannabes from college. A Grammar School Fluff Boy.

Maybe he'd sneered at the Fluff Boy whilst in the company of his punk friends, but he genuinely meant him no harm. Evidently he was just envious of slider's self-confidence and his friendship with Jasmine.

"I don't even know you, mate," Nick lied. "You seem like a nice guy to me." He then introduced himself. "I'm Nick, my friends call me Chopper," holding out his hand.

With a throat-filling ascending hiccup The Fluff Boy twisted around, leaned over the wall and honked a humongous, bile-pile onto the white pavement. Wiping spew from his mouth with the back of his right hand he then pushed it forward and shook hands with Nick, "I'm Geoff." Geoff brought Nick in for a friendly hug patting a spare bit of sick onto the back of Nick's dad's jacket.

"Don't you have any other names?" Nick encouraged, prying for a 'friends' name.

"Geoffrey?"

"You must have a NICK-name! It's a badge of honour. A sign of true friendship. What about 'Big-G' or 'The G-Man'? Like an FBI agent."

Heff had walked over with both carrier bags. "G-Man? More like G-Spot. What about 'Pussy'? Nicknames are given not chosen. Come on Chopper."

"This is Heff... Heff, Geoff. Are you okay? It was quite a smack."

Heff menacingly crouched sumo-like in front of Geoff eyeballing him with bull-like nostril exhalation. He then raised two fingers in a 'V', "How many fingers am I holding up?"

Geoff curtly but accurately returned the two fingered gesture. Touché.

Heff rose, towering over Geoff declaring in an angry boom, "He's fine. Can we please just go in while the door's still open, for fuck's sake."

With his father's chilling demise plaguing his conscience Nick ignored Heff and offered more assistance, "Come on mate, let's get you inside. You'll catch your death in this thin jacket, you bloody poser!" Lifting Geoff's arm over his shoulder to help him up.

At that moment, another huge black motorcycle with leather-clad rider thundered towards them. With rear wheel locked he skidded on the ungritted ice and slid to a halt on the road outside the party, right boot controlling stability. The biker gently manoeuvred the heavy, purring black and chrome Norton into a position next to the Triumph. He flicked the stand and calmly lifted his elasticated flying goggles above his eyes onto the open-face helmet, pulling down the bandit scarf to reveal a handsome youthful face. He coolly surveyed the party crowd with a finely-tuned smoulder.

Geoff's thrill-seeking audience quickly moved their attention towards the daredevil in a swarm recklessly begging pillion rides. The leather-clad biker broke through the crowd and waded to Geoff. His steel blue eyes weighed up Nick and Heff in a sultry attempt to look hard. What a poser! Definitely one of The Fluff.

The biker surveyed Geoff's crash scene with disdain taking the helmet from the wall and without a word gently whacked Geoff on the back of the head with his leather gauntlet, returning to his adoring fans.

"Who was that?" Nick asked hoisting Geoff from the wall with counterbalance.

"John."

JOHN? No nickname? Did no one from the grammar take the piss or have a sense of humour?

"Oy Heff, there's 'John', you'd better give him that message from 'his sister, no his mum'," Nick chuckled.

Heff turned and shouted cockily, "Oy, before you take your mum's scooter home, you'd better fix her shopping basket back on the front." He had some balls.

It wasn't a scooter it was a supercool road hog. A real Chopper.

Another life? Maybe. Nick had promised his parents. Promised. In an alternate universe his dad might not have had his motorcycle accident. Nick would have passed his eleven plus. His dad would still be alive and Nick would have been allowed to ride motorbikes with his Grammar School mates. He then reconsidered that if his dad hadn't had his accident and met his mum he'd probably still be with the blonde beauty, so Nick 'as he is' wouldn't have existed. His mum's ingredients would have been missing. Everything happens for a reason.

Nick quickly scanned the foolhardy crowd, turned and the three returned to the party, bold as brass lions through the open door into the bright palatial double-height entrance hall.

* * *

Leading ahead, Geoff disappeared as Nick and Heff lagged, gawping in wonder at their luxurious surroundings. The resplendent hall was a lavish vision of perfect symmetry. A pair of wide curvaceous staircases flanked either side of the grand hallway with Cinderella balcony. At ground level, open doors compassed the hub and an ornate centrepiece table displayed a huge crystal vase overflowing with freshly cut exotic non-seasonal flowers. Balanced around the periphery, back-lit antique cabinets displayed priceless heirlooms and ornately-framed picturesque paintings opened unseen windows. A single grandfather clock kept time at the head of the central meridian and ornate hands pleasingly stretched the horizontal plane at nine-fifteen. But the most impressive and imposing feature was an enormous 'Close Encounters of the Third Kind' UFO crystal-glass chandelier hanging luminous centrum to the round table, twinkling grandeur ambience. It certainly put the chandelier in Nick's lounge to shame.

The room was generously populated with a sophisticated crowd: selected for their beauty, wealth or pedigree. Well-mannered individuals politely excusing their way through channels in the central hub. Unfledged singletons cordially conversed and blossoming couples eye-batted, exchanging tactile whispers in order to become acquainted.

Uninvited, but with great ease, they had walked into a wonderfully lavish, exclusive private party full of the most popular, fashionable, beautiful and wealthy people... Sale's elite... They were in with the in crowd... As gate-crashers!

Unfortunately, the beer-packing, 'freshly-arrived' interlopers stood out like gloved sore-thumbs. They were the only ones wearing coats drinking from cans, hoarding their entire evening's supply on their person in milk-bags like miserly, alcoholic dromedaries. Their coats couldn't go into the cloakroom, Heff's frightful Kentucky Fried Chicken employee-shirt would definitely draw the wrong attention in such refined company. It was time to go deeper into the party, head for the kitchen 'safe-haven' and relinquish their gifts immediately.

An attractive clique standing at the floral display caught their eye, in particular a pretty girl with long blonde hair wearing a white jumpsuit with pert bottom and pink VPL. Nick was interested to see how, or if, the boys dare chat her up. They seemed to already know each other and were deep in conversation, even the beautiful blonde smiled on cue with every ripple of laughter. The boys' Grammar was about three miles from the girls' so how did people of the opposite sex get to meet, mix and befriend? They didn't school together. Neighbours? Siblings? They all seemed confident, articulate, mature and sober. They even addressed each other by their full, multi-syllable Christian names. Each appeared to have a drink's glass but none were in a hurry to see the bottom of it. Some had rested their half full glasses on coasters. Pacing themselves perhaps? Evidently Nick and Heff were the only people drinking to get pissed from beer cans.

As coursework curriculum conversation abated, one of the boys held his hand up pretending to be 'Harry Corbett' the puppet master from the children's TV show 'Sooty and Sweep'.

"Hello Sooty, say hello to the children." Giving a believable impression with 'purse lips holding his teeth in', broad Lancastrian accent making all 'S's' into 'Sh's'.

"What's that Sooty?" The boy asked holding his hand up to his ear, thumb and little finger being Sooty's arms. "You like Aelsa do you Sooty, but you're too shy to tell her?" His fingers wagged a nod. "You're embarrassed. Don't be embarrassed. Why are you embarrassed, Sooty?" The hand went back to his ear. "Because you haven't got any clothes on!"

Beaming awkwardly, Aelsa gently smacked Sooty's bare bottom as the others laughed encouragement.

Nick gave an uncontrollable snort of laughter, which attracted unwelcome attention. He raised his can to Heff's with a toast and slurred, like an anaesthetised Sooty, "Izzy, wizzy, let's get dizzy."

Wham's 'Freedom' started to boom from the disco room on the right. Aelsa jumped on the spot with clapping hands and dragged the girls away to cut the rug. The bare bear Sooty timidly followed. The remaining two were now glaring nervously down their noses at the drunken, beer-swilling, uncouth reprobate and his yeti ogre standing in the open doorway with their shopping. An urgent plan of action was whispered and they darted off in different directions for back up.

Sweet social serendipity, as the bolting snitches parted, Nick was delighted to see by the round table two friendly faces, Pip and Todger from psychology. Pip looked smarter than his usual 'sports casual' attire in a pleated white evening shirt with open wing collar, smart black trousers and black suede slip-on shoes embroidered with a crest. He also wore a diamante broach Nick's gran would have loved, had she been alive.

Todger was in his usual 'wacky' fashion wearing a black pork-pie hat and oversize blue teddy-boy jacket, sleeves rolled to the elbows, with a thin tie The Colonel would have loved, had he been alive.

With a welcoming cheer, Pip shouted, "Ah, Nicholas, come and give us some therapy!"

These two clearly weren't from the grammar, they had nicknames! How had outsiders managed to infiltrate the in-crowd and gain favour? Nick introduced, "This is Heff, he's an old friend from school. Pip and Todger are new friends from college."

Heff gave a rude belch, wearily crushed his can and tossed it onto the antique table like an Evel Knievel landing. But something caught his eye. He gently rested his laden carrier bag on the floor and crouched eye-level with the table. Holding the table-edge he closely studied two wonderfully vivid blue luminescent drinks, purring like Lesley Philips, "Well, Hello… Ding dong!"

In one finely-tuned movement, Pip and Todger proudly raised their crystal-glass chalices which now shone even brighter, emitting mystical phosphorescence under the chandelier. Excalibur? No. Holy grail? No. Their tall slender incandescent tubes glowed luminous blue like lightsabres! Nick had never seen a liquid, let alone a drink this colour. He was mesmerised. But Nick also noted that their cool, water-vapour covered cocktail glasses were full. Untouched. Like they'd not even been sipped. Their drink was a fashion accessory rather than an intoxicant or thirst quencher. This illuminating performance was probably why they'd chosen to stand beneath the light. You can't have your cocktail and drink it.

Todger declared, "This gentlemen, is a 'Blue Bols Lemon-sabre'... May it be drunk by you with force. It attracts the ladies almost as well as Nick's 'Endros' cologne."

"Easy tiger!" Pip said, then in an American accent added, "Save it for the birds."

Nick asked, "What's Endros?"

"The 'Mr Big' stallion lotion you wear for college... Girls are on him like Spanish flies!" Todger told Heff.

"Are they?! Which one's?" Nick asked keenly.

"I bet they are," Heff growled. Then turning back to Todger's drink he reasoned, "There's only about 20% alcohol in Curacao and you only put a splash in before you add the lemonade. No fucking point. You should add a double vodka, make it a Blue Russian... Now that would be nice. Nostrovia!" He said smacking his lips and then looked around. "Have they got a drinks cabinet?"

"More like a cocktail bar! There's all sorts in the kitchen," Pip advised.

Heff beamed, rubbing his hands together and began to sing Human League's, "Cocktail bar..."

At that moment, the civilised chatter was broken as a baying lynch-mob burst into the hall with 'intruders' in their sights corralled by the two snitches. The civilised gentry turned to face the commotion. Nick looked to Heff who was already preparing for battle, cracking his knuckles and flexing his neck, adopting a 'horse riding' stance, ready to spring into action a-la 'Kung-Fu'. Nick's knuckles tightened around the handles of his carrier bag as he drew it back behind himself, primed to launch one almighty left swing. But the two snitches immediately halted, dumbstruck in reverence to someone in their vicinity. They stopped in their tracks and were knocked to the ground by the clambering force behind. As the confused posse picked themselves up, each surveyed the situation, turned and timidly exited back to the room they had come from as quickly as they had arrived. The two red-faced snitches, without making eye-contact with anyone offered a sincere apology to the collective for their 'ill-conceived error of judgement' and 'high-jinks' as they skulked away.

The hallway returned to noisy chatter as Pip turned to Nick, "How do you know Simon?"

"Simon who?" Nick replied.

With an incredulous laugh Pip declared, "Simon, the party host? It's his eighteen's birthday."

"Don't know him."

"So what are you doing in his house?" Todger asked accusingly.

"Pure skill!" Nick announced modestly with an air of mystery, embarrassed to declare his love for Jasmine in front of his classmates, blowing his clenched fingernails then buffering them on his chest.

"We weren't invited. We GATE-CRASHED!" Heff boomed.

"RESPECT!" Pip declared.

"You're such a dark horse, Nick. I'd never put you down as the gate-crashing type! So you don't know anyone? I've got to admire your balls," Todger complimented, raising his arm onto Heff's shoulder.

"Funny that, because I admire your Blue BOLS," Heff replied, flicking Todger's glass with a 'ping'. "Gentlemen, the kitchen beckons and I'm shaking. Lead the way Todger!" Heff declared.

Nick thrust his beer package into Heff's arms, "I need a slash. I'll catch up with you in the kitchen, make me one of those blue drinks, Heff with vodka, yeah? Where are the bogs, Pip?"

Nick was pointed to a door under the right stairway. For a moment, Nick stood and watched Pip and Todger escort Heff across the hall, introducing him to acquaintances who returned welcoming smiles, nods and handshakes. It was nice to see Heff receiving a welcome. Nick felt a wonderful sense of shared belonging.

With a slight detour on his way to the water-closet, Nick walked to the 'disco' room hoping to see Jasmine or maybe catch a glimpse of Aelsa doing 'Tales of the Unexpected'. Michael Jackson's 'Billie Jean' bass was pumping out as Nick popped his head in at the door.

The room would have been in darkness if not for the large brightly coloured, rhythmic, flashing disco lights, strobes and glitterball, illuminating the room like a fairground. No furniture but bespoke-fitted, wooden floor-to-ceiling shelving ran the length of the opposite wall, heavily stocked with hundreds and hundreds of singles, albums and tapes. The centrepiece focal point was a top-of-the-range hi-fi, multi-levelled composite system with separate record player, amplifier and graphic-equaliser with rhythmic LCD flashing lights, the likes of which Nick had never seen. Four huge wall-mounted quadrophonic speakers pointed to the centre of the room. Thriller's record sleeve was visible under backlight on top of the smoked-glass deck as the record rotated. Nick surveyed the densely packed, silhouetted crowd who were pressed to the walls in a big circle, clapping in time to the beat as one person held the dancefloor.

As his eyes adjusted, Nick recognised the dancer as being one of the Fluff Boys he had seen in The Little B earlier. He had everyone's attention and was unashamedly doing the most amazing dance-moves just like Michael Jackson in his video. He must have recorded Top of the Pops and studied every step with freeze-frame accuracy painstakingly perfecting every move, strutting around like a superstar.

'Tosser', thought Nick as he turned away.

* * *

In the downstairs loo, Nick leaned into the small porcelain sink. A judging ancestral reflection looked back under the strip light. He was pale but had healthy rosy cheeks and his lips were full and red. His dilated pupils were dark and his long eyelashes gave his doe-like eyes a beguiling, emotionless expression. He swept his scruffy long dark hair back in a side parting and stared back at himself. Fresh, innocent and youthful. Pouting he observed his cheek bones, his dimpled chin and then he stared deeply, hypnotically, soul searching into the black pit of his pupils.

He considered his poor choice of words in polite company... 'Bogs'... 'SLASH'.

He pulled down his burgundy scarf and raised his chin, looking at his white throat: Adams apple, taut tendons, veins and arteries. The mirror was his father's escape route. Slash. Destiny. His father had been so mentally troubled, woefully desperate and alone, pushed beyond despair to take his own life. The reality was harrowing. Nick shouldn't dwell on this alone. He ought to talk to someone.

He then considered happy thoughts. One Very Important Person was the sole reason for this lavish party. All the sophisticated, beautiful and popular people were here to celebrate that individual's eighteen years. A celebration of life. Boys wanted to be him and girls wanted to be with him. His family were obviously rich and powerful. But who was the silver-spooned host? Where was he? His respectable cocktail Soirée was the perfect antidote to Nick's miserable time of late. In just three hours Nick's life had changed in so many ways: He thought of his dead dad covered in blood being discovered by police officers in the snow, his mother, free at last, granted a separation rather than the divorce she had sought but at what price? All the frightening and sad thoughts that had raced through his mind. Doused in alcohol. The wonderfully exciting Little B. This fantastic party where he had been accepted by genuinely nice people. Thank you Simon, whoever you are. Only one thing… Nick wasn't supposed to be there. Simon didn't know him. He was an imposter, a gate-crasher; the snitches were right to try and throw him out. Jasmine was Nick's real reason to be there. His raison d'être. Thank you Jasmine. But where was she?

Nick gave himself a cold water cheek splash, towel dried and with one last mirror-filling Paddington hard stare, walked back out to the party with not a care in the world.

Looking up, he saw Geoff walking down the opposite stairway alone. Nick gave him a friendly hand raise. Geoff, being an 'inner circle' special guest, had been upstairs to smarten his appearance, he'd definitely used a hairdryer and hairspray. It looked like he had a bouffant and may even have been wearing make-up!

Nick politely excused through the crowd to the bottom of the staircase to greet Geoff.

At that moment, the dancing Fluff Boy 'moonwalked' out of the disco room, his body moved backwards like he was going the wrong way on a conveyor belt.

He stopped near Nick and Geoff then spun around. With gyrating hips, he pulled up his pants, grabbed his crotch, then mimed running a comb through his hair. He slid and twitched his feet, kicked a foot in the air, then jumped onto his tiptoes and raised his 'invisible' jacket collar. To Nick all this erratic movement was like Monty Python's 'Ministry of Silly Walks' and he tried to hold back a smirk, thinking everyone else would be doing likewise.

For the finale, as the song faded out, he mimed taking off and throwing a hat up to the balcony. As he held the outstretched panting pose, Nick was amazed the hallway crowd applauded with genuine cheers and whistles. No piss-taking. With a theatrical bow the Fluff Boy squawked a Michael Jackson trademark "Hee Hee!" to Geoff, throwing up his collar and holding a painful looking knee-forward tiptoe stance. This Fluff Boy was a complete and utter show-off.

This must be the party host. Nick politely asked Geoff, "Is this Simon?" Although undeniably good looking, this narcissist was so self-absorbed and big-headed he obviously thought he was God's gift. Nick thought he looked 'cooler' when he was doing nothing, sitting silently on a sofa in the Little B.

Geoff said, "No, this is Daran."

Duran-Daran blatantly fawned over a tailored look. His big hair was dark with a hint of auburn and long straight, blonde highlight's masked his demure eyes. The bouffant was dramatically swept back, tall and wavy on top, shorter at the sides. All sprayed into place, flowing like a mane long-and-curly over his collar at the back. Nick could now see make-up: subtle acne-covering cheek bones, 'Smash Hits' eyes and 'natural' glossy pink lips. Daran certainly got his money's worth out of his mirror! He was dressed in a cool baggy dark-blue and black diamond pattern jumper with white upturned-collared shirt beneath. Both tucked into his thick leather belted black pleated carrot-shaped baggy trousers which were thinly-tapered to cuffed ankles. He wore white socks and grey pointed, slippy smooth-soled winkle-pickers.

Perhaps Geoff had forgotten his new friend's name so Nick turned and introduced himself with a handshake, intuitively using his 'Nick' name.

Daran said, "Like Nick Rhodes." And with a robotic body-popping arm flex pointed, "Cool coat."

"Thanks, It's my…" he paused remembering not to say it was his dead dad's, "…Abercrombie!" Unseemly flashing the inside pocket of the expensive coat.

"Nice label!" declared Daran, eagerly reaching over his shoulder to stretch the jumper's collar to one side, showing Nick the Matinique logo. "I'm a label-guy as well," He proudly admitted.

The silence was broken as the next album track started. With a mimed raising of a hat 'adieu', Daran quickly slid-reversed into the disco room with his forward leaning, knee-bent leg-drag, this time playing an imaginary air-keyboard to 'Human Nature'. A group of adoring girls ran into the darkness after him presumably in a race to catch him for the slow dance. No chance, he only had eyes for himself. But bloody hell, the girls adored him and Nick was pleasantly surprised at how friendly he had been.

Nick beamed to Geoff, "Where did all these girls come from? I mean how did you get to know them? You went to an all-boys school."

"Do you know Old Saliens? It's a sports ground and club-house joint owned by both schools. We had shared discos there in the fourth and fifth year."

He added, "It's great for parties, bar staffed by old-boys who'll serve anyone. At school some girls would come over for drama and debating classes and we'd also go on field trips and foreign holidays with them."

"Bloody Hell!" Nick exclaimed. "The only bars we ever saw, were on the windows to keep us in school! The PTA banned any disco's with 'our' girl's school because of the alarming rise in teenage pregnancies... Who the fathers were was 'debatable'! 'Drama' was always when the police showed up... And the nearest we got to a 'Field Trip' was the headmaster's 'Litter Pick' campaign making all pupils clean the streets in our own free-time, reassuring neighbours that most of us weren't burglars and juvenile delinquents!"

Shaking his head Nick put his arm on Geoff's shoulder, coaxing him forwards, slurring, "I've been held back. Let's get a drink, I need to drown my sorrows. Can you introduce me to some of the girls, Geoff?"

They navigated through the crowd under the balcony towards the kitchen door.

Chapter Fourteen
Di Di Mao!

As Nick and his new companion entered the plush, quarry-tiled, oak-cabinet kitchen an excited crowd huddled around the central island generating an enthusiastic buzz, passing and shaking something. People on the periphery were peering in with great interest.

To the left of the cooking station was a vacant lounge area with twin-sofa, reading-lamp and telephone table. Strangely, and probably because it was so tidy, Nick spotted under the 'Yellow Pages' four cans of 'Finger Walking' Scandia Green: Heff's secret stash? Against the wall a wide bookcase and photo frame shelving housed a portable Colour TV Ceefax listing this week's Top 40 and a very cool Sharp portable stereo twin-tape radio cassette player playing Duran Duran at a quiet level.

On the right of the luxurious kitchen, under-unit spotlights illuminated a mighty impressive room-spanning 'DIY Cocktail Bar'. Dozens of branded spirits stood neatly to attention as well as a spectrum of liqueurs and mixers, branded soft drinks and juice. A dozen clean highball crystal glasses were lined up for the next customer and a huge ice-bucket was set back on the left. A silver cocktail shaker and recipe book were both ready and waiting to be 'self-served' on top of a neatly folded tea-towel on the chrome sink side. It was like a do-it-yourself booze buffet.

Excusing himself momentarily from the close-knit scrum, a tall guy in black with blonde wedged hair, wearing a similar coat to Nick's dad's went to the tape player. He pressed 'Stop' and 'Eject', replacing the tape with one from his pocket. He closed the deck and hit 'Play' twisting the volume. As he walked back to the crowd, 'the man in black' yanked the tape, unspooled about four feet then messily wrapped the spewed brown tape around the cassette. Looking up the saboteur noticed Nick and mouthed a silent 'Oops' as he lobbed the 'damaged' tape into a wicker wastebasket. With a smile and an apologetic shrug, the blond man said: "I am Will" as New Order's 'Everything's Gone Green' flooded the chatter.

'I am Will. Will I am. William.' Deduced Nick. Clever semi-nickname word-play introduction. A bit harsh to destroy someone else's tape though. Nick had been under the impression 'The Fluff Boys' all modelled themselves on Duran Duran but Will was clearly not their biggest fan. Definitely a faction of Simon's 'pretty boy' gang though. Whoever the illusive 'Simon' was!

From the centre of the crowd, Heff's head popped up. He'd taken his coat off. The horrific chicken 'worker's shirt' was paraded for all to see. "AH, CHOPPER! You're just in time."

Pip and Todger's smiling faces rose on either side of Heff as well as classmate Jane, next to Pip in the scrum. She immediately started to make her way around to greet Nick.

Sitting at a stool with her back to Nick was the blonde 'Barbie' who turned her head elegantly with a pout to observe over her shoulder.

"Who's CHOPPER?" Pip asked loudly.

"Your basket-case mate, Nichol ARSE…His real name is CHOPPER."

Thanks a lot Heff, Nick thought with a sigh. Just when he'd started to fit in with 'normal' people Heff had to drag him back down to his level of pleb-like immaturity.

"Why do you call him 'CHOPPER'?" Todger encouraged as everyone stared at Nick.

"How rude of me. Let me introduce ourselves… I'm HEFF. My uncle is the millionaire Playboy magnate HUGH HEFFNER!" He then coughed a huge secondary-school 'secret-code' 'Mwodge!' "And he's Chopper because he's got A BIG TOOL!" Heff boomed. The crowd roared.

The blonde coolly gasped, "My God!" Sucking bubbles noisily up a straw to clear her G&T.

"Here Chopper, I've saved you one. Bombs away!" Heff lobbed a whirling missile upwards over the sniggering crowd, dinting a partition in the suspended ceiling as it plummeted down into Nick's hands.

"Oh, Thanks!" Nick shouted sarcastically then said to Geoff quietly. "Saved me one? I bloody well bought these!" Then back to Heff, "Have you got one for Geoff?"

"No. We've run out, soz." Head down, rooting in a utensil drawer.

"Don't worry Geoff, I'll get you one," Nick said glancing at the secret stash Buzbie had sent down the line. But was suddenly distracted.

Barbie twisted her bar stool around pointing knees directly at Nick. Her thighs were tanned, shaven and smooth and her red mini skirt had ridden up into her lap. She slowly uncrossed her brown tennis-player legs and with knees apart pushed her heels into the base of the stool leaning forwards to hold out an unopened can, "Here Geoffrey, take this. I don't drink from tin cans." She then noticed Nick ogling her inner thigh chasm and with a playful upturned nose and knowing smile she began to rock cheek-to-cheek rearranging her short skirt, smoothing creases to an almost respectable upper-thigh cover.

As Geoff was studying the foreign can in his hands, Nick had seen on the unit in front of Barbie another import, a white packet of Marlboro Lights. The exotic, lightweight paper-thin pack only available abroad. A real status symbol to show the owner had recently been on a foreign holiday.

"Fag?" She said, tapping the pack as a 'Pez-like' cigarette neatly popped out.

"No!" He said abruptly, "I mean, no thanks… I'm trying to cut down."

"I smoke like a chimney! I'd eat them like sweets if I could." The posh blonde said proudly, placing a long white-tipped cigarette horizontal between her soft cushioned pouting red lips. She gave no attempt to reach for a lighter or request a light. For any fire-carrying red-blooded-male it was obviously a great honour to attempt to be her match.

Remembering the box in his coat pocket, Nick fumbled to offer a light. Barbie leaned in and sucked on the amber sparking flame with no escape of smoke, then coolly blew Nick's match from the side of her pursed lips, without waving the perfectly balanced cigarette.

With a squinted observation, she asked, "Have we met?" The cigarette gently bobbed in her mouth.

"I was in The Little B earlier. You wi…" Nick then considered it was best not to say 'you winked at me', "walked past me at the entrance. You were with Jasmine I think. Hi, I'm Nick."

"Yes, you were talking to Jasmine," She purred with a smile. "Hi Chopper, I'm Grace. It's a pleasure to meet you," choosing NOT to call him Nick.

She held out her upturned hand, but in a way Nick didn't know whether to shake it, kiss it or click his heels together and bow. He chose to hold the end of her tips with horizontal forefinger and gave her manicured nails a smooth up and down movement. He then realised how scruffy his trampy fingerless gloves must have looked to such a refined lady.

By this time, Jane had navigated around, mutely cadged a cigarette from Grace and positioned herself between. She took Grace's cigarette to light her own, turned to Nick and with beaming smile blushed, "Hi Nick or should I say CHOPPER?" She teased blowing a puff of smoke into his face. "Your friend is so funny. What's all this about a big tool?" She elbow-nudged Grace with a chuckle.

"Hi, Jane. Yes, he's a real card," Nick said dryly. "It would be fascinating to study his brain in the lab. 'Abby Normal' I'd say. But anyway, look at this… You, Pip, Todger, me and… Oh, I've not seen Jasmine is she here?" He said nonchalantly surveying the crowd.

Jane's reply hit him like a sledge to the back of his head.

"Jasmine's upstairs with Simon."

It took a second to register… Then boom! JASMINE'S UPSTAIRS WITH SIMON! It was worse than hearing his father had just died. He couldn't pretend this hadn't happened. He never could have expected such a cruel, lethal blow. Jane stuck the knife in further, "They've been up there since we arrived." She then tried to emulate Nick's expression of anxiety, gazing nowhere as she dragged pensively on her cig, hoping Nick would notice her moral support.

Heff had wrapped the white cocktail tea-towel around his forehead like a head-bandage and boomed, "You came to play BEER HUNTER!"

Nick became blood-drained faint, his snow-white face ashen as his legs buckled with no power from his broken heart. Devastated, dizzy and nauseous he pushed between Jane and Grace slumping on the work surface. What was the point in being there now? He raised his frail head towards Heff and jabbered nonsensically, pleading for this cruel night to finish, all he wanted was to go home. The crowd thought this was all part of the act. Heff glared at Nick, then barked angrily, "Di di mao!" thinking Nick was playing along with his 'Beer Hunter Prisoner of War' charade. Heff leaned across and grabbed Nick by the collar roughly swinging his breeze-block arm with a slap across Nick's cheek, repeating his furious "DI DI MAO!" rant as he back-slapped Nick's other cheek. Throwing Nick down, Heff gave an appreciative thumbs-up and wink as the excited crowd roared.

As the red-faced laughing-stock, teary-eyed clown slumped head down on the unit he knew 'upstairs with Simon' could mean only one thing: Jasmine was being ceremonially 'deflowered'. This 'party' was literally a coming-of-age consummate entry to 'manhood' shagathon for the lucky bastard birthday boy. Whilst his green-behind-the-ear virgin guests giddily drank poncy colourful cocktails, laughing-at and beating-up the green-with-envy losing suitor downstairs, the winning-host was having his evil way with Jasmine upstairs. A virgin sacrifice. Heff had been right, she was getting humped by a spotty Grammar School Fluff Boy. Why had she even invited Nick? It was just cruel to rub his face in it, introducing him to her spoilt boyfriend's privileged life. Perhaps this was her 'sad news that she wanted to tell him later'. Well, bloody thanks! As he dwelt on the devastating news his cold blood warmed, then boiled. He became enraged, lifted his head and found himself facing nine other grimacing players who were all equally wild-eyed, revved up and hunched in to play 'Beer Hunter'.

Heff commanded everyone's attention with his best Robert DeNiro impression, "You wanna play games? All right I'll play your fucking games."

Each player pushed their innocuous can into a cluster in the centre. Nick had witnessed Heff's Beer Hunter 'parlour game' before. An adaptation of the 'Russian Roulette' scene in the Vietnam war movie 'Deer Hunter' but instead of a barrel-rolled single-bullet revolver aimed to one's own head, the 'roulette' was a 'pot-luck' one-in-ten chance of a heavily-shaken pressurised can of Scandia Smeg blasting into one's own ear lughole. Nick reasoned that 'IT' was surely his can, the ceiling scuffing grenade. He noted a slight indent on the rim and pushed it amongst the dud placebos, hoping to never come into contact with it again. Geoff did likewise with Grace's can. Everyone tried to stay focussed but Heff shuffled and shimmied like a 'cups and balls' street corner confidence trickster until ten identical cans were presented.

Nick had a demented look in his eye as he focused on an untainted-rimmed can within reach. This perverted pleasure dome was going to experience an almighty smegma eruption and no, not the birthday boy upstairs chucking his muck into Jasmine's tainted rim; the climax of this sick-and-twisted voyeuristic gathering would be a high pressure hosing, a saturating sanctification of splurged sticky Scandinavian sweetness. Skol! Nick rubbed his hands together baring his teeth with a maniacal grin. Bring on the floody lager baptism. Heff had ensured everyone present was culpable; all players had vigorously agitated the can, even spectators. Nick anticipated the ensuing pandemonium would put a stop to Simon's sordid soirée. The party would be ruined, Simon would have to zip up his designer pants and get the mop and bucket out, Nick and Heff would be frog-marched to the front door and shown the boot. Good. They'd come under false pretences anyway.

A range of utensils had been scattered on the surface and each player chose their own 'tool': small knives, metal skewers, screwdrivers, keys and corkscrews. Nick then realised Heff was planning a combination of both 'Beer Hunter' and 'SHOTGUN' two separate, but equally messy drinking games. Nick reached for the potato peeler. It was broad, pointed and sharp on both sides. He then chose a penknife which he opened and slid towards Geoff, whispering, "Copy me."

Nick advised Grace and Jane, "I wouldn't sit there unless you want to get soaked! Stand behind us and as soon as you see spray, duck." Grace took a long drag from her cigarette and picked up her box of fags with an expression to say 'what on earth am I doing here?' Pushed her stool backwards then stood behind Nick tottering to adjust her tight skirt again, gently exhaling as she held her left hand on Nick's shoulder, leaning her curvy, warm bosom in. Jane had her arm around Nick shielded to his right. It was a very strange feeling to have two smoking hot girls cuddling either side of him.

As news spread, more excited spectators crammed into the kitchen to witness the 'Beer Hunter Shotgun' challenge. The crowd filled every corner, jostling to witness the imminent explosion.

Heff piped up again, "ONE SHOT IS WHAT IT'S ALL ABOUT." The crowd fell silent. "The winner is the first person to finish their can, then stand it on the top of their head. But UNFORTUNATELY, one of us is not going to get that far. Oh no! ONE OF US is going to get a DISCHARGED DANISH DRENCHING! One shot is what it's all about. Ready? Okay, Let's Beer-Hunter SHOTGUN the smeg out of this Scandia SHITE! Three... Two... One... Go!"

Ten hands darted to the centre. Nick grabbed a can with undented rim. He quickly nodded approval to Geoff's. He placed the can on its side, picked up his potato peeler and aimed for the lowest of the four white printed hops below the logo at the bottom of the can. This is it. Suddenly a merciless cataclysmic explosion and riotous jet spray blasted from the other side of the table. It was Pip. His can exploded.

Accompanied by screams and screeches, a forceful spray of foam fired indiscriminately hosing everyone present. Pip ducked down under the unit pushing the grenade into the middle of the surface as it spun around like a firecracker furiously jetting beery throf everywhere. Nick and Geoff's faces were sprayed as the highly pressurised can changed direction. Todger was quick to grab and lob the erupting canister into the double-sink as it continued to spin-around like a Catherine wheel dousing kitchen units, window and ceiling. Nick pressed down sharply on his can and a small jet escaped. Phew! He punctured a hole about half an inch round, careful to bend the sharp edges inwards then leaned forwards, placed his mouth over the hole, stood upright with his head tilted then ripped the ring-pull off the top of the vertical can. Gravity pressed the Danish grog down as Nick chugged. Glug, glug, gone in a second.

Heff triumphantly crushed his can down on the top of his head like an accordion top-hat, opening his mouth wide triumphant. Clearly unbeatable as he screamed in a semi-gargle, "Did you see that? Whumph, fuck off straight down the back of me neck!"

Nick was second. Geoff bronze. It was refreshing to meet someone with a similar respect for the drug alcohol.

"How does it feel to be shot?" Heff asked as Pip sheepishly appeared from under the unit, giving a friendly back slap with a big wet hand.

The washing-up bowl had been upturned onto the grenade in the sink so the damage was nowhere near as bad as Nick had anticipated. Heff took his headband off and used it to wipe the surface. The kitchen was relatively unscathed although it now smelt like a brewery.

"It's not a proper party until a drink gets SPLIT! You've had your poncy cocktails and lager frenzy and Pip got shot... now who's ready for a knockout punch? It's HAPPY HOUR and I'm mixing!" Heff shouted as an excited crowd of dripping-wet boozy lads gathered around Heff keen to be involved in his next game, eager for drinking wisdom. Heff took the plastic bowl from the sink and placed it in the middle of the bar upturning half-bottle shots into it, two at a time, bellowing, "We'll start with a cheeky little concoction I like to call 'Window-Licker'!"

Geoff whisked a bottle of Jack Daniels away from the bar showing Nick, "Help yourself!" Then removed the lid with his teeth, spat it out and took an upturned swig staggering blindly with head up towards the sofa.

"I just want to make one of those blue drinks before Heff uses all the ingredients," Nick said, taking a tall glass from the right. He poured in a generous double vodka from 'Varrington', a single shot of Blue Bols grabbing an ice cube before Heff poured the entire contents of the ice bucket into his boozy trough. Then topped his glass with lemonade. He sideways-inspected his concoction as he walked to the sofa to join Geoff. The room was now packed with soaking-wet noisy revellers, chattering excitedly as beer dripped from the ceiling, units and brows. Now it felt like a REAL party! Nick could see Heff lifting the washing up bowl to his face to cries of, 'Drink, Drink, Drink!' Grandmaster Melle Mel was rapping 'White Lines' as the fun-packed kitchen came alive with overflowing alcohol and laughter.

Geoff took another swig from the bottle and contemplated distantly, "I used to go out with Jaz."

Humph, another one. Reputation precedes, Nick thought enviously. But then prompted, "Why did you split up?"

"We were only fourteen. We met at Saliens. I used to go around to hers to revise French." He turned to Nick and they both laughed.

"Seriously nothing happened. Puppy love, we were just good friends really, she's like a sister to me. I adore her. Her dad's a nightmare though. An absolute tyrant. I gave him a bottle of whisky for Christmas one year and he practically gave me his blessing. Alchy bastard. Pierce on the other hand lives in fear of him, poor sod," Geoff added.

"Who's Pierce?" Nick asked, not another bloody suitor surely?

Geoff looked at Nick, "Pierce, Jasmine's BROTHER. He's wearing a long camel coloured coat tonight."

"Camel coat, did he arrive at The Little B with Grace?"

"I think so."

"Peter Perfect!" Nick said with great relief, relaxing a little and taking a swig from his delicious cocktail. "So is he going out with Grace?"

Geoff coughed, "He's gay. If you think he's 'perfect', I can let him know. I'm sure he'd like you."

"No! No, I'm straight. It was Heff who Christened him 'Peter Perfect'. Put a good word in for Heff," Nick chuckled, remembering how wise Heff's 'Gay-dar' was to observe they weren't a match.

Geoff continued, "You were asking Jane about Jaz. I'll invite her over when she comes down. She should be finished soon."

Nick gave Geoff a contemptuous look.

Geoff added, "I was up there before. She was just finishing Simon off."

"Look I really don't want to know what she's doing, okay? How can you be so calm, you said you still have feelings for her, you sick bastard?"

Geoff put the bottle down on the coffee table and turned to Nick calmly. "Chill man, don't have a thrombie. Pierce was up there as well."

"Oh, I've heard it all now! Incestuous-threesome rumpety-pumpety?! Jesus Christ! You're all sick in the head, seriously deranged."

"What are you going on about?" Geoff started but everyone was suddenly distracted.

The white jumpsuit wearing blonde Aelsa was first to sound the alarm. She dashed into the kitchen, pushing through the crowd shouting, "TURN THE MUSIC OFF… THERE'S BEEN AN ACCIDENT…WE NEED TO PHONE AN AMBULANCE!" Nick felt a cold blast and the scent of fresh air as she lunged towards the phone stand. Kneeling in front of the beige telephone she picked up the receiver and dialled around the first '9'. The whole room fell silent.

Duran-Daran appeared at the door, "WAIT, AELSA, STOP!" All eyes turned to Daran. "Simon doesn't want to call the Emergency Services. He's going to drive them to the hospital. It will be quicker. He doesn't want his parents to know the police were called. Put the phone down."

Aelsa looked up with a worried expression on her face as the second '9' dial clicked its return. Geoff leaned over and put his finger on the telephone plunger.

Daran then piped up to the crowd, "Sorry everyone, party's over. Everyone has to leave right now. There's been an accident outside, someone's been hurt and Simon is taking them to the hospital. Go now, please."

Geoff stood up and added soberly, "I'll clear the kitchen. Come on everyone. Get your coats and go." Nick turned to Aelsa whose face was as white as snow, "What happened?"

"John was giving out backies on his motorbike, skidding on the ice but then crashed into a car by the gate." She covered her mouth and started to cry, then ran out to the hall realising she was wasting time talking to a stranger.

Geoff had started herding people out of the kitchen, allowing no-one to dawdle. Nick downed his Blue Russian and stood up buttoning his coat. He accepted that the kitchen mess was their fault but the motorcycle accident would have happened if Nick and Heff hadn't been there. That had been totally out of their control.

Heff joined Nick in the lounge area and said, "My advice to you is to start drinking very heavily," upturning a glass of Pernod and black which left a huge blackcurrant stain above his lip.

Looking at Heff in disbelief, Nick pointed to his own upper lip and pulled his bottom lip up with a 'copy-me' tongue lick but Heff smiled widely and raised his eyebrows a couple of times to accentuate the Groucho Marx blackcurrant moustache, then swung his long coat around like a matador's cape and leaned down to grab the four-pack of beers from under the telephone table, stuffing two deeply into each pocket.

"What?" he said, "Waste not want not", wiping his mouth with the back of his sleeve.

"Someone's injured and you're joking around. You don't give a shit, do you?"

Heff shrugged and said, "Unlucky but tough-titties. What's it got to do with me? People die every day."

"Every day," Nick repeated angrily.

"Hey, back off. It's not my fault. The only questionable thing I've done here is shake a can everyone else has shaken. Arrest me! If anyone's to blame it's that greasy toss-pot biker, John," Heff defended.

Nick wasn't mad at Heff; he was mad with himself for believing he had a chance with the host's girl. He contemplated the post-coital concubine standing by her man; supporting her heroic boyfriend's gallant rescue act racing to assist and selflessly terminating his special party to save someone. Nick was no longer required to have an awkward, defeated conversation with the victor's girlfriend and thankfully he hadn't embarrassed himself by foolishly asking her out, minutes after she'd been bonked by 'The Great Gatsby'. She didn't know Nick was heartbroken, that he had built his hopes up. Weeks of love sickness and now this. His heart couldn't take any more bashing and his head was mashed. He was an emotional wreck. His dad's suicide was an enormous burden; he didn't need additional mind games, to add to his confused state. He ought to try and forget her. Not mention her again. Heff was a good friend. He'd prepared Nick for this scenario. He was very wise. Nick ought to ease off.

As the house was evacuated, party guests collected their coats and streamed out into the cold night, down the snowy drive to form rendezvous clusters outside the gate on the white pavement. Pip and Todger were standing together with Grace and Jane, as Nick approached. Jane reached out and dragged Nick into the scrum with an armlock.

Pip declared, "The night's still young Chopper. We're getting the last train into town, burning the midnight chuff. Fancy coming clubbing?"

Geoff was last to leave the house and flicked the UFO hall light off as he pulled the front door shut, taking another swig from his bottle of JD he zipped up his leather jacket and surveyed the clear driveway from the step. Nick beckoned Geoff and asked if he wanted to join them. "Why not?" He nonchalantly replied closing the gate. Grace linked with Geoff.

Turning to the garden Nick shouted, "Come on Biggus Dickus!"

Heff was the last person on the property, artistically vandalising a six-foot snowman on the lawn. He'd quickly remodelled it into a massive snow-cock-and-balls erection with sculptured cod-piece head. Abandoning his ice-phallus he leapt over the low wall into fresh snow covering Geoff's pavement-pizza with an arms spread 'ta-da!' skid. Todger graciously welcomed Heff into the fold. With a forced smile Heff simpered to Geoff, "Can I have a swig big fella? Cheers easy."

Party pedestrians quickly dispersed and kerb-banked cars drove away. Close to the drive, one young man was checking his Ford Escort's rear bumper. The scuffed Norton was parked next to the Triumph as previously. Nick could see faint marks in the road where the bike had obviously slipped as fresh snow began to cover the trail, erasing any memory. With a shudder Nick wondered who must have been involved in the accident, some of those girls looked like they weren't wearing much protection at all.

Chapter Fifteen

In the City

The dissipated party gang headed towards Brooklands Station, carefully walking single-file in two lines along freshly made tyre tracks until they arrived at the arterial road's, wider slushy pavement. Now with room to walk together, Jane eagerly linked arms with Nick; Grace was quick to follow on his left, saying with a smile, "Two's company, three's a party!"

"And four's an orgy!" Heff's gurning face appeared between Nick and Grace like an annoying sprite. With a sudden upward twitch of Nick's left shoulder Heff recoiled to swig from Geoff's bourbon.

As if Nick wasn't there Grace huskily asked Jane, "Where did you find him? He's gorgeous." Nick started to blush, he could never have dreamt of ever being sandwiched between two adoring girls.

Jane quickly replied, "Hands off he's mine. I found him in my psychology class. I've got dibs."

She snuggled her face into Nick's soft shoulder with both hands clasping his warm under arm. Grace counter-balanced by addressing him directly, "Hold me steady Chopper or I may fall for you!"

Nick courteously offered equal support, secretly knowing he was out of his depth as his cheeks indicated with a glow.

Jane's incessant chatter entertained Nick and kept his shyness at bay. She was 'Plain Jane' in comparison to Grace though, a stunner, a beautiful sexy young woman who could easily have anyone she wanted and probably did. Nick wasn't stupid, he knew Grace was only interested in him because of Jane's infatuation. There was a game being played, a competition to see who could win. He didn't mind being their porn, should it come to that. He was loving the attention.

The group cautiously walked up the steep, rock salt scattered pavement to the station entrance at the top of the bridge. No stationmaster, the glass kiosk window said 'closed'. Next to the timetable Geoff was chatting to another group Nick recognised: Aelsa, Sooty and the two snitches. Grace broke away from Nick's arm link to ask the smouldering Aelsa for a light.

Heff whispered into Nick's left ear, "I bet she's had more cocks than the good colonel himself!"

"What's that?" Jane's ears pricked up turning to Heff.

"Oh, I was just asking Chopper if he'd told you about the colonel's Rat Meat Wall." Flashing the logo on his Kentucky shirt as Grace returned to cuddle Nick's left arm with a shudder.

Warmed by her cigarette and picking up on what she had misheard, "Tell ME about when the Rat was born."

"Ah well, I'm glad you asked me that Grace," Nick started as the group walked over the dank, puddle-reflecting, pedestrian bridge descending to the Manchester-bound platform. "You see, the rat was actually born in the Chinese year of the Rat and that is why it was given the name RAT." Nick scowled at Heff over his shoulder silently ordering him to 'piss off'.

The brass platform clock indicated it was nearly X:VI. They were just in time to catch the last, ten-forty train to Manchester. Glancing south along the tracks Nick could see a distant light on the horizon. With precious chilly minutes to spare they joined Aelsa's group in the warm waiting room and huddled in front of the dying ember coal fire. Silence fell as a tall grandfather clock hypnotically kept time, pendulum swinging like a musician's metronome. Heff started to chant:

"Me brother's in Borstal me sisters got pox,
me mother's a whore down the Liverpool docks:
me uncle's a flasher, me aunty's a slag,
and the Yorkshire Ripper's me dad.
Na-na-nah, na-na-na-naa-nah, na-na-na-na-nah, Oy!"

He finished his performance with an imaginary, 'Doosh, stitch that!' skinhead's headbutt and Aelsa eagerly started a round of applause. This crowd appreciated Heff's japery; polar opposites to The Bang Gang who would have dissed his poetic performance. Nick whispered to Heff with a smile, "I thought you said girls go out in two's. How come Aelsa's on her own?"

With the oily screech of heavy metal brakes, the tired old electric train arrived, pulling along three tall, seemingly unoccupied rickety carriages. Geoff staggered to the nearest door and tried the ancient latch which was too stiff to slide. The wet, steamy window above was slightly ajar so he forced it down, grabbed the roof-rail above and coolly hoisted himself in, feet first through the opening. A shrill whistle sounded, like an angry referee. Jane unlocked the next door with ease as everyone boarded. A red faced peaked-cap official appeared at Geoff's open window, balling, "Are you on WACKY-BACKY, you fucking idiot?! There's 25,000 VOLTS going through that cable above the carriage. Don't try to toast yourself on MY watch. NEVER do that again, you daft twat."

The furious conductor glared at Geoff for a few seconds then angrily scanned the chastised group who returned sheepish, pursed-lip, apologetic and angelic looks of silent contemplation. Order seemingly restored and warning clearly understood the guard returned to his engine as the group burst into hysterics. With a calmer whistle-pip the train departed, instantly picking up speed, steamy windows rattling irately as the carriage accelerated, thundering into the dark night along the track city-bound. Geoff stood up on his tall tartan seat, looked around and shouted, "It's RACE NIGHT!"

Nick watched the group scurry to rearrange themselves into position at the start of the carriage, all facing forward. Geoff held his nose creating a racing commentator's nasal tone shouting, "Welcome ladies and gentlemen to THE GRAND NATIONAL…"

Steaming stallions clambered onto the first row of springy old seats: bouncing, neighing and champing in anticipation. Refusing fillies Grace and Aelsa cantered down the central walkway to the carriage end 'finish line', checking 'The Chairs' and 'Belcher's Brook' enroute for sleeping obstacles as well as 'Valentine's Brook' for silent love-birds. Blinkered Nick and Heff climbed up to join what must be the 'steeplechase' start line. Heff laughed. "I'd rather do the KENTUCKY Derby!"

Geoff continued, "The going is fair to piddling. The race is about to start… As they assemble, they're under starter's orders…"

He slammed a window up to replicate the boom of a starting pistol. "AND THEY'RE OFF!"

At that moment, the sprawling mass clambered and vaulted over the first bank of seats. Jane held back, choosing to duck down and cut through the walkway, boots and arms flaying dangerously close for leverage. Todger was ahead, the front runner, missing out cushions and diving from seat tops in his bright blue jockey silks as he scrambled over furniture fences in a race to the end. Geoff could see he was out of the running and lifted up a loose seat cushion, hurling the discus down the carriage with a mighty spin to clip heels and add injury to insult. Jane had found a safe gap and ran down the central corridor. Utter carnage at the home stretch and photo-finish as Todger and Jane crossed the line, down to the wire. Grace's slimline pocket camera Supa-snapped conclusive photo evidence which would be available for an official examination in fourteen to twenty-eight days.

Geoff slipped down the final fence sideways then Heff shouted 'PILE ON!' as he threw himself onto Nick. They all lay in a heap across the warm, underheated seats at the front of the carriage catching their breath. His new friends had been charming at the soirée but they'd become mindless hooligans in public! This 'scourge on society' were Grammar School educated, high-society… Sale's finest.

New passengers joined at Warwick Road Station. The group rearrange themselves assuming formal, upright-seated positions, feet off the furniture, squeezing in next to one another in two bays as the train began urban entry. Grace at Nick's side and Jane opposite. Polite introductions ensued: 'Sooty' was Eric. One 'snitch' was called Tom. Then Jane asked, "Have you met Tracy?"

"I don't know, who is she?"

Jane snorted back with an embarrassed laugh, "Tracy's a 'HE' not a 'SHE'!"

"Tracy's my Christian name." The freckled carrot-top snitch introduced himself proudly with a wisp of an Irish accent and a rugby player's handshake, eyeballing Nick for any hint of ridicule.

He added intimidatingly, "It means 'fighter' in Gaelic."

"I bet it bloody does!" Nick said shaking his crushed fingers as he leaned back. A cruel name for any parent to give a boy; a 'get tough or die' name, like the boy named Sue… 'Tracy by name, fighter by nature'.

"I'm used to it, had it all my life. Some people call me Tray."

Nick wiped the window considering how he and Tray were similar in one respect. They had both been dealt something at birth that they had grown to live with and considered normal, something that had toughened them up physically in Tracy's case and mentally in Nick's: Tracy's girly name and Nick's father's schizophrenia. Although Nick thought it was strange how someone so physically tough cowered to harmless Pip and Todger at the party. Why had he revered them?

Tray started chanting, "Warwick Road, Warwick Road, Warwick Road!" To the tune of 'Here We Go'. Eric and Tom joined in.

Grace's warm cheek leaned in touching Nick's. They fell silent, peering out through their condensation-cleared steamy window as the sleigh-like train flew through the flour-sieve sky into the city. White flakes fluttered gently down as the ride dashed rhythmically through a monochrome multi-level metropolis maze of ascending and descending industrial heritage: viaducts, arches, Christmas-past workshops, warehouses and factories with towering, sky-stretching chimneys. In a blink of an eye the steamy carriage whip-cracked through layers of magical sugar-coated lamp-lit Dickensian heartland: freezing icy ripples sparkled in the fragile Venetian waterway, below a twisted, cobbled Fagin's-lair warren where tinsel contrast twinkled in the moonlight as the train entered the city through castle-fields in the air.

Grace, in wide-eyed wonder, started slowly, "What a…" Then added resolutely, "Bloody eyesore! That Brownfield shit-tip ought to be flattened then bulldozed into that stagnant, rat-infested, cesspit they call a canal!" She then sighed, "Give me a light, Chopper." Leaning back into her chair, shutting her gob with a fresh ciggy.

Passing unguarded Deansgate, the group agreed to pay the price alighting party central at Oxford Road Station. Hopping off Tray lead the way to the manned turnstile delivering a cheery, 'Warwick Road student single, Herr Kommissar!' With a heel click. Following likewise the pay-what-you-like fare-dodgers congregated in a huddle on the icy white Cornerhouse approach alongside juddering diesel Hackney cabs.

Emerging onto Oxford Road, the imposing Palace Theatre didn't entice under the influence: Reserved cultural performances with parents had been his only experience of Manchester by night. 'Jesus Christ Superstar', of late. There would be no more theatrical performances from his dad. He'd gone to meet his maker. Jesus Christ. But 'Following every end there is a new beginning' and Nick was alive on the city stage embracing every exciting new adult sense and watershed experience with gusto.

Congested pavements too busy for snow to settle, reformed slush into perilous puddles of churned dark ice, abstractly mirroring lights through flickering matchstick-legs as Lowry's mentor Valette had perceived. Furious wipers and impatient skid-row red-lights fought a hazy chain of porous orange and white double-deckers as they rocked the camber, skimming waves of stinging slurry and frozen backdraft onto the exposed.

It was chucking out time and the quagmire was spewing rock-hard, salt-of-the-earth debauchery. A wet hedonistic thoroughfare of decadent nightclubs and discotheques guiding the wrong way with the allure of enticing bright neon lights and thumping music. Packs of screeching, wonky heeled and cold skinned 'fur coat no knickers' harpies dragged suitable tie-wearing drunks into dance halls. Nick was now strutting like a Chorlton-Street pimp, rocking confidently supported by blonde and brunette on each arm, both vying for his attention. Another was towards the back of his mind, agonisingly history.

Two suited Rotters who couldn't see eye to eye had attracted a crowd, 'taking it outside'. One huge 'tash wearing walrus was wading into another, stirred on by a foul-mouthed damsel in distress who assisted her gallant knight with a bitter pint pot. The crowd closed in on 'a sight for sore eyes' with a gasp as eye-catching, glistening shards merged with ice crystals underfoot: Diamonds in the rough.

"Must be grab-a-granny night, no thanks!" Grace laughed, swerving to chaperone her rag-doll across the road in a tug of war with Jane. Startling sirens and flashing lights made Nick look over his shoulder: machine-gun fire, ringing bells, whirring dib-dob sounds and jackpot teasing electronic medleys merged as slot-filling pack-men battled invaders and armed bandits in an 'all the fun of the fear' arcade. The fascinating strip of revelry ended at a crossroads with a triple-X fleapit promising loners show-and-tell flicks. In his girl cushion Nick turned his head forwards with a smile through a blurry carousel of neon as they passed an exotically aromatic kebab house and the erotic desert island, bamboo and palm tree entrance to Club Tropicana where spiked drinks are free.

Onwards past the overflowing chippy, under the cinema's sheltering facade and then the all-night drunken chemist: equally handy for hopeful, fingers-crossed night-sock dodders or fearful, fingers-crossed morning-after pills. Nick watched Heff stop in his tracks and start punching the air, leaping for joy as the group continued oblivious. Heff had stumbled upon his very own 'Mecca'...

The Central Manchester branch of 'Kentucky Fried Chicken'! He tore his coat off using Todger as a coat-stand and shot through The Colonel's door, sliding with 'Hello Mammy' arms wide, waving his hands and beaming excitedly, as if he was expecting a hero's welcome from long lost friends. The staff behind the counter, wearing identical shirts looked back at him in bemused confusion. Tray, Geoff and Tom ran in behind Heff and grabbing his legs raised him off the ground and hoisted him up towards the counter. With an almighty heave they pushed his bulk over with a thud, demanding, "Serve us!"

As Heff picked himself up dusting himself down, he was suddenly aware he'd crossed the line. A staff member with badge name 'Mo' asked warily, "Which branch are you from mate? Help yourself to drinks and fries but NO CHICKEN, okay?"

Heff confidently stated in slow assured words, "I'm the new Deputy Manager of Sale Branch and I'm on a secret mission. I have direct instruction from HQ, Colonel Harland Sanders' personal orders." Tapping the side of his nose.

"I'm ordered to sample this branch's chicken with no warning. You're not allowed to serve me because you might try to select the best pieces, which wouldn't be fair, would it? It's a regional competition and there's a prize for the 'Ooer Missus, Best Breasts'." He gave a floury 'Mwodge' as he hygienically crowned himself with a paper overseas cap and boldly reached for the hallowed silver pincers. It was a dream come true to fill a bucket with the finest chunks of golden chicken, no scrawny legs or thighs. He tucked the contraband under his arm and Fosbury-flopped a counter-roll back to the customer side as his co-worker keenly served supporting marauders fries and fizzy drinks.

As the raid exited, Heff stopped in the doorway and pushing his luck turned to ask, "Oh, by the way, what's the secret recipe?"

There was a pause as the staff looked to one another, Mo replied helpfully in his North Manchester Asian accent, "We don't know, it comes ready mixed."

"Very good, very good I was just checking you weren't blabber-mouths. 'Loose lips' and all that. At this branch, do you use eggs in the batter?"

"No, no batter." Worried, Mo looked to his colleague for reassurance who nodded encouragingly.

"We dip the chicken in brine then breading mix... Which is dry. I think there's powdered egg and powdered milk in the pre-packed flour spice."

"Excellent. I like you Mo, I'll let you in on an insider's secret 'Harland' told me just this evening... White AND black pepper!" He delivered proudly with a theatrical wink as he turned with a chomp.

Standing just outside the door Nick shouted in, "Just this evening?! Were you at a seance, he's been dead five years!"

Heff pointed at Nick with a chunk of chicken, shouting over his shoulder, "Don't listen to him, he's drunk and stupid."

The posse crowded Heff like a winning goal-scorer, dragging him away, his white paper hat tilted on his head like a sailor on the town. The overflowing golden bucket was passed around until the choice cuts were shared. If the staff did actually read the January Newsletter, they would have a sur 'prize' recognising Sale's Deputy, The Colonel's number one fan, a schoolboy in front of his very own 'Rat-Meat Wall'.

All hands occupied, everyone enjoyed their free supper contentedly on the hoof. With no arm linkers Nick was able to walk with Geoff across St Peter's Square and through the curved pedestrian ginnel between Central Library and the Town Hall.

"Haven't we left club land?" Nick asked.

"You have to wear a tie and shoes to get in those places, no jeans or trainers. Keeps the 'riff-raff' out. We wouldn't get in!" He smirked with a bite, then after a contemplative pause with greasy lips added, "It's rough in there anyway and they play shit disco and chart music."

"Chart music? I thought you were into Duran Duran."

Geoff stopped mid chomp and turned to look at Nick with a high-pitched voice nearly choking, "Who told you that?"

"I don't know. I just thought you and your mates tried to look like New Romantics."

"My clothes don't reflect my taste in music. I like Bowie, Roxy, Japan... New Wave, Indy, Punk, Goth, you know? I just dress in designer gear with style and confidence. Look at Simon, if he's a New Romantic I'm Metal Mickey." Geoff stopped to throw his bones into a bin, wiping his greasy mouth with a smear along the sleeve of his leather jacket then towelled his oily hands on his jeans.

Nick didn't want to 'look at Simon', he didn't even know what he looked like but all the girls apparently did. He didn't want reminding of Jasmine's connection. He reached into his pocket and handed Geoff one of the Kentucky-lemony finger-wipes he'd saved from earlier, then reshuffled around the group, distributing the remaining cleaners. At the corner of Albert Square they all paused to freshen as a suitable passer-by, lit Grace up.

Todger drew Nick and Heff to the wall. Tom joined them.

"Pssst! You like Kentucky, poultry, yeah? Well, come here and I'll show you something really fowl," Todger coaxed them towards the street-level windows of the Indian which looked down to the basement restaurant with a dozen or so round tables of diners, twelve feet below.

Looking quickly up and down the pavement and across the square, Todger unzipping his flies, whipped out his pecker and leaned in, squashing his midriff against the window.

"Pressed chicken! Fowl... Do you get it?"

Todger clucked over his shoulder but at that moment, Heff knocked furiously on the glass window; 'BANG BANG!' making all the startled diners and waiters look up at Todger's flattened old cock sack.

The leaning flasher struggled to stand then quickly darted to his right, tucking his manhood away as he and Heff fled in hysterics into the crowd. Tom turned to the window, dramatically held his stomach and lurched forwards with a hurl, splattering the glass pane with chicken and chip spew then turned and ran after the others. Nick was now standing alone, watching their heels disappear. Astonished and unsure what had just happened and why, he slowly turned to look at the technicolour-yawn covered window and the angry diners and staff below looking up. Some were clearly distressed and covering their eyes. Nick realised that Tom and Todger's faces hadn't been seen, but his had! 'Todger by name, todger by nature' he thought, and after a split-second turned and hot-hoofed away from the scene.

At the mouth of Lloyd Street, Nick joined the group and heard Tom explaining he could control his stomach muscles to vomit at will; an unusual skill that occasionally came in handy.

"Come on lads, behave. I can get all of us in free, all you've got to do is shut up, be cool and not act like twats. Do you think you can do that?" Pip ordered angrily.

The group hushed as tiny Pip walked confidently over the street to the doorway alone. He received a hearty greeting from the two doormen, handshakes and a silent deal was made. They were outside DeVille's, a real indie basement nightclub. Another first for Nick. Heff hunched over, reducing his height by a couple of inches and shuffled to the back of the group to join Nick.

"Ditch the chicks, you're better off not taking Reenie into a club; you'll only have to buy them drinks all night. Stick with me."

"Ha, and buy you drinks all night?" Nick scoffed.

"No, I've still got these smeggers. There's one for you as well," Heff said revealing a can of Scandia Green in his magician's pocket. Nick put his arm around Heff's back and from behind discretely removed the white paper Kentucky cap, refolded it neatly and slid the sure-to-be-treasured, origami souvenir into Heff's inner coat pocket for safe-keeping.

Pip beckoned the group and the guards stood aside at ease. With clear entry they all descended the dark, rabbit hole staircase to the curious basement. Talking Heads' 'Slippery People' was booming from below as they passed the pay-booth and cloakroom with smiles as payment and one-by-one burst through the spring-hinged black door into the nightclub.

Chapter Sixteen

Nightclubbing

Oxford Road had gone to the zoo but here in DeVille's, THE CIRCUS had come to town! A big-top shaded carnival tent of fancy-dress performers and uninhibited kooks: androgynous sultry new-romantics in sequinned costumes and elaborate make-up glided in syncopation, demure raven DeVille worshipping goths lurked darkly in the shadows and colourful spiky-leather-pinned-bleached punks bounced off the walls. With rhythmic beats, out come the freaks. The flamboyant procession was complete with a thrilled audience of sexy cool new-wave 'norms': Many familiar, pale and colourful faces from Nick's art block.

An autonomous searchlight caught a glitter ball, momentarily bursting hundreds of rays into light-deprived cavorters. Theatrical exhibitionists shot in the crossfire feigned spasmodic convulsions of electrified-fits as pogoing punk rockers jostled alongside laid-back lounge-room lizards.

Pillar-mounted TV's overhead silently screened, independently of the DJ's music, video tape montage: split-seconds from action movies, snippets from pop video's and clips of stunts, crashes and nuclear mushrooms painstakingly 'pire-edited' tape-to-tape as a mesmerising flickering generation-x lifeline.

The music playlist was random, cool and edgy: Seriously tough, raw and tribal indie. No popular or 'sold out' aural bubble-gum. The vinyl ringmaster, in his own private booth held one side of a headphone to his ear seamlessly blurring records together: conducting the genre, mood and tempo, drawing in dancers like the pied-piper.

Local lad Billy Duffy and his unmistakable guitar started The Cult's 'Spiritwalker' as a new wave hit. Members of all tribes and their kinfolk stormed the erupting dancefloor, leaping into action as the drums kicked in. Illuminated mannequins and dark pillars on the periphery became wavy shadows as all lights turned to jostling heavy-beat self-expression performance art.

Grace flung her coat at Nick and launched herself into the choppy sprawling mass below. A magnetic space formed as she whirled into a ring of sleeveless, tattooed, stray-cat psycho-billies. She looked super sexy, throwing her arms in the air shaking her hips, writhing like a vamp, wiggling her backside as the tall trio of hostile Brylcreem-quiffed urban alley-cat hillbillies pushed and punched each other, in time to the music. Agitated close-by stomping goths marked their territory waving their wing-like arms at the elbow, fluffing feathers in a chicken dance. Grace was teasing Nick, beckoning him, daring him to join the rut.

Geoff shouted into Nick's ear, "Lovely isn't she? But you're playing with fire if you're out with Grace. She's a free spirited femme-fatale. She can't help attracting the wrong attention. Someone always gets hurt." He patted Nick's shoulder then turned and vanished into the crowd. Nick's mind and heart had already been broken today, he didn't need his teeth and nose breaking as well. A self-inflicted punch would do. He passed Grace's coat to Jane and left the parade, pushing through the blackness in search of liver-pickling amnesia.

Surprised by an unexpected evacuation and with a palette cleansing cross-fade, the DJ stormed, full throttle into The Smith's grinding 'What Difference Does It Make?' whisking the whole place into a wild frothy frenzied spinning vortex.

Nick recognised Heff's back leaning over a resting place for drinks. "Oy Heff, your round!" He shouted with a tap.

"I'm ROUND?! That's a bit rude! My mum says I'm big boned!" Heff shouted turning with a grin holding up two pint pots.

"Cheers! Have you been to the bar already?" Nick beamed, graciously accepting the drink. But then his smile deflated as he looked at the shelf noticing two crushed cans amongst the parked glasses realising Heff had merely 'decanted' his Scandia Green into used pint pots. Nick inspected the edge of his glass.

"Skengy! There could've been anything in these glasses, Heff! Puke... Glue... Ash... Poppers... Mandies... Are you sure they're clean?"

"They were empty. Get it down you, Howard Hughes!" He said with a gulp, "I thought you liked lipstick rims."

Remembering Jasmine's straw, Nick quickly checked his coat pocket: Safe and sound. Embarrassed that Heff had noticed his pucker-print fetish, he retorted angrily, "Yeah, off pretty girls, not transvestites! I'm not drinking from that! I'm off for a mosey. See you later." Rejecting the glass, he pushed it back to Heff.

"Suit yourself, but you've changed! I know the rules of the game," Heff said with a twinkle in his eye as he quickly necked his pint down in one and made a start on the other but stopped his throat opening gulp act as Nick, his best friend and childhood playmate, rejected him and walked away.

With a change of direction, Simple Minds 'I Travel' washed a new wave of graceful, eyeliner-wearing synth-heads into the limelight. Nick juddered past the deafening black wall of sound which throbbed and pulsated, reverberating electronic core-quaking shock-waves throughout his entire body. Feeling like he'd been through an x-ray machine he unsteadily aimed for the bar to shout himself a pint of oral contrast lager. Aelsa and her friends were at the other end of the bar laughing at their stooge Tracy who was doing a breakdance parody: mime-artist at a window, electronic robot, body-popping arm wave, space invader and spurious moonwalk. Nick didn't feel like going over or laughing. He just held up his pint and smiled a toast walking over to a neon arrow that flashed 'Lazy Lil's'.

Hesitating for a moment at the arched doorway, Nick then wandered through the portal into a strange, surreal, polar-opposite environment. He wasn't entirely sure whether he was permitted to be there. It was a bright, rodeo-themed American diner with seating booths on either side and a strong smell of chilli, grease and salt and vinegar in the air. Displayed on the walls were 'wild west show' posters, cowboy Stetsons, coiled lassos, boots and spurs and a huge five-foot tall real trophy buffalo head. Weirder still, in the middle of the room, was a circular 'crash-mat' arena, the centrepiece an imposing electronic, bareback bucking bronco ride! To check he wasn't hallucinating from Heff's ergot-laced dregs Nick looked back into DeVille's: The dark pact goth club was booming Killing Joke's 'Eighties'. The quieter, sister club/diner 'Lazy Lil's' appeared free to enter so with muffled tumble-weed music behind, Nick sauntered into the wild, wild west.

With fresh pint in hand, he propped himself at an unmanned bar, disappointed not to see a wax-moustached, sleeve-garter wearing bartender sliding shots of sarsaparilla along it. He turned and leaned back on the bar in a cool, relaxed manner like the comic-book character Lucky Luke to watch the rough stock competition.

The challenge was simple enough. Balance on raw-hide the longest to win a free drink. An operator manned cubicle on the circumference of the wrestling-ring cushioned arena controlled the speed and difficulty of the mechanical rodeo bull. A powerful spotlight above helped the bovine-master illuminate, embarrass and shanghai reluctant victims. To play, every contestant had to sign the 'life is cheap' waiver form. The ride would then start nice and slow, with the bull lurching from side to side lulling the rider into a false sense of security, then suddenly the contraption would waz into a wild frenzy, abruptly hurling the dummy into the air like a sack of spuds! Their inevitable impact was heralded with a clattering, grave-tolling handbell. Nick wondered, who in their right mind would go out in their trendiest clothes for a drunken night out at a goth club hoping to end the night wrestling a bull?

Geoff was in the limelight at the end of the long queue.

One after another, macho players were gracefully launched into the air with spectacular landing(dong)s. A poster read 'Pain is guaranteed, suffering is up to you'. Sore-losing, earth-bound Buckaroos appeared shocked to discover their fine clothing ripped. Nick turned his back on the rodeo and leaned his forearms onto the bar, pensively rotating his amber pint between his palms contemplating other inspirational words of wisdom ahead, 'Life is a rodeo and all you have to do is stay in the saddle'.

A barmaid appeared but didn't approach Nick, seeing his full pint. She made herself busy clearing the bar of used glasses pushing them two at a time up and down into the watery brush glass-scrubber, grateful as Nick moved a stack towards her. As he swept in glasses from his right, he looked up and noticed Grace entering arm-in-arm with a tall leather-clad punk; Biker John! He wasn't a punk-rocker, just a punk. He was walking with a limp and Grace was propping him up. She guided him to a vacant booth and quickly ordered a hostess.

Nick turned back to face the wall contemplating. The crash-dummy John was now here in the club after hospital treatment. He hadn't been given a crutch so couldn't be badly hurt, no broken bones anyway. He'd thrown someone off the back of his bike though: Tosser. How could he go dancing after doing that and who had brought him here? Nick then wondered what serious injuries the passenger must have suffered to need to terminate the party and rush to hospital.

But who had been the passenger? Surely it couldn't have been Jasmine, she'd been upstairs being bonk...

"OF COURSE I KNOW THE RULES OF THE GAME!" Nick shouted for the whole room to hear and quickly gulped his pint down in one, slamming the empty pot on the bar. Too late for Heff's ears. Nick hazily remembered dismissing his drinking partner. Giving his best friend marching orders.

He didn't hear the ring-master's excited bell and tannoy announce, "Do we have a volunteer at the bar?"

"Drinking alone and talking to yourself? That's not a good sign," a voice said.

"Hmmf! Another pint please," Nick slurred to the barmaid pushing his empty tankard forwards, remaining in the same gloomy slouched position, facing the wall.

"Cheer up, it might never happen," the voice said.

"It already has," Nick sighed sorrowfully, compelled to break his silence and spill his overflowing beans. At that moment, a heated, intensely-bright light beam-from-above shone down, a fire in the sky like Heaven's gate opening. Nick slowly turned to his right to face his unknown conversant, the good-Samaritan haloed guardian angel with whom he had been prepared to reveal his torment.

Nick squinted in the dusty torchlight, raising his right hand in a salute to shade his eyes. A petite silhouetted girl was standing next to him. With vision blurred, unfocused eyes, the alcoholic tempest in Nick's head churned his mind like he was a 'china shop bull' but below-deck in a force-ten typhoon.

Stunned and elated, he saw the light... it was Jasmine!

Fathoming the lucidity of this truly unexpected apparition, Nick's senses awoke and ignited, cleansing his addled mind with sobering adrenaline rush. His demeanour switched in the flick of a bull's tail from maudlin self-pity to euphoric jubilation; prayers answered, standing before him was the girl of his dreams.

"Jasmine!" Nick gasped wide-eyed, springing to attention, as his tell-tale choppers beaconed crimson.

Turning his cheek on love's-betrayal his mind raced, calculating the risks of potentially presenting himself unguarded: All his heart desired was Jasmine's soft and tender embrace... The action could easily be feigned as a friendly greeting. But the prospect of a 'cold shoulder' was too much of a gamble. He tried to summon inner strength and courage but the emotional split-second passed. Senses urged contact but sadly, he remained motionless. They were still together. So close but yet so far. What he yearned-for was not possible. Thwarted by self-doubt and fear. He could never be so bold. He was far too shy and inexperienced. He was frozen to the spot like a snowman: like Narcissus: like his dad.

Admitting defeat, Nick timidly recoiled, clumsily crossing his arms in a tormented self-hug, leaning on the bar hiding both extreme joy and extreme sadness with an untelling smile.

But Jasmine stood her ground. She was clearly there to see Nick. They stood silently, eyes locked for an infinite soul-searching moment.

The spell was broken with an alarming wrestling-ring bell. The room was full of noise again and Nick discovered his voice shouting garbled words, "Okay… ARE YOU OKAY?"

He was genuinely concerned Jasmine may be in-shock following her ordeal. He was. So much had happened since last they met. Jasmine gave a brave nod and uncertain smile. Nick decided it best not to bombard her with questions; after all, it seemed he couldn't even string a sentence together. Act calm, breathe and be cool. Formulate structured conversation. Work backwards.

"H-how did you find us?"

"Aelsa and I had arranged to come here after the party. I saw her next door and she told me you were in here… What a night!" Jasmine said with a sigh.

The wisdom of Heff: Girls DO always go out in two's. Aelsa hadn't planned to go out on her own, Jasmine was supposed to be with her! But more importantly, Jasmine had wanted to know where Nick was!

"Can I get you a drink?" he asked signalling the barmaid again, a fresh pint sitting in front of him.

"Yes please Nick, a lemonade with no ice would be lovely, thank you. I'm parched. I've had such a traumatic night."

Ice had been the cause of so much misery of late.

"Two lemonades as well, please. No ice." He placed two pounds on the bar then turned to Jasmine hesitating, "Shall I get a drink for… your… boyfriend?"

"Boyfriend?"

"Well, I thought… Simon… you were upstairs with him… then accompanied him to the hospital…"

Jasmine retorted with a defensive scoff, "SIMON?! No… We're definitely just good friends. He's a very sensitive, loyal and dear friend. I was upstairs styling his hair and doing his make-up. I went to the hospital because my brother, Pierce, was screaming in agony having broken his arm!"

Of course! Jasmine wasn't the grand finale, raving-nympho concubine Nick had concluded in his drug-addled state! She was in fact a kind, caring, sweet and innocent loyal friend, expert hairdresser and talented make-up artist… Simon was red-lipsticked not red-blooded!

'Be cool and don't blow it', Nick thought to himself, backtracking to repair the distortions in his weak, perverted mind. Lovestruck, once again he listened attentively with an adoring smile, wishing he could just lean over and kiss her sweet lips.

Jasmine continued, a little confused by Nick's doting reaction to the news of her brother's injury, "The nurses were marvellous, x-rayed him and found only a minor fracture, thankfully. He was much calmer then and insisted John and I come to DeVille's. Simon kindly brought us here while Pierce's arm was being set in plaster. He's gone back now to take Pierce home. What a birthday! He's such a caring, self-less friend. God knows what my dad will say, he'll be furious. Now Pierce will be no help in the move."

"The move?" Nick asked dreamily. Perhaps he actually stood a chance with Jasmine, after all, it sounded like she could be single and she clearly wanted to be with him.

"Yes sadly, that's my bad news." She paused and reached out placing her hand on Nick's in his folded arms: Goosebumps tingled orgasmically around his entire body. "I've known for a few months: We're moving away after Christmas."

Suddenly alarmed, Nick leapt to attention. "Moving away, where? You'll still be here though." He automatically put his right hand on Jasmine's upper arm anxiously searching her face for reassurance, but Jasmine looked down.

"Far away," she said gloomily. "To the toe of Cornwall. My grandparents own a farmhouse with caravan park and campsite in Polzeath but since my grandad died Grandma can't run it on her own, so she's given the estate to my dad. We're moving there for 'a new life in the sun'." She gesticulated inverted comas in the air with an attempt at a smile.

"The move is my dad's dream, his retirement plan. He's been out of work for ages, so depressed. He threatened my mum with divorce if we didn't go. He said he'd break up the family and go alone!"

Nick's whole world suddenly came crashing down on his weakened shoulders, knocking him to the ground and pummelling him under the floorboards. The devastating news of Jasmine's imminent departure, permanent exit was the backbreaking straw. 'Loved and lost' was an understatement. He was crushed. Goodbye cruel world. 'Sod's Law' and negativity reigned supreme. Sadness had finally defeated happiness extinguishing all guiding light. In darkness he was drowning in tar at the bottom of a dark pit with no escape, motionless, unable to scream: No one knew he was lost and broken. Just like Narcissus he was in love with someone he couldn't have. His love was in vain.

With dry mouth, he croaked, "I wouldn't wish that on anyone. My dad was depressed, wanted to break away from his family and went far away." Realising he had unwittingly started announcing his sad news he quickly swerved, reached for both refreshing glasses and offered chirpily, "Lemonade?"

Mirror image holding glasses, Nick's left hand reflected Jasmine's right, they straw-sucked thirst-quenching sugary citrus pop through moistened lips, curiously studying each other through sweet, nose-tickling, effervescent fireworks.

Looking deep into Nick's eyes, tongue and lips playfully exploring the straw end, Jasmine attempted a smile and asked, "Penny for your thoughts?"

To Jasmine it was probably just an innocent, flirtatious, fresh-slate opener to advance from her bad news but to Nick it was the key to finally unlock his anguish; willing him to reveal his inner torment…

His seriously-ill schizophrenic father had escaped from mental hospital. On the run, the subject of a three-day regional manhunt involving three police forces, penniless with nowhere to go, he'd waded day and night through icy blizzards in his nightwear. Earlier today, he'd been found, by a farmer's gate far away in the middle of the countryside, alone, frozen to death. But it gets worse… It was death by self-inflicted, broken-glass, neck and wrist artery-hacking bloody-gruesome, life-hating suicide.

'No, wait!' He thought to himself, 'I can't tell her that! Retain the outcome but condense the drama… Water it down into a brief palatable statement.'

Accepting his whole life would change following his next utterance, Nick bravely summoned the painful few words to the tip of his tongue. He was now prepared. Scared, exhausted and drained he took a deep breath and announced sorrowfully, "I've got some bad news as well." Then leaned forwards, speaking softly into Jasmine's ear.

Frozen to the spot, he closed his eyes in disbelief as he heard himself say out loud the harrowing words he had been so afraid to say all evening. Preparing for the unknown consequences he bit his quivering lips as his eyes welled.

Jasmine looked up horrified with tear-flooded eyes, "Oh no Nick, I'm so sorry." Then pulled him close hugging tightly, tears streaming down her cheeks.

Guardedly rigid for a moment, Nick succumbed, melting into Jasmine's tender embrace, slowly relaxing to wrap his arms around her shoulders reciprocating a comforting compassionate hug. Gently squeezing and stroking the suede tassels on the back of her squaw jacket Nick buried his head into her floral, perfumed bouquet of sweet velvet ringlets. The heartfelt, sombre embrace was blissful. He could have statuesquely held this position forever but overflowing eyes compelled him to reach into his coat pocket for the neatly ironed, clean handkerchief. He dabbed his cheeks then passed his dad's soft white truce-flag into Jasmine's hand, clasping her tenderly. Locked in an emotional consoling embrace.

Heff appeared over Nick's shoulder, drunk and red eyed, growling slowly, like he'd caught Nick in an act of betrayal, "Well, well, well… Et tu, Brut-33."

"Fresh pint there for you, Heff," Nick sniffed solemnly gesturing the bar with a nod, his arms tightly hugging Jasmine.

"Oh, don't try to sweet talk me you Judo, Indian-giver," Heff slurred angrily, grabbing the pint and gulping. "I've had enough of you. You've been trying to get rid of me all night, what with your poncy new arty-farty, shit music, pretty-boy 'fluffy' friends; fobbing me off and avoiding me. I bet you've not even been ill. You've just trying to get rid of me for the past few months; keeping drugs to yourself. Well, I won't leave without a fight, do you hear me?"

"Go away and leave him alone, you bully!" Jasmine blurted as she dabbed her tears.

"Oh, I've only just started… Prepare for an undressing. Not only are you handsome, thin, popular, rich and talented and you've got a cool car and fit mum, but… WELL DONE! CONGRATULATIONS!" He said clapping his hands, "You've actually grown some balls and GOT the girl of your dreams. You're a jammy git, do you hear me? You always get what you want. And what's more… What really drives me insane with jealousy… Out of all of us… You've got the best fucking PHONE NUMBER…" He mimicked Nick picking up the phone, "Double-one double-four." Grinding his teeth together with a snarl he continued, "I envy you Chopper, YES ENVY. You're a lucky bastard. Always was… Always will be! Everything always goes right for you. Coasting through life with a silver spoon up your arse. Easy Street, that's you. Not a care in the world."

"His dad died today!" Jasmine balled.

"WHAT? Come here you!" Heff bellowed, throwing his grizzly arms around the bereft couple with an almighty bear hug. Nick raised his mournful face from Jasmine's locks and buried his head into Heff's chest. A grieving trinity, Heff towered face upwards, hiding his anguish in the ether in a blind screwed-eye grimace. He started making a psyched-up and strained air-release emanation whilst clenching every muscle in his blubbery body as if he was punch-preparing, 'bracing himself' for the imminent impact of pain, with an inaudible primal scream. Like the sleep paralysis exhalation of a frozen dreamer's nightmare: Probably the last noise Nick's father ever made.

It was the only way Heff knew to deal with pain. He'd never felt grief. Jasmine and Heff both had no comprehension of Nick's horror, but their embrace was all he needed to accept the truth, openly grieve and start healing.

Then with carefully controlled breathing, Heff started, through bravely gritted teeth, "You're alright Nick, do you hear me? It's okay to cry. Go on, let it out. Boys are taught not to cry, yeah? Well, that's wrong… Fucking wrong. Crying when hurt is wrong, but this is different; this is when you're supposed to cry. Let it out. Cry. Don't worry. You're going to be alright. I'll look after you. Do you hear me? I love you like a brother. Brothers stick together through thick and thin, yeah? Always and forever. We've both lost your dad. You're not alone."

Relieved of his heavy burden, Nick felt purged and comforted by the caring embrace of Heff and Jasmine. They could now share the weight and relay Nick's sad news outwards on his behalf. His sorrowful disclosure had passed respectfully, if a little late and it hadn't been as harrowing or traumatic as he had anticipated. Tragic news delivered, Nick's mind was now flooding hopelessly with despair, heartbroken by the realisation of Jasmine's devastating news.

Heff then addressed Jasmine sternly, "I'm no bully, luv… I'm his best friend, his protector, his guardian angel, okay? I'll be here long after you're gone. But soz, I didn't mean to shoot all over the messenger."

"Shoot the messenger?" Jasmine asked, pulling back looking at Nick.

"And what did he mean, 'Got the girl of your dreams?'" Jasmine was trying to look Nick in the eye. But he was distracted, noticing a huge crowd had formed around the bronco arena to cheer on the latest death-defying greenhorn who was being tossed around like a wasp on a lolly… Geoff!

Clinging on for dear life, he was fighting the centrifugal force, clockwise then anti at dizzying, break-neck speed. Geoff was the 'G' in G-Force! The fuming genus-bos terminator, raging bull nearly blew a gasket, hurling him backwards and forwards, up and down, any which way but loose, determined to eject the infuriating straphanger from its robotic hide. The wrangler had one hand tightly gripping the bronc rein and the other counterbalancing the frenzied movement, with lightning reflex; one minute using his legs as pincers seemingly glued to the saddle then a moment later floating above as the bionic-bull kicked angrily over and over again, hovering over the blurred saddle with rhythmic spurlicks yelling, "Yee-Haa!"

The humiliated and enraged bull operator saw red and flung the rotate lever to max launching the bronco-buster forward. Geoff was almost upside down, head locked between the bull's horns, backside above in the air, both hands trapped on the rein between his legs as the death roll, graveyard spiral started. Unable to move even if he wanted, the contraption started to spin faster and faster in one direction, no more bucking or direction change, perhaps the pistons had broken. It was a Lazy Lil's record and Geoff had drawn in a massive rodeo crowd leaning in close cheering him on.

He was now completing revolutions in under a second and his distorted face was rippling like an astronaut in space-flight simulator. He wasn't letting go, of the reins anyway; but Nick could see Geoff's eyes had lost control of direction, they were spinning around his head like bagatelle marbles. Another revolution, his eyes closed and his face faded to white: Then green. Nick had already been in close proximity to Geoff's ralfing outside the party but the excited ringside crowd were unaware of his yo-yo digestion. With tightly sealed wet lips Geoff's cheeks started to grow, it was only a matter of seconds before his churning stomach succumbed to the whirling force.

"THERE HE IS!" A scary-looking 'Bride of Frankenstein' Siouxsie Sioux yelled, identifying Heff as culprit to a brawny bouncer who descended intimidatingly towards the barside trinity, putting his giant hand firmly on the shoulder of the prime suspect as the banshee claimed Heff was the person she'd seen stealing drinks next door.

At that moment, Geoff's gizzard forced an almighty flood-gate opening, exorcist-style Catherine-wheel projection... Spraying congealed bourbon-marinated beery-chicken-barf through the air over the unsuspecting audience in Nick's direction.

Nick ducked and pulled Jasmine and Heff close, shielded by the doorman, whose broad back acted as an umbrella and his dinner jacket became GEOFF'S DINNER jacket!

Gagging and retching, chunder-doused victims quickly fled the fallout scene to decontaminate themselves as the horror-show finished and the knackered steaming terminator finally seized up and rasped to a halt. Ringside, Tom the puking-prince, obligingly returned a free sympathy spew. Geoff flopped off the defeated machine onto his back and dizzily scanned the crowd for applause but heard only shrieks and screams. Sweeping his ruffled wet hair back and with a self-clasping handshake above his head he lay back in the puddles and gave a weak, audience-less underwhelmed, "Ye-Har."

With a savoury pause-in-proceedings, the malcontent master quickly assumed his other, less glamourous role 'a la school caretaker' with sand, brush and shovel and the disgruntled barmaid also sprang into action in his wake with ready-and-waiting bleachy mop and bucket.

Nick slowly looked up from the shielded protection of the looming bouncer. With fixed eyes, the great doorstopper ground his neck with a satisfying crack, well aware that globules of rancid puke were dripping from the back of his head.

"COME ON THEN, YOU PEBBLE-DASHED PENGUIN!" Heff knocked the shovel-like hand off his shoulder and rotated to face the humiliated doorman, beckoning a confrontation by raising his fisticuffs Queensberry stance.

"You're first better be your best," Heff goaded. Possibly an ill-conceived, masochistic self-destruct attempt to feel something like Nick's pain and empathise the only way he knew: Physically offering himself up for a good kicking. This wasn't going to end well.

Nick quickly moved Jasmine out of harm's way and bravely leapt between the two giants, like a boxing referee, outstretched, parting the imminent clash, seconds before a knockout punch could be delivered. "Wait, STOP! He doesn't know what he's saying. His dad died today, do you hear me HIS DAD DIED TODAY!" Fear and genuine tears in Nick's eyes. It seemed to be working.

Nick continued calmer, "He's sorry, he doesn't mean any harm. He's upset, drunk; drowning his sorrows. We shouldn't be here. We're going to leave now, okay?"

Within seconds Nick and Heff were unceremoniously escorted by the scuff of their neck's to the nearest exit and roughly ejected from the club, forced to overbalance head-first into ice-cold slurry piles.

"You're barred," the bouncer said calmly with a tired vaporous sigh, brushing his hands together as the emergency door slammed shut. A few seconds later, the door reopened and Geoff was hurled out head-first with a boot up his backside into clattering dustbins on the quiet narrow street.

"Hey, what did I do?" Geoff puzzled, rubbing his head. "And where's my prize?"

Heff helped Nick up and they began wiping ice from each other, then started smirking, well aware they had side-stepped a very tense situation. Heff then solemnly said with his arm on Nick's shoulder, "I'm sorry to hear about your dad…"

Then with an attempt at humour, "Our dad, I should say… Thanks for that. Not all it's cracked up to be this nightclubbing-lark, is it?"

Lying in the snow, Geoff delivered a Deputy Dawg drawl to the closed door, "Sakes alive! 'Shoot the cat' scared up scamper juice goes with the territory in these here parts, dagnabit!"

Heff walked over to Geoff and hoisted him up, finally accepting him. Geoff then staggered dizzily to the closed door drawing holstered fingers like a gun-slinger, shooting from the hip, "Take that you yellow bellied cotton pickin' varmint!" Blowing clouds of water vapour down the barrels of his smoking fingers.

Heff returned to Nick and pulled him in for an almighty bone-crushing bear-hug and added in a whisper, "You don't have to say anything. Talk when you're ready."

Moments later, Pip, Todger and Jane appeared at the top of the stairs via the dignified exit, followed by Grace, John, Aelsa and Jasmine. Relieved to see the ejectees unharmed the group gathering in a solemn huddle. Nick was offered gentle words, pats, hugs and sympathetic nods. Jasmine had obviously relayed Nick's news, which finally reached Geoff. Aelsa's chaperone group of 'outsiders': Tracy, Tom and Eric remained in the club.

Todger approached solemnly, "I feel your pain kiddo, my dad died when I was younger." He was the only person who could truly empathise.

Nick pulled Todger in for a hug, hoarsely repeating the overheard maudlin-mantra, "I'm sorry for your loss." Todger's wardrobe of oversize dinner-suit and Teddy-Boy jacket were no longer 'wacky' but emphatically respected.

Pip sighed blowing his lips out and announced wearily, "I wasn't really 'FEELING' it in there tonight, were you? I don't know what it was. Something just seemed… Off!" He flicked a chunk of congealed vomit off his shoulder and double-take scowled at Geoff adding with furrowed brow, "Anyone got Junior Aspirin?"

Pip then turned to Nick and said seriously, "Sorry to hear about your dad. It was brave of you to come out tonight but we're going to take you home now, okay?"

Nick didn't have to talk. He just nodded. The group walked down Lloyd Street with Nick cushioned in the middle to the bus shelter opposite the Deansgate Picture House.

Within minutes, the orange and white Altrincham-bound 264 double-decker night bus juddered up. Racing aboard permitted students shot up the narrow spiral staircase to the top deck racing to claim the back row.

A central 'pile on' of the back seat, Nick cushioned in the middle with his big boots outstretched down the aisle. Heff was squeezed in to Nick's right with Aelsa at the window: Jasmine had squeezed between Jane and Nick with Geoff at the end. Grace and John sat on the row in front to the left and Pip and Todger to the right. The exhausted diesel chugging bus was warm and cosy, reassuringly homeward-bound but the closed windows were dripping with condensation, stagnant air stale with tobacco fumes and the floor was littered with ash and dimps.

Pip shouted, "Why don't you take a bit of time in life. Spread the love. Let's GET CLOSE!" Stretching to hug Aelsa and Todger, Nick and Heff.

"I can't reach you! I'm SHRINKING!" He squealed immersed in a seat-diving smile-cracking communal embrace. Jasmine rested her head on Nick's shoulder and Heff leaned his arm over the back of the seat with his hand on Nick's other shoulder. Heff turned to his right to wipe condensation from the dark window aiding Aelsa's view. Settled in for the six-mile journey, church-like silence was only broken when Jane whispered Grace, "Crash the fags." Aelsa cadged a cig and John joined in blowing smoke rings. All collectively united in silence contemplating kindred mortal fragility.

Intermittent streetlights flashed either side of the tearful windows as the in-crowd huddled motionless at the back of the silent, smoky charabanc. In front of Nick, John made a move, slowly stretching his creaking leather arm around Grace intimately advancing. Nick began to glow with embarrassment, witnessing their budding romance, inches from his face as they started French kissing. Nick couldn't look away, the movement would have just drawn attention. Heff started tapping Nick's shoulder, sure to be staring comically wide-mouthed with bulging eyes to make Nick laugh. Nick wished he could be so bold and reach out and put his arm around Jasmine, but his arm was trapped at his side, she was leaning on his shoulder. Surely Jasmine was also watching the unavoidable 'peep-show'.

At that moment, Jasmine turned to Nick, inches away saying softly, "I'm getting off."

What? Nick's mind raced… He had a semi-on! He pulled his arm up and leaned it on the back of the seat turning to face her.

Awkwardly, Jasmine said, "Sorry. I'll need to get past you. This is my stop."

"Oh, sorry, of course." Nick retreated in an uncomfortable bent stance to clear route and pressed the red button. Jane and Pip also stood to leave at the Odeon cinema stop.

Grace looked up to Jane from her reclined position making no attempt to move and said with an amorous smile, "I'm going to John's. My parents think I'm staying at yours so I'll call you in the morning to check they've not phoned."

Jasmine, Jane and Pip passed, offering brief formal farewells with no looking back and vanished. A moment later, Geoff, John and Grace prepared to get off at the Vine/Rat-Meat stop.

Now sitting in front of Todger Nick shouted, "Wake up Heff, it's your stop."

"I'm walking you home," Heff calmly announced crossing his arms and closing his eyes as seven became four.

* * *

Todger and Aelsa remained on the bus as Nick and Heff waded down Homelands. Walking side by side along tyre tracks in the middle of the quiet road, with neat moonlit gardens Heff said, "Your dad was a good man."

"Was he?"

"Well, he made you, didn't he? He did a good job. I thank him for that. My mum said he was very handsome and always impeccably dressed; that he always wore very smart, stylish suits to parents' evening."

Nick didn't rise to the bait. They walked on in silence. At the T-junction they turned left onto freshly gritted and wider Joule Road, now choosing to walk on the pavement.

"Did you get Jizzum's phone number?"

"No," Nick said quietly.

"FOR FUCK'S SAKE, YOU MONG!" Heff bellowed.

"Shhh, this is a respectable neighbourhood," Nick whispered. "I don't even think she likes me."

"'Course she does, you wazzock!"

"Well, she didn't go for a kiss or hug when she went... She didn't even look at me or make any fuss."

"You're such a fuck up. She was being solemn and respectful, you tit. Sympathetic to the fact your dad just croaked it. She wasn't likely to start tonguing you and dry-humping. You really are a mental bastard. You've got your emotions seriously mixed up you fucking psycho. I think you need therapy."

"Maybe. She's moving away soon. She'll be gone forever."

"Well, strike while the iron's hot, my friend. Just think, if you were on a summer holiday, nothing would stop you trying to get off with a girl you fancied, even though you're never going to see her again."

"Really? I don't know about that. Anyway, I might have to move as well. I might not be here much longer either." He looked at the snow-capped telephone box and the locked ornate iron-gated park entrance, his childhood playground.

"Plenty more birds in the sea. Hey, she might give you a sympathy shag for Christmas."

"Fuck off, I'm probably never going to see her again and Shhh! We're nearly at my house and our neighbours are sleeping. Have a bit of respect. My parents can hear a pin drop outside their bedroom. Well, my dad can... I mean could..."

They stopped and turned to face. Heff put both hands on Nick's shoulders.

"You've never been good with emotions, expressing yourself and saying what's on your mind; you clam up and get defensive. It's like you build a barrier that you don't have to. It's sad that you're so damaged... Parent's eh, who'd have 'em?! 'You can't live with 'em and you can't kill 'em.' You didn't... did you?"

Nick rolled his eyes and pursed his lips, shaking his head slowly with a scowl through 'I'm not surprised, just disappointed' squinted eyes.

"Sorry… Too far? Too soon? You're always welcome at my house. Have Katies room, then we'd be like real brothers," Heff whispered excitedly.

"There will be a lot to sort out here and I'm the man of the house now. I won't be out for a while. Thanks for everything. I love you… like a brother. Please, no talking now."

They walked to Nick's house in silence. He was relieved there were no police cars outside. With a gentle pat Heff stepped cautiously over the slushy pavement edge then started to jog slowly up the snow-cleared, gritted road. Surprisingly he kept pace into the distance. After fifty yards or so, respectfully out of neighbourly earshot, he started to sing loudly a drill sergeant army cadence, "*I KNOW A GIRL FROM NEW ORLEAN'S, SHE'S GOT A MOUSTACHE IN HER JEANS…*"

Chapter Seventeen

Forever Young

An alarming bell rang, awakening Nick. He instinctively swung his arm out blindly to hit 'snooze'… But the annoying chime continued. Dazed and confused his groggy eyes opened and squinted at the LCD alarm clock; it was only 9:22am! The impatient doorbell rang again. Why would anyone call a r o u n d at this unearthly hour on a Saturday morning? Perhaps it was a scheduled support-officer check-up. In which case why hadn't his mum answered? Or maybe the police again, they did love Nick's mum's coffee. Dehydrated with a stonking headache and the whiff of stale cigarettes in his hair he kicked off his warm continental quilt revealing nothing but Y-fronts, then leapt out of bed. Stumbling into yesterday's 'doubled-up' thick woollen socks, he grabbed his dressing gown and practically streaked downstairs.

"Alright, I'm coming!" He shouted half-way down, whirling past the delicate windowsill display of colour catching honesty dried flowers as he swung a r o u n d the banister, cotton cape flapping behind. From the bottom step he opened the door, leaned into the porch to see who was outside… Or in this case WHAT. To get a better view, he pulled the door wider and stepped down into the cold quarry tiled porch, edging over the 'WELCOME' mat towards the window in disbelief.

In the snow, he could see the long thin muscular legs of a massive animal and a huge taught brown underbelly. He walked forwards and opened the glass door looking up with a squint to see Jane, sitting on the back of a tall, elegant horse. She was smartly dressed with knee-length leather riding boots, tight cream jodhpurs, padded jacket, gloves and helmet. She even appeared to be wearing make-up.

Nosy park-bound neighbours pointed; snow shovelling drive-clearers stopped to stare and twitching curtains secretly spied Nick's unusual equine visitor. To them, a 'Mountie' was quite a different sight to the usual squadron of police cars visiting the juvenile delinquent.

With door wide open, Nick looked up, leaning on the doorframe and said, "Tally-ho!" Jane chuckled.

"Well, good morning to you, my oh my! Your reputation precedes you, Chopper. You certainly know how to greet a girl! I'm blushing."

Nick wasn't sure what she was going on about. He'd only just woken up; riddles were wasted on him at this time of day. He yawned and stretched his arms, hands clasped behind his head, touching the doorframe with his elbows.

"I'd have put you down as more of a boxer short kind of guy myself. More, roomy." She was now blatantly staring down at Nick's nether-regions.

Suddenly, the penny dropped. Realising his gown was wide open and Jane was ogling his skimpy-duds, he quickly 'drew the curtains' and securely tightened the sash. Totally embarrassed that the ever-intrusive neighbours had also copped an eyeful of the jockey parade.

"Gone in a flash... Pity. Interesting colour though; as an artist how would you describe them?" Jane quizzed, obviously leading somewhere.

Nick cautiously surmised, "Canary yellow, I guess."

"CANARY yellow!" she echoed with a snort. "Canary yellow budgie smugglers? You're too funny. I'd describe them as Banana-Split!" She chuckled, adding flirtatiously, "Sorry but they're clearly too small; your BANANA was SPLITTING out of them!" She laughed out loud and snorted, covering her mouth.

Malcolm, the pools man, was hovering around at the end of the drive. Nick wished he'd just bugger off as well as all of the other prying eyes. This was a private conversation. Why did people think it was okay to stop, stare and listen? He hated being watched, but he could hardly invite Jane and 'Mr Ed' in.

Then without any warning, the horse started to piss: A steaming gallon melting a huge black hole in the driveway. Nick was mortified and stared wide-mouthed in disbelief at such blatant disrespect for property.

Malcolm was skipping around with a big smile on his crooked face, grinning at the horse.

"YOU DON'T OFTEN SEE HORSES THESE DAYS. THEY'RE GOOD," He shouted excitedly. "MANURE'S GOOD FOR THE ALLOTMENT."

"Shit!" Nick affirmed coldly.

Keen to hurry Jane along, he cut to the chase, "I don't mean to sound rude but, is there a reason you're here? Or was it just to TAKE THE PISS out of ME and then HOSE it onto my own DOORSTEP out of YOUR HORSE'S DERRIERE?" With a pause, he then added in a defeated tone, "And how did you even know where I live?"

"The phone book silly," Jane replied smugly with a cheeky smile, "There's only one 'F Hopper' on Joule Road."

"Not anymore," Nick said impassively.

"Yes. Sorry. Anyway I just wanted to check you got home safely. It was an 'eventful' night. I've never known anyone get chucked out of a club before. We're all going to a college party at 'Checkers' tonight. Tickets sold out weeks ago, but I've got a spare. We all wondered if you might like to come? Take your mind off things. It's fancy dress."

"Nah, I don't think so; things to sort out here. Who are you going as, Princess Anne?"

"You're funny," She chuckled. The horse clopped its feet in the cold snow and shook it's head impatiently, like it knew it was time to go. "Well, if you change your mind, I've written my phone number on the back of this." She passed an envelope down to Nick.

"College closes soon and we go in The Little B practically every night. There'll be loads of parties around Christmas," she said excitedly. "Just come and find us." She pulled the reins and steered away.

Fortunately, the horse wasn't on his drive when it decided to release the huge steaming 'compost' pile Malcolm had anticipated. Delighted with his 'wind-fall' the pools-man reached into his pocket and unfolded his one-and-only carrier bag, disgustingly scooping up his winnings. Evidently, 'Where there's muck there's brass', and vice-versa.

"Absolutely unbelievable!" Nick said as he dropped Jane's unopened card into his gown pocket and leaned forwards to pick up the daily pint, carefully checking the silver top for tit-holes and horse-piss splashes.

Closing the glass outer-door, he reached down to pick up the post then returned to the carpeted hall closing the front door. Amongst his parents' bills was a large square manila hard-backed envelope addressed to 'MR BIG'. It was thick and sturdy, about seven inches square and franked with a 'Rowntree's' logo! Definitely from Heff to him.

Nick strolled through the morning room into the kitchen, placing milk in the fridge and letters by the phone then opened the thick envelope. Inside was a record, 'Forever Young' by Alphaville and a note from Rowntree's: Heff had sent enough Jelly coupons to claim a free record. He must have already claimed in his name, as the rules state 'Strictly one per household' so he'd ordered this for Nick.

As usual, Nick's mum had left a note by the telephone. Good-vibes header: 'Stay positive, work hard, make it happen.' Then her handwritten message, 'GONE TO THE POLICE STATION AND CORONER'S OFFICE IN NORTHWICH. FINGERS CROSSED.' Then at the bottom of the note one word 'PETROL.'

An arrow pointed to a five-pound note. Nick put the fiver in his pocket with Jane's card.

He took a run up into the kitchen and leapt onto the linoleum sock-sliding, left foot forward, facing sideways with hands in pockets for about six feet as he slid to a halt in front of the kitchen sink chuffed to observe his nonchalant front-on reflection magically 'glide' into view along the mirror-like window.

'Fingers crossed, what does that even mean?' He wondered. Then calmly said out loud, "Yes, I know the rules of the game." Gulping a tall glass of tap water down in one. With a gasp and cough, he refilled. Repeating the statement and action twice again, without cough. Carefully studying his reflection each time.

He went into the front room and put Heff's record on, turning the volume up he left the door open and two-stepped upstairs, slipping into his parent's bedroom.

Discretely parting the voile under-curtain, he checked the drive, then soft-footed to his dad's wardrobe like a rooting child before Christmas. But instead of snooping for pre-wrapped presents he browsed the smart collection of tailored suits. Although flawed in many ways Nick's father had certainly known how to dress with style. Nick selected a black 'Frank Rostron, Manchester' single breasted jacket.

He had felt cool in his dad's Abercrombie the previous night, although admittedly it had been padded with many layers of clothing, including a thick denim jacket. He lay his gown on the neatly-made bed, lifted the suit down and slinked into the cold soft silky sleeves. The garment clearly swamped him but, only wearing socks and undies he accepted the fitting required 'an imaginative assessment': It may look better than it felt. He presented himself confidently upright with chin up and shoulders back looking hopefully into his mum's dressing mirror... But sadly, he looked like a first year pupil in a fifth year's blazer! A look Todger could get away with but not Nick. He was still a growing boy, not developed enough to step comfortably into a grown man's clothes. He browsed the extensive range of one-size-fits-all ties, selecting solid-black knitted silk Turnbull and Asser; a conservative formal noose his father had thought appropriate.

Nick needed a black suit that actually fit to show ashamed relatives, insincere family-friends, whispering neighbours and curious judging onlookers that he was not a woeful, poorly-prepared, wretched child-of-the-damned; but a strong, independent, proud son. A dashing look was absolutely essential to respect his father's memory. He marched resolutely to his own bedroom, retrieved the 'Life' Savings Account booklet and returned to the 'Music Room'.

For many years, the front room had been saved for 'best' as dining room when entertaining guests or special occasions like Christmas. There was a fireplace with ornate surround and large framed mirror above. Since they'd had a fourth bedroom and dining-area extension at the back of the house, the front room was now Nick's 'music room'. There was a piano, which no one could play and an antique mandolin in the side window; again, which no one could play. But the room's 'music' defining feature was the Sony hi-fi composite system with all Nick's records and tapes stacked below. The huge, wide music appreciation 'sprawling-sofa' was covered in a Chewbacca-like, long brown faux wooky-fur covering which reached the floor all around. Loads of scatter cushions also helped disguise the fact it was, in fact, actually a bed. It had been Nick's elderly grandmother's bedroom when she used to visit.

With feet up, Nick lay flicking through his mum's Marshall Ward catalogue. No 'Matinique', whatever that was: Nothing appropriate. Anyway, even if he'd found something suitable in his size, it would probably take weeks to arrive. Funerals: burials and especially cremations, are literally hot-on-the-heels of death.

He had six hundred pounds in his building society and life had undoubtedly saved for today. With a bleak future and household income chopped, Nick and his mum would definitely be poor. His extravagant 'blow out' could be a final present to himself, his mother wouldn't have to spend a penny on him for Christmas. He thought about Jasmine's rich Fluff Boy friends in their expensive designer gear. He could get a lot of wear and tear out of a smart suit, to rub shoulders with the in-crowd.

With his remaining savings, he could live like a prince, partying in a dream-world bubble, drinking himself into oblivion. Surely it would take at least a month to sell the house, he could then fall back down to earth, skint. Exit with a bang. Shuffle back to The Bang Gang in The Vine, having lived the most wonderful, magical dream.

There wasn't a moment to lose. His mind was made up. A lavish expensive European, cool and trendy, slim-fitting, tailored designer suit. Respectfully in black: In the name of his father.

He would transfer the money on Monday; but for today, crossed-cheques would cover.

Washed, dressed and with wallet and folded-chequebook in back pockets he trudged out to his snow-covered igloo. Foot on clutch he crossed fingers and turned the key... After a 'cut, cut' the beast kicked in chugging-noisily with a splutter as the old engine thundered to life. Nick turned the tape up loud: 'Space Age Love Song', A Flock of Seagulls. In the small, dark cocoon he air-guitared and revved the engine, then got out and cleared windows and bonnet, occasionally hopping back in to peddle-rev and avoid stalling.

A city-centre shopping extravaganza followed: Fiver on Elf Three-Star... £120 Lewis's Sony Walkman...£200 Royal Exchange, Matinique boutique... Pocket-change lunch at Meng and Ecker's... £60 HMV cassettes and 12" singles...

Finally on Mosely Street, Nick summoned the courage to enter The Midland Hotel's Unisex hair salon to get a real hairstyle! Drawn-in by the 20% student discount, he kissed goodbye to another £40! The hairdresser coerced him into a 'John Taylor' Duran Duran 'look'. Bouffant top, short sides swept back, long parting with over-eye demure strands, long and wavy mane at the back. Nick was gobsmacked when she revealed tin-foil bleached 'highlights'. There was no going back now. Finally, his hair was blown dry and carefully 'sculptured' with all sorts of gunk: mousse, gel and spray... Which he ended up buying to guarantee similar results at home.

He felt incredibly self-conscious and under-dressed walking with his 'everyone look at me' hair-style to Tommy Duck's free parking.

Returning home triumphant, he parked at the front of the house blasting out the crescendo of The Fixx's 'Red Skies at Night'. He waited for the song to finish before turning the engine off then got out, pulling his seat forward to lean into the back and gather his smartly packaged purchases.

He looked through the rear window and saw the pop-up headlights of his mum's sleek silver Nissan Silvia ZX Turbo DeLorean-esque sports car approach. He wondered how long she'd be able to keep that. She gave a wave then accelerated up the drive. Nick decided to save unloading until later and walked down the side of the house to greet her. She stepped out wearing her cool black Ray Ban Wayfarer sunglasses, smart Coco Chanel jacket and black dress. The grieving widow was smouldering and dropped her cigarette into the snow with a sizzle, her red-lipped face lit up as Nick approached. Feeling guilty about his extravagant afternoon he decided not to mention his shopping spree, he'd smuggle the bags in later.

"I love your haircut, Darling... Very 'with it', have you joined a band?"

She kissed his cheek and wiped the smudge with leather thumb as Nick opened the back door and stood aside for her to enter. She was clearly trying to hold back a smile and as Nick shut out the cold she announced excitedly, "I have some wonderful news." Walking towards the fridge, pulling off her leather gloves she grabbed a chilled bottle of Chardonnay and an ashtray.

"Following an autopsy the coroner's report has concluded that your father died from hyperthermia." Her face lit up.

Nick flinched at the word 'autopsy' then sighed.

She continued, "His cuts didn't kill him, it was the cold weather. It WASN'T suicide, he died from NATURAL CAUSES... Thank GOD!"

Nick looked solemn and said slowly, "Does that mean he's not damned... He'll go to heaven?"

Knocking back the wine, his mum looked at him quizzically as if he was joking, then said, "Yes, darling, he's gone to heaven."

She then came close and put her hand on Nick's shoulder with a huge smile and added excitedly, "But also the life insurance will pay out, the mortgage will be paid off and we will get your father's pension. You are going to get an allowance... a tidy sum of money every month until you finish education!"

"So we're not going to be poor and have to move?" Nick asked.

"No, on the contrary Darling, WE'RE GOING TO BE RICH!" She declared, hugging him with a huge sigh of relief. Nick didn't return the hug. He remained solemn. His dad's gory inners had been painstakingly removed and analysed.

His cut up body was lying in a mortician's morgue somewhere, not even in the ground yet and his mother was celebrating. It just felt wrong.

He felt guilty about his hedonistic afternoon.

Sensing Nick's mood, she added sternly, "Look I'm sorry Darling but this really is the best outcome for all. You'll get over it in time. No one need know what happened, as far as everyone else is concerned your father died whilst out walking in the cold. I had to pull a few strings with my journo colleagues so there'll be no 'wild' news articles, so events leading up to your father's death won't ever be reported. Would you like to go out to dinner?" She asked, lighting another cigarette.

"No," Nick said sadly.

"We could get a Chinese take-away then… with meat for you if you like."

"I don't want to celebrate."

"Well, we've nothing in. I've hired some films from the video shop. We can just stay in and snuggle up on the sofa. What about beans on toast?"

"Okay."

"'Skinheads on a raft' it is then!" She said with a smirk.

Chapter Eighteen
Beautiful Armour

A few days later, when his mother approached the subject of funeral-attire, Nick became nervous; had she discovered his secret stash of designer threads? When she declared it was unjustifiable to buy a 'dowdy' suit he'd never wear again, he was relieved his treasured outfit hadn't been unearthed but equally disappointed she considered his appearance unimportant for the internment. He should wear whatever he 'felt comfortable in', it 'didn't have to be black' and he 'didn't even need to wear a tie'. She just sounded disrespectful: He wasn't a child. She clearly wanted all eyes on herself, turning heads in sombre fashion. The 'weeping widow' putting on a brave face in killer dress with the heartless ragamuffin paternal-orphan in tow. He'd show her.

Secretly blaming 'The Ice Queen' for his father's death, Nick banished his mother to exile with the silent treatment. In a teenage-psychologist passive-aggressive manner: Ignoring her, choosing solitude, avoiding conversation, giving disdainful glances… Knowing the rage he would unleash if she dared to ask, 'What's wrong, Darling?' They'd eat and watch videos side by side, parted by Nick's cold shoulder. In her eyes he was dumb with grief, emotionally mute. His divorce-dodging patronising mother was clearly upset too, with blood on her hands. She tried to win Nick back gushing tearfully exhaustive speeches, covering every subject apart from the glaringly obvious one… Suicide.

Somehow she had convinced herself that the events leading up to her husband's death hadn't actually happened. He'd just gone out for a walk in the cold and died. But she neglected to tell Nick the rules of this 'code of silence'. His mother was intelligent, articulate and manipulative and could easily rewrite the truth; he didn't want a confrontation.

Distraught with guilt, shame and self-loathing, Nick took a good, long look in his dad's shaving mirror. So much pain underneath. Mentally torturing his mother and casting stones was selfish and dangerous. But someone had to pay. With defensive-shield locked Nick's silent duel was crushing his mum's heart, with no possibility of a positive outcome. He knew his cruel, childish and stubborn behaviour would gradually wear her down and he certainly didn't want to push her too far, as he had his father: It had to stop.

The first step was to accept his dad's death was not their fault: He hadn't pushed his father over. Neither had his mother. Mental Health had. They should mourn his death, celebrate his life and move forward lovingly supporting each other and enjoying their lives as best they could with this awful tragedy behind them. Nick conceded buying his dual-purpose suit had been a thoughtful considerate act and equally the grieving widow was right to want to dress immaculately in memoriam.

So Nick dropped his guard and offered his mum a loving hug. He started conversing and laughing at the funny bits in movies; he even revealed his new Sony Walkman. He was back to normal, his mother's son had returned! It was better than being alone. He never wanted to make her unhappy again. This change of heart was just the tonic; all his mum had wished for; her son's acceptance to get through difficult times. Celebrating her son's return the prodigal mother recklessly splashed out on something that couldn't be hidden in a wardrobe…

It's true, people deal with grief in different ways. During her tightly scheduled week of 'compassionate leave', Nick's mum ticked through her Filofax 'To Do' list: Hair, Florist, Buffet, Return car to dealer…

Yes, she took her beloved silver sports car back and traded it in. Knowing exactly what she wanted, no smarmy sales-patois required, within minutes she brazenly drove out of the forecourt with the most beautiful, prestigious top-of-the-range cover-star pin-up 'centrefold', suped-up sports car 'wet-dream' pride of the showroom. Nick was gobsmacked when the brand-new shiny red Porsche 928 purred up their snowy drive. He knew it was wrong to celebrate, his emotions were all over the place, chuffed to bits but equally aware he ought to be in mourning! No one knew what hell his mother had been through, the psychological torment she had endured for the past twenty years. Nick's nightmare family-life was history and his financially stable future, a dream.

Nick considered Dali's painting: Narcissus had tried to cling on to an 'out of reach' love and look where it got him! Jasmine would be out of reach after

Christmas. The gods' 'Love comes from within' message was clear, Nick had to love himself first to fill the echoing void in his cavernous heart. He needed to work on confidence and self-esteem. Thankfully positivity was Nick's greatest strength.

Wealth was an exciting prospect, a fortuitous privilege to embrace, opening new doors, affording materialistic comfort and security, but blood money comes at an agonising price. Nick had been the weak link holding his loveless parents together. His handsome father ashamed of his own refection, couldn't be stopped extinguishing his sorry soul, married with the self-preservation vanity of his glamourous mother who protected herself at all cost behind beautiful armour.

His mum looked at Nick over the brim of her Wayfarers holding up her car keys with a smile and said coolly, "Let's take her out for a spin. Come on, let's show ourselves off. Grab the videos!"

Chapter Nineteen

An End/Ascent

Friday soon arrived, the day of the funeral.

Warned not to 'dilly-dally' the bathroom would soon be public domain, Nick took a quick shower and unnecessary shave. Flaunting new baggy boxer-shorts, the slender towel-turbaned 'Sheikh of Araby' teased a 'Wilson, Keppel and Betty' music-hall sand-dance across the landing into his mother's bedroom as the doorbell rang again. Discarding the damp cloth and reclining head upside-down over the edge of the bed, he chilled-out to the soothing wind-tunnel sound and massaged foamy mousse into his power-dried mane.

Upright at the curious-counter dressing-table with finger-palm gel, he artistically slicked, swept and teased the three mirror reflected coiffure, perfecting the golden coma of hair over his right eyebrow. Finally, with a pucker-pout he held breath and closed eyes behind handy protective goggles to fix hairspray-guild with a long spray. Close to asphyxiation, he fled the toxic area still donning the freshly-solicited cool dark shades. Door-crack spying over Wayfarer-frames, the coast was clear to sneak out and tiptoe to the safety of his own room as ominous, slow and heavy footsteps creaked the staircase. The bell went again. Stop the clocks... Cover the mirrors... This house-full was no party.

Downstairs, maudlin mourners could be heard arriving in respectful close-lipped clusters but Nick wasn't on 'door duty' today. Mrs Burns, bless her, had arrived early to offer her services: Take coats, make drinks, be maid and stay-behind to prepare the reception. Nick slid a tape into his cassette player and hit play; Psychedelic Furs 'Heaven'. Surely a good omen. He sprayed musky Brut deodorant under his armpits, catching window-reflected mirror moves remembering Heff's 'Ghostbusters' dance with a smile.

On went his new starched white shirt and smart, slim-fitting suit trousers with leather belt, notably fastened 'American Gigolo-like', anti-clockwise. Black socks and shiny leather brogues. He then adorned his ultra-cool pop-star's thin collared, shoulder-padded single-breasted European imported, designer jacket. The expensive material had microscopic silver criss-cross flecks woven into the black wool complimenting his wind-swept, bleached-blonde summer-sun hair strands. He felt super-cool, dressed like a million-dollars: A Matinique male model mannequin.

He then upturned his collar 'a la Elvis' to attach the finishing 'piece de la resistance', his father's black funeral tie. Assuming respectful solemnity, he reflected on the white winter window as he tied the simple schoolboy knot his father had taught him.

'Who's tying whose tie now, attention-seeking puff?' The cruel, mocking heir goaded his new-found air of confidence. A chilling contradiction warning Nick the disdainful mental battle was far from over, it lived on inherently within himself.

He knew he had to earn self-respect and stop hating himself.

Bravely denouncing anger and fear he stared his visual echo in the eye and sought absolution. He took a deep breath, looked at the ghostly white garden reflection with pity and whispered to the translucent self, "I'm sorry you were ill but I've done nothing wrong. All my life I've tried to make you proud."

He then recited his mother's healing mantra, "I am not to blame… You are not to blame… We are not to blame… No one is to blame."

Strengthened, he spoke confidently, "I will NOT be defined by negativity, I choose a positive life. I love you, Dad. Today is all about you, you will never be forgotten but please rest in peace." A sudden movement in the still winter wonderland made him snap out of his window-reflecting face-off as a collared dove on the greenhouse roof launched into flight flapping to rise above the house.

There was a gentle knock at his door and Mrs Burns popped her head in, "Sorry to disturb you, Dear… My, don't you look handsome. The cortege has arrived and is ready for you." She was wearing her hearing-aid, a black frock with frilly white apron and a dab of make-up.

"Thank you, I'll be down in a minute," he said softly, folding down his collar. The voice hadn't been his father's ghost or 'shoulder angel' versus 'Little Nick', it had been his own emotionally frayed conscience; his id and ego, screaming automatic knee-jerk defence, although no longer under attack.

Summoning inner strength, he banished self-blame and negativity. His pitiful father's disappointment was a thing of the past. Today was a time to accept and mourn his father's passing; show respect and forgive.

Switching focus from close reflection to distant garden and back, he contemplated how fortunate he had been to witness a dove's angelic ascension the moment his father's cask had arrived home for his final journey: Prey to the heavens.

At ease, confident and introspectively absolved he admired the immaculate image: The metamorphosis of Narcissus. He reached for his dad's Parker pen and the 'conversation-opening' matchbox, containing the enigmatic hieroglyph note, slipping both into jacket pockets along with his mum's Ray Bans. He then remembered he'd given his father's monogrammed hankie to Jasmine. What a blissful yet tragic memory, a split-second of life, locked heart to heart in an emotional embrace he could have held forever, sadly accepting Jasmine was the love he couldn't have. Finally, he kissed and pocketed Jasmine's lemonade straw and with a deep sigh left his bedroom suitably sombre and forlorn, descending the banister-guided staircase to make his appearance to the dark crowd below.

The hall was packed with tall, black-wearing strangers, just like the last time he had seen his father alive. This time they weren't police officers they were press-officers from his mother's work as well as his father's colleagues, family-friends and distant relatives. There was a strong smell of sherry. They could have been 'Rentacrowd' he didn't recognise anyone. The chattering stopped as everyone turned to face the new 'man of the house' as Nick froze on the final staircase landing. He held back childish blushes and with dignified poise gritted teeth and pursed lips scanning the crowd for his mother.

Unusually, the sitting room door was propped open with a heavy velvet cushion. Nick's father would never have allowed such blatant heat-wasting. The socialite hostess glided out looking elegant with black-widow lace-veiled fascinator and clinking gin and tonic. As their eyes locked, the Ice-Queen melted for a micro second but composed herself, theatrically hankie-dabbing her dry cheeks for the audience as the solemn crowd respectfully parted to form a path, coaxing mother and son together.

"Look at you… You look so handsome Darling. Just like your father on our wedding day." His dad was the last person Nick wanted to be compared to but he kept quiet.

"Come on, it's time." Nick's mother beckoned reaching into the cloakroom for her smart new black winter coat. All the murmuring stopped as Nick assisted and linked arms to lead his mum out of the house into the cold. All the visitors knew the drill and followed suit to their cars.

Blocking the drive was an elegant, black Rolls Royce Silver Shadow. In front of it a long hearse parked centrally in front of the house, his father's wooden casket on show. Nick had been dreading an 'open casket' but thankfully 'closed' suited this occasion. He wondered who all the floral tributes could be from. He hadn't ordered them and they didn't have many relatives. The invitation had instructed only 'family' flowers. One particular bouquet caught Nick's eye, a beautiful spray of maybe fifty Narcissus daffodils.

"Those flowers, were they all from…"

"Yes, Darling."

"I like the yellow ones. Can they be from me?"

Elderly neighbours peered out from twitching curtains. Nick had personally posted invitations so he knew they'd been invited. Maybe it was too icy for them to venture out, perhaps they'd show up to the buffet.

He carefully guided his mother, arms-linked along the gritted drive to the pavement he had spent hours clearing the day before as the limousine door was opened. Taking a final drag his mother discarded the ashen coffin-nail with a flick and boarded, closely followed by Nick who sat to her left. He'd never been in a Rolls Royce before, the luxurious dark leather and mahogany interior was like a posh taxi. Facing out towards the park Nick took the sunglasses from his pocket and slid them on, out of sight.

The silent car cruised south slowly behind the hearse. Nick twisted to look out of the rear-window and was amazed to see a procession of about twenty cars following, bumper to bumper. His mother tugged his sleeve, silently instructing him to sit forward with dignity so he obliged gazing out of his side window. An old man, a generation older than his father possibly in his sixties, was walking a dog. He stopped and removed his hat as the procession passed. Another couple stopped and respectfully bowed. Most people were elderly. If the old folk had known the deceased was only in his forties, they may have contemplated the horror of losing their own beloved offspring. Nick had never met his paternal grandparents; they'd died before he was born. They must have died very young. Perhaps an early death was hereditary for Hoppers. Alphaville's song 'Forever Young' suddenly took a sinister twist.

The procession crept slowly up the main road, past Nick's College. He sank back in his seat, far away from the window, hiding behind his shades. He didn't want to be recognised, being part of this openly public display of grief. Thankfully the hearse was invisible to the students who ran across the road in front of the slow traffic, unaware of its significance.

As the cortege drove through Broadheath, Nick spotted 'Market Dave', Altrincham's eccentric rag-and-bone-man. He stopped his hand-pushed wooden barrow, blocking the busy north-bound lane, much to the annoyance of motorists and removed his flat cap, which he held over his heart. He stood solemn and respectfully finger dotted a cross on his chest, 'spectacles, testicles, wallet and watch'. Nick was genuinely touched by the heartfelt gestures of strangers, pushing a finger under his sunglasses for a secret wipe.

At Altrincham Crematorium, the motorcade dispersed to park as the Silver Shadow escorted the hearse to the covered chapel entrance. Within seconds the crowd of mourners appeared navigating neatly excavated, heavily gritted paths to the chapel as four funeral directors gathered in formation to carry the coffin to its final destination. Nick wondered why he'd not been asked to be a pallbearer but his mum clutched his hand tightly as the undertakers ceremonially raised the coffin onto their shoulders; clearly Nick's role was to support the living. As the reverent coffin-bearers stood to attention, a dignitary, the master of ceremony opened the limousine door, offering a solemn welcome and brief guide to proceedings. Nick's mum quickly reached across to remove Nick's sunglasses, folding them away into his inner jacket pocket with a gentle whisper, "Be brave Darling, no hiding."

Nick supported his mother as they walked slowly into the chapel behind the coffin-carrying pallbearers along the central aisle leading the assembly to stand respectfully to attention; solemn, still and silent. The ethereal 'An End/Ascent' by Brian Eno played softly as if synthesizer-playing angels were in attendance. Nick scanned the room ahead; there were no religious church-like signs, crosses or artifacts. His father's large colourful bouquets were now displayed at the front, brightening up the room and the daffodils were displayed in a white, oval vase. His mum had requested a 'Humanist' none religious ceremony, possibly due to the fact her husband had been trying to commit suicide when he had frozen to death.

Right on schedule at the top of the hour, the joyfully maudlin footman, approached the lectern to begin the carefully scripted order of ceremony and theatrically conducted everyone be seated.

With throat-clearing murmurs, the congregation fell silent, lowering in unison to behind-rest. The Celebrant waited patiently with hands clasped offering a forced-smile and impatient-eyes as Nick's mother's older sister, Aunt Hilda lowered herself slowly backwards. Her ruddy ham-like arms gripped tightly to lower her blubbery-bulk onto the creaking pew with the assistance of her Zimmer-frame counter-balanced by her Skeletor husband, the dog-collar-sporting, faithful-whippet Uncle Clarence, a reverend, gentleman of the cloth. Fortunately for Nick's mum, she had absolutely no resemblance to the Viking battle-axe Brawn-Hilda twenty-years her senior who assumed the role of matron today.

Nick noticed Uncle Clarence was already piously reciting his own protective incantations under his breath holding a vial of what must be holy water. Sitting rigid facing forward, all Nick could now see was the master of service and his father's coffin. The 'celebrant' started badly by calling his dad 'Francis'. No one called him that: It was Frank.

Nick prepared himself, anticipating the unimaginable, horrific and harrowing event's leading up to his father's death would soon be revealed to all. Would mental health be mentioned? Suicide attempts? Absconsion from the psychiatric institution? The police force's three day, three county freezing-cold search? No, this wasn't an obligatory, factual police report it was a carefully crafted eulogy his mother had written to peacefully close a chapter. The service was a brief C.V. mentioning youth and schooling, employment history, interests, his 'devoted' wife, 'beloved' son and 'suffering a recurring illness, Francis was taken too soon'… No shit! What a bloody understatement! No mention of the shocking and traumatic facts everyone ought to be made aware of. Nick felt robbed! Anyway, the majority of people in the room already knew the truth: They'd been involved in the manhunt.

And so his father faced his final curtain. Nick's mum gripped his right hand tightly, clearly dabbing real tears as the conveyor belt ferried the coffin out of sight to another realm and the electric curtain closed. The poignant 'An End/Ascent' began again louder this time, drowning automated sounds to refocus attention as the inevitable ashen process fired-up. The celebrant's voice speeded up and became louder as the ceremony closed with a crescendo climax.

Before he stood, Nick wiped his eyes, hoping not to be seen. The coffin had gone. All that remained was the egg-shaped vase of forty-four Narcissus daffodils, one for each optimistic/pessimistic spring of life, depending on mother or father's point of view.

The celebrant led Nick and his mum out first, arm-linked through the assembly as Nick spotted a familiar face on the back row. Good old Heff! This alone brought a tear to Nick's eye which he quickly wiped with suit sleeve, snivelling to offer an embarrassed smile as he passed.

On the other side of the chapel doorway, Nick and his mother stood in the foyer thanking everyone as they pooled together in a hub of sympathy. Receiving handshakes, pats and kisses from strangers, Nick repeated the same two lines over and over, "Thank you for coming. Please come back to the house for the buffet."

When it seemed everyone had left the chapel Nick and his mum were ushered towards the open door Rolls Royce. But Nick stopped, backtracked and said, "Wait, Heff's not come out yet."

The clock-watching celebrant whispered impatiently through gritted teeth, "Please be quick."

Nick walked back inside to find Heff standing alone at the front of the chapel. All the flowers had already been removed.

As Nick approached, Heff turned and said, "Look at you, you bloody poser! What the fuck have you done to your hair, did a bird shit in it? And do the Fluff Boys know you've been raiding their wardrobe?"

Nick patted him on the shoulder and said, "If this was a church you'd have burst into flames by now. What are you doing, casing the joint? You do know there are no priceless artefacts left unattended."

"I was just having a quiet word with the big man."

"My dad or God?"

"Yeah."

"What did you say?"

"I just told him I was going to look after you now. That you'd be okay."

"Thanks Heff. But we have to go, it's someone else's turn. Do you want a lift back to ours? There's plenty of room in the Roller."

"I'm on my bike, I'll see you in a bit. Save me some cheesy henna vol-au-vents and a bottle of Southern Comfort."

"You're not going on the piss, Heff," Nick cautioned.

"I've got a surprise present here to cheer you up." He patted his pocket. "I'll give it you later. And a card from the boys… Oh, and one from Jizzum."

Nick was suddenly delighted; Heff had seen Jasmine! Then he became worried; Heff had seen Jasmine.

Chapter Twenty
Sweet Mary-Jane

With morning passing, the reception started with shameful high spirits for a dead-air house. Curtains drawn and lights illuminated, the atmosphere was like a taboo speakeasy. Guests were lapping up the hospitality: Red-demonic faces, crying with laughter, guzzling limitless free booze, raucously back-slapping, stopping only for seconds to gorge on tasteful canapés. Nick couldn't believe how disrespectful guests were. Had they forgotten why they were dressed in black? They ought to be miserable and contemplative; this 'send off' was evidently a reunion piss up.

Nick sat alone at the bottom of the stairs, unwelcoming strangers with his glum expression. Everyone had clearly moved to pastures new, grazing on the well-stocked veggie and meat free-for-all. As far as Nick was concerned, sipping tea was acceptable but the alcohol-drinkers could burn in hell. He saw Malcolm, the pools man, standing alone in the morning-room by the buffet merrily scoffing vol-au-vents: Blessed tea-drinker.

He started wondering what his dad's 'Marilyn Monroe' girlfriend might look like these days and whether she was here. She'd be in her early forties, probably still beautiful and blonde, or could it have been dyed?

Two smartly dressed women that age, walked across the hallway with overflowing glasses of Chardonnay and Nick overheard snippets of their conversation, "Northwich of all places. Wasn't that where? Oh, how romantic."

He was intrigued and left the self-imposed naughty-step to eaves-drop further in the music room but an old couple stood in his way. With a craggy smile the 'Grandma Clampett' look-alike said, "Well, haven't you grown into a handsome young man, Nicholas. You've inherited your father's good looks. A heartbreaker for sure. I expect you're quite a lady-killer!"

Her husband's white caterpillar-eyebrows arched and his jowelled-jaw dropped as he excused themselves and whisked away for hot tea and an out-of-range scolding. Why was everyone being so cryptic? In Nick's current 'frame of mind' no one could say or do anything right, everyone was getting his back up.

It wasn't healthy assuming the pious role of Saint Peter at the Pearly Gates. As host he ought to relax and mingle, gain ancestral insight from his parents' acquaintances, many of whom had travelled a great distance to pay their respects.

A shriek of laughter came from the music room. Nick's blood was boiling, why couldn't people keep the bloody noise down and show a modicum of respect? He poked his head around the door with a scowl and was surprised to see his mother surrounded by a gaggle of screeching harpies: How bloody disrespectful.

"Isn't he handsome?" One said to the group, eyeing Nick up and down.

"Yes," his mother smouldered proudly through smoky veil. "Oh Darling, these are friends of mine from university. I won't say 'OLD' friends." Her Chardonnay guzzlers thought 'that' hilarious too.

"We're having a reunion! This is the first time we've all been together in nearly twenty years! We're having a superb catch up. Can you put some music on… something tasteful? I don't know how that thing works."

Nick gave his mother an incredulous look of disbelief, muttering to himself, "Sorry for getting in your way all my life."

His dad had loads of classical dirge but finding something suitable would be a fluke. He chose one of his own instrumental records, Jean Michel Jarre's 'Oxygen', turned the volume down to 'one' and left the room appalled. He walked through the busy hall to the far end of the crowded sitting room and sat alone on the chaise lounge covering his head in curtain as he peered out at the still white garden. He felt the seat bounce as someone immediately came to sit beside him. God, not more hypocrisy, why wouldn't people leave him alone? With a sigh he turned to face the latest unwelcome conversant: Fortunately, it was Diane.

Diane worked with his mum. She was pretty and slim with shoulder length, shiny straight dark brown hair. After au-pairs 'au-revoired', when Nick had started secondary school, Diane used to babysit when he was about eleven and she was seventeen. He'd had quite a crush on her. Now she was about twenty-three the age gap didn't seem too far so he was able to talk to her on the same level.

He poured out his heart, "It's like he never existed. No one is talking about him or mourning his loss, they're having a whale of a time getting pissed like it's last orders or happy hour."

Diane paused for thought then replied sympathetically, "In my understanding the reception after a funeral is a celebration of life. What you see are ripples of friendship and love your father created. Your father brought these people together; for some, he is their only connection in this house but they're still here paying their respects. The fact they're all getting on is a sign he was well-liked and a good person. Some of these people may not have seen each other for a long time and are really pleased to see each other again. You have to allow them a friendly catch-up over drinks. It's a good thing really. You should be proud to have such a loving, happy house full."

"It's like they knew a different person. Ironic really, I spent most of my life hating him and him me. I feel daft, like the beaten dog that licks his master's hand," he said distantly.

After a contemplative pause Diane put her hand on Nick's thigh and continued, "You're very tense. Would you like to go outside for a smoke?"

He leaned back and reached behind the curtain to the windowsill and revealed a clean crystal glass ashtray, passing it to her. "You don't have to go outside."

"You do if you're smoking what I've got," she said with a wink flashing a ready rolled joint in her bra. "Come on, some pot will do you the world of good, help you 'chill out'."

Nick was about to explode. He sat for a second looking at the wall battling emotions: outrage, anger, disdain, contempt... but then instead of spontaneously-combusting he rose, and said, "Fuck it, why not?"

Scanning the over-crowded room, they both slipped behind the curtain and sneaked out into the cold back garden quietly closing the French doors. They walked up the snow-cleared narrow footpath at the side of the detached house, ducking down under the four small uncurtained stained glass windows to Nick's car at the front. He'd certainly not anticipated that he would be smoking weed with a girl at his father's funeral.

"Funny, I'd never have pencilled you down as a drug addict," Nick said.

"NICHOLAS!" Diane quietly hissed, offended. "The occasional joint doesn't make me an addict. You're such a square for an art student. Have you never smoked draw before?"

"Oh, yeah… My friend gets it from a drug dealer in Brighton. China white, mother of pearl, he re-flakes what we need."

"That's a 'no' then. You're just quoting 'White Lines' which is about cocaine not grass. Brighton's cool though, very bohemian."

"Where should we go?" Nick whispered taking his car key from his pocket and starting to wipe the wind-screen with his hand. There was no way he was going to smoke marijuana outside his house. Even though the curtains were closed, the exotic smell might linger through porous walls. Driving his car high on drugs for the first time was probably not a good idea either.

"Let's go over there." Diane pointed to the red telephone box at the park entrance. "It'll be dry and you can keep me warm, JOHN TAYLOR," she said with a cheeky smile. Strangely aroused and with heart thumping in his throat they crossed the road. Nick pulled the heavy red door open as they entered the intimately close, stale fag stinking, puddly telephone box.

Diane took the ready rolled reefer from her bra and grinned as she rotated it in front of Nick's face. He stared at the neat, long, carrot-shaped doobie with a mix of excitement, fear and apprehension.

"I've never had wacky-backy before. You'd better be gentle with me. Do you know the kiss of life?" He said passing Diane his box of matches.

"That I do," she said, quickly sparking up the spliff with a deep inhalation. No smoke came from the joint or her mouth as she drew in filling her lungs, tilting her head back, eyes closed. She then gave a slow and long exhalation, filling the telephone box with pungent smoke and expertly blew a beautiful smoke ring into the purple haze.

"Sweet Mary-Jane," she said slowly in a relaxed tone, holding the amber smouldering joint steady in the air inches from Nick. The phone kiosk was a confined space and they were pressed close to each other. He was intrigued to see how calm it suddenly appeared to have made her. This was a first for Nick: One up on Heff who had only ever eaten dope, never smoked.

"I won't go schitzo, will I?"

"There's a distinct possibility," she said, passing the joint to Nick who graciously accepted it in his left hand. He flicked the cardboard roach end and ash fell to the puddly floor, the lit end burnt bright. Practicing inhaling without it in his mouth he hesitated.

"Holy moly, I don't have a clue what to do with this, you know," he said, petrified.

"Have you ever smoked a cigarette before?"

"I'm not a child, of course I have," he said, lowering the joint away from his face.

"Well, just smoke it like a cigarette. Take a small puff to start with, to see if you like it." Diane coaxed his arm back up. Smelling the peculiar aroma of Diane's exhaled air Nick then examined the doobie, turned it around in his hand and sniffed the mouth end of the smouldering joint. The cardboard 'roach', although very neatly made, was just a rolled up piece of orange Rizla card. There was no cigarette filter. Inhaling burning embers was sure to be fiery. He carefully put his lips around the peace-pipe and gently took a small inhalation, sucking the devil's-exhaust down but instantly rejected the noxious-pollution with an uncontrollable bellow, coughing his lungs up, red-faced and asphyxiated. He pushed the heavy door open and gasped for fresh air.

"Shut the door its freezing! We won't get the benefit."

"GET THE BENEFIT? There's nothing beneficial about this! It's disgusting. Not for me," Nick shouted clearing his mouth, dropping a glob of saliva onto the floor as he leaned out.

"Look, I'll give you a blow-back," Diane said inhaling deeply then holding the joint over the telephone behind, leaning towards Nick's face as if she was trying to kiss him, smoke gently wafting from her nostrils.

"Give me a WHAT?" Nick said incredulously.

Diane burst with laughter, expelling the unused purple cloud into Nick's face.

"No silly. I'm not THAT easy, although it is tempting, I'm a MAJOR Durannie. A blow back. We cup mouths and I pass the smoke into your mouth. It's a gentle way to try it."

"Like a kiss?" He asked excitedly suddenly keen to give drugs another go. He wasn't going to tell Diane that he'd never been kissed before.

"Yes. I pass the smoke from my mouth into yours. Are you ready?"

Nick nodded enthusiastically as his cheeks started to glow red. She put her head to one side and gently dragged on the joint, then holding her breath and resting the joint on the telephone she turned to Nick who put his right arm around her back and went in for the kiss. As their soft lips touched gently, they both

165

relaxed and their mouths opened as Diane gently passed the smoke into Nick's mouth, a perfect seal kept the smoke in. Nick had his eyes closed as he'd seen in films. He couldn't believe it, he was actually kissing a girl and having drugs for the very first time. He inhaled the soft, pungent smoke deep into his lungs then instinctively pushed his tongue into Diane's mouth as he'd seen John with Grace on the bus. Diane gave a squeak, but they were both enjoying it and she did likewise. surprisingly he became calm and relaxed, quite the opposite effect he ought to have from his first kiss. He became aware of a peppery hinge at the back of his jaw and he felt dizzy. He opened his eyes and realised he was exhaling smoke through his nostrils. Something he'd always wanted to do with cigarettes but had never managed without making himself convulse.

Still locked in embrace, Diane pulled her mouth away and said with a sweet smile looking into Nick's eyes, "How was that? Would you like to do it again?"

"Yes please," he said eagerly. Closing his eyes and puckering up. He heard Diane draw on the crackling joint and then locked lips again. He pulled her close and their mouths pressed together, opening wide. Diane tilted her head slightly so they weren't tooth to tooth and it happened again. Their tongues darted at each other, exploring whilst warm smoke gently travelled from Diane's mouth into Nick's lungs. He was loving the dreamy effect.

His head was becoming dizzy but the kiss was intoxicating. His arms held her tight as he explored her torso, moving up caressing her body, pushing his fingers down the back of her skirt to feel the top of her panties and then pushing down further to touch the beginning of the crack of her bottom. Diane didn't flinch, she was receptive to Nick's advances. Smoke went backwards and forwards between their lungs and out through nostrils. Nick's left hand moved up, under her jacket around to the front, through her blouse and touched her right breast. At this point she smiled and broke the seal of their mouths saying, "Your hand's cold."

Embarrassed, Nick pulled away, but Diane gave him a smile.

"My, you're quite a kisser. You do know you're not supposed to use your tongue with a blow-back? But it's okay. I liked it. What do you think?" She had a pretty smile.

"Thank you," Nick said dizzily. Two heavy hits on that joint had gone straight to his head. "That's the first time I've ever touched a girl's breasts. Well, since I was a baby, which I can't remember. You know, since I drank my mum's milk."

Diane put her finger on Nick's lips with a smile, "Ssssh, stop it. You're stoned. Stop talking about your mum's tits. It's weird."

"Okay sorry. But thank you for letting me touch your tits."

"You don't have to say 'thank you', that's weird as well. I enjoyed it. You're very gentle and sensual. I was very aroused."

"Sorry but I feel like I have to tell you everything I'm thinking." He then recited the first thing that came into his head:

"May we remind you, that for the convenience
of those patrons who prefer not to smoke,
seating areas on the right hand side
of this auditorium
have been designated as 'No Smoking Areas'.
Your cooperation is appreciated."

It was an intermission message that appeared at the cinema announcing the interval as the lights turned on and the curtains drew. Where had that come from? Some distant recess of his smoking mind.

Nick then spotted Heff arriving at the house on his bicycle. He cycled up the drive, then appeared on foot walking to the front door. He was about to ring the doorbell so Nick opened the kiosk door and shouted across the road, "PSSST, HEFF!"

Heff's hand lowered from the button and he looked at the curtained front room bay window then up at Nick's parent's window.

"HEFF, OVER HERE!" Nick shouted.

Heff turned and looked at Nick's car, wiping snow off the rear window.

"NO DIP-SHIT, OVER HERE!" Nick yelled louder, waving his hand out of the kiosk. Heff looked up and then ran over, opened the telephone box's door and stood looking gobsmacked at the embracing couple.

"Here he is, the man who put the 'fun' in funeral, this is my friend Heff. This is Diane, my babysitter. We're having drugs. She was just giving me a blow... Back?"

"You jammy bastard, in broad daylight? Squeeze together, incoming!"

It became very cramped, Nick sandwiched in the middle. Heff was shoe-horned behind Nick who still had his arms around Diane intimately close now. Heff asked, "Is this the shit my sister sent?"

"Whatchoo talkin' 'bout, man?" Nick asked dopily, taking the joint from Diane's upheld hand and having a baby puff in front of Heff. This time he managed not to cough.

"We agreed, Katie would send an 'Enry here," Heff said then relieved Nick of the joint and discerningly studied it closely, "Ah a perfectly embalmed mummy's finger! No doubt rolled on a virgin's inner thigh, mwodge!" He then took a 'cool as fuck' deep fireball drag, which he couldn't hold in and coughed out onto the back of Nick's head.

Nick asked in a very laid back way, "You've asked your sister to post drugs to my house? Cool."

"Don't you remember? You owe me three quid. So where did this come from?"

"Diane brought it to help me chill out," Nick said, taking the spliff back to have another drag as he passed it to Diane.

"This is why I love you Chopper, finding you in such weird situations! Copping off with a drug addict at your dad's funeral." He waved to Diane. "No offence."

As Diane took the final drag on the joint and dropped the spent roach into the puddles below with a hiss, Heff bragged, "I can tear a telephone directory in half with my bare hands."

"Why would you want to do that?" Diane scowled.

"I don't know. To impress you I suppose."

"Well, I wouldn't be impressed." She stuck her tongue out at Heff then looked at Nick, "Shame, this could have gone somewhere, I'm going back. It's too cramped in here now and I'm not into ménage à trois." She reached for Nick's jaw and planted a kiss on his lips. "You're absolutely gorgeous, don't ever change. I'll leave you two love birds to it." She squeezed her way out of the phone box crossed the road and disappeared up the side of the house.

"Babysitter eh? You jammy bastard, how much is she a night? Are you still banning me from drinking or have those drugs changed your mind?" He took his hip flask out of his pocket and waved it in the air.

"No. Go for it, man," Nick said light-headedly.

After a long swig Heff said, "You know when I snuff-it, I'd like you to hire professional mourners for me like they do in China."

Nick looked at Heff vacantly.

"You know, fit young girls dressed in black, sobbing behind a veil. Beautiful actresses who never knew me really but no one need know that. Even if it happens when I'm an old man and married with children. It would make everyone else wonder what the fuck I'd been up to. About five will do. I'll bequeath you the money. If you don't do it, I'll haunt you forever. Oh, here's the cards from me and Jizzum."

Nick took the cards and gave Heff a hug. "Wow man, that's really cool and considerate."

He looked at the cards, one simply scrawled 'CHOPPER' and a thicker envelope, addressed in neat, girly handwriting to 'Nick & Mrs Hopper'. He knew Heff would be offended if he didn't open his card first so quickly opened it. Heff, Salty, Eggy, Lanks had all signed their names and written at the bottom, 'L.U.L.A.B.' (Love you like a brother).

"Thanks dude," Nick said and gave Heff another hug.

"Go on. You can open her card now," Heff said enviously. Nick gave a big grin and studied Jasmine's thick card as if it was Valentine's Day. He gently tore it open, aware that Heff was watching him like a hawk. Her actual tongue had licked the gummed seal, if Heff hadn't been there Nick would probably have tried to lick it as well. A tasteful picture of iris flowers. Inside Nick found his father's neatly ironed, floral smelling handkerchief.

Heff declared, "Ew what's that, a snot-rag? Hate mail!"

Ignoring Heff, Nick raised the opened card close to his nose and inhaled the sweetly scented fabric conditioner, then gently turned the neatly folded hankie over to read the message written with a black fountain pen in beautifully calligraphic, girly handwriting:

To Nick and Mrs Hopper,
Our sincere condolences.
Love from
Jasmine and Family x

Nick slowly prodded Heff. "Hey man, you were supposed to give me the card before the funeral, so I could wipe my tears with the white truce flag. Do you know the smell of Jasmine? It's the most beautiful smell in the world. Look, she said 'LOVE' and gave me a kiss."

"Yeah, yeah, yeah, one more thing," Heff said and passed Nick a TDK C-90 tape-cassette box. "I was going to give it to you later, at the end, but you seem to be in the right frame of mind now."

Nick held the tape box close to his face. It had lots of different signatures in different colours on the index. He slowly looked up to Heff.

"It's a mix tape. I started with one of my favourite records then I took it around to Salty's then Lanks and Eggy and got each of them to record their favourite songs for you. Then I went to Boots and gave it to Jizzum. She took it and passed it around her friends and The Fluff, got them all to record a song for you. We signed our names instead of listing tracks. I just thought it would be a nice thing to do… Considering I know how much they all meant to you. There's room for you to record some of your own songs as well.

"I called it 'Chopper's Smegma-Mix'! Jizzum gave me the card when I went back to pick up the tape. It's supposed to make you happy. I didn't want you to be 'down' when I gave it to you. But you seem pretty chilled out to me. Good gear that. Can't wait until my sister's stash arrives. We'll have to make brownies with it though, my throat is rasping."

"Thank you Heff. You really are the best friend ever. I love you like a brother too. I think I got to first and second base with my babysitter." He put his hand on Heff's shoulder, who pushed the door open and put his arm around Nick.

"Do you know if the buffet has been served yet? I'm starving. Come on let's get you some sugar. You must have the munchies."

They sneaked back through the unlocked French window and Heff went straight to the kitchen as Nick turned right into the front room where music was playing louder than before, 'Avalon' by Roxy Music. His mother staggered up to him and flopped her arms on his shoulders with a boozy sigh and excited smile.

"Darling, I've been looking all over for you. It's been decided, I'M GOING TO SOUTH AFRICA FOR CHRISTMAS to stay with an old University friend!"

"Cool," Nick said stoned and non-plussed.

"Don't worry darling, you can spend Christmas Day with Aunty Hilda and Uncle Clarence." She pointed over at the old battle-axe Brunhilda and the Skeletor reverend looking as sour-faced as the farming couple in Grant Wood's 'American Gothic' painting.

"Groovy."

"My, you're taking this extremely well, darling. I was anxious about telling you, you were like a coiled spring before. Thank you for being so calm and understanding. I thought you might get upset, being left home alone for Christmas."

"Ag Naaah. 'Soud-Afrika' izit? Be sure to git y'self some gold or 'doimonds', Merry 'Kristmis'!" He said in a strange accent.

He turned away to the fireplace and took Heff and Jasmine's cards from his jacket pocket, pushing others aside to place them centrally, pride of place on the mantlepiece. As he lifted the neatly ironed hankie to his nose, a small piece of paper hidden within fluttered to the floor. He reached down and unfolded the note which read: 'My last night will be Christmas Eve. I'd love to see you one last time in the Little B, Love Jasmine x.'

There's that word again 'LOVE' twice... It's a date!

Chapter Twenty-One
Small Packages

It was Christmas Eve morning. Nick's mother was ready to be driven to the airport as he carefully reverse-levered her heavy leather case downstairs into the steamy-windowed porch. Wearing a light continental jacket and silk scarf, she was ready to fly with freshly applied red lipstick, looking like a jet-setter heading to the sun. She beamed at him, saying they ought to quickly exchange gifts, grabbed his hand and led him to the end of the sitting room to stand under the huge, ceiling-touching Nordic-spruce Christmas Tree which filled the room with the most wonderfully, aromatic seasonal alpine scent. Prompted to go first, Nick reached down to hand his mother a very small, golden box neatly wrapped with red ribbon.

"Happy Christmas, Mum," he said, giving her a peck on the cheek then recited his father's traditional Christmas message, "Good things come in small packages." He gave a nervous laugh as she unwrapped. Carrying his father's baton, he'd bought the same gift his mother had received every Christmas for as long as Nick could remember…a small but extremely expensive bottle of Chanel No. 5 perfume. He had thought it a nice sentimental idea, but now felt embarrassed, worried it could have been seen as a 'dig' to ensure she didn't forget her husband too quickly.

"Thank you, Darling, my favourite. Now, I'm in a hurry." She clapped urgently.

"Take the one labelled 'Hilda and Clarence' with you to Yorkshire tomorrow. It's only a tin of biscuits, I gave up buying them nice gifts years ago! All the other presents are for you to open tomorrow morning. Sorry but there's nothing terribly exciting… I've been too busy."

"Oh, and for goodness' sake, don't sit in the darkness feeling sorry for yourself; put the tree lights on and crank up the telly so you're not like 'Little

Orphan Oliver'." She paused, dabbed a tear from her eye and continued, "I'm such a bad mother, how will you ever forgive me, Darling? Finally, there are two Christmas presents you can open now." A smile reappeared.

First, she passed a white envelope from her handbag. Before he could open it, she said, "It's obviously money... Two hundred and fifty pounds. Don't 'blow' it all on alcohol, it's terribly ageing. Buy yourself some nice 'threads' and 'tunes', something to remember. I never know what to buy you these days, your fashion changes so frequently."

"Wow. Thanks mum." Nick leaned over and gave her a hug. "I'll be fine, stop fussing. I won't be alone. I'm going around to see my mates later. I want you to have a wonderful time, come on, let's go," he said, pulling keys out of his pocket.

She paused, looking at him with the most demented smile then reached under the tree, handing him a tiny, neatly wrapped red box with golden ribbon, similar in size to the one he'd given her. He gently shook it with a rattle, giving her a quizzical smile. She said excitedly, "Good things come in small packages."

Nick unwrapped the box, peered in at the curiously small, pocket-sized object... And couldn't believe his eyes. Christmas *had* come early as Nick realised he had received the most incredible, unexpected surprise ever. He felt like he'd won The Pools! He couldn't contain his excitement, he leapt with joy, hugged his mum and spun her around, smothering her with kisses. She was undeniably on a major guilt trip, leaving him over the festive season but she had magically regained favour with the most amazing, lavish present ever. Apparently he *could* be bought! Nick's wildest dreams had come true. He held up the heraldic-striped rearing horse logo-crested key with 'Insurance Paid' fob attached, permitting him to drive her brand new, super sexy sports car... the Porsche 928 S2!

Grinning from ear to ear with sudden change of carriage, Nick took the luggage from porch to Porsche, unlocking the boot with his very own key as he carefully lifted the case into the hatchback. His heart was racing as he lay back in the cream leather body-hugging bucket seat and the dashboard cockpit fitted around him, turning the key revealed a mesmerising array of pilot-like dials and LCD indicators.

His wing-woman warned, "Only necessary trips, don't drive fast and no showing off, it's icy."

Nick turned the key further, igniting the engine then cautiously reversing the snow-cleared driveway. A seventeen-year-old behind the wheel of the fastest street legal production car of 1984.

Revering, as opposed to revving, the 'red-bullet's' powerful V8 fuel injection engine, Nick drove at an incredibly slow pace as if he was taking his driving test again, ambling along the inside lane towards Ringway, Manchester Airport. He ignored other drivers' tooting as they shot past giving him the V's and wanker signs. With great concentration, he barely heard his mother's last-minute instructions.

"I couldn't have you driving to Yorkshire tomorrow in your love bug, it would never make it over Sadleworth Moor! The tank is full so you don't need to buy petrol. Hilda is expecting you at one. Don't be late and don't forget the present. Do try to have a nice afternoon, they're really pleased you're going, honestly. At home the fridge is fully stocked with goodies so you don't have to buy food and don't eat 'Rat Meat' every night. Don't 'fridge-graze' either, sit at the table and eat from a plate. Are you listening?"

"Eat from a plate, it'll taste better from a plate!" he recited obediently.

"I'm only away eight days. If you do invite anyone around, close friends only. The... *Bang Gang?* I always hesitate saying that. Mrs Burns will be popping in to check on you. Try to keep the place tidy for her. I'll be back New Year's Day and I'll get a taxi home. Invite your friends around on New Year's Eve, they can stay over if it's okay with their parents. I've written daily notes for you in the kitchen and I'll phone at eleven tomorrow morning to wish you happy Christmas! I think that's everything."

* * *

Standing in the twenty-four hour departure lounge, under the enormous 'tears of joy' smoke-tinged, dripping-glass focal-point chandelier, Nick bid his mother farewell as she quickly vanished upstream into the approaching crowd of homeward-bound long-distance travellers, reuniting wide-arms with doting family and loved-ones: There's always a bigger chandelier with longer tears.

He walked back to his cockpit. Both parents were in the clouds, mutually touching heaven. His distant mother, travelling 8,500 miles down the earth's meridian.

Sitting in the Porsche, Nick checked his reflection in the rear view mirror. 'Independent or unwanted?' He pulled out his bottom lip sulkily in a self-mock.

Leaning across the passenger seat, he popped the glove compartment open, retrieved the abandoned Ray Ban Wayfarers his mother was missing and slid his 'Smegma-Mix' into the Dolby Stereo cassette player and cranked up the dial. The drums started... ZZ Top's 'Gimme All Your Lovin'.

Looking himself in the eye with an over-frame glance at his grinning reflection, he revved the powerful engine, floored the gas and ripped up the clutch...

"Yeee-Haaar!" With tyres screeching and the smell of burning rubber left behind, G-force threw him out of the air park like he'd stolen a jet.

Tempting history to repeat itself the reckless adrenaline-fuelled father's son threaded through amber lights at breakneck speed, barely gripping grit, shimmying and sliding with counter-turn to skate over unexpected icy twists. No pedestrians: He wasn't driven by anger, loneliness or self-pity, he had no one to miss.

This narcissistic material boy was perfectly happy living fast in his ivory bubble speeding towards his raison d'être. Jasmine returned to the front of his mind and he immediately released acceleration.

His designer suit awaited it's second airing with the addition of a stylish silver, black and white plaid patterned Matinique tie to compliment his cool blonde streaks. He had to be immaculately groomed for his final rendezvous.

Chapter Twenty-Two
The Elephant Man

T'was the night before Christmas when all through the house,
sweltering heaters radiated a humid greenhouse.
Every light was illuminated and electrical appliances on,
as utility metres clocked; controlling parents gone.
Nick opened windows in an attempt to cool down,
Not considering bills would give his mum a meltdown!

He propped doors with cushions and turned on the TV,
for a week-long screening no one in the room would see.
The hi-fi played loudly, filling the house with tunes,
As Nick recorded his mixtape in the festive front room.
When out on the road there arose such a clatter,
Neighbours sprang to their windows to see what was the matter...

Toasting living-flame in the dimly-lit room, Nick studied the Christmas card framed mirror with contemplative reflection. The immaculately groomed, hot and cool, rosy-cheeked peacock in the other realm smouldered a melancholic pout.

Outside, an angry air-horn blasted 'Dixie', the 'Dukes of Hazard' theme, forcing an end to the dark trance-like ancestral abyss-search. Pulling away from the mirror's possession, without a scratch, Nick silenced the room, returning the needle, diamond-tipped stylus tonearm to its grip and with a final eye-to-eye father's pupil glance, uttered his first word in hours; an incredulous gutsy, "Odgeamowey!"

He ran to the end of the sitting room to close windows. Overjoyed, saved and alone no more, 'It's a Wonderful Life's George Bailey was wishing Bedford

Falls a 'Merry Christmas'; nightmare over, returning to his beloved family thankfully on Christmas Eve. No doubt at that precise moment the nation was united in joyful tears, relieved for the troubled man's safe return. For Nick it was oddly satisfying to know the exact same colour film was airing in his bedroom on his black and white portable TV to no audience. Upstairs windows remained open to thermostat the temperature and he kept all lights and appliances on, not wanting to return to a cold, dark, silent house. Pulling the door shut he ran out to Lanks's yellow Beetle and with a slide, thumped himself against the open passenger's window with both arms raised and with his best 'James Stewart' shouted excitedly, "Hey, Merry Christmas, Mr Potter!"

He jumped into the car expecting a friendly welcome but Lanks was shouting into his CB radio's hand-held microphone, "Ten-four for a copy, come on… Barn-Owl you got your ears on, over?" He was putting on an American accent and gave Nick an authoritative 'wait' signal. The dashboard-box crackled like a badly-tuned radio. He leaned forwards to twist a dial, transmitting again and Nick noticed a can of 'Long Life' beer tucked between Lanks' thighs, "Come back Barn-Owl, good buddy. Negatory, Chopper's-twenty, copy. Roger that. Ten-seven. Over and out." He hung the speaker on the dash-hook and flicked the incoherence off; turning with a proud smile and raised eyebrows, observing Nick's eye-catching, fashionable new look with questioning wide eyes and pursed lips.

Nick smiled, "Dream on, there was no one there! And why do you want to talk to big hairy truckers?"

"You should get one Numb-nuts, it's not just big hairy TRUCKERS… it's also big hairy GIRLS."

"Yeah right! I bet you're hard-up and working nights for Dial-a-Ride. Put your foot down Joe Baxi, there's a tip if you don't spare the huskies."

Lanks revved, "You cheeky twat, your house is miles out of my way. I should charge petrol money, it's treble rate at Christmas."

"See!" Nick declared smugly then leaned forward to reach into his jacket pocket avoiding the open window's icy gust.

"Chuddy, dog-breath?" He offered a green paper-and-foil wrapped stick of Wrigley's Doublemint, advising with a wide grin, "Gotta be minty-fresh for Christmas kisses!" He puckered up and smacked his lips.

Lanks offered no witty come-back and was clearly thrilled with the cool breath-freshener. Nick popped the dusty chewing-gum into his mouth and as he inhaled, cool sharp peppermint intensified freezing air, painfully stinging delicate sensitive nasal airways. He yelped dramatically and cupped a hand over his nose to warm, quickly winding his window up. Lanks did likewise in Steptoe gloves. He always copied Nick.

With his over-styled hair secretly saved, Nick sat back in his seat then spotted a stud in Lanks' left ear. "No way, have you had your ear pierced, you toppy-dreck? You've had the wrong one done... You're telling everyone you're a shirt-lifter!"

"No! 'Left is right and right is wrong!' I researched."

"Researched? Hanging out at the BLUE OYSTER BAR?"

"Says John GAYlor!" Lanks retorted pointing at Nick's hair, delighted with his 'Taylor' rhyming wordplay, then inspected his ear in the rear-view mirror, "I think it makes me look hard and cool... Edgy."

"Butch?"

Stopping conversation, Lanks clunked a cassette in, twisting the volume as the predictable guitar started to grind.

Since watching a video on Top of the Pops featuring a yellow beetle, Lanks had become obsessed with the movie 'Footloose'. So much so, he'd recorded a tape to play Kenny Loggins' title track on loop; over and over on both side.

Nick groaned, "Not this! You know what you need for Christmas? A new bloody tape. It's Christmas Eve for Christ's sake, what about something festive, Band Aid or Wham! Even Aled Jones would do."

"If you don't like it you can get out and walk, IN THE AIR!" Lanks sneered popping a bubble and can swigging. He then pushed into first gear and wedging can between thighs, looking at Nick quizzically. "WHAT, you want one? Cheeky freeloader! Free rides AND beer, what do you think it is, Christmas?"

As the beetle spluttered up the road, Lanks reached into a plastic bag behind and performed his party-trick. Passing a can and removing its ring pull with his gangly long pianist's forefinger one handed. At the same time steering with his knees and supping right-handedly.

Chugging towards the end of the road and cemetery overflow parking, the way ahead narrowed to a single lane; but instead of yielding, Lanks accelerated towards the tight space and oncoming vehicles. Terrified, Nick recoiled and pushed his feet forwards, urging brakes. He turned to Lanks for reassurance but was horrified to see his eyes were closed; he'd let go of the steering wheel and was bracing himself, as the car freewheeled blindly non-handed, somehow squeezing through the gap! Now hurtling towards the busy junction and wall beyond Nick shrieked, pushing Lanks to force his eyes open and slam foot to brake and pull handbrake as the car slid sideways, gliding through banks of slurry across both lanes of Marsland Road to a buzzing medley of angry car horns. Miraculously avoiding traffic, they kerb-halted with a jolt, sending the car onto its two side wheels and hurling an ice-rink jet-stop wave of slush across the pavement onto the factory wall beyond, thankfully jolting down to four wheels with a thud. They were facing the wrong direction, without a scratch.

"Holy-shit Lanks, how many've you had? Are you trying to kill us?" Nick screamed.

Lanks took another swig to calm his nerves, "Close. I didn't see that coming!"

"Of course you didn't… You had your fucking eyes shut!" Nick hissed through gritted teeth, secretly finding his seatbelt and passing it over himself to buckle unseen.

"No one sees an accident coming that's why it's called an 'accident', Dick-less. My dad had a motorbike accident twenty odd years ago. No more CRASHES. Today, this week OR THIS YEAR, OKAY?" He screamed, then forced silence with a long gulp, then gasped, "Long Life, huh? I'll drink to that."

"Yeah, must've been a real mind-fuck. My sincere condolences to you and your mum at this difficult time," Lanks delivered awkwardly.

* * *

Heff's house was a futuristic ideal home with minimalistic Bauhaus decor and sliding frosted-glass panel interiors. The staircase had open-rise steps with a beautiful, exotic and rare-coral, living-jewellery marine-life tank beneath; a fish bowl within an aquarium.

As the doorbell chimed, Nick watched the beer-fish, flounder from the kitchen into the hall and throw the glass door open as Bang and Olufsen played 'Love of the Common People'. Holding a boozy clinking-ice, crystal-glass tumbler and short stubby cigar between his teeth Heff was half dressed in a vest, unbuttoned festive-red Rat-Meat shirt, baggy striped boxer shorts and socks; but no trousers.

"Hark, carol-singers! Come listen Tiny Tim. How joyous, the local povs have come begging! A shiny coin if you can harmonise, street-urchins," Heff said playfully, conducting Paul Young and blowing smoke in their faces. He held hand to ear as Nick and Lanks stood silent, staring wide-eyed at Heff's glowing face; for some reason he was beaming, swollen, red and scabby.

Bait not taken, Heff switched to his best Noddy Holder impression and bellowed excitedly, "IT'S CHRIIISSTMAASS!" With welcoming outstretched arms.

Nick gasped, "Jesus, what happened to you, Freddy Krueger? You've got a face like a baboon's arse!"

"A spot of acne needed 'blitzen' so I washed my face with TCP. Three times! That'll teach me! I'm glowing like a Windscale lab-rat. Come in I'm nearly ready, just need to rub ice into this new layer of skin and get some kecks." He chugged back his drink and held the glass upside down, encouraging soothing ice-cubes to glide over his blistering-raw crimson face.

"Fuck me, zit-head. It's like a leper colony in here with that antiseptic smell," Lanks sniffed as he passed. "Topex not strong enough?"

"Cheapies!" Heff said, puffing on his cigar then pointed a circle at his face excitedly, "THIS is the least of your worries. Wait 'til you see Salty! He's been ON THE LASH! His dad's 'Work's Christmas Do', a lock-in with comedians, strippers-with-pythons and chicken-in-a-basket! He's talking to Huey on the great white telephone."

The downstairs toilet door slid open and Salty's grinning, drooling white face looked out weakly, slumped on the floor; he raised his head exhaustedly to rest face-cheeks inside the cool Thomas Crapper.

The bulldog Winston's head appeared sideways at the kitchen entrance, strangely about four feet off the ground with a hand above giving two fingers which were rotated from Churchill's 'victory' sign to Vicious 'V's' as the dog and hand slowly descended then slid back.

Lanks ordered, "You need to sober up Salty to go out on the piss. Eggy make coffee. Give him some chuddy Chopper." Walking into the kitchen Lanks sneered, "Don't bother giving any to John Merrick, the Elephant Man, he's no chance of copping!"

Filling his cheeks with ice-cubes, Heff gurned, "I am not an animal, I am a human being!"

Nick looked at Salty's slimy-wet hands and decided to place the chuddy-stick directly in his jacket pocket with a pat, "Save that to freshen up." Then whispered caution. "You two better not sabotage tonight. We're going in The Little B whether you like it or not. I know the bouncers so there's no stopping us!"

Salty slurred back, "I'll be gradely shipmate, jus' need to get me sea legs."

Then louder, Nick addressed all, "Talking of chicken and being sick, when's the home-brew ready?"

Salty sprang to life, "Thish week! We can have it on New Yearsh Eve and do it all over again." He then blasted the porcelain.

"We've not done anything yet," Nick said walking into the kitchen. "You can all come around to mine for New Year's Eve. My mum will be away." He was careful not to say she was already away.

"Oh-aye?! Your mum'll be out all night? Bringing in the New Year with a dong?" Heff grabbed a banana from the fruit bowl and held it upright, waving it from side to side, continuing, "Dong! Dong! Dong!"

With Heff's brutal enlightenment, Nick then realised he couldn't assume his mother's South African 'friend from University' was a woman! He gave Heff a scornful 'who needs enemies' look but controlled anger calmly continuing, "You can all stay over. Make Rat-Meat and dope brownies, drink gut-rot and watch video's all night long."

"An all-night party?" Eggy turned on his kitchen stool open-mouthed.

"Brownies?" Heff yelled delightedly.

"Video-nasties?" Lanks grinned. Salty retched incomprehensible bile.

"Banana-skins?" Heff continued the circle of quick questions excitedly, puffing on the unpeeled banana instead of his cigar.

"What do we want them for, we've got REAL drugs. An envelope arrived today from Brighton addressed to 'Mr Big'. Thanks for that, Heff. Drug-squad've got my cards marked and are probably casing the joint as we speak!"

Eggy asked excitedly, "Can we invite girls?"

"We don't know any," Lanks added.

They all turned to Nick apprehensively. Even Salty stopped chundering.

"Okay, you're going to meet girls tonight in The Little B, I promise you, it's wall to wall! I suppose we could invite some, but Jasmine's moving away before then and IT'S NOT GOING TO BE A PARTY!" Nick realised it may have been a bad idea to mention his free house and quickly changed the subject, "Are your fossils out, Heff? Where's Katie?"

"Bridge Tournament on Christmas Eve! I'm telling you, they live the bloody high-life! I think it's code for Swinger's Club and they all chuck their keys in to swap wives. Katie's driving her boyfriend up tomorrow morning, you know… the black drug dealer. I can't bloody wait to see my dad's face! Anyway, come here you two, we're playing a traditional festive parlour game to test your speed, skill and dexterity."

Heff led Nick and Lanks to a tea towel spread out over the work surface.

"Now then, dear brothers… WHAT'S THIS?" Heff yelled excitedly in a theatrical voice, quickly snapping the tea towel like a magician's table-cloth to reveal a neat line of large brown King Edward's potatoes. At the end two had been peeled and next to them were two small potato rectangles.

"A don't' knoo, it's all covered in't mud!" Eggy entertained, reciting lines from a crisp advert.

"Oh dear, it's a potato… GAME!" Heff shouted excitedly, "The challenge is to be the fastest potato peeler. You get two goes each and there's a prize for the quickest! Eggy is the current champ. Ignore those two, they're Salty's shite efforts." He pointed at the two rectangular chips, "The drunken-twat said he could skin his in six chops, hacking at my mum's marble… Twice! He's disqualified." He bent low and brushed the surface with his hand like a snooker player carefully inspecting for scratches then tossed Salty's chips into the bin as Salty tossed his into the Crapper.

Lanks went first, eager to show-off his dextrous long fingers and then it was Nick's turn as Heff counted gleefully, "Kodak one, Kodak two, Kodak three, Kodak four…"

"Judicator inspects and yes, perfect. May I say I think you'll both go far in the catering trade; manual labour is clearly your forte. Are you sure you didn't sneak out for Home Economics at the girl's school? Seriously though, John's Chippy are looking for someone of your calibre. Chopper's winning with 6.34 seconds. Now with your second go, try to beat your personal best. Feel free to have a third go Eggy but it's a difficult target. I'll just go and finish getting ready."

Paul Young's 'No Parlez' side two continued playing as Nick, Lanks and Eggy took it in turns to peel and time, over and over.

Heff reappeared zipping up the flies of his school pants, wearing his familiar big black coat and monkey boots. Lanks presented Heff with the peeler and said proudly, "Try to go faster than 5.8 seconds, NIKI LAUDER!"

"Enlighten me, dick-splashers," Heff said, coolly picking up the two remaining potatoes and returning them to storage, then grabbing a large pan to fill with water. "When have you ever played this at home as a 'traditional Christmas Eve parlour game'?"

"Never, but I demand a rematch! WE NEED MORE POTATOES!" Eggy yelled in an Irish accent.

"It isn't a 'traditional' game, you MUGS! I can't believe you SAD CRETINS fell for it, willingly doing the skivvy chore my bids' set for ME! Have you never heard of TOM SAWYER'S FENCE?!" He literally beamed, placing a lid on the hob salt-watered pan, ready for his mum's roasties tomorrow.

He walked over to the drinks trolley and coolly started topping up his hip flask. "You feltchers are all winners in my eyes and the prize is either a can of beer or a shot from the drink's trolley PLUS one dodder each." He unravelled a foil concertina-folded pack of twelve condoms and swung it around like he was holding a dead snake, parading the revered skin high above.

"IT'S TIME TO CUT THE SERPENT'S HEAD OFF… 'DU' durability, 'R' reliability and 'EX' excellence… DUREX!" He distributed, sliding one into Salty's top pocket then peered back into the kitchen as if waiting and said, "What are you lozzing about for? It's time to go snowballs-deep into Christmas with the birds and The B's!"

Chapter Twenty-Three

A Christmas Miracle

"Don't go in the pub car park Lanks, pull up here on the left. We don't know the bouncer at the back door." Nick directed blindly, squashed into the back seat with Eggy crammed uncomfortably on top of him. Filling most of the rear space was a large bucket which Salty's head was leaning into. Heff, being the largest, was afforded the passenger seat.

Prising themselves out of the compact car, Lanks joined the Bang Gang posse on the pavement, ducking down in the slush to hide behind the beetle. Heff propped Salty on a wheel arch so they could observe the pub entrance from afar to agree a plan of action. Nick reasoned, "The bouncers are just there to make sure you're over eighteen, that you've followed their dress-code and that you respect their authority. They limit numbers, want more girls than boys, no gangs, no one who looks trouble and no one who's already pissed."

Eggy and Lanks laughed.

"You may laugh shit-for-brains I'm serious! I'll be alright, I look the business but you geeks will struggle to get in." Nick rose and stood tall, brushing creases out of his suit.

"You said you knew the bouncers AND COULD GET US ALL IN!" Eggy squealed, continuing his protest exasperated. "That was the whole reason we got dressed up tonight."

"Normally I could have but it's packed, the bouncers can be selective tonight… and have you seen the state of these two?!" Nick barked pointing at Heff and Salty.

"What do you mean?" Heff asked innocently.

"Well, look at you."

"What?"

"He's clearly shitfaced, can't stand up or open his eyes; I think he's unconscious. And you, well, look at your face."

"What about my face?"

"WHAT ABOUT YOUR FACE? You look like DOCTOR BLOODY PHIBES!"

"They let me in last time," Heff sulked.

"Yeah, well, they're not going to recognise you now, are they? Why would they let you in? You'll scare all the girls. Seriously though with a face like that, and I mean before the TCP, who would ever fancy you?"

It hadn't been the harshest dig but Heff looked down. Nick had hit a sensitive nerve. The group fell silent. Looking at the dark slushy ground, Heff paused then squinted at Nick with dagger eyes and a carefully considered question, "If the rest of us get turned away would you still go in on your own?"

"You're bloody dead right luv!" Nick retorted.

"Splitter!" Heff barked angrily, the others mumbled, "Twat," in agreement.

"I've got a date with Jasmine! It's her last night. If I don't get to tell her how much I like her tonight, all this would have been in vain."

"All this in vanity, you mean! Your suit, your hair, your reflection, it's all false! I don't even recognise you anymore. Who are you and what have you done with our mate, Chopper? It's not about Jizzum really is it? When she's gone you'll still want to be with The Fluff Boys instead of us. They're superficial posers and you're just trying to infiltrate their girly clique. You could get girls without them if you had any confidence but you've got no balls… In fact, I bet a fiver I dip-my-wick before you."

"Ha, fat chance! deal!"

They locked hands, glaring at each-other like raging bulls. Squeezing tightly and staring into Nick's eyes, Heff warned, "But remember this: We're not life-long friends because you have a pretty face and wear fancy clothes, it's the sensitivity, beauty and fragility that shine within you that will always make me love you like a brother," He snarled, close to tears.

Lanks nudged but Eggy didn't respond.

Nick replied calmly, "Look, I'm not going anywhere. You don't have to lose a friend. You just have to make some new ones. I love you too, I love all of you and always will. You, my brothers, are literally the closest I have to family this Christmas. But I also love Jasmine and it's my last chance to tell her. Please help me get in," Nick begged.

A crack appeared on Heff's face which became a grin and then a painful, flaky smile. He pulled Nick in and hugged him lovingly.

With a new verve, Heff threw his arms around Eggy and Lanks as well, rallying the troops in a team scrum saying confidently, "Okay, I guarantee I'll get us ALL in, *even* Salty... Friends stick together forever. Here's the plan: We go in two groups. See all those girls at the back of the queue? Me and Salty will mingle with them, pretend they're our girlfriends. I'll prop Salty in the middle and do his talking for him. Then after a few minutes, you three join the queue and act like you don't know us. But if there's a problem make sure Chopper gets in and you two go around to the back door and wait out of view of the bouncer. Seriously, good luck with Jasmine, Nick; I mean Jizzum, Chopper. Merry Christmas Brother, I love you!" He hugged Nick and kissed his cheek then frog-marched Salty across the road to mingle.

After a few minutes, Nick said, "Add a year to your birthday and you're eighteen, okay?" He crouched to check his hair in the wing-mirror then the trio walked over the road to join the queue. In the few minutes that had passed, no one else had joined the line so they awkwardly stood directly behind Heff and Salty. The queue was quickly reducing as the bouncers were turning a worrying number of people away.

Nick then realised the bouncer he knew, Steve Benson, wasn't working the front door tonight. Another Neanderthal thug had taken his place.

A girl in front shouted angrily, "Hey Doorman, he's pushing in!" Another said, "Ew, hanging! Get away from me, you smell of sick!"

Salty's eyes were closed as he swayed backwards and forwards with a wide gormless grin fixed on his face. In his semi-conscious sleepwalking state, motor skills prompted him to reach into his jacket pocket and unwrap what ought to have been breath-freshening Wrigley's but was in-fact prophylactic-lubricated latex as he popped the germicidal Durex into his mouth, chewing rubber noisily. Watching Salty like a hawk the new bouncer was clearly disgusted and grimaced an angry scowl at the perverted delinquent as he gave little attention to pushing boys away and allowing girls in, keen to get the offensive drunken halfwit closer for a knuckle dusting.

Salty blew a huge bubble with the condom which shot out of his mouth, fired overhead with a high pitched flap as it deflated, rudely landing on the shiny boot of the enraged doorman.

"Jesus Christ, we need a Christmas miracle! I don't know either of these bouncers," Nick whispered in horror.

The group of girls Heff had infiltrated were next in line but there was a sudden commotion, shouting inside the pub and the bouncers quickly withdrew, closing the door and noisily latching it shut. A moment later, the door burst open as the two heavies used a white-bearded man in red as a battering ram to barge the door. As the line turned to watch the bouncers drag Santa Clause across the snow, knocking him to the floor for a good kicking, Heff slipped Salty through the door into the pub unnoticed, vanishing into the crowd.

The bouncers returned to their post, pleased to have been required to legitimately beat someone up. The replacement bouncer declared boldly to the horrified crowd, "That low-life sneaked in, in disguise. He's a known criminal, a DEALER, ladies and gentlemen and has previously been barred from this establishment for attempting to sell DRUGS. You witnessed us DEFENDING YOU. Out of the kindness of our hearts, we just gave him some bruises, a kick in the balls, etcetera rather than have police officers throw him in a cell; because tomorrow is Our Lord's birthday, even for scumbags. The good book says, 'Matthew 7:15 Beware of false prophets. They come to you in sheep's clothing, but inwardly they are ravenous wolves'. He, ladies and gentlemen is not Santa, but the devil himself, Satan! The same letters but rearranged. He'd love nothing more than to turn you all into drug addicts, rent boys and crack whores this Christmas. We, The Little B Security Team, have saved you all from a good bumming," the gruff doorman said proudly, brushing his gloves and surveying the shocked crowd.

Without moving or drawing attention, Eggy's eyes opened wide in surprise with pursed mouth he then sucked in his lips and blinked contemplatively.

The bouncer then realised someone was missing. He quickly scanned left and right, squinting beyond the queue up the street, clearly disappointed not to be able to stick his steelie up Salty's arse as well.

As the group of girls entered, and the trio moved forward towards the entrance the bouncer blocked Lanks, weighing him up.

Lanks jovially offered a polite greeting to a fellow Christian, "A very merry, Mass of Our Lord to you, good Sir."

"What did you just say?" The bouncer growled sternly as if he'd heard his mother being insulted.

"Nothing, Sir. Sorry Sir," Lanks said, suddenly bricking it.

"Fuck me, you're a big cunt, aren't you?"

"Yes, Sir. I mean no, Sir," Lanks wailed.

"How tall are you?"

"Six foot seven, Sir," he whimpered politely.

"I bet he's got a massive cock. You've seen it haven't you?" The bouncer said leather-glove thumb pointing at Lanks winking at Nick with a smile.

"No," Nick replied curtly.

The bouncer snarled aggressively, "NO, WHAT?"

"No, thank you."

"That's more like it, manners cost nothing. In you go gents, Merry Christmas. No trouble big-balls, yeah?"

Chapter Twenty-Four
Winter Wonderland

As if stepping through a magical portal into a dream, Nick found himself staring up at a dense forest of fir tree branches, interwoven with pine-cones, holly and ivy, filling the warm air with the sweet citrus scent of spruce and cedar wood. The enchanting floral decoration covered the entire ceiling of The Little B, creating a wonderful Christmas tree canopy above the festive party grotto.

Decorations added colour as bright baubles rotated, tinsel glistened and fairy-lights flickered but it was the predominance of a fresh white-berry decoration that intrigued Nick. A profusion of romantic mistletoe sprigs dangled seductively like unctuous ripe vine grapes, abundant throughout the venue, coaxing Christmas kisses beneath every encounter.

'Steal a kiss and take a berry' appeared to be the 'jeu du jour' as excited sprig-hogging clusters pushed bashful mates together with perfect strangers to canoodle under mistletoe and claim their berry trophy. From shy cheek-pecks and brave lip-kisses to full-on darting tongue snogs comme Les Français!

One familiar blonde boy with ruffled hair looked like he'd been dragged through a conifer; Nick nodded a greeting to I Am Will. The unscrupulous lipstick-smudged Lothario showed off his bountiful berry-count as he passed, shamelessly circulating to the next sprig to graze on pastures-new.

Slow drums started then the first star sang, "It's Christmas time…" Dry ice blasted, lights turned and lasers fired as the festive mass swayed to the new super-group charity Christmas number one record.

Nick was back in his favourite place. Lanks and Eggy were nowhere to be seen so he set off with the confident, self-assured stride he'd perfected, to the VIP area for his first-and-final date with Jasmine. A path instantly appeared as the melee parted to admire the smart newcomer.

Nick strode deeper into the overhead fire-hazard woods as the guiding path continued to part. But The B was packed tonight, much more crowded than last time and the channel disappeared. His route was blocked by a girl in a sparkly silver dress who's back was turned; but on seeing Nick, the girl's friends excitedly instructed her to turn. Sadly, not Jasmine, she was a tall, pretty-faced, leggy brunette with curly shoulder-length dark hair. Her freshly-applied red lipstick smiling-face lit-up as she raised an unplucked never-been-kissed mobile sprig, pouting sultrily.

Nick hesitated with a reluctant smile. He'd hoped Jasmine would be his one and only tryst but it appeared random kisses were the only way to advance. The brunette opened her eyes and cautioned, "I'm VERY selective and you DO know it's bad luck to refuse a kiss under mistletoe?"

Nick needed all the luck he could get. Her friends leaned in to watch as he accepted the harmless game and politely kissed cheek as she twisted to lock lips with his. With deafening screams and maniacal screeches, the 'Saint Trinians-esque' delinquents mobbed Nick, grabbing him, stealing kisses, smudging fresh lipstick all over his face, stripping the new mistletoe sprig bare of its precious berries like a plague of locusts.

Pressing-on Nick squeezed through the mob and arrived at the mirrored-pillar overlooking the dancefloor to compose himself and check his reflection. As he suspected, his face was covered in 'war-paint' of which he quickly removed all trace with his father's handy personal cloth.

He surveyed the VIP section on the other side of the dancefloor recognising familiar faces of the Fluff Boy entourage congregated around their sofa. Pip was on the periphery by the stairs wearing a deely-bopper, one long spring centrally dangling a plastic sprig of mistletoe in front of himself like a donkey carrot. G-Force Geoff spotted Nick and beckoned him with a friendly wave.

"No tongues!" Pip said, planting a gentle kiss on Nick's cheek as the mistletoe danced overhead. Todger, wearing red and blue lensed 3D-glasses greeted Nick then Pip took the deely-bopper off, wrapped it around his waist to dangle over his flies and said, "Christmas isn't just about the north pole, the south pole needs conquering as well!" The pair then strutted onto the dancefloor with Pip proudly gyrating his appendage through halls of ivy.

Nick was now standing above the in-crowd's Imperial Box and below, centrally seated was Emperor Simon. He was tall and had a look of Japan's frontman David Sylvian wearing a smart black suit and tie, with stylish manicured hair. He had a handsome face; feminine cheekbones and lips but masculine jawline and brow. He was leaning forward observing the crowd below, consulting Daran, "The girl in silver dress? Yes, fit. I love the way she's done her eye make-up. She'll be stunning in a year. Jail-bait for sure, not even sixth form. Is she signalling me?"

Nick looked down and realised the girl they were referring to was trying to catch his attention, the pretty brunette he'd just kissed! Possibly a year younger than himself but seemingly unripe forbidden-fruit, given Simon's assessment.

Prior to this, Nick had assumed Simon would be gay. Jasmine had described him as 'Definitely just good friends', and that he was a 'very sensitive, loyal and dear, caring and self-less friend' to her broken-wristed brother. 'Methinks she doth protested too much', Nick surmised. It was clear that the Adonis's penchant was for beautiful girls, no doubt devouring the lion's share from his position as alpha-male leader of the well-groomed pack.

Geoff stood to welcome Nick with a friendly handshake and patted his shoulder politely relocating himself to the sofa's arm, offering his seat and introducing Simon, who instantly rose tall.

"It really is my pleasure to meet you, I've heard so much about you, Nick."

"Really?" Nick declared, flattered by Simon's cordiality.

"Join us, please."

Nick was bursting with pride, welcome amongst the beautiful ones as he took his seat at the inner sanctum on cloud nine, rubbing shoulders with the decadent in-crowd's highest echelons as his heart had so desired.

Simon began to regale his friends, "Jaz asked me to tape my own record onto a cassette for Nick as a present to him after my birthday. He was already a friend of mine apparently, but I must have amnesia. I invited him to my party but I have absolutely no recollection of doing so."

"Ah yes, well about that…" Nick began awkwardly.

"It seems to me that YOU OWE ME A PARTY," Simon said, looking Nick in the eye with a calm smile. Was this a trap?

"A debutant party to introduce you to our friends," Simon continued less intimidating. "I can see us becoming good friends, you fit in Nick and will go far with the right people. I love your suit. Matinique?"

Nick glowed. "Yes it is!" There was no harm in befriending the elite, in fact it would be an honour to invite such respectable and polite people to his house. "Actually I'm having a party on New Year's Eve."

"Perfect," Simon purred shaking hands to seal the deal.

Lanks appeared below, over the heads of the tallest on the dancefloor shouting excitedly, "Have you SEEN the talent in here, it's bursting with totty! How did you get up there? I couldn't get past."

Through the railing he started to hand Nick a dark beery pint-mug glass tankard, "They don't do mild so I just got bitter."

Daran repeated in a high-pitch, "Mild!" Laughing at Lanks' warm frothy old man's grog.

"That's not for me, it's Heff's," Nick said, winking at Lanks, starting to glow as he turned back to Simon with 'puzzled' gesture.

"Suit yourself, but I'm not dishing out for lager at these prices." Lanks turned to join Heff who had greeted Todger and Pip on the crowded dancefloor. Nick could see Eggy standing at the side nursing his pint, shyly ogling dancing girls. Salty was sound-asleep at his side wall-leaning on a stool.

"What is that idiot doing?!" Simon laughed, pointing into the crowd. Nick added to the roar but realised they were ridiculing Heff's special dance. Heff looked up into Nick's eyes and his red-faced expression flipped from utter joy to extreme sadness in the blink of an eye. Nick instantly stopped laughing and looked away noticing Jane to the right of the dancefloor. As soon as she saw him, she leapt up to rip a sprig like an Amazon and made a beeline.

Thankfully at that moment, Jasmine arrived with her slinged-arm brother, both fending off opposite-sex mistletoe-wielders. Wanting Jasmine to see him at the high seat Nick gave a cool wave from his VIP position. She was wearing a blue In-Wear logo jacket with cream silk scarf loosely wrapped over figure-hugging white dress, big buckled belt, tights and blue slouch boots.

He pulled his feet forward preparing to stand, but Simon pressed down on Nick's thigh hoisting himself up first to stand in his way, putting his arm around Jasmine under mistletoe.

"Merry Christmas Jaz," he bowed. Jasmine looked at Nick and pecked Simon's cheek.

"Is that it?" Simon scoffed. "You're under mistletoe. You'll have to try harder than that if you want to come to the party with me tonight."

"Sorry Simon, I can't," Jasmine said nudging closer to Nick, out of sight her hand secretly fumbled for Nick's in a blind and brave 'leap of faith'. As skin touched skin, the magnetism was electric and a sudden boost gave Nick the confidence to interlock fingers then dare to clutch her tiny hand within his, affirming mutual attraction. Courtship sealed, Jasmine had chosen Nick.

"Can't come to the party? That's a pity."

Simon then addressed Nick. "Would you like to join us? We have a spare seat in the car now. We're going to Liv's party in Hale. Do you know Olivia? Fantastic legs; she has a swimming pool, sauna, sunbed and well-stocked wine cellar, all open to the right people."

Nick squeezed Jasmine's hand and said politely, "I don't think so, I didn't bring my trunks."

"Neither did we!" Simon guffawed, slapping his hand on Daran's shoulder. "To skinny-dip with Hale's most beautiful all you need is a smile! She has plenty of towels to cover your modesty out of the water. Sure you don't want to join us?"

"Thank you but no. I am where I want to be," Nick replied, secretly squeezing again.

"Grace, it's your lucky night!" Simon shouted over his shoulder, then whispered to Nick, within Jasmine's earshot. "She looks even better in the buff."

Grace replied, "I'll come if Jane can squeeze in. She's only twiggy, she can sit on my lap." Simon turned to Jasmine. "Oh well, Jaz dear sister, is this goodbye? When do you actually leave?"

Jasmine looked at Nick with a smile and told them both together, "My parents are taking the removal van on Boxing Day but because of Pierce's arm, we will be staying with family for a few more days, taking the train down on New Year's Day."

Nick was elated at this wonderful news and begged, "You've got to come to my New Year's Eve Party!"

Jane suddenly appeared and forced herself between Nick and Jasmine's locked hands thrusting mistletoe overhead, "Merry Christmas Nick," she panted throwing herself at him.

Nick had hoped it was obvious he and Jasmine were now 'an item'. He reluctantly leant forward to peck Jane's cheek under the pallid parasitic plant, at the same time Simon re-planted his lips on Jasmine. Still finger-entwined Nick and Jasmine both turned to watch each other being kissed, unwittingly forcing their own mouths directly onto Jane and Simon's adhesion.

"That's more like it, hot-lips. We can say goodbye properly at Nick's party," the gratified conqueror smouldered as he walked away.

"Are you sure you don't want to come Nick? This invitation really is a golden ticket," Geoff advised.

"No thanks G-Force, All I want is here."

As the crowd dispersed, Jasmine hugged Nick and glanced longingly at the overhead mistletoe, gently squeezing his arms. Nick looked around, aware they were standing alone above the crowd.

"Can I ask you something?" He said nervously.

"Please do," Jasmine said with a dreamy smile, pushing her chest into his, heart to heart and gazing into his eyes.

"Will you go out with me?"

Jasmine pulled away with a sigh, looking sadly down.

"Oh Nick, why? Can't we just have a Christmas kiss? I can't go out with you… I'm leaving in a week, forever. I don't want either of us to get hurt. Can't we just be friends, what's the point?"

"WHAT'S THE POINT?! I like you, you like me and a Christmas MIRACLE has granted us some more time! I admire you too much to just 'go with you', publicly sucking-face to add to a seedy, berry count. I want to 'go OUT with you' as your boyfriend until you have to leave," He smiled, remembering Heff's words of wisdom.

"If we lived at other ends of the country and met on holiday we wouldn't hold back would we? We'd open our hearts and enjoy every moment together, then after a blissful week we'd part and return to our separate lives." He held Jasmine's chin up and looked into her tearful eyes.

He continued, "There's nothing I'd like more than to kiss you. You're the only one I want. I could never request kisses from random strangers. If anyone is lucky enough to follow their heart and kiss the one they truly love, why would they ever want to kiss anyone else?"

"I agree," Jasmine sighed sadly. Her eyes fluttered as a heart-felt saline tear cascaded down her cheek tipping silver into Nick's begging hand, encouraging him to continue softly.

"Please go out with me Jasmine, if only until midnight on New Year's Eve then we can part and toast new beginnings as 'just good friends'. Start 1985 with an end. They say 'it's better to have loved and lost than never to have loved at all' so let's enjoy this brief split-second of life with no regrets, for one week only, opening our hearts to each other's love."

He put on a brave face as his eyes welled, he'd said his piece, it was time to hold his peace. After a pensive pause, Jasmine's head rose. Her blue eyes sparkled and she smiled, "YES, I'll go out with you," She said with an enormous grin, "But…" She cautioned. "I have two conditions, you're not going to like them and they're non-negotiable. Firstly, our house is upside down, we're living out of tea-crates, I have to pack, clean and leave the place spotless. Then living out of a suitcase at my mum's sister's house, I have to be helpful, volunteer to do more chores and duties than usual, so I can't come and go as I please. I'll be cooped up all week but I'll make sure I'm allowed out to say goodbye on New Year's Eve.

"Secondly, since I've known about the move, don't be mad. Many nice boys have asked me out and I've said no to them all. I don't want to upset ANYONE so our relationship has to remain a secret, no one must know. If you agree to these terms, I'll be your secret girlfriend at your party until the stroke of midnight. Then we walk away from each other: No more tears and no regrets."

"And tonight?" Nick asked.

Jasmine quickly drew Nick close to seal the deal, her breasts merged into his chest, forcing his bulging, attention-seeking pants into her midriff. As his eyes shut he closed in on lustful, thrilled smiling teeth as their mouths met; touching, pecking, then caressing, tasting and testing love's luscious lips, life's sweet appetiser for Nick's first true kiss. Briefly pulling back with rosy beams and puffed up lips they gazed wantonly into each other's eyes. Hungry for more they relocked, tilting to secure application. Too close to focus and regardless of their surroundings they closed eyes and blissfully pressed on, interconnected blind and mute. Forceful desire broke seal to meet and explore tongues, sucking, stirring and tasting passionate pleasures together.

Weak kneed, Jasmine abandoned herself into Nick's strong, safe arms with eyes closed and connected tongues they barely heard the rapturous cheers and wolf-whistles from the whooping crowd below.

Lights dimmed and the DJ announced orders at the bar and thirty minutes to Christmas as Wham!'s 'Last Christmas' filled the dancefloor with amorous, smooching couples. Colourful inflated balloons were released and the floor was swamped with dry-ice as an inflated condom patted towards the lovers.

For the finale of their tonsil-tennis snogathon, Nick pretended it was 'just a Christmas kiss' and reached up to pluck two precious pearl-like mistletoe berries from the overhead sprig. After parading them to the crowd, he gently folded them into his handkerchief giving Jasmine a secret wink. He then guided her, hand-in-hand to the edge of the dancefloor where Eggy, Lanks and hungover-Salty were eyeing up nearby dancers. Eggy shouted, "This place is spondicious!"

Nick coaxed them all onto the dancefloor to find Heff, Pip and Todger locked in embrace then asked Heff with a hug, "Teach us your dance, Brother."

* * *

When the 'Time gentlemen please' last order's bell rang, Lanks looked at his wristwatch, "God help me, I'm going to be late for midnight service. I've got to go."

"Wait, Lanks. If you're going to The Methodists, can I scrounge a lift home? It's on your way. I'll pay full taxi fare."

"Okay, but it's treble rate at this time."

Nick then turned to Jasmine, "Would you like to come back to mine for a bit?"

"You're a fast mover! A bit of what?" Jasmine laughed.

Nick started to glow. "I didn't mean like that." He then whispered in her ear, "My mum's gone on holiday. I don't want this lot to know I've got a free house; they'd treat it like a drop-in. I'd just like to see a bit more of you; I mean, spend a bit more time with you, that's all."

* * *

Nick's house was lit up like Blackpool Illuminations; expensively cosy and festively atmospheric. A choir sang softly from the sitting room as Nick guided Jasmine straight to the kitchen in search of sweet rehydrating lemonade to replace fluids literally sucked out of themselves.

Jasmine said, "I can't stay long but I hate to think of you on your own. Can I phone a taxi before they get busy?"

"Are you leaving already?" Nick pouted, holding the fridge door open.

In the spotlight, Jasmine held Nick's jacket collars and pulled him towards herself, planting a seal on his sultry lips, "No, I'm definitely spending the first hour of Christmas Day with you," then rubbed an Eskimo kiss. "I'll book a taxi for one. I'd get into trouble if I stayed later."

As an 'All the nines' taxi was booked, Nick poured lemonade into two tall glasses with no ice then handed Jasmine hers, declaring habitually with a smile, "Do you know the rules of the game?"

"Well, you're going to give me the 'grande-tour of honour' and then we end up in your bedroom," Jasmine said with a mischievous smile as she clinked and gulped.

Nick gulped, "No! Sorry, that's not what I meant. It's a drinking game my friends…"

"Shhh!" Jasmine placed a finger on Nick's lips and silently guided his hand to the hallway where they stopped at the bottom of the stairs. She turned to roll Nick's arm around herself, leading another course of sweet, lubricated heavy petting. But with the sitting room door cushion-propped open and Aled Jones singing his little heart out Jasmine was distracted. She opened her eyes, lured by the enchanting sight at the far end of the room; the evergreen festooned with brightly-coloured glass-baubles and a glittering array of colourful fairy lights.

"Oh, I love a real tree. Yours is beautiful!" She whisked Nick away from the stairs to the seven-foot-tall Nordic Spruce which was clearly glad of the attention, shining prouder and brighter than ever before. They dropped to their knees in admiration like praying children. Jasmine scooped cupped hands of fallen needles and shared the Christmas scent delightedly.

The best under-tree gift ever was to watch Jasmine's adoring child-like face in the flickering light as she explored the enchanted forest of delicate heirloom glass ornaments. After she had marvelled over every orb within reach, her expression saddened and she said softly. "We don't have a tree this year. We're not doing presents and we're not displaying cards. In fact, quite the opposite, we've taken pictures and ornaments down so the rooms are bare and cards went straight in the bin. It doesn't feel like home anymore."

"Home is family. Look at me I'm surrounded by all these luxurious decorations in warmth and comfort but I'm all alone. This isn't home, it's just a nice house," Nick said with a wistful smile, contemplatively turning his back on the attention-seeking tree.

Jasmine quickly turned to sit feet-forward, by the side of Nick holding his hand, "Sorry, that was thoughtless of me. I can't believe your mum has left you alone over Christmas. Do you have somewhere to go for Christmas dinner?"

"My aunt's in Yorkshire. I'll be fine."

Suddenly an eye-catching glint shone from Nick's jacket pocket, the Cupid's arrow pocket grip of the silver Parker pen. Jasmine reached in then wrote her address on the back of Nick's hand.

"Please come around to mine in the evening after your aunt's, it would make my day. We don't play games or entertain, we'll probably just sit and watch telly all night but I can't bear to think of you on your own. My dad's a bit grumpy but he's my dad and I love him."

She then lay back staring up into the tree. Nick, remained sitting upright with his back to her thinking about how grumpy his dad used to be and that he'd not see his present opening face this Christmas or ever again.

With head underneath the branches, Jasmine explored the glittering tree from its base with one eye closed then the other. After a while, she propped her head on her arm and leaned forward seductively to catch Nick's attention through the lowest branches. Giving up telepathy she gently prodded him.

"Oy, lie back with me, it's lonely under here."

Nick reclined to join Jasmine on a soft bed of aromatic needles cushioned by gift-wrapped delights and soft parcels for pillows, presumably new clothes. His head touched Jasmine's and they held hands gazing up into the tree.

Jasmine continued merrily, "When I was little I used to lie like this under our tree looking up through the tinsel, closing one eye at a time to see different perspectives of the lights and baubles like a magic kaleidoscope. I was the only one who ever saw the tree like that. I'd rather lie there in my own world than watch telly; It was so colourful and magical at such a black and white time. We should make a wish."

She turned to Nick but he was fast asleep, still firmly clutching her hand within both of his, as if he never wanted to let go.

* * *

Nick awoke suddenly with a jolt, knocking his head on a big red glass bauble and a confetti of pine needles showered his head and shoulders. He was clothed and still lying under the tree. Jasmine was standing over him putting her coat on and wrapping her scarf.

As he sat up, she knelt down beside him cupping his face with both her hands, kissed him and said sweetly, "It's Christmas Day! Merry Christmas Nick."

He stood and held her in his arms, "Merry Christmas, Jasmine." Then they shared the best present anyone could ever receive; embracing a loved one, heart to heart with a kiss.

An impatient 'clock's ticking' taxi horn beeped again outside as they walked past the black 'broadcast closedown', low-pitched tone of the 'now turn me off' telly. Nick knocked the cushion into the hall, instantly shutting the sound behind the spring-loaded door.

Outside in the snow by the juddering black cab, they held each other and kissed. As snow confettied down, Jasmine said with an adoring smile, "My wish came true! I woke up beside you on Christmas Day." Then with a smile added, "You can give me a private viewing of your bedroom on New Year's Eve."

The Hackney cab used the park entrance to turn around. Nick waved goodbye as the dark steamy window vanished into the distance as the night became silent.

Back in the hall, Nick glared at the velvet cushion then booted it as far as it would go through the morning room into the kitchen. Why hadn't he kept the sitting room door shut? He should have listened to his father.

December Twenty-Five
The Bleak Mid-Winter

At 9.15am, Nick's radio-alarm leapt into life blasting Wizzard's 'I Wish It Could Be Christmas Every Day', silenced when he flung his continental quilt back and hit 'Snooze'. Toasty-warm he reclined with fingers clasped behind his head studying the contoured ceiling, contemplatively.

Transfixed by the woodchip snowscape overhead, he was transported back to the bleak white tundra of Sadleworth Moor in the early seventies, his mother's Hillman Imp careering dangerously fast. The car was filled with smoke and she was hysterical. Nick was terrified and slid around the back seat as the car struggled to keep a grip on the snake-like road in the icy wilderness. There'd been horrific screams at home... Police and ambulance. Nick's distraught mother 'upped sticks'. Grandma hadn't been warned, she had no phone. His father didn't go with them; he was in hospital after hurting himself shaving.

Nick's grandmother's cottage was remote and cold. No Christmas decorations and no television. Nick was sent to bed with no supper; out of the way, as Grandma consoled her daughter. The crying went on for hours until he could hear only an exhausted whimper. Nick huddled under thin sheets in a small bedroom with no carpet, pictures or ornaments. He lay shivering and hungry but pretended to be asleep when the door crept open and his mother sniffed back tears to deliver an ominous sack. It became dark again, then more weeping downstairs. What had he done wrong? He was helpless and full of remorse but daren't look, fearing coal. Eventually he drifted off, shivering with fear. He was five.

He then recalled Christmas the following year, in his house. The excitement of waking to discover Father Christmas had actually been to his house! A huge white sack had magically appeared at the foot of his bed, overflowing with gift-wrapped goodies. Expensive 'wish-list' presents he ransacked alone in silence without parents present. Not out of selfish choice, he'd been instructed to open alone, forbidden from showing his face until lunch when he was expected to present himself, composed, with decorum.

As an adult, Nick now understood his conditioning. It was clear that his excited giddiness, pleasure and extreme joy could possibly have upset his fragile father and sent him over the edge again.

Concealing oneself and suppressing emotions isn't healthy, every budding psychologist knows that. The repressed will grow to crave attention. He glanced over at Narcissus.

If Nick could understand the reason for his father's torment he may be able to find closure. Questions his aunt may be able to answer. His mum was no use, she'd wiped her husband from her memory since the funeral and was likely to never mention him again.

Alone again on Christmas Day. But eight hours earlier, he'd had the most wonderful time with Jasmine and his secret Christmas wish had been granted. Jasmine, the fleeting love of his life, had requested a 'private viewing' of his bedroom on New Year's Eve.

He was in love. An adult with loving urges. Alarm bells were telling him he was 'on a promise', Jasmine wanted to experience pleasure and extreme joy with him; her parting gift. He rolled over, put his leg over the rolled duvet and giddily ransacked alone in silence.

* * *

After showering with band-aid on the back of his hand, Nick didn't bother with poncy hair treatments and dressed conservatively-smart for visiting relatives, then went downstairs to masticate oats silently alone in the morning room. He could hear cartoons playing in the sitting room so took his muesli to investigate, returning the velvet cushion. He roared with laughter at Donald Duck who was so furious unwelcome chipmunks were living in his Christmas tree, he smashed up the entire house trying to get rid of them.

His mother's presents beckoned from under the tree. He knelt where he'd slept with Jasmine, rubbed his hands through the needle carpet and lay back gazing through the branches at the colourful lights, baubles and tinsel, awakening senses, recalling observations that would become precious memories.

As he unwrapped silently alone, the cushioned ones were: socks, boxer-shorts, scarf, ski-sweater. The boxed ones were: Three handkerchiefs monogrammed 'N', sandalwood aftershave, deodorant and soap-on-a-rope, a box of chocolates and a bottle of whiskey. Whiskey?! His mother really didn't know him. Everything 'St Michael' branded from Marks and Spencer.

In the kitchen, he read his mother's note:

'Stay patient and trust your journey.' He liked that one.

'Christmas isn't the same without you Darling. (Humph, Nick thought. 'You wrote this before you left, I bet it's much better!') Big kisses from South Africa. I hope you like your presents but if not, they're all M&S so you can take them back for a cash refund, no receipt needed. I'll phone you at eleven o'clock before you set off. Boxing Day's message is under this one and one for each day thereafter until I'm back. Merry Christmas, Mum P.S. Don't forget Hilda's present and drive safely!'

He returned to the tree with a white pillowcase. Along with Aunt Hilda's wrapped biscuits, he bagged the whiskey, chocolates, scarf and handkerchiefs. He put the new sweater on over his shirt and tie, anticipating his uncle's vicarage would be frugally cold then put on his dad's boots and coat.

It was 10.43am, His mum would phone soon but he decided to leave now, it would give him more time to drive safely and cruise around the neighbourhood, posing in his Porsche.

* * *

The shiny red, turtle-wax polished sports car Nick had lovingly buffed and shammied was secure in the dark garage. With sack and coat on passenger seat he inserted key illuminating the spacecraft-like dashboard and the headlights automatically popped up reflecting brightly on the white garage wall. He sat in the comfortable cream leather bucket seat beaming over Wayfarer frame. The cockpit was tidy and smelt new, a green turtle-shaped air freshener disguised a hint of cigarettes. Paul McCartney's latest was smoothly accepted by the LCD auto-reverse cassette player, serenading, 'No More Lonely Nights'. His mum had a range of slushy cassettes on the dashboard including 'Diamond Life', 'The Carpenters' and 'Give My Regards to Broad Street' soundtrack.

He turned the key further and the V8 engine roared into life.

The problem with showing off your new toy on Christmas Day is no one sees you, everyone else is home with their loved ones playing with their new toys. Nick cruised silent roads with heating up and windows down. There was sure to be an eleven o'clock service at Lanks' church on the wide palatial Avenue, he might even see a friendly face to wish 'Merry Christmas'.

As he reached the Methodists, there were last minute stragglers scurrying but no crowd. This desperately needy detour had been a waste of time, he ought to get back on track. He turned the wheel sharply, quickly pulled the handbrake up-then-down, making the back end of the car slide out, slipped from fourth to second, eased the clutch up and quickly returned the steering wheel anticlockwise with rear wheels gripping as the car turned 180° to face the way he'd come slickly accelerating at pace. A pretty cool move if it wasn't for all the tapes and boxes jetting across the dashboard and hurling themselves out of the passenger window!

He skidded to a halt and leapt out of the car to run back and collect his mum's slushy tapes from ice drifts, sheepishly avoiding eye-contact with condemning parishioners. The church-bell started to toll 'eleven'. Nick guiltily imagined his mum worrying as the phone would have gone unanswered.

As he returned to his car, a voice shouted, "Hellraisers are not welcome here. Go back to your father's ivory palace and leave us in peace."

"Amen" said another. Nick looked into the stern face of the dog-collar wearing minister and felt ashamed. He hoped to get a better reception from God's representative on the other side of The Pennines.

* * *

As if fired from a gun, the Porsche shot straight up the main road aiming for the M63 motorway, changing direction with a rewarding screech powerfully accelerating up the wet slip-chicane with the prospect of no future lights, obstacles or restrictions. Nick removed his sunglasses for optimum vision, set the wipers to 'fast' and tightly gripped the sports wheel. The road ahead was dead, he pressed foot down forcing skull and spine back into the seat and his peripheral vision blurred into lightspeed. With heart pounding he focussed on the ever-approaching distant horizon not daring to blink, as perilous avalanche-threatening sweat beads threatened to obscure vision. No traffic on all six there-and-back lanes, he put his foot to the floor, thunderously galloping the three hundred light brigade thoroughbreds towards the fast approaching hills, travelling two miles a minute! Holding the outside lane like a Scalextric slot car, he could see the road dip dramatically down into Beal valley then whiplash up into The Pennines.

With gravity's assistance, he tore downhill towards the valley floor hurtling past the landmark cooling tower of Milnrow's looming mill with the stretched engine booming like a rocket. Ego-trip distracted, he gave the speedometre a split-second glance… One hundred and forty miles per hour! As he looked up with a proud grin, a dot suddenly appeared on the distant horizon moving from inside lane to middle, Nick was suddenly upon it like kestrel on prey and flew past overtaking cars at twice their speed. Fearing aquaplane, brakes would be dangerous at such force, he gradually eased his foot off the gas decelerating as the sports car shot up the steep hill into the man-made gorge, at this point he reached for the seatbelt and clipped it securely, returning back from lightspeed to whisk across the red and white rose Lancashire/Yorkshire border blurry pink finish line. His heart was pounding as he continued to ease speed to a respectable eighty-six flinging into the slip road at Sadleworth Moor to hum a judder across the cattle grid. A few miles down the reservoir-straddling moorland and then a twisting minor road up into the abyss of the moor.

Powerful wheels churned fresh snow to grip traction uphill through the gullied white-wall, tractor-cleared path which eventually opened to reveal the solitary old church he recognised from childhood. Parrock Nook or 'Parrot' Nook as he had known it as a child: Hopefully home to an insightful talkative old bird.

The chapel was in the middle of nowhere, centre of a long gone farming community.

Taking his mother's wrapped gift from the sack, he walked up the steep steps through the graveyard to the big wooden door and gently rapped the knocker. There were finger-wide gaps around the wooden door possibly welcoming church-mouse congregation. It would take Aunt Hilda some time to get to the door with her dodgy hip so he turned to admire 'Gods Own Country' exhaling condensation as the sun broke through the clouds casting a beam of light across the picturesque shepherd's moorland winter wonderland.

The old aunt eventually creaked the door open and said wearily, "Welcome Nicholas, it's nice to see you again. Do come in to the cold."

After cleansing his soles on the ancient wall-mounted boot scraper, Nick handed the present to his aunt holding her hammy shoulders and planting a kiss on her jowly cheek greeting chirpily, "Merry Christmas Aunty Hilda, this is from mum."

They walked through the great hall into a warm room with welcoming fire. Hilda placed the gift on a table overflowing with similar boxes of biscuits and chocolates, presumably gifts from Uncle Clarence's flock.

"Clarence is just preparing his robes for this evening, he won't be long, can I get you a cup of tea?"

Nick sat on a stool by the fire remembering the room. A big table in the middle covered by a thick table cloth and many seats of all different styles lined the walls as well as a wooden pew under the window. They too had a print of one of Salvador Dali's paintings on their wall: 'Christ of Saint John of the Cross'. There was an inactive radio and no television. Nick hadn't expected he'd be able to watch anything anyway and was happy to stare into the warm flickering amber flames of the fire. As a child, his favourite activity had been sparking coals and digging fiery pits with the poker which had always unsettled Uncle Clarence.

Hilda returned slowly, awkwardly balancing a tea-pot tray across the bar of her Zimmer frame. Nick quickly leapt to assist, "Let me help you with that." Relieving her of the burden. She declined his offer of any further assistance and returned to the kitchen to carry on cooking as a grandfather clock chimed once in the hall. The big old church house was silent and Nick could hear every second tick past.

Clarence eventually appeared, greeting Nick at the fireside. "Ah Nicholas, it's a shame you missed this morning's adoration, will you be joining us at seven?"

Nick knew his mother wouldn't have expected him to attend either service, but politely said, "Merry Christmas Uncle Clarence, I'm afraid I can't, I'd like to get away before it goes dark, the snow as it is."

"My, that's a fleeting visit, it goes dark at three thirty."

The wall-mounted black Bakerlite phone in the hall broke the silence alarmedly. Clarence answered and called Nick quickly to speak long distance.

"Yes, sorry. No, I'm fine. Merry Christmas Mum. You too. Oh, by the way who is the friend you're staying with from University? ALICE? My godmother?

Oh, send her my love as well. Have a great time. I will. Peaches? Yes, please. Bye Mum."

Back in the parlour, Hilda was bringing items to dress the table, a few at a time tucking her pinny over the frame as a cradle. Clarence gave no assistance and their guest was told to sit by the fire. Back and forth she painstakingly came until the table was set for Christmas Dinner.

As they sat, Clarence said grace. Nick closed his eyes and did his best Sunday School prayer pose, cheerily repeating, "Amen."

The meal was a plentiful feast. Nick loved Aunt Hilda's mashed potato heavily seasoned with white pepper and the crispy roasts in dripping were delicious.

Out of the blue Clarence declared enigmatically, "Frank of Sale."

Continuing to eat, Nick coaxed his uncle's conversation opener with a raised eyebrow contemplative nod.

Clarence went on pensively, "Your father's namesake 'Saint Francis de Salle' said, 'The Lord will shield you from suffering or he will give you unfailing strength to bear it.'"

He then placed his cutlery together on his clear plate and looked Nick in the eye and said, "Your father had unfailing strength to bear his suffering."

Hilda nearly spat out her sprouts, "Clarence that is no conversation for the Christmas dinner table. I am so sorry Nicholas."

"No really, it's okay. Tell me about my dad. I really don't know much about what happened and it would help me find peace. Do you know why he went to Northwich?"

Hilda said softly, "Oh, you poor lamb. Northwich is where your father had a tragic motorcycle accident in the early sixties."

"What?" Nick said in surprise putting his cutlery down. This was the first time he'd heard a reason for his father choosing the location of his death.

"Oh, I'm so sorry to bring it up," Hilda said, reaching for her frame preparing to hoist herself up.

"No please, tell me all you know." Nick insisted, putting his hand gently on hers.

"Well, your mother and father met at Liverpool University, studying together. Frank already had a girlfriend he knew from home who lived in Northwich, he would ride his motorcycle back and forth to see her at weekends with her riding pillion. One winter's night it had snowed and your father's motorcycle skidded on black ice on a tight bend in rural Northwich throwing them both off, the girl crashed into a wooden gate and died instantly. They had been engaged. What was her name now, Clarence?"

Clarence, who was tapping a cross on his chest, shrugged.

Could it have been the girl in his father's hidden photograph? Nick patted his pockets in search of his matchbox, but realised it was still in his suit jacket pocket. He remembered, 'lower-than' symbol, 'greater-than' symbol, v.

"V... did her name begin with V?"

"Yes, Valerie!"

Nick could picture his father sitting under a wooden gate, reflecting icily for the last time at the moment of death. It was the sad image of Narcissus on his bedroom wall. He asked solemnly, "Was Valerie blonde?"

"Yes, golden! Such a pretty girl I recall from the photograph in the newspaper. So sad. But everything happens for a reason, you wouldn't be here if that hadn't happened."

* * *

Choosing to no longer punish his mother's pride and joy, Nick emerged from the backbone of England, within the speed limit, to survey millions of beautiful shimmering lights illuminating the distant Cheshire plain and North Wales.

Nick remembered the old woman at his dad's funeral being scolded for saying 'ladykiller' and his mother's friends saying 'Northwich, how romantic'. His father had planned his death to rest in the same spot he had lost his love, Valerie: He WAS romantic. He HAD a heart. He FELT remorse. He DID love.

Nick had new-found hope and felt energised. No longer dwelling on negativity, sadness and insanity, his bloodline clearly oozed love, passion and romance.

Coming off the motorway at Stretford, he flicked the interior light on, peeled the band-aid off and headed for Jasmine's house.

* * *

Nick grabbed the sack and crunched past the unwelcome 'SOLD' sign staked into an overgrown snow-capped privet-hedge, buzzing the terraced house's bell.

After a moment, the hall illuminated and Jasmine's petite figure skipped excitedly to the frosted glass door. She beamed with delight but an angry voice bellowed incredulously, "WHO THE HELL goes out ON CHRISTMAS DAY?"

"It's okay Daddy, it's a friend of mine."

As the day Nick had fallen head over heels for her, Jasmine was dressed in skin-tight jeans and sweater with no jewellery or make up, ungilded, flawless and natural beauty. Wearing white ankle socks she tiptoed from the carpet to lean out, stretching to plant a luscious soft kiss on Nick's lips. She grabbed his hand and guided him through the crate-stacked hall. Whispering with a smile, "I'm so pleased you came. Come in, he won't bite."

The through-lounge was stacked high with a jumble of boxes. A sofa and two armchairs were clustered around an amber-glowing radiant two-bar electric heater and the only item on display was a deep mahogany boxed television-set commanding attention. Jasmine's father was sitting in profile, wearing a home-made newspaper crown; the ruler's eyes glued to the TV with control under his arm-rested fingertips, not remotely interested in Jasmine's guest.

In the curtainless bay-window, slinged-arm Pierce sat in an armchair facing the skewed telly, he was also sporting a home-made newspaper hat, in the style of one-armed Admiral Nelson. He gave Nick a bored nod. Jasmine introduced, "This is my friend Nick from college, this is my Daddy," She hugged her catatonic father, "Do you know my invalid brother, Pierce?"

Pierce teased, "Does Simon know you're going out with 'him'?" Lazily pointing his good arm at Nick.

"We're not OUT we're IN, Pea-brain!" She quipped, giving Nick an open-mouthed wink then raised her voice, "Mummy, come and say hello to Nick."

Jasmine continued, "Nick's mum's gone away for Christmas so I invited him around." She withdrew her left leg backwards onto the sofa and reclined to sit cross legged, tugging Nick's hand to join her.

"Merry Christmas Mr Banks; Pierce. I hope you don't mind my intrusion," Nick said politely and before taking his seat freed his hand to reach into the sack. "I've brought gifts; they're not wrapped. I didn't want to bring waste paper."

Without looking away from the television Jasmine's father 'shushed' angrily, waving an instruction to shut up and sit down.

From a crouched position, Nick leaned forward passing the bottle into Mr Bank's periphery, "It's a decent single malt."

Jasmine's father's concentration broke to cautiously accept the gift. He looked Nick in the eye for the first time, "Sit down and get warm lad, but don't talk while I'm watching telly. Give him a paper hat, Jasmine. Then he'll look as daft as us." He eagerly shouted, "CAROL! BRING ME A GLASS, LOVE."

Jasmine reached over the end of the sofa to retrieve her own Peter-Pan style paper-hat. This stretch revealed the tanned skin of her toned lower back midriff. Unable to look away Nick could feel himself getting aroused as he admired her athletic peach-like backside. At that 'bum-ogling moment', Jasmine's mother appeared from the kitchen wearing bubbly marigolds to present her husband with a damp tumbler.

"This glass is WARM! Why is it, everything I want COLD is WARM and everything I want WARM is COLD?!"

"Oh, give over, you grumpy old goat! I'm packing. It's a wonder I've managed to get through Christmas with no fridge. If you want ice, you can go out there and get some yourself!" Mrs Banks pointed to the rear yard and gave Nick a friendly smile saying, "Hello Dear, Merry Christmas."

"This is Nick," Jasmine said proudly placing the 'forever young' elf hat on Nick's head and adjusted it, leaning back with an admiring glance.

"Merry Christmas Mrs Banks, these chocolates are for you," Nick whispered, keeping his voice down and unable to get up because of his excitement.

Jasmine's mum returned to the kitchen and Nick reclined continuing quietly, "Pierce, I thought you might like this silk scarf as a sling. A bit more stylish than that hospital gauze dressing."

He reduced his voice even further so only Jasmine could hear as he clasped her hands, "And for you, a token of my love."

He reached into the sack and pulled out the 'N' monogrammed hankies, twisting the corner of one he gently kissed it and presented it to Jasmine, "Throughout time lovers have secretly communicated with white handkerchiefs. We have one each, a matching pair and this knot means I will never forget you."

Jasmine said, "Then I will do likewise so I will never forget you." She tied a knot and pulled it tight, kissed the handkerchief and squeezed it into Nick's palm.

"We must keep them forever," she vowed.

Nick was horrified as Jasmine rose to kneel and piped up dramatically waving her arms thespian-like for all to hear, "LEAVE US ALONE for our HANKY-PANKY, and SHUT the door BEHIND YOU!"

Thankfully, her embarrassingly dramatic projection had gone on deaf ears as her father 'shushed' angrily again. She grinned to Nick, "Didn't you do Shakespeare in O' Level English Lit? That was 'Othello'!"

"We read 'Adrian Mole'!"

She smirked holding the hankie from its middle and brushing it down through her thumb and forefinger, to hold it tall and thin. Another meaning.

Jasmine then hugged Nick and mouthed silently, "Thank you, I love it. You're so sweet and thoughtful. The whiskey was a great idea as well." She did an impression of her father being drunk and falling asleep, then led a constricting embrace guiding Nick's right hand between her crossed legs as she pushed her left hand between his thighs. For the next half hour, they sat in silence, all eyes on the telly, hidden hands caressing unknown territory.

When the adverts came on, Jasmine's father broke from his trance to top his glass then turned to Nick and said bluntly, "Are you the friend whose dad died?"

"Yes Sir." He'd never called anyone's parent 'Sir' before.

Mr Banks enquired, "How did he die?"

"DADDY!" Jasmine protested.

Her father added with a cautious sip, "If you don't mind me asking."

Nick deliberated then said solemnly, "He had a motorbike accident, skidded on black ice and… His heart stopped." He'd explained his father's twenty-year death sentence truthfully in a way that didn't require interrogation. Holding back tears he offered Jasmine a forced smile.

"I'm sorry to hear that, Son," Mr Banks said then pointed at Pierce barking, "You see! You're lucky to get away with a broken arm. Bloody death traps!"

Jasmine leaned on Nick saying, "Hold still, I want to Christen my hankie with your tears. There we go." She dabbed his eyes.

Nick's own family never watched soaps, Coronation Street was new to him but as the end titles came on and the brass band began its melancholic tune Nick was reminded of band practice playing euphonium, Heff on sax, Salty clarinet and Lanks piano: His true family. A snore indicated Jasmine's father was asleep. A signal for Jasmine to lean over and kiss Nick; pushing herself onto him, he cautiously reciprocated, terrified they'd get caught. Pierce was holding his scarf from neck to knee to mask vision of the sofa lovers. "You've made my Christmas," Jasmine whispered dreamily.

Reclined comfortably on the sofa with Jasmine on top of him, Nick gushed, "This has been the BEST Christmas of my ENTIRE life."

They spend the whole of the next 'sunshine bringing' programme kissing and cuddling in silence under the nose of the snoring guard. Jasmine whispered into Nick's ear, "It sounds crazy but I can't wait to be alone with you for our last night together on New Year's Eve."

Lost in Jasmine's amorous dilated pupils, Nick stroked her hair with his right hand, her chest pressed on his, hearts beating together as she slowly and deliberately ran the tip of her index finger up and down the palm of his hand with a cheeky wink.

Chapter Twenty-Six
The Time of Nick

The next few days were spent covertly party-prepping; tidying, vacuuming and polishing inside, window cleaning, snow-clearing and turtle-waxing outside. Cars were switched so the rusty old Beetle was hidden in the garage and the shiny new Porsche exhibited in the front bay. The house was spick and span on the afternoon of New Year's Eve, Nick insisted Mrs Burns go, waving her off with a 'Happy Hogmanay' and a twenty pound tip he said was from his mother: Undoubtedly a guilt-tip. Mrs Burns must have been sanctimoniously praising angelic young master Nick, as she passed an uncouth, cigar-toting Goliath reprobate, pushing a barrel of beer, deep fat fryer and gallon-bottle of cooking oil, in a wheelbarrow.

Nick turned the hi-fi on, closed curtains and hid photo-cubes and framed pictures of his younger self. He distributed crisp bowls, nut trays, Scampi Fries, plenty of disposable-ashtrays and rare beer-mats on loan from Heff. Upstairs he blu-tacked marker-penned 'No Entry' signs on his and his mum's bedroom doors but left the guest room and former au-pair's bedroom cum office with French-letters brazenly en vue.

Behind-the-scenes preparation had taken days. For what would be the sitting room's focal-point inspired by DeVille's, Nick had borrowed Lanks' VCR to tape-to-tape hired videos, pirating a super-cool four-hour sound and vision music-video compilation.

The music room was easy, his ninety minute 'Smegma-Mix' on auto-reverse all night, dimly-lit lights and a scattering of party balloons camouflaging an inflated condom. Lanks could play 'Auld Lang Syne' on the piano at midnight.

For the kitchen, he'd bought the colonel's secret herbs/spices, flour and powdered egg/milk as well as fifty pieces of chicken, currently brine-marinating in the deep veggie-salad section of the fridge. He'd also bought a packet of brownie mix for Heff's space cakes, to be offered to a select few.

Nick set up the morning room 'booze buffet'. Guests were sure to bring their own but to be on the safe side of the ominous, soon to arrive fifty pints of 'gut-rot', Nick contributed a case of Scandia Green, Coke, lemonade, red & white Thunderbird plus four bottles of sparkling Asti Spumante for midnight toasting. He made space for the keg and beside it placed disposable paper serviettes and sleeves of forty plastic cups.

His bedroom had undergone a complete revamp, maturing from nursery to boudoir. 'Metamorphosis' remained, but he'd removed childish posters and boxed toys. A shameless narcissistic full length mirror took up half a wall and a new arty poster from Athena: 'Neptune's Horses' by Walter Crane, both curiously captivating illusions. He'd bought an atmospheric larva-lamp and appropriately scented 'Midnight Jasmine' joss-sticks from Affleck's Palace. Action Man was replaced by a wooden artist's-muse poseable figure and he'd bought an American-import baseball bat-and-glove to display on his shelf, subtly hinting knowledge of first to fourth base, the mythical home run. 'Mr Big's cellophane-wrapped contraband ''Enry' was secretly hidden under the ball in the leather glove out of sight until Heff was ready to get baked.

He'd also recorded some of his mum's slushy cassettes making a slow mix-tape just for Jasmine, ready and waiting in his bedside cassette player. Since Nick's bedroom didn't have a lock, he'd installed a heavy-duty slide bolt so his room could now be secured from inside to ensure uninterrupted intimacy. The new dark and sultry art student's room looked, smelt and sounded perfect and more importantly, was completely private.

His mother's bedroom was out of bounds so Nick locked the door and kept hold of the key, happy in the thought there'd be one less room to tidy tomorrow! With yet more forward planning, he'd hired a professional carpet cleaner, hidden at the back of the cloakroom. He knew guests couldn't help walking slush in. It would be a nice surprise for his mum to see the house looking and smelling so clean and fresh upon her return.

With minutes to spare, he showered, hair-styled and mirror-dressed. This time he complimented his suit with an informal white V-neck t-shirt, jacket sleeves coolly rolled up to the elbows. He tried a white Duran Duran headband but discarded it, deciding he looked too much like the walking wounded.

He estimated: Along with The Bang Gang, The Fluff Boys' Duranie-entourage and Jasmine's friends, twenty-five to thirty guests. Quite a VIP shindig.

* * *

Two hours before the party was scheduled to start, The Bang Gang burst through the front door, darting to explore ready-and-waiting rooms, kicking balloons, cranking up music and helping themselves to snacks as Heff carted his barrow triumphantly across the hall; slush trail predictively in tow. His face was no longer crimson, the acid bath had erased any trace of acne and he'd improved other aspects of his appearance: A roguish hairstyle, a real professional cut with spiky-tipped flat-top, daringly highlighted blonde and he was wearing a brown leather biker jacket. For once, he actually looked pretty cool.

Sensing Nick's approval, Heff held out his arms declaring, "If you can't beat 'em, join 'em!"

Lanks had also had a trendy haircut, similar to Nick's and was wearing a Burton's 'office-boy' black suit and silver tie but Salty and Eggy still appeared unstylish schoolboys.

As Heff heaved Salty's home-brew keg onto the morning-room table he shouted, "Tell me again... Jizzum ran the tip of her middle finger UP AND DOWN the palm of your hand?!"

"Shhh! I told you that in confidence," Nick hissed, crouching to inspect the edge of the table with a tea-towel wipe then lowered himself to position the sink-bowl, looking up to assess spout-drip accuracy.

"A sure sign she wants to DO IT with you tonight, Big-boy! You and Jizzum are getting FROTHY, Man!" Heff released the tap, blasting Nick's face.

As Nick dried his blushes, Heff navigated his wheelbarrow into the kitchen to fill the fryer with viscous glugs. Lanks had discovered the piano and was expertly rag-time tinkling 'Blue Monday'.

"The secret formula is MINE!" Heff yelled, wrapping his arms around the Shwartz herb bottles like a wizened alchemist discovering the elixir of life. Keen to get started he hung his cool new biker jacket on the back door exposing his gaudy Rat-Meat shirt then hid his stylish haircut under the souvenir paper sailor's cap. Preparing for business he grabbed a pair of chrome pincers, thrust the serving hatch doors open surveying his pitch and poked his head through shouting, "FRYING TONIGHT!"

Half way between realms like a magician's assistant Heff admired the unoccupied dining room's tall Christmas tree with a nod, inhaling the sweet pine-fresh scent and castanet-clicking his tongs, cheerfully sang to the tune of 'O Christmas Tree', "Oh KFC, Oh KFC, how lovely is thy new branch!"

He proudly set up a Rat-Meat counter in the hatch: polystyrene trays filled with dozens of illicitly-acquired logo-branded lemony finger-wipes, salt packets and serviettes. Heff's very own Kentucky shrine bargain bucket would be christened, nay sacrificed, with a baptism of chip fat. Rubbing floury hands together, he dived in to messily prep the dry mix in a cloud of dust, pouring everything into one huge bowl, proudly assuming role of chief chicken dipper.

Nick was relieved to see the drinks-table looking healthier. Accompanying the barrel was now another three dozen cans of Scandia.

He gathered everyone together in the morning room for a pre-party toast, filling cups with Salty's gut-rot. "To The Bang Gang. Brothers, we're finally in with the in-crowd! Do you know the rules of the game?" They all force-chugged the warm effervescent, thick treacly home-made grog down in one and on cue with perfect gut-timing, Eggy flatulated a loud squelchy fart.

"That went straight through me, I think I've followed through!" He yelped and charged upstairs. The doorbell rang.

"I'll get it," Salty belched clearing the yeasty Marmite taste with a palette-cleansing mouthwash of fresh Smeg as he went to the front door. A second later, he darted back through the morning room, crashing the can on the table and shot to the back door white as a sheet crying, "Five 'O'… It's the dibble… The fucking pigs… A police raid! And you've got drugs. LEG IT!"

He swung the back door wide and disappeared into the garden. Heff and Lanks looked at one another for a second, considering drug possession far more serious than underage drinking and did likewise, scrambling outside to hide.

Nick hesitantly walked to the open front door, aware his music was playing loudly. The closed porch door windows had steamed up but there was clearly a policeman outside with white Rover behind on the road. Nick opened the porch door.

"Good evening," The silhouetted constable said.

Nick flicked the external light on and instantly recognised Cheshire constabulary's senior officer PC Murray, formerly the bearer of bad news.

"Hello again, how can I help you?"

Descending the stairs Eggy stopped and popped his head sideways through the top of the door-frame giving a friendly franglais welcome, "'Ello, oo iz it?" Then gurned feebly, "Je suis commando."

Realising it was the boys in blue, Eggy whispered, "Oh sheet." Slowly withdrew and ambled to the morning room then dashed a retreat crying, "Mon dieu le gendarme! Jambes rapides! Je vien!"

"Is your mother in?"

"She's, popped out. Can I help?"

"Shame. Well, it's actually you I wanted to see Nick. I'm returning this. I know how much it meant to you." Nick was handed a brown envelope he upturned, slipping his father's watch into the palm of his hand.

"There's no present like the time," the officer said proudly.

"Thank you!" Nick gasped.

"Sign here please and my card, be sure to pass it to your mother with my best wishes. I'll pop around another time to check on you both and hopefully have another cup of your mother's delicious coffee. Happy New Year, Son."

Nick noted no wedding ring as his shoulder was patted.

"Yes, Happy New Year, Dad," Nick said, closing the door to admire his new heirloom.

* 7.31 pm *

He walked through the empty morning room and outside, posting the envelope and card into the tall black-lined wire-mesh bin, careful not to slide its top-hat snow-cap off then followed a frantically ploughed snow trail out to the rear garden, across the lawn to the shed.

He popped his head in. "Hey twerps, the first place drug squad look for POT is the POTting shed! Come on we've got to be at The B for eight. You can have a few more and still drive, can't you, Lanks?"

Lanks said, "Yeah, but how did you shake off the fuzz?"

"I told the tit-head, I know my rights, come back when you've got a search warrant." Nick then coughed the loudest 'ODGEAMOWEY!'

As they left the house, a youngster carrying four-pack of Special Brew was loitering at the end of the drive. Nick laughed. "Where do you think you're going?"

The small boy said eagerly, "To the party! It is here, isn't it?"

"Where's your invitation?"

"My sister said I didn't need one, that's why I thought I'd get here early."

"Ha, listen to him, cheeky sprog! It doesn't start until nine. Come back then and I'll think about letting you in, if you've still got all four of those. They're dangerous, you know."

"The man at The Dairy said they're the strongest! You can have them all if I get in."

Nick laughed. "Suit yourself but don't freeze. Nothing over five percent for you in future, okay?"

As the five squeezed into Lanks' Beetle, Nick said cheerily, "Probably one of the Durannie's brothers. Respect for having the balls to gate-crash."

From the car park entrance Steve Benson heartily welcomed all five as the endless crush parted to guide Nick into the wild melee of the VIP area. Cool smartly dressed boys reached out to pat him and shake hands and pretty girls gave bosom-pressing hugs and two cheek kisses as streamers and party-poppers were thrown over him. Finally centre of attention, local hero Nick was greeted like a celebrity, mobbed by adoring fans. Geoff appeared handing Nick a Blue Russian and guided him through the parting crowd to a rapturous Fluff-Boy greeting worthy of a reunion. Pip, Todger, Grace and Jane joined them as the beautiful Durannies squeezed forward for invitation-qualifying introductions.

Simon hailed, "Tonight is your night, Nick. Enjoy. But first there are some people I'd like you to meet."

Simon escorted him towards the Club Bar, stopping to introduce so many movers and shakers Nick gave up trying to remember names. They approached a group of beautiful, tall model-like girls Simon cheek-kissed. "This is Liv; she throws the best pool parties in Hale. This is tonight's host, Nick. He's studying to be a commercial artist. Olivia's dad runs one of the country's biggest advertising agencies."

At that moment, Nick spotted Heff's blonde highlighted spikes and brown leather jacket over the crowd, chatting to Pierce, Jasmine's slinged-arm brother and Aelsa.

"Would you please excuse me?" Nick said quickly and pushed between Simon and Olivia. He didn't mean to be rude but finding Jasmine meant everything tonight, talking to strangers just wasted time. As secret lovers, they had until midnight then they'd part forever. Every second counted.

Nick was overjoyed when he found Jasmine at the bar and threw his arms around her savouring the heart-pressing embrace.

"Happy New Year," he beamed, eventually pulling back from the hug to gaze into Jasmine's eyes.

She put her finger on Nick's lips. "Shh, save that until we're alone at midnight." Then with a wide smile, pulled Nick into herself lip-locking and pressing together, hidden from view in the shadow of Lanks' tall bar-propping screen.

Lanks helpfully craned Jasmine's drinks from the bar to Pierce and Aelsa then looked down at the lovers. "Unfortunately for you, princess, this Hopper is still a frog." Placing his empty pint on the drip tray, he added, "Come on. Time to go."

Jasmine put her hand on Nick's heart and said, "I'll see you there." With a demure glow, she added, "I can't wait for my private viewing. Shall we say ten o'clock? I need to say some goodbyes. These are for you." She handed him a carrier bag, four cans of Long Life beer, pecked his lips and skipped off.

His mind was racing as he led the in-crowd out to cars. He now estimated nearer fifty to sixty guests. Six rooms downstairs, ten people per room wasn't too bad, but double the number he'd anticipated. Heff would have to ration Rat-Meat. Anyway, forget catering conjecture and paltry poultry, Nick had no appetite; for food anyway. There was only one thing on his mind. His heart was pounding and his cheeks glowed as he contemplated Jasmine's words, 'private viewing'. This together with Christmas Day's blatant palm finger-rub clearly meant one thing: imminent intercourse. In an hour he would put to bed the wet-dream obsession, the adolescent preoccupation he'd vigorously tossed over his mind since puberty: Consummately loving the girl of his dreams. Maturing from virgin to virgout. Playing the metaphorical baseball game: Batter up… Third base… Home run! Finger lickin' good.

Chapter Twenty-Seven
The Art of Parties

Driving down Joule Road, Nick turned to view the bumper to bumper motorcade procession, remembering his dad's funeral cortege but this time surrounded by his brothers. Lanks terminated Loggins as he saw a dark mass in the road ahead and slowly whispered, "Holy trousers."

The car fell silent as they entered the horde, passing clusters of carrier-bag toting party-pilgrims, all heading in one direction. An ominous chant could now be heard, "PARTY! PARTY! PARTY!"

Into the maelstrom disturbance outside Nick's house, a beam of torch-light flickered onwards but Lanks banked the kerb forcing cross pedestrians. A thick dark swarm of over a hundred birds and bees had crowded the drive, spilling onto the pavement, blocking the road.

Worryingly, a Trafford Council police car was already on the scene and two policemen were torch-directing traffic around the crowd.

"Looks like they got that search warrant," Salty announced mordantly.

As Nick pushed his way through the mob to the front door, he was confronted. "Is this your house?"

"Yes, officer. Is there a problem?"

The policeman replied, "Being drunk and disorderly is a disturbance of the peace and blocking roads is a traffic violation. This gathering commits numerous serious public order offences. We have the authority to disperse this crowd, many of whom appear to be underage drinking. How old are you?"

Booming out from the warm and friendly side of the door, Frankie Goes to Hollywood's crescendo bellowed layer upon layer.

"Sorry officer, sorry guests. Late for my own eighteenth, mwhodge! WELCOME… To the PLEASUREDOME!" He held the door wide with a cocky smile as the floodgates opened and dozen upon dozen of brightly dressed Little B evacuees streamed into the warm open house.

When the crowd had dissipated and the road was relatively clear, the policeman said, "That could possibly be the stupidest thing you've ever done."

Nick replied, "I don't know, I've done some pretty stupid things."

"I'm watching you. We'll be back in force later and if we don't like what we see, arrests will be made."

* 9.17 pm *

The house was packed with revellers. The Little B had moved in. All under control, if a little overcrowded. Due to the increased number of guests, possibly now two hundred, Nick designated The Bang Gang supervision zones: Heff kitchen/morning room, Eggy sitting/dining room, Lanks music room and Salty hall/front door. Doorman Salty was instructed to not let anyone else in unless they were on the original VIP list. Nick decided to do a final recce, then disappear upstairs for the final two hours.

All of a sudden, he sensed something wrong. A second later, the fire-alarm sounded. As he shot through the hall, the shrill high-pitched signal stopped but the noxious stench intensified as he weaved through the crowded morning room into the kitchen. He was instantly engulfed in a thick black cloud. Gagging for air he fumbled through the dank greasy haze and threw the rear door open swinging it back and forth to waft cool fresh air in and stale smoke out. As the fumes disbursed, the mess was revealed. The overheated fryer had clearly erupted through its filter, units and walls were splattered with flour bombs and the worktop, cookery books and linoleum floor were coated in a disgusting layer of oily flour paste. The alarm had been knocked off the wall; spewing out wiry inners, circuit boards and tombstone battery.

"Jesus, Heff, the whole house stinks of congealed fat." Nick went to the far end of the kitchen and opened windows, flicking the extraction fan on full. "Are you trying to choke us?"

"Choke the chicken. Like it," Heff laughed, sucking on a chicken leg.

"I'm not kidding, it reeks and LOOK AT THE STATE!"

"What's up? Calm down, there's nothing wrong. This is a working kitchen not a salad buffet. At my house if the fire-alarm goes off it means tea's ready."

"It's going to take ages to clear this rancid smell, the walls are thick with grease. The house needs fumigating and my mum's back tomorrow. She's a vegetarian and will go off her fucking tits."

Heff took the bargain bucket from the serving hatch and offered it to Nick saying in a southern drawl, "It may be rancid but it sure tastes good!" Then added, "Have some before it's all gone. It really is just like The Colonel's Rat-Meat."

Nick sighed, "No thanks. I've no appetite."

"Well, that's the last of the chicken." Heff placed the bucket in the serving hatch and slapped his hands together in a puff of dust.

"Thank God," Nick tutted opening the fridge door to gloomily survey his mother's healthy salad draw which was now contaminated with a disgusting fowl raw-stock of pink salmonella-juice brine. With a defeated sigh he grabbed a bottle of lemonade and closed the fridge, "I'm a bit nervous to be honest."

Heff continued chirpily, "I'm baking space cakes next so get the 'Enry. That'll calm your nerves. Anyway, fuck the Babylon. It's a private party. All they can do is ask you to turn the music down."

"It's not the police," Nick said unwrapping a stick of Doublemint. "I've got my final rendezvous with Jasmine soon." He reached to a cupboard for two glasses.

"Ah, it's time for THAT talk, is it? Okay, remember at school in 'Digging' we were taught about germination, big birds and little bees? Well, 'suck, squeeze, bang, blow.' No, that's the four-stroke engine in physics. Remember, remember; okay, here you go. When a grown up man and a grown up lady love each other very much, they have special cuddles. You know that dong between your legs. Well, that grows like Angry-Doctor David Banner's forearm and you thrust it…" Heff started gyrating his best 'Rocky Horror' pelvic thrust.

Nick looked at Heff scornfully, grinding the glasses together. "I know you mean well; you just have a funny way of showing it. But tonight would never have happened without you. Especially this." Nick pointed at the mess and continued with a smile, "So thank you, Lulab. Love U Like a Brother."

"Lulab: Now GET THE GANJA!"

"Do me a favour. If you see Jasmine, don't mention dope brownies and don't let her see or smell any ganja. I don't want to have to spend our last hours being counselled about drug addiction."

"Mum's the word," Heff tapped the side of his nose with a floury finger.

Considering how relaxed he'd become last time he'd taken drugs, Nick wondered whether his sex-drive would diminish eating an uncontrolled amount of the ominously drowsy substance named 'dope'. Tonight was too important so he decided to abstain but still get the marijuana for Heff. With friendly smiles he squeezed past Pierce and Aelsa in the morning room, his Jasmine-radar was now on full alert as he went into the hall and through Eggy's room. All the sofas were occupied with lap-sitting snogging couples, Tray was doing his breakdance parody and Daran's Durannies knew all the moves, dancing seductively to the X-rated 'Girls On Film' video. Fast-food diners including Eggy, Tom and Eric occupied the tree-end of the room but the acrid stench oozing from the kitchen was stifling. Nick pushed the grease bucket through and closed the hatch. The wilting forest-fresh magic tree was suffocating so he parted the curtains and opened the French-window patio-doors, welcoming a new gust of fresh air.

As he walked back into the hall, a line of girls was queuing against the wall from the bottom of the stairs into the music room and behind the door. He heard a tall blonde question what they were doing.

"We're queueing to GO with WILL!" A pretty brunette squealed, springing on her toes and with a shoulder tap it was her turn next. The blonde poked her head into the room to view what was on offer and accepting the eight-deep line, joined the back of the queue. Nick walked into the dimly-lit music room and sure enough, I Am Will was lying on the shag-pile 'Miss Willed' casting-couch bed, amorously French kissing and up-skirt fingering the next 'willing' contestant. Mute tongues speaking the universal language. 'Touched for the very first time', sang Madonna as trilby-wearing Lanks expertly tinkled the ivories boogie-woogie style, snowman-pipe gripped between his teeth. Another cool Wayfarer wearing Perspex-bangled musician dressed in black was seated on top of the piano jamming along on the antique mandolin. Pip and Todger were teaching dancers Heff's moves as Nick shimmied through to open upper windows. He was disturbed to see the dark crowd had reformed outside and drew the curtains on refreshing ventilation. Out of sight, out of mind.

In the hall, Nick thanked Salty and patted his shoulder, relieved to hear all invitees were accounted for then strode over step-seated guests and terraced can-shelves ascending to get Heff's drugs.

The landing was a bustling queue centred around the party's constantly flowing WC. Outside the au-pair's bedroom an acrobatic human totem-pole had formed, bodies stacked on top of one-another scaling the narrow door gap. Checking his mother's bedroom door secure and squeezing the key in his jacket pocket, Nick continued his patrol around the intriguing peep-show spies, cautiously easing the gap wider. He was gobsmacked to witness another pile-on; a writhing mass of limbs, breasts and bums flailing naked on the double bed in the dark. Judging by the bare limbs at either end, there were at least five entrants. A steamy sex orgy taking place at his party. How sordid and utterly brilliant! He could have made good money from 'Reader's Wives' if he'd had a camera, but undoubtedly the film-processing censors would never have allowed such debauchery to develop. He grinned and with a brisk knock pushed the door wide-open exposing the tumbling stack of Peeping Tom's to the embarrassingly exposed, light-adjusting dilated rompers. Nick bounded past the overflowing spare-bedroom which also sounded like a bed-squeaking free for all, clearly all bonkers; up the corridor to his room.

* 9.49 pm *

He turned the handle and pushed but it didn't budge. He tried again with a shoulder nudge but realised the door was bolted.

"Jasmine? Let me in, it's Nick," He whispered pressing his ear. He questioned louder, "JASMINE?" There was no sound and the exotic waft wasn't romantic joss-sticks, but repulsive black-market grade-A shi-iit!

With the realisation his plan was now seriously jeopardised, Nick became terrified then enraged, banging furiously, "WHO'S IN THERE? The sign says 'NO ENTRY' can't you read? This is MY ROOM, open up NOW or I'll break THE FUCKING DOOR DOWN!" The crowded corridor behind grew silent and curious heads poked from the spare room, anticipating the next move of the maddened huffing and puffing host.

Nick charged at the door with all his might barging like a battering ram, instantly winding himself. Forcing against the door, he held the handle down and pummelled, over and over until the weakened, splintering frame gave-way and burst with a loud wood-splitting crack. As the door swung open, the room appeared unoccupied apart from a pair of white knuckles suddenly vanishing from the bottom of the wide-open window. Someone had dropped to the patio. Nick ran over but was distracted as the duvet suddenly sat upright on his bed. There was a smouldering joint balancing on the bedside cabinet along with orange Rizla papers, a splayed tobacco-less cigarette skin and a white packet of imported Marlboro Lights.

"Sorry, Nick," the duvet-guarded girl said with an apologetic croak as she lowered the veil from under her eyes to reveal her face, then semi-naked boob-cradling bra. Apprehensively biting her lip was Grace.

Nick leaned out looking down but the unidentified culprit had just re-entered the house via the French windows. He threw the curtains together, furious with himself for breaking the lock and ruining any chance of privacy but equally mad with Grace and her leaping-lover for locking themselves in, to christen his bed before he'd had a chance and making his boudoir pong like a skunk's-lair. His amorous tryst had been well and truly sabotaged beyond repair!

"WHO WAS HE?" Nick snarled. It didn't even matter. The lock had been destroyed by his own fair hands.

"Why so tense? Have some of this, it's good shit." Grace toked on the joint and held it out, holding it in. Georgio Moroder's 'American Gigolo Love Theme: The Seduction' was playing on Nick's cassette player. He glared at Grace and went to his shelf to inspect the baseball glove which, clearly couldn't help drawing sport-fans' attention. Sure enough, the ganja had gone.

"Get up. Get dressed and get out. This is MY private room which is NO LONGER private, 'cos it's got NO FUCKING DOOR!"

Nick then remembered the key to his mum's secure bedroom. With a glimmer of hope the night may yet be saved. Still mad with Grace for nicking Heff's 'Enry he bellowed, "And you, stole MY DRUGS!"

This scandalous accusation was made for the entire corridor to hear as Nick tugged the duvet away to reveal, name and shame the thief.

A 'what the butler saw' crowd had gathered outside the door to witness the angry host, drug-addicted 'cheated boyfriend' rip the modesty off the blonde-beauty exposing her in all her glory: her athletically toned, sexy and bronzed body lying seductively on Nick's bed in nothing more than skimpy, scarlet bra and knickers. Nick gawped in disbelief, two in a room clearly caught red handed. Grace thigh-rotated downside-up to slink provocatively across the bed mischievously grinning, "Have you got those dirty, trampy fingerless gloves to hand?" Then more sultrily she rose on her knees, pressed herself against Nick and enticed, "Oh Nick, I thought you'd like me to come in your bedroom. I'll give you a blow-back. Marijuana makes me SO horny. Show me your chopper."

The warped door cracked shut.

"Who was that at the door?" Nick yelled. "Was it Jasmine, did you see?"

Sucking on the joint, Grace hopped out of bed, stepped into her dress in front of the mirror and slinked it up, slipping into shoes. She tutted sultrily, "I know when I'm not wanted. I thought it would be okay to help myself, it is a party after all. Colour me bad. Pip will give you some more."

* 10.00 pm *

Nick had meticulously planned this virgin-voyage: Destined lovers embarking on a 10 pm departure rite of passage, 'I-Spy' undressing onboard the private sleeper-carriage love train. A breath-taking, bone-rattling 'are we nearly there yet' journey, none-stop from adolescence to adulthood. But everything had gone tits-up and none of it was Nick's fault. Jasmine had discovered him taking drugs and having sloppy-seconds with a nympho! He yanked at the shattered door and darted down the corridor.

Desperately seeking Jasmine, he scanned the crowded spare bedroom and was shocked to see Olivia and John centre-stage publicly bed-springing. Olivia was wearing Nick's dad's Cebe leather-blinker, nose-shielding glacier sunglasses and they both wore white lip sunscreen whilst simulating energetic synchronised knee-bent, tucked-in downhill slalom ski moves bouncing on the bed fully clothed, repeating, "Whoosh, shush, jump!"

Nick ran to the landing where he met Jane ascending, she looked delighted. Breathless he begged, "Have you seen Jasmine? Did she just pass?"

Jane paused to consider her reply, "I'm not sure... I saw her saying goodbye with Simon."

"Was she leaving?"

"Maybe. It IS their last night together."

Jasmine had left, gone forever. Nick had been pipped at the post and defeated. Jilted Jasmine was undoubtedly being consoled by Nick's nemesis Simon. The better man had won. Nick felt dejected. This whole heart-breaking charade had been in vain and in the process his mum's house had been trashed. Realising he would never see Jasmine again, Nick leant on the bathroom door, hyperventilating. All of this for nothing. He looked around past Jane, to see if there was anyone who could possibly help him. He couldn't see anyone he knew.

To his left beyond the toilet queue, the spare room's sleazy open-door sex-show was now in full swing. Shameless performers were flagrantly getting off on the attention, some wearing nothing more than black stocking-disguises, robber-like pulled over-heads or erotically blind-folded over eyes masking identity. Equally perverted voyeurists passed a desk lamp in the dark highlighting body parts as uninhibited exhibitionists dominated one another. The spotlight occasionally caught embarrassed toilet-queue peeks, but when the burning bright white beam shone in Nick's eyes his stare was not that of a sex-spy but that of a terrified rabbit caught in headlights. Jane tugged at him to break the trance and save his retinas.

As if awoke by smelling salts, Nick was alerted to a disgusting aroma emanating from the other side of the bathroom door. Nauseated by the appalling stench, he covered his nose and entered warily. The sick and evil had clearly jumped queue to use this toilet-less room's plumbing for immediate emergency evacuations. The bathtub and tiled-wall were splattered with a pressurised pestilence of cloying disgorge, fetid diarrhoea and seriously-dehydrated tramp's-piss. Nick's mother's luxurious bubble-bath immersant, private-haven was now no more than a septic cesspool spawning mire of stagnant coagulated vomit, faeces and urine. Crushed beer cans and cups, shampoo bottles and soap bars, bobbing bereft in the repugnant languid gurgling swill, had fallen victim to the childish boy's fireman's-hose game. Expensive cotton towels were now excrement-encrusted bog-wipes clogging the swampy trough's plughole.

A smouldering cigarette abandoned on the edge of the bath had melted a long amber line into the white acrylic and unextinguished butt-ends burnt molten chicken-pox dots around the tub's edge. Heavily-soiled, abandoned 'gut-rot's revenge' skiddy-duds littered the gypsy's-kiss puddled floor and the shower cubicle had hosted a monumental pissing contest, reeking like a Glaswegian telephone box. Irn-Bru-like pee had been sprayed up the back of the makeshift-urinal pissoir, in a 'golden-shot' attempt to hit the 'up a bit, right a bit, fire' clean sponge target. As Nick queasily reached for the stained-glass window, he gagged and retched, looking down at a huge brown steaming turd curled into the sink.

Jane covered her nose and said, "Oh dear, but it's not as bad as it looks. I'll help you. I clean my grandad's house and he's incontinent. I use razor blades to scratch cigarette stains out. I'll scrub and bleach and have it good as new, if I can take a good long shower after everyone's gone? Is it okay if I stay the night, with you Nick?"

Nick ignored Jane's seemingly helpful advances and walked in a daze over the landing to stand by his mother's door and said distantly, "Who would do such a thing?"

Jane said, "Certainly not guests or anyone from The Little B. Have you not seen, downstairs has been overrun with gate-crashers! They piled-in causing trouble and wreaking havoc. Most of the nice people and our friends have left. Some idiot opened the patio doors for them. I think you should phone the police and get them to stop the party, it's out of control."

Nick leaned his head on the door, mentally drained and traumatised wishing it would all stop but then heard the scratching sound of a key exploring a lock. Then surprisingly, his mother's door inwardly gave-way.

A familiar face peered out through the gap. "Oops! Ah, Nick, I hold my hands up. Sorry." It was Simon, the libertine, caught in the act! He adjusted his tie and smirked awkwardly through the head-wide gap. Nick quickly barged the door and peered around to reveal, sitting demurely on his mother's bed, coyly adjusting her bra-strap under her party dress and reapplying her lipstick was not Jasmine, but one of Olivia's model friends from Hale.

Still holding the door, Nick gawped at Simon in disbelief for a second then looked sternly at Jane who looked just as surprised. With a huge sigh of relief but totally confused Nick reached into his jacket pocket and pulled out, plain as day, in the palm of his hand, his mother's room key.

Simon did likewise and held out a matching key, smiling apologetically.

"Sorry Nick, so many parties at these 1930s houses have perfectly good bedrooms that go unused just because they're locked. I don't steal anything, well, nothing you can touch! Skeleton keys never fail. Andrea and I just needed some privacy." Andrea blushed as she walked out to the landing and another lustful couple slipped into the vacant shag-pad.

Simon continued patting Nick's shoulder, "We're very similar you and I, Nick. We see opportunities and take them. If there's somewhere we want to be… We go! Regardless of invitation, permission or consequence. Laws can't stop us. It makes life fun. We're rule breakers. Gate-crashers. I can see us being very good friends and having some fantastic adventures. What do you say, even?" He presented his hand.

Overwhelmed with this unexpected turn of events, Nick squeezed and shook vigorously, gushing, "Yes we're even, THANK YOU. I'm delighted you're…" (not with Jasmine.) "With Andrea."

"For tonight anyway," Simon whispered in Nick's ear then roared with laughter. "This party is MENTAL Nick, BEST EVER!" He slapped Nick's back and coolly stretched his arm around Andrea guiding her to watch the juicy sex show. Jane had returned to the bathroom with sleeves up.

"It ain't over yet," Nick said morosely as he turned to face the stairs. He already had a fantastic adventure friend and didn't need another. Thankfully Simon was out of the picture, it was time to find Jasmine if she was still there. HAD she seen him with Grace? How hostile were the gate-crashers downstairs? Should he phone the police? Why did his hand smell of Scampi Fries?

He began the battlefield descent with courage and hope, strengthened in the knowledge Jasmine's heart would never be Simon's toy.

Chapter Twenty-Eight

Two Tribes

Haemorrhaging cans clattered cascading frothy dregs under-foot. The windows ill trash-mound was overflowing with empties, put-out fags and their combined slop-ash crud. The extinguished, beer doused, charred and smouldering remains of the honesty dried-flower display was now mockingly decorated with beer-cans 'budding' from black spindly brittle scorched branches.

Nick turned the final landing and ground to a halt. His legs buckled and he slumped down. For the third time his hall was over-crowded with tall dark strangers but this time he couldn't hide behind the banister or his mother. This house-full was no party, it was a nightmare.

The piano, now a tuneless cacophony of random plinking and dullard-glissando, accompanied Prince as he sang, 'When I woke up this mornin', could've sworn it was judgement day.' To Nick it was Armageddon!

An ugly crowd had hijacked the broken-hinged sitting-room. A rotation of pseudo-trapeze-artists were launching themselves from one sofa to grab the ornate crystal-glass chandelier then swing and bounce onto the other trampoline until its cushion-springs collapsed. One foolhardy swinger, clinging upside-down by knee-joints, yanked the fixture from the ceiling-joist bringing the heavy light-fitting crashing down upon himself in a shower of rubble, broken glass and teeth, casting half the room into darkness with victorious cheers. The long-since dead Christmas tree had toppled with drunken thugs trampling it flat as they glugged from Nick's mother's antique jugs as beer-toasting steins. Jigging around, they smashed the fragile pitchers together peevishly with every delicate glass-decoration targeted under heavy boot. The TV screen was a snowstorm of loud static-noise as the no-longer connected video player slipped out of the patio door under arm.

Passively surveying the gut-rot flooded morning room, Nick watched his mother's notes being defaced with vulgar messages and puerile knob tits graffiti as a whirling froth-spewing grenade whisked past his ear, exploding into the wall behind. He sat as beer dripped down his brow and his ashtray seat became damper.

* * *

"Chopper! Chopper! CHOPPER! Nick! Snap out of it... NICK, WAKE UP!"

Eggy appeared from outside, kneeling on a lower step anxiously staring into Nick's vacant, unresponsive eyes. He waved hands, clicked fingers then shook Nick's shoulders until he returned from mental shutdown; groggily whispering, "Was it all a bad dream?"

"Nope, it still is." Eggy brought Nick fully around with a slapped cheek. Nick registered the blow, "Ow, stop. Where's Heff?"

*11.00 pm *

"Fuck knows! It's kicking off out there. A gang are stoving Salty's head in for being Head Boy. They won't stop until YOU go out!"

In a high-pitch, Nick squealed, "ME?! Why ME? I was a Prefect and Cloakroom Monitor. Whoa. I'm not facing any trouble, I'm a lover not a fighter. I'm calling the police!" He started to stand.

Eggy snapped back, "Dur! Don't you think we would've done that? All your phones have been nicked!"

Nick slumped back terrified, "Shit. Has Heff left? No phones. What about Lanks' CB Radio, he could 'ten two-hundred' the 'smokies'."

"He's out there getting duffed-in as well. They're making an example of him because he's the tallest."

Nick surmised, "Neighbours won't call 999, they think I'm the ringleader, public enemy number one. What about the phone box at the park entrance?"

Eggy replied, "They've blocked the drive to stop anyone leaving."

In a cold sweat Nick asked, "How many of them are there?"

"About ten outside and ten inside. Skinheads! Don't even think about squaring up to them. They're psychotic mental bastards!" Eggy advised sincerely.

Nick shrieked back in horror, "Squaring up to them? Are you nuts? Do you even know me?"

Eggy said, "They want you."

Nick said with a nervous laugh, "Oh aye, so you came in to get me? That was well-snide!"

His mind was racing through every terrifying scenario as he jolted up, bolted upstairs barged to his bedroom to grab his baseball-bat then charged back down the corridor holding it over his head shouting, "Out of my FUCK-KING way!"

On the landing Simon blocked Nick. "STOP! What do you plan to do with that?"

"I'm going to break some fucking skulls, that's what I'm going to do," Nick panted dementedly.

Simon lowered the bat and asked sternly, "Are YOU ready to be beaten with that bat, Nick?"

Nick's rage passed and with a defeated sigh he countered in terror, "There's a mob of thugs outside beating up my friends. I have to try and stop them, even if it means sacrificing myself."

"Go out and fight honourably, with fists like a man. But if you take that bat outside and it's turned on you, you could be beaten to death. That scum out front will be charged with manslaughter, sent to Risley Remand Centre, crowned cock of Borstal and you're dead! Is today the day you die, Nick? Unarmed you may suffer cuts and bruises but live to tell the tale. He who uses a weapon in life will meet that weapon in death. Give me the bat."

Simon was suddenly like some kind of sensei, ancient sage. For a peacock, he seemed pretty savvy. But those espadrille ballet-shoes he was wearing couldn't kick through a cardboard box. He talked a good talk but it would be better if pretty-boy Simon kept out of the dirty work.

"If you know anyone hard, send them out to help," Nick passed the bat to Simon, then returned to the porch white as a sheet to face the music with Eggy at the eleventh hour.

* 11.08 pm *

Above the dark crowd, a short rat-haired scumbag clanked the roof of Nick's mum's car, brazenly using the hatchback as a platform to get to the windowsill and scurry into the house through the music room's upper window. Eggy whispered, "What a twat."

His under breath consternation was not delivered to provoke anyone but suddenly a scrawny thug lunged forwards, punching Eggy so hard in the face, he was instantly knocked unconscious and flipped heels-over-head, hitting the gritted ground with a crack; out cold, unable to cushion the impact.

Nick dropped to his knees and cradled Eggy's bleeding head in his arms. Horrified and with tears in his eyes he took his cherished handkerchief from his pocket and pressed the gauze onto the wound. The bully pushed the crowd back to isolate Nick on the outskirts of the hostile arena, returning to his car front post.

As Eggy slowly came around, he said, "I don't feel very well. I want to go home."

Nick assured. "Everything is going to be okay but you can't go yet."

Closing his eyes Eggy whispered, "I'm cold Nick."

Nick removed his jacket and lay it over Eggy. The blonde from the back of the queue bravely came forward to crouch with Nick, saying she was a nurse and rested Eggy's head on her thighs taking over pressing the blood-stained hankie.

Nick rose to his feet in his bloodied white t-shirt, trying not to shiver with cold or fear as he surveyed the terrifying assailants combat zone.

* 11.14 pm *

Two boneheads were pressing Salty into the Porsche driver's wing whilst Eggy's attacker now held Salty's hair and mercilessly bounced his bloodied, bruised head into the bonnet: Doosh, Doosh, Doosh! Unresisting, Salty was barely conscious. In 'no man's land' Geoff was struggling to tackle a skinny wrestler's armlock and Lanks had surrendered, leaning forward with an upright can behind himself, whilst a short skin held him in a head-lock parading him to the crowd giving occasional face punches. The drive exit was guarded by two trainee-bouncers and three cadets were standing at ease across the snow-lawn.

Nick spotted Tray and Tom and signalled them closer then took a brave step into the arena, "STOP!"

The eyebrow-less blood-splattered leader looked up, gave Salty one last press into the bonnet then swaggered menacingly house-side. Nick now recognised the head skin as school-dropout, Mental-Rentil.

"Cracked-Head boy and Humpty Dumpty," Rentil panted then held his bloodied hands high surveying Nick's house.

"So this is YOUR house? I like what we've done with it." He turned and laughed to his stooges. "Do you know what we like about you?" Turning away from Nick he walked clockwise around no man's land addressing hostages, "You've got money. We want to be your friends so you can share it with us. We like rich people. They've got stuff we want." He ended leaning on the Porsche driver's door and asked, "Is this daddy's car?"

"No. I don't have a dad."

"Oh, another little bastard!" Rentil laughed to his friends.

"No my father died; recently."

"Diddums. You look like you're managing without 'father'. Well, here's what we want you to do. Give me the keys to MUMMY'S car or… we start TAKING money, jewellery, designer coats and trainers. That's a nice watch, mummy's boy."

* 11.17 pm *

Rentil addressed the mass, "What would you prefer? Option one: We GO AWAY with this car, gone in sixty seconds. Or, option B: ALL OF YOU empty your pockets and purses and give us your valuables? Or option four: We do both! God help you if you've got nothing we want. Boys will get a Borstal-beasting and girls will have to show us their tits. Ugly ones can have the Borstal-beasting!" He cackled.

"So, which will it be?" He returned to Salty, grabbed him by the hair and pushed his bloodied nose into the red bonnet, sneering, "Brainy head-boy KNOWS the answer… GIVE ME THE KEYS."

Nick scanned the crowd. Unable to see Jasmine, he summoned the courage to shout, "Leave him alone. Three on one is unfair, you coward. Last time I saw you, you squealed 'fight your own battles' then ran away."

Enraged, Rentil stormed up to Nick and roared, "I'M NO COWARD! Oh, it's the Chicken Boy. Where's your big fat lard-arse boyfriend?"

"He'll be out in a minute to woop your scrawny arse," Nick lied.

Rentil turned to his cronies, "This cack-handed queer threw a piece of chicken at me then a tub of gravy but missed both times." They all laughed.

He snarled halitosis in Nick's face, "The only chicken around here is you." Then hawked up a greenie at his feet, skipping into boxing footwork. "Have you got nothing to throw at me this time? How about a punch? First throw is free, see if you can hit me from there. Or are you chicken, Chicken Boy?"

Tray and Tom had moved to Nick's side.

Within striking distance, the featherweight pugilist bobbed and weaved then pushed his face intimidatingly close provoking Nick with a noxious condensation gas cloud exhalation.

The battle-scarred runt looked even more psychotic and ghoulish up close: Bald bony skull, abandoned mossy graveyard teeth, ghostly red dark-ringed dead-eyes with blue Quink tattooed 'Borstal-dot' tear and spooky skeleton nostrils outlined black from an over-indulgence of marker-pen solvent-abuse.

Seemingly on a suicide mission, Nick goaded, "Jeez Rent-Boy, what've you been cleaning your teeth with, dog shit? Phew, that's foul, but I'll show you something really fowl?" Slapping Tom's back.

On cue, Tom the puking-prince hurled a stomach-full of regurgitated gut-rot poultry-porridge over the little dreck. Stunned and instantly dripping with steaming-spew Rentil stopped skipping to wipe his eyes and look down at his puke-splattered bomber jacket, drain-pipes and cherished cherry Docs.

Nick advised, "There's your free THROW." Then quickly right jabbed Rentil in the stomach winding him and forcing his head forward then completed 'the-old-one-two' with a cracking left knuckle punch to the side of Rentil's head, knocking him to the ground.

All hell broke loose as two tribes went to war. Tray stamped on Rentil using him as a gymnastic springboard to vault into the air at Salty's guards.

Fearing a dose of Doctor Martens prescribed brain-damage, Nick saw a gap in the brawl and fled across the drive towards the snow-covered hedge, choosing a large fuchsia-hiding white iced cap to dive head first into, disappearing through the middle of the delicate branches, spraying light powder dust into the air. He landed on the neighbour's clear white lawn with a forward roll then sprang to his feet, turning right to coax Rentil.

Rentil picked himself up and witnessing Nick's great escape also charged at the bounding shrubbery, diving head-first into the next untouched virgin-white peak; straight into Nick's trap. As a 'hedge-hopping' child, Nick had learnt which boundary plants were harmless and which were not. This innocent-looking soft white cushion of fluff hid the oldest, gnarliest, thickest rose tree in the garden. Twisted stems of razor-sharp, dagger-like thorns caught Rentil mid-flight in a painful barbed embrace. Impaled and unable to move he let out a blood-curdling scream.

With Rentil painfully entwined, Nick ran out of next door's drive directly over the road, now pursued by two more shaven heads, on the other side of neighbouring walls he turned right across white lawn, hopped over another hedge: Lawn, drive, fence, drive. But another boot-boy had predicted Nick's movement and cornered him on the final driveway. Knowing the other side of the next tall hedge was the park entrance and phone box goal, Nick blindly ran at the seven-foot-tall conifer bush, leapt into the air, curled into a ball and disappeared through the white wall.

On the park side, Nick's long-jump, leap of faith continued over knee-high snow-buried roses, skidding to the ground on the safe side of the low topiary-manicured border.

Nick scrambled to the telephone box and prised the heavy door open, safe inside. Three fearsome baldies closed in on his sanctuary as he cupped fingers around the door handle to secure. Spring-loaded in the occupants' favour the door was heavier to open out than pull closed and thankfully the outside handle was too small for more than four fingers at a time.

The three rabid skins bayed for blood as they hit, kicked and headbutted the thick glass windows, snarling and pushing each aside. Nick reached for the telephone with his spare hand, placed it on the telephone directory and dialled 'nine'. As it clicked around, he tried not to contact eye with the nose-pressed grunting savages. Another 'nine', click click click click… A Doc-Marten kicked through the side lower window with a smash. Then finally the third nine.

Nick was a sitting duck as bovver-boots de-glazed the lower window of the red frame white light. Choosing to focus beyond his imminent slaughter Nick looked to the heavens watching beautiful slow-motion clusters of soft white fluff gently settle on the starkly contrasting hard-hitting dark fluff-boy uprising. Simon had joined the allies, surprisingly taking on two at a time delivering karate chops, kung-fu cartwheel kicks and gravity defying martial art splits, swatting opponents like flies. Tray was also wading in strong, windmilling and cracking heads with his own. Nick regained his will to live.

"Emergency, which service do you require?"

"Police."

"Hold the line…"

"Police, what's the address of the emergency?"

"70 Joule Road, Sale. There's a riot! A gang of skinheads are attacking innocent people."

"Where are you?"

"In the public phone box at the entrance to Joule Park just over the road. Three attackers are trying to stop me. Hurry. I can't hold them back much longer. They're smashing their way in."

"What phone number are you calling from?"

"I don't know, I have to hold the door. The house is Brooklands double-one, double-four."

"Tell me exactly what happened."

"A party has been overrun by a gang of about twenty skinhead gate-crashers. They're smashing the house up and looting. Outside they're fighting and robbing people. They want to steal a red Porsche."

"Help is on its way. Stay on the line. What's your name?"

A hand appeared through the lower broken glass frame trying to hold a lighter near Nick's arm to burn release. Nick kicked and stamped until the arm retreated.

"My name? David Sanders. I can't hold the door. Hurry." He put the phone down then swapped hands with weakening strength, rising up to press his foot on the frame.

With an exhausted grimace, Nick blurted at his attackers, "COLONEL Sanders to you. Odgeamowey!"

The cavalry was on its way, just in the nick of time. Nick could see the hostage protecting duo Simon and Tray, fighting the good fight, but Rentil had returned to the car and was prising the top of the driver's door, peeling it back like the lid of a can. Nick was horrified to watch the bovver-boy enter the car, yank the radio cassette from the dashboard and hold it triumphantly out of the bent out window. Not enough for the psychopath, he then released the handbrake to roll the steering-locked Porsche into the gate.

From both directions, whirring sirens and flashing lights skidded to halt askew road-blocking escape from the chaotic battlefield. The balmy-army retreated, scattering over the park gate, traceably disappearing into the moonlight, chant clapping, "You're going to get your fucking head kicked in," and to the same tune, "You're going home in a Saint John's ambulance". Puke-splattered, bruised and bloody, Rentil was last to flee, calmly swaggering towards Nick, alone together outside the phone kiosk. Nick didn't cower or retreat but braced himself without flinching as grinning Rentil delivered a painful, balance-restoring blackened eye-for-eye then leapt at the park gates, 'wired for sound'. A Black Maria then crashed through the gate releasing an aftershock back-up of truncheon wielding bobbies in hot pursuit 'that-a-way'.

* * *

Self-hugging goosebumps, Nick looked skywards into the never-ending ethereal descent and with a condensed sigh, closed his eyes as soothing heaven-sent cotton wool swabs gently melted into salt-water.

Sure to face lengthy interrogation, serious repercussions and possibly criminal charges, he couldn't hand himself over to the police tonight; time was too precious. He'd face his mother's wrath tomorrow like a man but now he had to deliver a heartbroken, tearful farewell to his lost love Jasmine: Lost indeed. For the first time since childhood Nick prayed... Prayed to find Jasmine.

Awakening his pitiful black-and-blue, red eyes he observed the chilling gravity of the vandalised and looted flashing crime scene's apocalyptical exodus.

Unrecognisable as narcissistic party host, with bedraggled hair and blood-stained ripped shirt, the shell-shocked fugitive launched himself into the strobe-lit aftermath: On-the-run he dashed head-down through walkie-talkie clicking riot squad, around the abandoned open-door panda blockade; onwards past steaming adrenaline-pumped ninja-scrum victors, motormouthed willing-witnesses and battle-scared underdogs. He met the mangled, prised car-door gate-crash scene and continued upstream into the pirated sunken-ship police-forced eviction.

* 11.39 pm *

Amazingly, Salty was not on a life-support system 'in a Saint John's ambulance', the scrappy old sea-dog was actually in the hall on the stairs being cleaned and bandaged by the man-hungry queue-front brunette. He looked like a tough new romantic with Duran headband and Adam Ant plaster over his nose. Overcome with lip-twitching emotion Nick threw his arms around Salty in relief.

Salty said, "That's quite a shiner you've got there, Brother. I'm glad you got stuck in and didn't just leg it. There's a message I should've given you earlier but got 'distracted', sorry," He then whispered into Nick's ear, "Sneak out and GO TO HEFF'S."

Nick snarled, "Have you got brain damage? I thought you were dead. We needed Heff here, the splitter!"

With a swollen smile, Salty said, "I've had worse, 'tis but a flesh wound. Anyway Heff didn't know dole-scum were going to gate-crash after he'd gone. He'll be gutted when he finds out, he loves a good scrap and protecting you has always been his priority. He loves you but obviously wanted you to take Jizzum back to his house."

* 11.41 pm *

Nick replied sadly, "It's too late. She stormed off ages ago after she discovered me two-timing with a drug addicted nymphomaniac. I need to find her and say sorry and goodbye, but don't know where her aunt lives."

Salty advised, "Try the phone book."

Nick replied, "She's staying with her mum's sister. I don't know her surname."

Salty then patted Nick, "Oh well, go out there and find her in the evacuating crowd. Sorry about your house mate, but what a party!"

A helmeted policeman in black waterproof cape waded in and approached Nick's black back, rudely plucking the 'description-fitter' from lip-locking blonde-saviour to shine a powerful torch in Eggy's eyes, "Nick Hopper?"

Wearing the smart Matinique jacket, Eggy mutely pointed in the wrong direction to the dark sitting room where the flashlight spotted Lanks being comforted by a tall twiggy girl. Salty's brunette introduced her two friends. "We're nurses from Princess Christian College," she added. "We were told it was an all-nighter. We've missed our curfew so we're locked out of our dorm until morning. Please don't chuck us out, we've nowhere to go. Could we stay the night? We'll tidy up, monitor concussion and treat your brothers."

Nick whispered into Salty's ear, "Treat you, you jammy bastard. You can have my room."

239

Salty smiled, "We'll batten down the hatches all hands on deck and get this place shipshape and Bristol fashion from stem to stern before morning, just as planned. Up sticks and find your love shipmate."

* 11.44 pm *

As the host-seeking inspector beamed out of the silent music room, Nick slipped in. Dismayed to see the tape-deck open, his cherished Smegma-Mix had been half-inched and the only remaining LPs were a trash-mound of his dad's unwanted classical records trampled into the floor, doused in beer and ash. Crushed cans, popped condoms and an upturned empty bottle of Jack Daniels, pirouetted the record player.

Suddenly, a distant ringing came from above. His mum's bedroom.

Nick looked into the hall and said, "Eggy, I thought you said all the phones had been stolen?" Gobsmacked Eggy defended, "Yeah, DOWNSTAIRS. I didn't know you had a phone UPSTAIRS as well!" Salty ordered angrily, "Are you still here? Find Jasmine and go to Heff's now! I'll take the rap."

Nick prised his jacket from Eggy, handed Salty his keys then slipped out saying, "You're in charge Salty, Lulab!"

"Lulab, Chopper." Salty then raised his hand and called, "Over here, Officer. I'm the person you want to speak to," coughing a painful mwodge.

Chapter Twenty-Nine
Metamorphosis of Narcissus

An angry wind booed Nick's return. Facing the freezing blizzard, with upturned collar he clutched jacket lapels together hunching to evade sharp snow-blasting sleet and charged through the thick white veil past the police blockade. Sprinting up the road overtaking the banished mob of evacuees, Nick scoured for any friendly faces who may know Jasmine's whereabouts.

Overtaking clusters, he tirelessly repeated, "Have you seen Jasmine Banks?" Sadly, to no avail. One person carrying records under his arm recognised the host and barked, "I hope you're happy calling the cops, Party-pooper. You ruined my night, I'd just copped."

"I'm sorry, but at least you have a home to go to," was all Nick could remorsefully muster.

"I can't shag a girl at my parents', you selfish twat," was the indignant reply as Nick ran ahead, overtaking hecklers, far from the madding crowd.

* 11.52 pm *

At the end of the road, the crest-fallen peacock slid into the T-junction: No pedestrians, no cars; even the factory watchman's checkpoint was in darkness. Evidently at ten-to-midnight on New Year's Eve the entire nation was warm and safe indoors, gathered with loved ones celebrating Big Ben's imminent chimes.

As Nick clenched his lapels together preparing for another bout with arctic conditions, something poked his chest; inside his jacket pocket was Jasmine's lemonade straw! Surely a good omen. Clutching lipstick-kisses to heart, He dashed up the lifeless incline between God's acre, where all the lonely people belong. Over the bridge at the desolate crossroads he crossed fingers and stood under amber light, scouring the trackside pavement's distant mile, praying for movement on the final road of hope. But tragically he was out of luck and out of time: He'd been clutching at straws. This was no longer Jasmine's route home and never would be again. Jasmine had gone forever.

Devastated, sobbing and alone Nick abandoned hope turning to retrace his hollow, slush-quarried trail downhill as a furious, howling maelstrom whipped a torrential blizzard, relentlessly lashing its lonely, wretched victim with core-freezing hail. Wading past the foul stenching and dank crypt-kickers' convenience, weak and blue with not a soul around Nick faintly succumbed to cardiac fatigue as his legs buckled. Gripped by hypothermia, he collapsed to a kneeling crouch outside grave-digger's gates propping his head weakly on one knee to focus on a dark abyss seemingly opening the ground at his feet.

Life of late had been such a lonely struggle he just wanted to close his eyes and forget his troubles. No one would miss him at midnight. He'd rise after the saints rang their imminent toll but first he needed to rest, in peace: Unwittingly, surrendering to the grim icy cloak that had claimed his father.

* * *

In a transitional dreamscape, Nick found himself on an idyllic beach, lost in the shimmering ocean vista, contemplating ultramarine, cyan and turquoise; gouache colours he would palette-mix to paint the seascape. Powerful waves curled along the shoreline: A race of Neptune's vaulting horses boldly rising from the sea, peaking white manes streaming a blurred burst of speed through crest falling waves. As they crashed ashore, each new wash of effervescent foam explored further, whispering advance as it retreated to the next rhythmic cycle of aquatic-equine hurdlers: Waves goodbye. Behind him, the enclosed dusky horseshoe bay was deserted but for a group of revellers, dancing naked below an amber-hewed mountainous cliff-face. No shadows, in fact no sun; yet the scene was bright, warm and seemed safe. Wearing yellow swimming trunks, Nick was crouching ankle-deep in the wide moat of a beautifully sculpted sandcastle with Jasmine by his side.

She looked radiant, happy and tanned in red two-piece bikini with a daffodil tucked behind her ear. She smiled, pointing to Nick's reflection in the shallow water. Conscious of his lifeless appearance, he kept his face hidden and with head propped on knee, leaned over the heated sandy pool but could see nothing. Suddenly, the water turned dark and cold, then iced over and froze, trapping his foot. The ice reflected a menacing violet tempest overhead as the sky blew away in a rain of glass, tearing day into night. Reflected by his side in the mirror's fiery-red underworld was not Jasmine, but a blonde impostor and on terror-firma blood-soaked nudists kicked sand in Nick's face, trampling the sandcastle as they fled, clambering at the impassable rock-face.

A colossal sky-scraping version of Nick dressed as black as the night's sky, with shooting star flecks, loomed down from the heavens, eclipsing light, crouching over the snow-capped peaks, crashing his titanic leg through the ice-mountain as if it was snow, shattering the cliff and causing a deadly avalanche. Beneath the falling rock precipice was a chequered board with single player, a statuesque pedestal-standing mirror-image of Nick, admiring his naked self in a hand-mirror, blissfully unaware of his impending doom. Crystal-glass chandelier shards struck down, cracking the mirror-moat, tearing a gateway to Hades.

Out of the corner of Nick's eye, he could see Jasmine had turned her back on him, mirroring his crouched pose, shielded behind armour. He sorrowfully whispered, "I love you, goodbye." Sadly, too late, Jasmine had turned to stone. Alone in purgatory, petrified with jagged glass-like ice hacking the nape of his neck, Nick braced himself to hunch forward and looking down at the reflection, echoing his words 'I love you, goodbye' was the blood-dripping face of his father.

With a jolt and the blink of an eye, Nick was back in the land of the dead crouching in the snow and staring into a dark kerbside puddle; slush dripping from his face. Recognising himself, he welcomed his safe return with a grateful smile and mirrored self-hug: The abyss had stared back and shown him love.

Popularity wasn't friendship. Being popular hadn't made him 'respected' or even 'liked' and his pursuit of Jasmine had been in vain. The hedonistic ego-trip with the beautiful ones was over. An end to wanting to be seen and a start to wanting to see. With dishevelled armour he accepted he was an unloved, lonely boy. Dusting snow off himself and beginning afresh he rose tall vowing to live the most fulfilled, rewarding, positive and happy life possible: In the name of his father. Awakened, a shiver ran down his spine as he remembered he was welcome somewhere warm and safe, by someone who loved him; like a brother.

Hearing the angry mob nearing the end of Joule Road, he started to jog, run then sprint across their path. He passed The Vine whose 'drink and drive' road-fronting car park now showed-off an impressive legion of mirror-heavy polished chrome, scooters. The old man's pub had been given a new lease of life, resurrected by youthful suit and parka wearing mods. Nick slid to a halt noticing trouble ahead: Skins evading the long arm of the law were antagonising customers in the Rat-Meat. He gave them a wide birth, crossing the four quiet lanes to continue on the other side, facelessly observing the fracas through window reflections: Derek Smith's, Mrs McCarthy's and John's chippy.

Final Chapter

Illuminations

A crippling stitch stopped Nick in his tracks, moments from Heff's. Bent double and gasping icy air he brow-scanned resplendently-festive wreathed-door houses, each proudly exhibiting generations of loved ones through open curtains. Excited children nose-pressed windows as their father waved 'see you next year', stepping out coat-less into the snow, humorously wafting a fan of notes, juggling bread and coal, fire-breathing clouds of steam and self-hugging a teeth-chattering countdown. At the stroke of midnight, he'd ring the doorbell, welcomed home a hero, 'First Foot' of the year bearing good luck symbols: money, food and fuel to bring prosperity home. A tall, dark, handsome man's role, traditionally, Nick's dad.

Emerging from darkness, a pretty sorry first-footer carrying shrapnel-stitch and empty stomach limped the final stretch to Heff's glass-fronted home, bearing nothing but brotherly love. He cupped hands against the hall-window stretching a numb smile in anticipation of the warmest welcome.

All was still but for gliding marine-life exploring illuminated coral. Fusuma partitioning opened the dark hall into ambiently-lit lounge as Bang and Olufsen serenaded U2's melancholic 'The Unforgettable Fire'. Nick then noticed two glasses and Heff's saxophone beside a pile of clothes and more than two boots at the end of the wide leather corner-sofa. Widening his field of vision, he nosily window-dragged right to see Heff, dressed only in vest and boxers sprawled across the sofa clearly grafting. Nick stretched tall to identify the cigar between Heff's lips... A GIRL... In white jumpsuit with long blonde hair and visible panty-line... Heff was face-sucking Aelsa!

Nick was gobsmacked! What he saw made no sense. Yet somehow here was Heff, HEFF with this stunner. Perhaps she was a sax maniac and he'd wooed her with his 'Careless Whisper'. Nick then remembered Aelsa being the first to applaud Heff at the station, the same night on the bus home Heff had sat next to Aelsa and gallantly wiped her steamy window; secret seeds planted long ago. They'd been chatting earlier in the pub and at the party she'd positioned herself in Heff's view outside the kitchen. Surely Aelsa was way out of his league but Heff did have charisma and he'd scrubbed up tonight: Perhaps opposites attract. Like a jilted bosom-buddy Nick felt envious of Aelsa for luring his impressionable, drunk, fat and stupid best friend away but equally envious of confident stud-muffin Heff for pulling a cracker.

* 12.00am *

At the stroke of midnight, celebrations echoed across the land. Church bells rang, fireworks lit the sky and good-looking heroes were welcomed home. As loved one's hugged nationwide, this cold wretched and heartbroken outcast could not have felt more destitute. The losing third-wheel shrank out of sight, conceding defeat.

Plucking himself from the hall-window, Nick noticed at his feet on the warm side of the door, tail-wagging Winston looking up at him quizzically. Nick glumly fluttered a goodbye wave and turned to limp into the shadows. Freezing and exhausted with nowhere to go, his stomach churned. Remembering he'd not eaten all day, he pulled a handful of shrapnel from his pocket and slid coins across his palm counting eighty-six meagre pence. Not quite enough for two pieces, but one succulent morsel could be his. He'd request a rib and savour the delicious take-away inside by the counter, warm and safe for a moment, then face the inevitable confrontation; hostile skins seeking redemption: So be it. Perhaps he'd wake up in hospital with his mother by his side shedding genuine tears. Home again.

As Nick's shadow disappeared behind the neighbour's tall hedge, Winston whimpered then jumped to his feet with a whine.

Cuff-wiping snowflakes from coal-black eyes, Nick enviously watched 'Father Time's' family gather by the piano to sing 'Auld Lang Syne'. Turning right onto Barkers Lane, he clutched lapels as his walk became a run, sprinting to the finish-line to acquiesce the last supper, pleasure pain atonement of Colonel Sanders and Doctor Martens.

* * *

Alerted by the deranged barking of his rabid guard-dog, Heff leapt into unlaced boots and flung the front door open; emerging trouser-less, barely covering underwear in brown leather biker jacket as he belted up the cul-de-sac churning snow to follow the fresh trail with Winston unleashed, hot on Nick's heels.

As Winston ploughed ahead, Heff shouted, "Chopper, stop you fucking dildo!"

Heff reached Winston hugging Nick at the main road and panted exhaustedly, "Fuck me, what happened to you?! Even I know that's not how fluff-boys do their make-up!"

Nick's blackened eye looked up and snivelled, "You won fair and square, Heff. I owe you a fiver. I think I owe each of the Bang Gang a fiver as well."

Heff helped Nick up, "You owe me more than a fiver, you nutter. Come back to mine, you're going to catch pneumonia. My bollocks are shrivelling up like brass monkeys'!" He hula-hooped his bare-legged boxers then gave a shudder and Michael Jackson high-pitched, "Hee hee."

Nick turned to scan the Rat-Meat skinhead-territory over the road and bravely declared, "I'm not going to play gooseberry."

Heff gasped, "Gooseberry? Woah, did Salty not give you the message, the dozy twat?"

Nick then broke down in tears, "He told me to find Jasmine and take her to yours, but I couldn't, okay... I looked all over and I couldn't find her... I lost her, Heff."

Heff put his hand solemnly on Nick's shoulder, "How far did you get with the blonde, Joe DiMaggio?" With a grin and a wink, he performed a swinging baseball bat action, "Home run?"

"How do you know about that? No, nothing happened," Nick protested.

"Yeah, yeah, yeah, save it for the birds! I've read all about 'premature ejaculation' in the problem pages. It's nothing to be ashamed of, ODGE; but smoking OUR drugs after sex with that red-knickered spunk-bucket IS! That's why you owe me a fiver, isn't it?"

Nick was confused, "No we had a bet. Five-pound prize for first to pop their cherry. How did you...?"

"Ah, so you DIDN'T do it!" Heff looked delighted and rubbed his hands together. Nick could almost hear cogs churning as Heff continued to ramble incoherently, "I thought you were still at it, Studley! Good job I kept shtum...

You're not double-dipping, ha!" He chuckled to himself then turned to put his arm around Nick, guiding homewards, "Finally, you're learning to show emotion and express yourself, I think you might just be ready. I can't wait to show you WHO I GOT."

"Yeah, I know, I saw. Congratulations," Nick said glumly, "I'm not being funny, but how the fuck did YOU pull Aelsa?"

"Pull? Don't be sexy. I wooed her. I told her my mum's called Aelsa and that I could play 'Edelweiss' on the sax."

Nick retorted, "Your mum's called SANDRA!"

"Don't be mean," Heff sulked then turned up his jacket collars, strutting and singing Wham! proudly, "'I've got street-credibility…' Aelsa complimented my new jacket and haircut and said I looked like Simon Le Bon."

"Another one? As if! The world's gone mad!"

Heff stopped and turned to face Nick holding both his shoulders and said seriously, "You! Not someone trying to look like someone else… YOU could be with any girl you want; but sadly, you're touched."

Nick shook his head and scowled at Heff in disgust, "You know there's only one girl I've ever loved. But 'touched?' That's low Heff, even for you."

Heff retracted, "Touched in the head. I didn't mean PHYSICALLY touched. God no, I don't think your dad fiddled with your botty. But mentally, yes, you're nuttier than a fruit cake. One day the men in the white coats will come in the yellow-van with a man-sized butterfly-net to whisk you off to the funny-farm."

Nick's eyes rolled then after a moment's contemplation, he smiled. "Say it like it really is, why don't you? You're as mad as me but you've no excuse. You bought that jacket and had your hair cut to look like Duran Duran to join the Fluff-Boys, didn't you?"

Heff owned up, "I didn't want to join them, I just wanted to keep up with you. I admire you."

"Then you asked Aelsa if you looked like Simon-le-Bon didn't you? She didn't suggest it herself." They walked on in silence.

Looking at the ground, Nick said quietly, "Why do you always go on about loving me, Heff?"

Heff said distantly, "Because you're the loneliest, saddest, most fucked up person I've ever met but despite that you have the biggest heart and an infectious, relentless and fearless love for life and adventure. Someone needs to tell you, you are loved, every day." He then returned to his normal pitch scoffing defensively, "Just because I love you, doesn't make me gay, you jizzum-monkey."

"It does," Nick retorted.

Heff then pointed at Nick triumphantly. "See what I mean! Touched in the head, mad as a box of frogs. You've no understanding of love, you've never known it."

Nick returned seriously, "Oh, believe me Heff, I know love and it hurts. It has given me nothing but heartache."

At the end of the drive, they faced one another and Heff looked earnestly into Nick's eyes, "No matter what happens after tonight, you'll never be alone. I'll always be here for you."

Nick patted Heff's shoulder guiding him home, "Thanks. You're the only family I've got. I love you too and always will."

As they reached the door, Heff finally noticed, as well as black eye Nick was covered in cuts, had a bloodied shirt and torn clothing. He put his finger through a hole in Nick's blood-stained shirt and asked, "So was she a bit of a dominatrix, Miss-whiplash Barbie? Was she into that kinky M&S shit?"

Nick wearily replied, "No, it's a long story."

Standing on the doorstep, Heff reached over to pat Nick's hair into a schoolboy parting, "Well, you look like you've been dragged through a hedge backwards. Don't get me wrong I like a bit of bondage as much as the next man; handcuffs, whips and oranges, it's all good fun until someone gets hurt, 'Razzle' say you've got to agree on a safe word to stop."

Nick tutted and said wearily, "Odgeamowey."

* * *

In the warm hall, Heff whispered excitedly, "It's bedtime for Bonzo! You're in Katie's room, first right. It's got an en-suite to freshen up but remember it's not a race. I'll bring you some grub... And coffee."

"I don't drink coffee," Nick said, "Do you have any lemonade with no ice?"

Heff replied, "There's something sweet in the room but you need coffee to keep awake." Then explained, "Sugar for lost energy and you might have concussion so I don't want you falling asleep yet."

They parted at the bottom of the stairs with best-friend handshake: right palms locked flat together down once, pivoting thumbs to cupped arm-wrestler grip for another downward shake then with thumbs still interlinked they released palms, gently fluttering fingers upwards whilst tweeting whistles, flapping a two winged bird above their heads into the air with ethereal release.

* * *

As Heff headed to the kitchen, Nick ascended to Katie's room and pushed the door. Striped beams of golden street-lamp shadows parallel projected across the dark room silhouetting venetian blinds. Nick raised his hand in a light-shielding salute, sensing he wasn't alone. He wondered if he may have disturbed Aelsa but as he bowed a retreating apology the bedside-lamp flicked on and in-a-flash Nick's tired departure switched to euphoric arrival. Unheard prayers answered, impossible wishes granted and shattered dreams repaired... Heff had somehow reunited Nick with his lost love! Reclining seductively on a bed of cushions Jasmine wore the new red shirt the Kentucky had sent for Nick, but as a sexy nightie. It was barely buttoned teasing a glimpse of secret breast and thigh tan-lines.

Nick froze as Jasmine outplayed his doting child-like gaze of puppy-love with a sexy smoulder and sizzled sultrily, "It's finger lickin' good!"

Unable to contain her excitement, she burst with laughter and leapt off the bed in a flash. With shirt flapping like a cape, she launched at her beau, wrapping arms and legs around, passionately welcoming a wash of kisses. Nick cupped cold wet hands under Jasmine's warm bare bottom, thumbs embarrassingly supporting privates.

"Oh Nick, thank heavens." Jasmine's delight suddenly became concern, "What happened to your eye and your clothes are soaked? You're FREEZING!" She climbed down and ordered, "Take everything off and get into bed before you catch your death!"

Nick didn't need telling twice. With Jasmine in the en-suite he quickly stripped off and swung into bed cocooning himself in soft, luxuriously pre-heated, sweet-smelling girly comfort. Enveloped head to toe he shuddered contentedly basking in the warmth, giddily aroused contemplating inevitable pleasures to come. Jasmine returned carrying a folded fluffy white towel and asked anxiously, "Are you still cold?"

With duvet up to his chin, Nick shook his head; ballsing-up James Bond's survival rule number one.

Jasmine placed the towel and a flannel on the cabinet then sat beside him. She studied his wounds with nurse-like concern as she gently brushed hair from his brow, checking his temperature and sighed, "You poor little thing." She leant forward and kissed his forehead then stood up and turned the bedside light off.

The room was now once again in semi-darkness, shadowed by parallel lines of venetian shade as amber lamplight beamed in. The horizontal pattern cast a beguiling, half-hidden descending mask across the back of the red shirt as Jasmine walked across the room to open the wardrobe; then reached for her jacket. Horrified Nick quickly slid up and tearfully begged, "Don't go, please stay. I love you."

Jasmine was motionless, with her back to him. After a few seconds, she closed the wardrobe and returned with a cassette in her hand, taken from her jacket pocket. She leaned in close to Nick and through the shade of a letterbox-shadow said softly with a sweet smile, "I love you, too… And a promise is a promise." She leaned over and gently kissed his lips.

She then slid her tape into Katie's bedside ghetto blaster, pressed play and quickly assumed a position by the bed with her back to Nick, as if she was preparing to perform gymnastics. Over her shoulder she said, "I want to do this as a parting gift. I hope I get it right; don't laugh. Just lie back and let me entertain."

Nick's heart thumped as Sade's cool, sexy and sizzling 'The Sweetest Taboo' started to play. Stripe-shaded Jasmine moved slowly, seductively in time, teasing the shirt over a tanned shoulder like a burlesque dancer and slipped it alluringly down to reveal an angel's-wing shoulder blade, then another; flexing both together to raise her hidden breasts and tease a nipple glimpse as the red collar rippled down her toned back. Catching the shirt on her forearms she stopped at the small of her back to push her bottom out and wiggle her hips. She then slipped the shirt to wrists, lowering briefly to expose the crack of her bum unveiling a deliciously secret white tan-line.

Jasmine then turned her head to pout sultrily at Nick's reaction as she casually dropped the shirt to the floor, exposing herself for the first time completely naked, showing off her innocence, her white peach-like bottom and long brown athletic legs through camouflaged horizontal shadows. Uninhibited as if it was an act of performance art, she slowly and confidently turned to face Nick standing elegantly tall, posing like a centrefold to reveal perfect upstanding breasts swelling with pride as she observed the delight on Nick's face. Nick's first love truly was the most stunningly beautiful girl in the world. She whispered sweetly, "You've got the biggest heart. Sometimes I think you're just too good for me. Every day is Christmas and every night is New Year's Eve. Will you keep on loving me, will you keep on bringing out the best in me?"

She skipped a triumphant gymnastic salute bow and with a grin said, "Now, for MY prize." Then pulled the duvet back and jumped into bed pressing her naked body into Nick's as the next track on her slow mix-tape began to play the soft, sexy and steamy 'Illuminations' by Swansway.

"My, my Chopper... It IS true!" She cooed.

They entwined, tactilely exploring male and female differences for the very first time. Jasmine raised her leg sliding across Nick with an inner thigh straddle and sat upright taming his manhood into submission, pushing her magnificent breasts into his face as she leaned over to take the flannel from the bedside-cabinet then started to carefully tend to Nick's cuts and bruises with gentle dabs. She leaned in for a lip-peck and with wide eyed smile whispered, "Slow down, we've got all night."

Then she started to explain how she and Aelsa had ended up at Heff's, "I was going to your room at ten as we'd arranged, when Heff came out and stopped me, saying drug addicts had taken over your bedroom: He called it 'Operation Barbie' and said it called for 'Plan B', which meant you wanted me to go to his house. My aunt thinks I'm staying at Aelsa's and her parent's think she's at mine so we had to stay together, he was so kind saying Aelsa could come as well. Aren't we naughty?"

She giggled and brushed a strand of hair behind her ear, wiggling to adjust her breasts on his chest and slid her fur gliding saddle down Nick's midriff to rub an Eskimo nose-kiss and continued, "But that was ages ago, we've been worried sick. We tried phoning but no one answered. What's 'Operation Barbie'?"

Nick gulped, now was not a good time to reveal his unbelievably compromising encounter with Grace and said, "Oh yeah, 'Barbie' is code name for barbiturates. I think he does them in chemistry. In the same way 'Mandies' is short for... Some other psychedelic drug."

"How awful. Anyway, I began to wonder if Heff was just trying to get Aelsa alone and whether you even knew 'Plan B' was to come here, so I came to bed. I'm so glad you got MY message."

Nick asked, "What message?"

"The message I gave Jane as I left: I asked her to tell you to come to Heff's."

"Oh, I got the message alright," Nick said coldly.

Putting her head sideways on Nick's chest listening to his heart she whispered, "Oh Nick, do you really love me?"

Nick replied sincerely, "With all my heart I feel warmth and love. You've touched a part of me no one else has ever done."

Jasmine leaned to kiss Nick sweetly on the lips then slipped to his side, keeping one thigh over his legs and cuddled within his arm. Studying him in profile she brushed Nick's wet hair through her fingers, then traced a goosebump-tingling orgasmic line with her forefinger from his forehead down the bridge of his nose over his lips, down his neck and over his chest. Continuing her virgin voyage exploration over his flat stomach and belly-button down to his pubic hair then she gently reached his manhood. She licked her bottom lip and bit it, then leaned over to suck Nick's bottom lip. Looking into his eyes she said sadly, "You will write, won't you?"

Nick replied with certainty, "Every day, and I'll phone. Calls are free for my mum, even long distance. Fair to say I'll be grounded for months, so I'll be the best pen-pal ever." He reassured brushing an auburn tress behind her ear.

She smiled nervously and blushed, "There's no stopping us now is there, my darling? Two people in love doing what comes naturally. I've dreamt about this and it feels right. Boyfriend and girlfriend hopelessly in love, sharing each other for the first time, for one night of passion. It won't hurt, will it?"

"I'll try to be gentle," Nick whispered gallantly but his darling paramour led the advance sliding onto him receptively guiding courtship coitus. She plunged her mouth down upon his, forcing his teeth apart with her tongue and pressed deep into his mouth, penetrating an oral yin for his pelvic yang. Coupling together her hand ardently guided, gliding his unsheathed girth into her tight warm honey, nectar-oozing love-pocket promise. Glistening striped bodies groaned with delight, fervently panting into each other's hot salivating mouths, sucking tongues, lips, ears and nipples exhaustedly until Nick could press no further, adult eyes rolled back exploding with ecstatic release: Flesh and blood magnetised, feeling total pleasure. With orgasmic sighs woman and man were replete, sized; climactically coming together as one.

They had each other for tonight, sunrise would summon the inevitable, heart-breaking disengagement but for now, alone together, they had all the time in the world.

There was a brisk, knock at the door. They stopped panting and looked each other in the eye, perspiring, red-faced and conjoined, caught in the act like naughty children.

Heff shouted from the landing, "Keep the noise down, you randy sods! I'll leave this tray outside: Jam-butties and a flask of coffee to keep you up all night. A bottle of lemonade, shaken not stirred and an unopened catering pack of extra-large rubber-Johnnies." Then he drummed the door, "Oh, and a fiver... You won Slick-Wick!"

Unable to hold back laughter he finally mimicked, "Try to be gentle." Then blurted, "And don't forget the safe word, 'ODGEAMOWEY'!"

Nick Hopper will return in 1985.